Prince of Outcasts

Prince
of Outcasts

A NOVEL OF THE CHANGE

S. M. STIRLING

ROC
NEW YORK

ROC
Published by Berkley
An imprint of Penguin Random House LLC
375 Hudson Street, New York, New York 10014

(Penguin colophon)

Copyright © 2016 by S. M. Stirling
The author acknowledges permission to use the following:
"To Njord" © Diana L. Paxson

Map by Jade Cheung

Library of Congress Cataloging-in-Publication Data

Names: Stirling, S. M., author.
Title: Prince of outcasts: a novel of the Change / S. M. Stirling.
Description: New York City: New American Library, [2016] | Series: Change
series; 10 | Description based on print version record and CIP data
provided by publisher; resource not viewed.
Identifiers: LCCN 2016019575 (print) | LCCN 2016012398 (ebook) | ISBN
9781101603390 (ebook) | ISBN 9780451417374 (hardcover)
Subjects: LCSH: Inheritance and succession—Fiction. | Regression
(Civilization)—Fiction. | Voyages and travels—Fiction. | Kings and
rulers—Fiction. | Princes—Fiction. | BISAC: FICTION / Alternative
History. | FICTION / Fantasy / Epic. | GSAFD: Alternative histories
(Fiction) | Fantasy fiction.
Classification: LCC PS3569.T543 (print) | LCC PS3569.T543 P75 2016 (ebook) |
DDC 813/.54—dc23
LC record available at https://lccn.loc.gov/2016019575

First Edition: September 2016

Printed in the United States of America
3   5   7   9   10   8   6   4   2

Jacket art by Larry Rostant

To Jan, and it always feels good to say that

ACKNOWLEDGMENTS

Thanks to Kier Salmon, unindicted co-conspirator, who has been my advisor and helper on the Change since the first.

To Gina Tacconi-Moore, my niece, flower-girl at my wedding twenty-eight years ago, Queen of Physical Fitness and owner of CrossFit Lowell, who gave me some precise data on what a really fit young woman, such as herself, could do.

To Steve Brady, native guide to Alba, for assistance with dialects and British background, and also natural history of all sorts.

Pete Sartucci, knowledgeable in many aspects of Western geography and ecology, including the Mojave and Topanga.

To Miho Lipton and Chris Hinkle, for help with Japanese idiom; and to Stuart Drucker, for assistance with Hebrew.

Diana L. Paxson, for help and advice, and for writing the beautiful Westria books, among many others. If you like the Change novels, you'll probably enjoy the hell out of the Westria books—I certainly did, and they were one of the inspirations for this series; and her *Essential Ásatrú* and recommendation of *Our Troth* were extremely helpful . . . and fascinating reading. The appearance of the name Westria in the book is no coincidence whatsoever. And many thanks for the loan of Deor Wide-Faring and Thora Garwood.

To Dale Price, for help with Catholic organization, theology and praxis.

To John Birmingham, aka that silver-tongued old rogue, King Birmo of Capricornia, most republican of monarchs.

To Cara Schulz, for help with Hellenic bits, including stuff I could not have found on my own.

To Lucienne M. Brown, Pacific Northwesterian and keen wit, for advice and comments.

To Walter Jon Williams, Emily Mah, John Miller, Vic Milan, Jan Stirling, Sarena Ulibarri, Matt Reiten, Lauren Teffeau, and Shirl Sazynski of Critical Mass for constant help and advice as the book was under construction.

Thanks to John Miller, good friend, writer and scholar, for many useful discussions, for lending me some great books, and for some really, really cool old movies.

Special thanks to Heather Alexander, bard and balladeer, for permission to use the lyrics from her beautiful songs which can be—and should be!—ordered at http://faerietaleminstrel.com. Run, do not walk, to do so.

To Alexander James Adams, for cool music, likewise: http://faerietaleminstrel.com/inside.

To Johnny Clegg for permission to use the lyrics of his beautiful song "Digging for Words," which can be found at www.johnnyclegg.com.

Thanks again to William Pint and Felicia Dale, for permission to use their music, which can be found at www.pintndale.com and should be, for anyone with an ear and salt water in their veins.

And to Three Weird Sisters—Mary Crowell, Brenda Sutton, and Teresa Powell—whose alternately funny and beautiful music can be found at http://www.three weirdsisters.com.

And to Heather Dale for permission to quote the lyrics of her songs, whose beautiful (and strangely appropriate!) music can be found at www.heatherdale.com, and is highly recommended. The lyrics are wonderful and the tunes make it even better.

To S. J. Tucker for permission to use the lyrics of her beautiful songs, which can be found at http://sjtucker.com, and should be.

And to Lael Whitehead of Jaiya, www.laelwhitehead.com, for permission to quote the lyrics of her beautiful songs. One of which became the Montivallan national anthem.

Thanks again to Russell Galen, my agent, who has been an invaluable help, advisor and friend for decades now, and never more than in these difficult times. I've had good editors, but none who've helped my career and work as much.

All mistakes, infelicities and errors are of course my own.

Prince of Outcasts

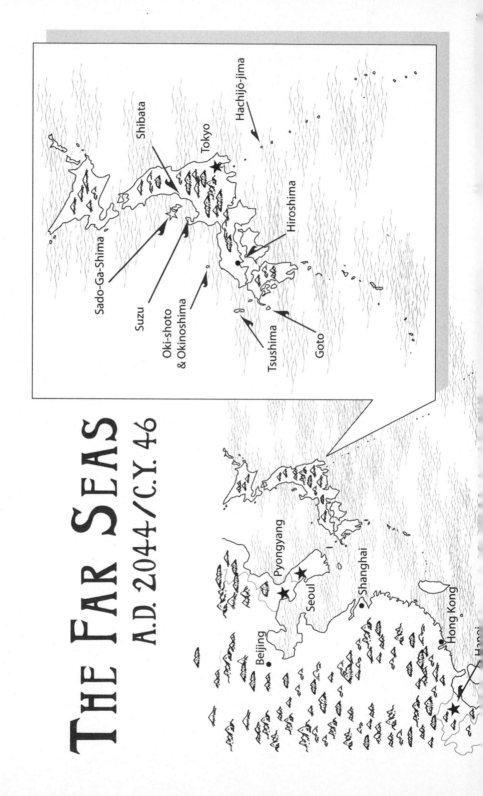

The Far Seas
A.D. 2044 / C.Y. 46

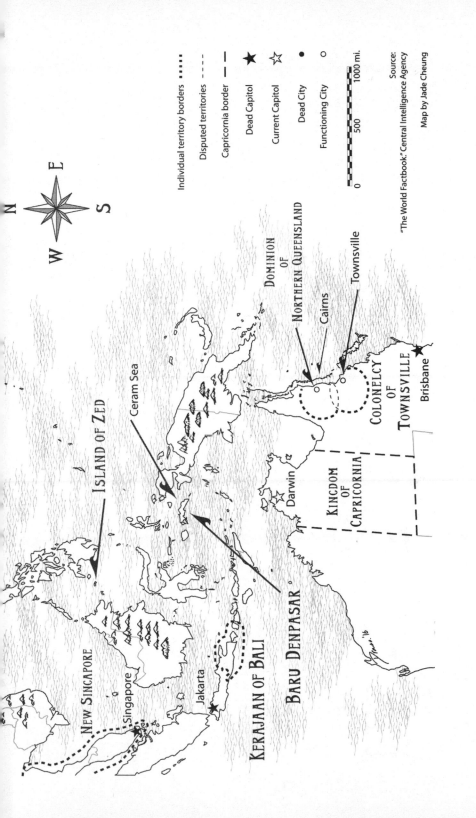

N
W ⊕ E
S

NEW SINCAPORE

Singapore ★

Jakarta ★

KERAJAAN OF BALI

BARU DENPASAR

ISLAND OF ZED

Ceram Sea

Darwin ☆

KINGDOM
OF
CAPRICORNIA

DOMINION
OF
NORTHERN QUEENSLAND

Cairns

Townsville

COLONELCY
OF
TOWNSVILLE

Brisbane ★

Individual territory borders ▪▪▪▪
Disputed territories – – – –
Capricornia border — — —

★ Dead Capitol
☆ Current Capitol
● Dead City
○ Functioning City

0   500   1000 mi.

Source:
"The World Factbook," Central Intelligence Agency

Map by Jade Cheung

CHAPTER ONE

PARTICIPATORY DEMOCRACY OF TOPANGA

(FORMERLY TOPANGA CANYON)

CROWN PROVINCE OF WESTRIA

(FORMERLY CALIFORNIA)

HIGH KINGDOM OF MONTIVAL

(FORMERLY WESTERN NORTH AMERICA)

AUGUST/HAOCHIZUKI 26TH

CHANGE YEAR 46/SHŌHEI 1/2044 AD

Prince John Arminger Mackenzie stood and sweated in his suit of chrome-steel plate, glad of the shade of the raised visor that stuck out from his flared sallet helm like the bill of the ritual cap baseball players wore. The fierce southland sun glittered off the rocky ground and sank into the faded asphalt of the ancient roadway and blinked in endless sparkles from the surface of the Pacific to the southward.

There was a familiar smell of hot horse, hot human, sweat-soaked leather and metal greased with canola oil that always went slightly rancid, a composite scent common to wherever warriors gathered, no matter how polished their appearance; it was fairly powerful since his sister, their men-at-arms and crossbowmen and Mackenzie archers and McClintock caterans, the Japanese contingent and several hundred local levies from Topanga and the Chatsworth Lancers were all standing and sweltering together. The score of robed *bnei Yaakov* from the Mojave were a little to one side—a people apart—but their mounts added hot camel to the mix, which was indescribable.

Despite the tension of the moment as everyone stared out over the water towards the quartet of enemy ships, he smiled to himself, remembering his parents inspecting troops once. That had also been on a hot day, in the County Palatine of Walla-Walla far up the Columbia. There had been a rather sheltered town-based cleric with them and he'd asked what the smell was. His mother had considered gravely for a moment, and said:

"Esprit de corps."

She'd said it deadpan, but he'd noticed his father working hard at not bellowing with laughter.

Today that familiar almost-stink went with the odd alien scents of fennel and sage that summer baked out of the chaparral here, harsh and spicy at once.

We're back in the stewpot just when we thought the adventure was over with, he thought. *Though everything's grist for the mill.*

He was a prince and warrior by birth—second child of the first High King and Queen of Montival—but a troubadour and bard by aspiration, and he could appreciate the irony of the situation from an artistic point of view. They'd dared the desert and the supernatural perils of the Valley of Death . . .

Well, to be entirely fair, mostly Orrey and Reiko dared them in that last bit. Good ensemble cast, some comic relief from the heroic characters' points of view, someone for the groundlings to identify with too . . .

. . . they'd reclaimed the fabled Grass-Cutting Sword that their Nihonjin friends had crossed the sea to find, made unexpected allies of the desert-dwelling *bnei Yaakov* to bring it back through the desert and the just-barely-friendly lands of the Chatsworth Lancers and the Topangans . . . and now four enemy ships were sitting out there waiting for them, instead of the clear passage back to the northern heartlands of the realm that they'd expected.

It would make an excellent startling reverse in the epical chanson he'd tentatively entitled *The Desert and the Blade*. A quiet interlude in the music, then a hint of doubt, minor key, crashing chords building to a crescendo—

Artistically fine. In my all too mortal person, it's a bloody menace. Not to mention those ugly-looking Eaters the Koreans have picked up from the Los Angeles ruins.

The locals had a powerful pre-Change telescope set up. One look had been enough. The Korean vessels swarmed with the naked savages, scrawny and scarred and ferocious as great rats among the ordered, armored easterners. The diabolists could control them, somehow.

This bunch look even worse than the ones we fought up on the Bay, and those were bad enough.

He swallowed and blinked as the stink came back, and the screaming faces and the ugly feel of edged metal hammering into meat and bone vibrated up into his hand. And the taste, when a gout of blood landed on his face. He hadn't had time to be frightened during the actual fighting, mostly that had been drilled reflex working.

But the times in between the rushes waiting for the wild men to work themselves up to another attack and listening to their mad squealing brabble . . . that had been fairly bad. Having to keep up appearances had helped, and so had giving everyone some verses from *La Chanson de Roland*. He found that a bravura gesture could convince one's own mind just as thoroughly as it did an audience.

And the Koreans may not be savages, but they're outright diabolists. Or at least their rulers and lords are.

His eyes narrowed. It had been servants of the Korean ruler who killed his father the High King only a few months ago, a spillover of their long war with Dai-Nippon, and a chess-move in the game Heaven and the Malevolence were playing in the Changed world. There was a blood-debt yet unpaid. *That* would be part of the song too.

"Reiko, can I borrow your Captain Ishikawa, and his men?" Crown Princess Órlaith said.

John's ears perked; when his older sister . . .

. . . three years older. I'm almost twenty and it's not as if we were children any-more . . .

. . . adopted that crisp tone, things were about to happen. She sounded like their father when she used it, allowing for her being a woman of twenty-one and not a man in his forties.

The Empress of Dai-Nippon nodded decisively, and spoke a word of command to her followers. She was actually a little older than Órlaith, though her almost-delicate features made some layer of his mind see her as closer to his own nineteen summers. He'd been half in love with her since they met at Montinore Manor in June, when his sister had brought him into the conspiracy. It was more or less required of a young knight when confronted with a beautiful, absolutely unobtainable foreign princess. The romaunts made that clear enough. And of course her father had died in the same skirmish as his, just too late for rescue. He hadn't been there, she had, and somehow that made her a link to that tremendous absence, the loss that still broke through the shell of his life at times with a jarring suddenness that he never expected.

In actual fact as opposed to aesthetic theory he found her very capable, and very likeable on the rare occasions when she relaxed . . . and more than a little intimidating.

"Johnnie," Órlaith went on in a clipped tone.

Her chiseled face was utterly intent as she weighed the situation. The cooler sea-breeze cuffed at the little wisps of sun-faded yellow hair that escaped her tightly-clubbed fighting braid; she took more after their father's side of the family, while he had the hazel eyes and brown hair and blunter features of the Armingers. She was also an inch taller that he was, but since that made him a very respectable five-ten he didn't mind.

Come to think about it, she's getting very focused too. *Granted this is a* good *time* *for it.*

They'd always been fairly close, and the gap in their ages mattered less now. He gave her the Associate salute, a martial clank of gauntlet against breastplate.

"Take Ishikawa and the Nihonjin sailors, and go there."

She pointed westward and downslope from the low ridge that bore the old coast road.

"There are some longboats at the Topangans' saltworks. Take them, and . . . the crossbowmen from the Protector's Guard, and a few others, say four, pick them yourself. Feldman's short-handed; you reinforce him. And tell him to be cooperating fully with the *Stormrider.*"

He shot her a swift look of surprise; for weeks now they'd been dodging the Royal Montivallan Navy warship their mother had sent to drag them back as if they were naughty toddlers to be hauled in by one ear. And there it was, to seaward of Captain Feldman's *Tarshish Queen,* their own hired ship, which in turn was slowly cruising back and forth south of the four Korean ships at anchor just offshore.

Órlaith stepped closer and spoke softly; there was no need to broadcast the facts about their little disagreement with their mother, High Queen Regnant Mathilda.

"Johnnie, Reiko *has* her Sacred Treasure the now. We've done what we set out to do. Now we clear this up, go back to Mother, roll on our backs, wave our paws in the air and whimper for forgiveness. We'll get it, too. Eventually."

He didn't let the jolt of raw fear that image brought show on his face.

I knew we'd have to confront Mother eventually. Ah, well, better to seek forgiveness than ask permission! And we did bring it off. Success has a thousand fathers and failure's an orphan.

"She'll recognize a magic sword when she sees one!" his sister said, echoing his thought.

Her hand rested on the moon-crystal pommel of the Sword of the Lady, the heirloom of their House that their father and mother had won on the Quest.

"So will anyone with the least bit of the Sight, without Reiko having to do anything too . . . dramatic."

John gave the not-really-a-katana-anymore at Reiko's side a glance and suppressed an impulse to cross himself. The Sword of the Lady was disturbing enough, but his Church officially regarded it as the gift of *the* Lady, Mary Queen of Heaven and Mother of God, which pagans like his father and sister unfortunately conflated with their mythology. Coming from a mixed family could be awkward at times; his mother was a devout Catholic, and he was too or tried to be, but Órlaith followed the Old Faith as their father had. It wasn't like having the old wars of Clan and Association in the same household—the union of their parents had laid that to rest, with many other feuds—but it could be . . . difficult.

Kusanagi-no-Tsurugi, the Grass-Cutting Sword, was something else entirely, altogether outside Montival's complex of religions and all their mixed history and old grudges and sometimes grudging common life. As far as he could tell from what Órlaith and Reiko had let slip, the pieces of it had been *absorbed* into her Masamune sword as the Empress fought her way through that lost castle and his sister stood guard outside with the Lady's blade. There had been something about a monster with eight heads as well. . . .

Deor Godulfson was standing close. The wiry Hraefnbeorg poet nodded. Among his folk, a scop was likely to know something of rune-craft too, the arts of magic reborn since the Change. The angular raven image on his round shield wasn't just the symbol of his people, but also of Woden Allfather, and a protective sign.

"It *burns*," he said. "Like carrying the very sun in your hand . . ."

John nodded himself, giving it a glance. He felt it like a prickling on the skin. A little like the feeling of the Sword of the Lady, but . . . he could hold the Sword; he didn't like to, but it was in his blood and if his sister fell—*which God forfend!*—he would have to bear it.

Kusanagi was wholly alien.

"Then why not just have everyone go out to the *Tarshish Queen* and show them our heels?" he said quietly to his sister and liege-lady. "*Storm-rider* would be glad to escort us back to Portland, since that was what Mother tasked them with in the first place."

She shook her head. "They've some on those Korean ships who could sense Reiko and me moving, given what we bear," she said.

The enemy called their adepts *kangshinmu*, and John swallowed at the thought of meeting one again. Especially on his own. As their father's heir Órlaith carried the Sword of the Lady, which was proof against all fell enchantments and a great deal else besides. All he had was his own entirely mortal and fallible self and a length of very skillfully reworked leaf-spring at his side; and while he was a faithful son of Mother Church, he didn't delude himself that he was any sort of saint, or as armored in sanctity as he was in plate.

I'm the son of a great hero-King and a great and powerful Queen, he thought as he pulled out his crucifix and kissed it before tucking it away again. *What I am myself . . . isn't entirely apparent yet. There would be better ways of finding out than being thrown in over my head, though!*

Órlaith went on: "They'd be waiting for us on the water, that they would. For you, not so much."

Deor Godulfson made a soft sound of agreement at that, too; and John remembered how he'd tracked the Haida shaman at the battle on the shores of the Bay.

"Also I'm not inclined to leave our new subjects in the lurch," Órlaith said, and tapped her titanium-sabaton-armored foot on the dusty faded asphalt with a clank.

Her voice rang. "This is Montivallan soil now, and by Macha Red-Locks and Nemain of the Blood-Shout and Badb of the Crows, these are our folk, every one of them, and House Artos stands with them! The Shadow Queen bear witness!"

John nodded; he agreed with every word of that, barring the paganism, and he knew that she meant it too. But there was an element of performance to ruling. He'd been surprised to find so many similarities to the family business he'd been raised in when he also took up music seriously.

Except that if you're born to our House, you never get to step away from the limelights and sit backstage laughing with a glass in your hand and a towel around your neck.

Now he saluted again and decided:

"Deor, Thora, Evrouin, you're with me. Sergeant Fayard, your squad. Captain Ishikawa. Thora, get mounted and scout ahead. Let's go!"

Deor was a valuable asset for a whole clutch of skills, and the scop's oath-sister Thora Garwood of the Bearkillers was a warrior's warrior who went where he did . . . and neither of them was part of a larger unit that would be disrupted by tagging along with him, and besides, he liked them both.

Though not in the same way!

Evrouin, John's valet-bodyguard-minder, wasn't going to go more than arm's length from his charge anyway: they hadn't been able to shed him when they skipped out to begin all this, despite vigorous efforts. Before they'd gone more than a dozen paces someone else dashed up; it was one of the young Mackenzies who'd come on the journey with them, Ruan Chu Mackenzie of Dun Fairfax. He and Deor embraced fiercely for an instant, and they were both grinning as they caught up.

John's Catholic-reared mind disapproved, but that was a matter of dutiful conscious thought, not feeling. For one thing he'd spent a lot of time among Mackenzies, who had their own customs, and you were supposed to hate the sin and not the sinner, anyway, as St. Augustine had put it, and he just plain and simple liked Deor as a person and admired his talents.

And for another, his confessor had always told him that it was a good idea to concentrate your hatred for sin on the ones that you were vulnerable to yourself. Sloth tempted him, and women tempted him a *lot*, he even felt the tug of gluttony, occasionally, and he'd been known to envy a bit, and he couldn't even confess and be absolved for feeling wrath against those who'd killed his father because he had no intention of reforming on *that* one yet and you couldn't even ask forgiveness unless you sincerely intended to repent. But spending a lot of energy hating a sin that simply didn't attract you was entirely too easy.

To be real virtue had to be hard-won.

And Deor's a good solid fighting man as well as a poet and runemaster, and Ruan's a healer and a first-rate archer, and both are men to trust. Glad to have them along, if it comes to bad trouble. Worse trouble.

Thora had a horse at hand, and Bearkiller A-listers like her rode as soon as they walked, rather like knights but even more so. She swung into the saddle, pulled her recurve bow out of the scabbard and galloped ahead, then back to meet them.

"Four boats, big fishing boats by the look of it, and some smaller stuff," she said. "The hamlet's completely deserted, as far as I could see from the saddle."

The dust of the path on her handsome bony face and reddish-brown hair made her look a bit older than her thirty-two years; she was wearing what her folk called cataphract armor, a bit lighter than an Association suit of plate, with the helm slung at her saddlebow.

"None of the fisherfolk there?" John said, and she gestured assent. "That's a relief."

He'd leave some gold anyway, but they didn't need to waste time and trouble arguing with some screaming local determined to protect her family's main asset against armed strangers. John had seen that Topangans didn't react well to toploftiness.

"Whoever owned them just took off uphill when the enemy showed up, looks like. Didn't even take their gear."

She fell in beside him, and he gratefully grasped her stirrup-leather as he jogged with a clang and clatter of plates, as much to even his pace as for actual support, and he forced himself to breathe deeply and hold it for an instant rather than the shallow inefficient panting that his lungs *wanted* to do. He was a big young man, broad-shouldered and long-legged and very strong, but this would be hard work for anyone.

"Don't worry, Johnnie. I'll protect you if they try anything with fish-hooks," she added, then grinned at his flush. "Sorry, sweetie. Couldn't resist."

It wasn't the first time he'd been involved with a woman older than himself. It was the first time with anyone like the Bearkiller, who'd traveled literally around the world in the past six years with Deor. It made things . . . interesting.

And Thora doesn't want anything from me but my company for a while. Which is . . . refreshing. You can just take what's offered and ignore the unspoken hopes . . . but while God knows I'm a frail sinner and I like women, I'd have to be a worse man than I am to enjoy a woman under false pretenses.

Topanga's harbor was an accident of the Change; the coast ran east-west here without any natural protection against wind or surf, rising immediately into canyon-fissured hills or low mountains. In the first winter after the old world fell one of its vessels had come ashore in a storm here, what they'd called a *container ship*. It was a monstrosity, at nearly a thousand feet long and a hundred wide, and the rust-eaten hulk lay canted with its deck inclining westward, looming more like a geological freak than a human artifact to eyes born generations later. It had settled to the bottom with its bow to the eastward, making a sheltered V-shape in its lee.

And it's ugly. It would have been ugly when it was floating and moving around. Odd. Oceangoing ships are beautiful, among the most beautiful things humans make; I'd have thought they had *to be, to work at all.*

The longshore current had piled sand against it almost to the rail, and storms and human hands had tumbled the steel freight containers overboard to mingle with the sand and break the waves. The rickety dock—empty now that the few foreign merchantmen had fled a conflict they didn't see as theirs—was on the inner, eastern side. Ships stopped here now and then, more lately as trade picked up.

West of it was a rather crude set of stepped evaporating pans built of salvaged concrete rubble, with the skeletal windmills for pumping brine inactive now. Tools lay scattered about, and sacks and barrels where the laborers had been shoveling the beds of glittering white crystals stood half-empty, abandoned when the alarm went out. Shacks of reused cinderblock for the workers stood in a clump, with incongruously pretty roofs of red tile from some ancient mansion, and at a little distance more for the fishers. An abandoned mongrel dog barked at them, and then ran off, and a cat raised its head and looked with cool insolence from the fish-drying racks. Gulls were swarming on the rest.

War was waste. His parents had told him that more than once, and now he was seeing it with his own eyes.

Thora slid down as they halted, unbuckling her saddle and throwing it over her shoulder before she left the borrowed beast loosely tethered. A baby carriage lay tumbled on its side near one of the huts, with an arm protruding from it. He took a horrified step towards it, then saw it was a doll; a thing of the ancients, of that smooth ivory-like substance they called plastic, but painstakingly dressed by the hands of love in miniature modern clothes. He flushed, hesitated for a moment, then stepped over and set the toy carriage upright and pushed it into the little cottage and pulled the door closed so that the latch fell.

As he looked up a couple of the others were glancing at him; Thora met his eyes and nodded soberly. He felt obscurely cheered, for no reason he could think of. The brief incident made him remember his father somehow—well, so many things did, nowadays.

Rudi Mackenzie, High King Artos, had been a mild-tempered and gentle man for the most part; it often surprised folk who met him for the first time in person, after hearing of his deeds on the Quest, and in the storm and thunder of the Prophet's War. One of the High King's prerogatives under the Great Charter was to review death sentences where a petition for clemency was made, and it was one he'd taken very seriously, enough to risk the touchy care for their autonomy of Montival's many member-realms. He'd commuted about one in ten to exile or hard labor or some other lesser penalty, and pardoned about one in twenty altogether.

Don't be over-quick to deal out death in judgment, he'd said to John once, two years ago, after explaining a case to him and patiently taking him through the testimony, showing how the bone and muscle of fact could be traced beneath the fatty tissue of interpretation.

But one thing that had turned his father savage had been harm to children; he still checked the facts of the matter carefully, but in those cases he'd almost always written:

Let it be so, and let him make accounting to the Guardians of the Western Gate. Mercy to the guilty is cruelty to the innocent. Artos, Ard Rí in Montival and first of that name at the bottom.

And stamped his seal into the wax more forcefully than usual, too.

"Let's go," John said sharply, shaking off the memory.

It was only a few steps to the high-tide mark. There were four of the boats, long double-ended things of sheet aluminum hand-riveted to metal frames and waterproofed with heated plastic, honestly made but crude to his eyes.

"We'll take those three," John said calmly, indicating the closest; there didn't seem to be much difference between them.

Don't shout unless you have to and if you have to shout bark it out and don't let your voice wobble. Don't hesitate. A perfect decision made too late is worse than a second-best one in good time. And don't look worried, he could remember his father saying. *It's part of what you owe them. Nothing disheartens like seeing a leader doubt himself.*

Then a grin. *You* will *doubt yourself, lad, and that often, or at least I did, but keep it private.*

"Fayard, you and half your men with me. Thora, you take Deor and Ruan and the other half of the squad, you're in charge. Captain Ishikawa, you're in the third. Let's go!"

The boats were chained to posts and the chains fastened with twists of wire designed to hold against sudden squalls, but the rusted metal gave way easily to a few blows with the steel-shod butts of a *naginata* or crossbow. He tossed his shield into the first boat with a clatter and helped in the brief labor of throwing out the coils of net and boxes of very smelly bait and lines and old plastic tubs and bottles reused as floats. The Guard men weren't expert boatmen, but they could all pull an oar, more or less. And the Royal family had enjoyed sailing and fishing.

He dropped a purse of rose nobles on top of the heap of discarded gear, and put his shoulder to the hull with the others, staggering a little as the boat hissed down the wet sand into the waves and began to pitch. As the cold Pacific swirled round his feet he rolled into the boat cautiously—there was a layer of tattered ancient plywood at the bottom but he suspected if he was wasn't careful he could punch his armored foot right through the hull. Then he pulled the lashings on the tiller free, holding the end of it down so the rudder wouldn't scrape on the sand.

Evrouin grinned at him as he swung in with John's lute-case and his glaive both held carefully high, stowed them and took an oar. He was a stocky, muscular man in his early thirties, black-haired and olive-skinned. The jewel-hilted, foot-long dagger at his belt proclaimed him an Associate, but he was of the lowest rank in the ruling order the Portland Protective Association had established after the Change. Until recently John had strongly suspected that the man regarded him as something like an absentminded, dim-witted younger brother, behind a façade of imperturbable good manners and due deference to his birth. Since the battle in the Bay he'd been promoted. To *promising* younger brother.

The rest of the scratch crew came over the side as they ran the boat out deeper, seizing the oars and running them out through the rowing locks with thunks and clanking sounds as they slipped the retaining pins home. The underofficer Fayard used an oar to hold the boat against the sand and keep it from being shoved backward onto the beach by the incoming tide.

"On the mark . . ." John said.

The men bent forward, the oars rising on both sides.

"Stroke! Stroke! Stroke!" he called, letting the rudder drop down into its working position.

The blades of the oars dipped and bit and threw spray back at him. He felt his heart lighten; it was a bright day and he was young and healthy and a prince and the tiller was coming alive under his palm as it bit into the moving water. . . . Life could be worse.

He risked a quick glance behind him. The other boats were following to either side, spread out in a shallow V. Thora and Deor had traveled the world around, mostly in ships, and knew boat-handling a lot better than he did. Captain Ishikawa and his men were professionals who slipped into a boat and put the boat into the sea like otters off a rock, and could have overtaken the others without raising much more of a sweat. Ishikawa was what the Nihonjin called a samurai—roughly like a knight—as well as a naval officer. His men weren't, but John suspected they'd all been born in fishing villages and had grown up as amphibious as seals.

He steered as close as was safe to the wreck and the sandbar that had piled up against it, for concealment and because it damped down the waves, and in places that meant the ancient ship hung over them and cast a shadow like a steep hillside. It was noisier than he'd have expected, sighing and soughing where the water ran in and out of jagged holes in the time-eaten steel, and loose cables and fittings went *bang . . . bang . . . bang* hollowly like drums beaten by skeletons.

The choppy slap of the waves when they rounded the canted bows of the wreck came as a surprise, and the cold spray struck his face. The surface of the harbor proper had looked as smooth as a manor millpond, but they were seaward of that now, and he could barely see the mast-tops of the *Tarshish Queen* at all. He thought for a moment, then turned and pointed.

Ishikawa waved back, and his boat moved into the lead. John grinned wryly as he passed; even with unfamiliar equipment, the Japanese commander and his little crew—all the survivors of his lost *Red Dragon*—were demonstrating the difference between *passable* and *expert*. Very much like what happened when someone who carried a sword for self-defense against ruffians and practiced a bit ran up against a knight. He took up counting the stroke again, and the crossbowmen-turned-oarsmen worked doggedly. He also followed just as closely in Ishikawa's wake as he could.

Then the sleek shape of the *Tarshish Queen* turned sharply, more sail blossoming in off-white curves as she heeled to the northwest wind. They must have seen the boats from the masthead lookouts, up there nearly a hundred feet above the surface. He could also see the bow-chaser catapult moving, the eighteen-pounder rumbling along metal tracks laid into the deck until the throwing trough jutting from a slot in the middle of the sloped steel shield pointed straight at them.

The *Queen* was a merchantman, not a warship, and flew the beaver-head flag of the city-state of Corvallis as well as the High Kingdom's crowned mountain and sword. But Feldman & Sons of Newport—Corvallis' window on the Pacific—traded in the sort of places where a respectable broadside and a fast pair of heels were costs of doing business. Or of living to see home again, for that matter. That and an old link between House Artos and the Feldmans, dating back to their grandparents' time, was why Órlaith had sent John to talk her owner into providing the ship. It hadn't been hard. . . .

"Ahoy there!"

He recognized the musical tones in the voice as the big schooner came near despite the distortion of a speaking trumpet and water purling back from its sharp cutwater; that was First Mate Radavindraban, who'd been born a long, long way from Montival.

"Who comes?"

He'd asked the man why he'd left home, and he'd shrugged and answered: *Most unreasonably angry bloody-minded bloody Raja, Your Highness.*

"Prince John and party!"

The ship slowed in the simplest possible way, turning directly into the wind and letting itself be what sailors called *taken aback*. It stopped in its own length . . . if you didn't count the violent pitching up and down, accompanied by sailorish cursing from the crew trying to deal with the effect of the drastic measure on the rigging. The shadow of the hull fell over them as they approached, and the crew threw a net over the side to lie flapping against the thin sheet metal anti-flame sheathing that covered the Douglas fir planks. The *Queen* was a big ship but not enormous, a three-masted topsail schooner of about four hundred and fifty tons displacement, and a bit over two hundred feet long from fantail to bowsprit. The rail was only a little more than a tall man's height above the waves.

"Permission to come aboard!" John shouted.

"By all means, Your Highness," the Captain called from near the wheel, a slight irony in the flat, neutral and rather old-fashioned Corvallan accent.

"Send ropes too!" he shouted to the deck crew; his parents had taught him never to take an avoidable risk. "Everybody use one and secure yourself first, that's an order!"

The Bosun up above shouted her own commands, which boiled down to *lines for the dimwit lubbers*. Lines duly came whirring down, with loops on the ends. He took one gratefully and snugged it up under his armpits, slung his shield and jumped to the netting. One armored foot slipped, sending his stomach twisting and lurching even if the only real risk was getting his feet wet; a sabaton made your foot rather rigid, for all that it was articulated, and the motion of the ship slapped the net against the side at unpredictable intervals as he swarmed up hand-over-hand. One of the tests for knighthood—if you were knighted in peacetime, not on the battlefield with a bloodied sword slapping you on the shoulder—was hauling your armored self up a twenty-foot rope using only your arms. He'd probably gotten the *opportunity* to seek the golden spurs rather young because of his high birth, but nobody got to fudge the *results*, if only because it was all done in public.

John waved to the Captain, but turned immediately to make sure Sergeant Fayard and his guardsmen were coming up safely, lending a hand here and there. Ishikawa's contingent came over the other side as if they were strolling up the path to their homes, and immediately headed for two of the portside catapults; the *Tarshish Queen* had eight a side plus her stern and bow-chasers and the Nihonjin sailors had trained on them coming south, getting used to the differences between these and the similar-but-not-identical models the Imperial Navy of Dai-Nippon used. The crews of those two nodded thanks, then split up to bring the others closer to full complements.

Thora and Deor waited a moment and then came in where John's boat had come alongside. He took the loop of rope he'd used and tossed it accurately to her; she sent her saddle up on it first, then looped it under her arms as he had before she stood and leapt, and he pulled her up hand-over-hand while she held the line in an experienced rappeler's grip and fended off the side with her booted feet.

"Thanks, lover," she said as she turned and caught Deor's wrist. "*Up* you go, brother."

Thora and Deor weren't actually related; their birthplaces were almost exactly half a thousand miles apart. They'd just been comrades and very close friends for half their lives, starting when they'd been younger than he was. They came at his heels as he trotted quickly up to the quarter-deck; the owner was rapping out a series of orders, and the ship heeled sharply as it fell off into the wind and the sails cracked taut. The pitching motion gave way to a long smooth rocking-horse gait.

"Mission accomplished, Captain Feldman," he said. "Except for those Korean ships in our way. My sister says you should cooperate fully with the *Stormrider* and her Captain, and we're here to reinforce you."

"Captain Russ RMN commanding," Feldman said, looking southward at the frigate. "We've been playing dodge-'em and I don't think he's very happy with me. He couldn't shoot when we slipped away like a wet watermelon seed . . . but I think he very much wanted to."

He grinned as he said it; he was a slender dark man in his mid-thirties, black-eyed and black-haired and with a single streak of white in his close-cropped beard over a scar, dressed with plain practicality in a peaked sailor's hat over his kippah and brass-buttoned blue coat and pants and soft-soled boots. He stood for a moment with his thumbs in the belt that supported his cutlass, tapping his fingers on the walrus-hide. Then he turned to his signaler:

"Run up *Prince aboard, Crown Princess ashore* and *will conform to your movements*," he said.

"Aye Aye, Cap'n."

The signal hoist went up, worked by a sailor universally known as "Rat" McGuire, for his face and general attitude. Feldman turned his telescope on the frigate.

"*Acknowledged*," he read. "Brief. My, my, Captain Russ *is* in a temper. He's actually not a bad sailor . . . for an Astoria man."

Astoria was the main port for the southern Association territories, just within the dangerous bar at the mouth of the Columbia; Newport was Corvallis' sole seaport, linked to the inland capital of the city-state by a busy rail line. Their rivalry went back well before the High Kingdom.

Then he turned to John: "This situation is unstable, your Highness. May I ask why the Princess and the rest of your party didn't accompany you?"

John hesitated, then told him. Feldman whistled slightly between his teeth before he spoke.

"Magic swords and wicked sorcerers. I don't suppose they're more dangerous than catapult shot or storms, but . . ."

"I grew up around a magic sword, Captain. This . . . What they brought back out of the desert . . . it's most definitely the genuine article."

"Like the Sword of the Lady?"

Feldman's voice was dry. He acknowledged the force of the thing the Quest had brought back from haunted Nantucket; you couldn't see it and not do so, especially if you were a Montivallan yourself. That didn't mean he had to like the fact that in the modern age such things walked abroad in the light of common day.

"Not exactly. It's more . . . more for battle. They have . . . other Sacred Treasures . . . for some of the things the Sword of the Lady does. *Kusanagi* is more purely a weapon. It's a symbol of the ruler as Power. The power to protect and to punish; symbol of it, and the thing itself too. And it scares me silly."

He shook himself and returned to things less mysterious, to their mutual relief:

"Who'll win if it comes to a sea-fight?" John said.

"A close-run thing, given all those savages they've picked up."

"They can't storm the shore," John said, and Feldman nodded.

"Right, we'd move in on them," the Captain said.

"And the Crown Princess and the locals could just pull into the mouth of the canyon there. It's fortified."

"They must be planning something else," Feldman said meditatively.

"Perhaps," John said, and then smiled. "Or perhaps they're not as clever as you, Captain. I've noticed that extremely smart people tend to assume that there's a deep-laid plan when they may be facing blundering incompetence. My grandmother the Queen Mother Sandra said *she* had to watch that tendency in herself, and she only had to walk into any room on Earth to be the smartest person in it."

Feldman chuckled, but grimly. "Ordinarily you might be right. But the things we're fighting . . . they're not stupid, worse luck."

"True, but a lot of their followers are dumb as a knapsack full of hammers," John pointed out. "I think it goes with the territory. *I'll eat you last* isn't really a recruiting slogan to attract the intelligent."

Feldman gave him a considering look, and then a respectful nod. John was flattered . . . and slightly annoyed. If you were a young, handsome prince with an eye for the ladies and artistic inclinations people tended to assume you were a lightweight, for some reason. Nobody ever thought that about Órlaith, she was always taken seriously . . . though to be fair, *Órlaith* had never underestimated him. She knew he was perfectly *capable* at anything he put his mind to; she just thought he was lazy, and was always shoving work onto his plate like a second helping of boiled broccoli.

Feldman turned his telescope towards the shore again. Time stretched. He'd noticed that happened when things got tense. A while ago, in fact— the same thing happened at tournaments, or before a performance, but never quite like *this*. Some of the younger sailors—younger than him— were looking a bit anxious, peering shoreward. Some of the others were relaxed enough that there was a quiet game of skat going on behind one catapult, though he'd have bet himself that the grinning woman who was raking in the pot had been the one who started it.

One of the bits of barracks wisdom Evrouin had taught him was that you generally did a lot better at cards if you were focused and the other players weren't.

"*Hello*," Feldman said. "Something's going on there. Boat going ashore from the Korean flagship—just one. White parley flag . . . no, and that's a Japanese flag it's flying too."

John's eyebrows shot up. Reiko and her followers had made very clear that Dai-Nippon and the realm that called itself *Chosŏn Minjujŭi Inmin Kong-bwaguk* were deadly enemies. *Chosŏn* was ruled by the descendants of the man who'd run the northern part of that country before the Change. He'd been a spectacularly bad ruler then by all accounts, managing to starve his people even in the abundance of the ancient world, and he'd brought himself and his immediate followers through the chaotic aftermath of the Change by *eating* their enemies—not to mention many of their subjects. That had opened the way for certain *things* from beyond the world of common day; extreme evil often did, and his descendants had become far worse as they spiraled down that trap. They'd been raiding Japan's less numerous survivors ever since, too. He had a strong impression that the grimly warlike cast of the Nihonjin was a result of that long merciless struggle.

John stretched out a hand. Evrouin put his binoculars in it, and he leveled them. It was surprisingly difficult to keep them trained on the shore from a moving ship, and the way the picture swayed and pitched made his stomach swoop in sympathy for a moment before excitement drove it out of his awareness.

"Reiko's coming down the road to meet the ones under the Japanese flag. . . . Two of them are in Nihonjin armor, whoever they are," John said. "She's got Egawa and six of her samurai with her. Mother of God, but I wish I could hear what's being said. . . . Wait a minute. . . . That weird little kid she picked up at the castle in the desert is there . . . The Koreans are attacking! They're fighting!"

He opened his mouth to say something more, then gave a quick gasping grunt. *Something* had punched him in an entirely non-physical way that still felt like a paralyzing blow to the pit of the stomach. The Sword of the Lady had been bared, and then thrust into the living flesh of Montival, the land it had been created to embody and protect. John could *feel* that protection spreading, like a skin of invisible steel rooted deep in the bones of Earth.

What came next was a hurricane wash of flame. For a moment he drew breath to scream as his skin was flayed off, then realized that there was no pain and no heat. Feldman and a few of the sailors were looking at him oddly. Deor wasn't; he'd stumbled to his knees, and Thora was beside him with an arm around his shoulders and stark concern on her face.

"Kusanagi *has been drawn in anger,*" he said, or Something spoke through him. "*Amaterasu-ōmikami's* daughter takes the Grasscutter Sword to war."

Feldman was frowning slightly, but no more than that. As if he was mildly frustrated that things were happening which might involve him in a deadly fight at any moment. There were things that being of the High King's line gave you; he wasn't at all sure that they were advantages, though.

"Captain, something very bad is going to happen," John said tightly.

He hadn't known exactly what he was going to say until he'd said it, but when he had it rang with the brazen inevitability of utter truth.

Feldman nodded cautiously. "With those *mamzrim*"—he inclined his head towards the Korean warships—"I'm not surprised."

John swallowed. A good deal depended on his being very clear. *Including my life*, he thought.

And while he was good with words, he usually wasn't talking for his life. Fortunately he wasn't the only man of words on the ship.

"He's right, Moishe," Deor said; he and the Captain had first met when they were both in their teens and were good if not exactly close friends. "The Prince doesn't mean bad as in evil. Just . . . *terrible*. Something terrible is about to happen, not wicked, but powerful and very dangerous to anyone who gets caught in it. Like an earthquake or a storm."

The word the *scop* used tripped something, and suddenly John was very certain. "Storm! There's going to be a storm!"

Feldman looked at him, waiting. He swallowed again, conscious that his life, all their lives, might depend on what he said next.

"*Kusanagi* . . . the Grass-Cutting Sword was named after a battle where a Japanese prince used it to turn a blaze back on its makers. It commands the spirits of Fire and Air . . . what they called it before then was *Ama-no-Murakumo-no-Tsurugi*. The Sword of the Gathering Clouds of Heaven! A fragment of the sun embodied in the world of men. Like . . . like a flail of flame and wind. And the Sun drives the Earth's tempests; even the ancients knew that much."

Feldman met his eyes for a long moment, glanced at Deor's face gone pale under its weathered tan, then nodded slightly, a single quick jerk of the chin. Then he turned to his First Mate:

"Mr. Radavindraban, strike all sail. Storm canvas only. Batten down around, and have a sea anchor ready to go over the stern. Lively, if you please. McGuire, signal *make storm preparations* to the RMN ship."

The deck officer called out instructions through his speaking-trumpet. Sailors exploded into motion. The catapults were uncocked and doubled tarpaulins lashed over them. The sails came down at a run, all but the narrow triangular staysails that ran from the foremast to the bowsprit, and the crew lashed the furled canvas round and round with lengths of rope tied with complex knots. The hatches were battened, which turned out to mean putting heavy tarpaulins over them too and hammering home hardwood rods in grooves to keep them there. Everyone else went below, except Deor and Thora; both of them had years at sea, if not exactly as sailors, and they'd shown on the voyage down from the Bay that they knew enough to be useful and not get in the way. Thora murmured as she worked:

"Fair-footed father of Freyr and Freya,
Wave-rider, winning us wealth from the sea,
Shielder of ships, send us good fortune,
Hear us and help us to prosperous harbor,
Bring us a blessing, oh brother of Nerthus,
Pledge of the Vanir, by our prayers be pleased
In Noatun, Oh Njordr, Know Now Our Need."

John knew he and Evrouin were on the quarterdeck because of his rank, not for anything he could do except take up room and pray, which he was doing silently.

But I gave the warning. That was something worthwhile.

"And rig manropes—everyone on a line," Feldman went on. "Everyone but the deck watch below, but warn them to be ready to hook on when or if they're called up. The Lord alone knows if Captain Russ will pay attention, but we tried."

Radavindraban looked up at a sky still calm, at the masts, then at his employer. "Double the backstays, Captain? Preventers?"

It took a moment before John realized he meant putting extra ropes between the masts up at the top; he knew that was a major job. Feldman was looking at him again . . . and the feeling of pressure was building, building. Whatever was going to happen would be soon, very soon. He shook his head.

I'm sort of the hero if I was right. If I'm imagining things, I'm the goat.

"No, Mr. Mate," Feldman said. "Yes if we had time, but we don't. Proceed with orders."

The whole process of readying the ship took mere moments. John watched with fascination; he was used to masses of people moving in quick unison—everything from the Guard on drill to dances—but this had a grimly utilitarian flavor. Everyone was acting as if their lives depended on doing the right thing quickly, which it very probably did, and they trusted their skipper's alarm even if they didn't know why he was giving the orders.

A quick inhalation of breath brought his head up. The sky had been blue and streaked with a little high white cloud. John blinked, uncertain for a moment of what he was seeing. Then the Captain's incredulous grunt told him that it wasn't an illusion; the clouds were thickening as he watched, the skies darkening. Streamers of wolf-gray appeared, turning, curving as if an invisible giant spoon was stirring. . . .

Suddenly the sky northward was covered, bulging downward in a blackened rush like a huge hand rising over the Santa Monicas. Rising like an avalanche of flaying wind. Lightning crackled within the clouds and between cloud and earth, its actinic blue-white suddenly very bright in the darkening day. Each stroke seemed closer, and he could feel the small hairs on the back of his neck trying to stand erect.

"*Baruch ata Adonai, Elohanu Melech Haolam she kocho u-gevurato maleh olam,*" Feldman said, and John recognized it as a prayer even before he repeated it in Montival's common tongue:

"Blessed are You, Lord our God, King of the universe, whose power and might fill the world."

"Amen," John said wholeheartedly. *I feel like an ant on a pavement!*

Then the Captain went on softly: "It's like a typhoon over in Asia. I've seen them coming on, but . . . not like this. Never like this."

He turned his head and snapped: "That sea-anchor! Lively!"

The Bosun went by with a party of sailors, an apparatus of canvas and chains in their arms, their eyes wide and flickering up to the mass of cloud.

"Just reeving the cable to the anchor bitts, Cap'n!" she called, her voice carefully controlled.

"Good," Feldman said. "At the wheel there, port your helm."

The ship heeled and turned a smooth steady arc, until the bowsprit pointed nearly southward.

"Thus, thus, very well, thus. Steady as she goes. We'll head away from that"—he jerked a thumb at the gathering clouds—"for now."

As the ship's bow turned they had a good view of the frigate; it seemed to be in a similar state of upheaval, but a bit behind, and of course it was a more complex task on a much bigger ship. Evrouin came up, knelt, and began stripping off John's suit of plate, fingers quick and deft on the buckles and snaps. John gave a start, and then began to work himself on the pieces around his shoulders and arms and the bevor around his neck, the ones you could come at yourself. The peril driving down on them wasn't one steel armor could protect him from. His valet-cum-bodyguard dropped the pieces into a canvas sack—for once not wrapping them carefully and individually—put John's thick supple swordbelt back around his waist, cinched it tight and tied some of the points from his arming doublet through the metal-rimmed eyelets in the leather, snapped a line onto a loop and ran it to one of the manropes.

Then donned his own just before the prince could open his mouth to order him to do it.

"Devoted to duty, Your Highness, but not suicidal," he said.

There was a shiver in the air. John looked shoreward again, finding himself curiously reluctant—it reminded him uncomfortably of the way he'd felt as a child when he'd convinced himself something ugly was hiding under the bed and he tried to make himself look because he thought he was too old to cry for his parents or the nanny, but oh how he wanted to do just that. When he did look the breath hissed between his teeth and he crossed himself reflexively and murmured a brief prayer to invoke the aid and intercession of St. Francis, who'd been a musician too. The thunderheads were piled mountain-high now, and they covered everything he could see left and right. Already the mountain peaks had disappeared in a silvery-gray mass that must be scourging rain. The chaparral on the stark hillsides bent before the wind like the fur of some great mangy beast, and then a line rippled across the water that churned it into white foam, swifter than a galloping horse.

John ducked his head instinctively and threw up an arm as it struck and staggered him, as much by its own force as the way it made the ship buck. The staysail cracked taut like a catapult releasing, and the ship heeled sharply and seemed to jerk forward. The leading edge of the wind had grit and twigs in it, whipped up off the dry scrubby hills to the north, and he slitted his eyes and threw up his hand. Then it was full of flying salt-spume. Rain followed hard on its heels, cold and stinging, soaking his arming-doublet and hose instantly. The note of the wind in the rigging deepened to what his musician's ear recognized as bass for a moment, then tore up into a shriek.

"There's an old saying," Feldman shouted with a grim smile, holding to a stay. "*We beat Pharaoh, we'll get through this.* I *thought* this expedition would be interesting and my judgment was sound!"

The wind built from second to second. John squinted through the stinging wet, then shouted himself:

"One of the Korean ships just capsized!"

It had been a glimpse, the masts crackling and toppling, sails and ropes flailing through the air, the hull heeling farther and farther and then suddenly pitching over in a flash and the weed-grown keel showing for an instant before a wave hid it and threw bits of wood and he thought people up into the driving darkness. He couldn't see the others at all, and then for an instant he could, one of them was heading towards him on the crest of a wave with its bow headed nearly straight down. They must have cut their anchors and were trying to run before the storm.

"*Get that—*" Feldman shouted.

There was a sensation underfoot, as if the ship had *jerked* somehow, but soft and elongated, as if the jerk had been through a cushion. John felt his feet skidding across the wet-slick deck, and then Evrouin had him by one upper arm and Deor by the other, with Thora gripping his belt and the back of his doublet.

"Got it!" he said.

And he did; he clamped his hand on one of the manropes and used it to haul himself back to near the helm. Feldman hadn't even staggered, and he shouted again.

"That was the sea-anchor taking hold. It'll keep our stern to the wind!"

He had to do it louder this time; the gale had risen until the sound in the rigging was a roar and a shriek in one, and the masts were bending visibly. Then there was a huge series of popping cracks from the bow, like a whip miles long snapping. They all looked that way, and John saw Feldman's lips shape the word *shit!* Perhaps he'd said it; ordinary speech would be inaudible right now. The jib and the other forestaysails had blown out of their boltropes and were flogging themselves into scraps of pale canvas, just visible across the hundred and fifty feet of heaving deck, with banks of half-solid spray rolling across it in between. The ship gave another jolt, then settled into the same heaving roll.

Feldman glanced back over his shoulder. His eyes went wide, and his mouth shaped *shit!* again. Then something else, which John suspected was:

Hear, O Israel, the Lord our God, the Lord is One!

That was the prayer Jews spoke in the face of imminent death. On its heel came a shout of:

"Lash the wheel, now, now!"

Unwillingly, forcing his head to turn, John looked in the same direction as the sailors frantically hooked the loops of cable around the spokes to keep it steady if their hands came off.

There was a wave behind them. Towering, a wall of water rising nearly like a cliff. A moving cliff topped with a line of white, visible in the stark flicker of the lightning bolts.

"No!" the prince shouted into the wind that tore the words from his mouth. "I haven't finished making the song yet!"

And the world fell.

CHAPTER TWO

Castle Todenangst, Crown Demesne
Portland Protective Association
(Formerly northern Oregon)
High Kingdom of Montival
(Formerly western North America)
September 15th
Change Year 46/2044 AD

"Johnnie's alive, Mother," Órlaith said softly.

She'd gone to her knees as the High Queen—Mathilda Arminger Mackenzie—entered and now she stripped the sheathed Sword of the Lady from the leather-and-brass sling that kept it angled back from her belt and held it up on her open palms. Her blue eyes met her mother's hazel-brown, and she saw a slight thawing in the cold anger there as the older woman put her hand on the black staghorn and silver inlay of the hilt.

She knew much of the anger had been born of fear for her and her brother, not just that a masterful will had been successfully defied. And it was natural enough to fear, when they put themselves at risk so soon after her father's death. That didn't make the anger any less real, and perilous. It was even a bit justified, if you looked at it from her perspective.

She'd have been mad at Johnnie too, if he was here. He's not, he's still in danger, and I'm safe to take both our shares out on.

Their faces both went blank as the Sword linked them to things beyond the world of common day, and to each other. There was a moment of communion on a level Órlaith found impossible to describe even to herself. She felt a single word, as if it hummed in her mother's mind and echoed across miles and years:

Rudi.

A ghost of her father's presence, faded but still there in the Sword and the land it embodied, the land he had died for and blessed with the sacred King's own blood, as the very Lord in whose power he had walked died each year for the ripened corn that fed human-kind. An echo that would live forever. Beneath it were the linked lines of blood that connected her parents to her and to her siblings—even to the unnamed babe that her mother bore, stirring now with six months' growth.

"Yes, we'd know if John was . . . if he wasn't," the High Queen said. "But he's . . . far away. I can tell that much. Beyond Montival. And that's all we know. The western Pacific is . . . very large."

She released the hilt, implicitly not demanding that the sacred blade be turned over to her. Who had the better right was moot, and her daughter was the High King's heir.

"What can we do?" Órlaith asked.

The Pacific was indeed very large, and sending the whole Navy haring off into the beyond would be like looking for a particular grain of sand on a beach. It was hard enough to keep the piracy problem down, and they *knew* that started in the northern isles. Even sending a second warship down to Topanga had stretched things, though it had given them a quick safe journey home.

"For now, you've done more than enough, Órlaith; you've lost your brother, lost the *Tarshish Queen*, and lost the *Stormrider*. Rise," she said.

She made a palms-up gesture as she did and sank back onto the throne of wrought and inlaid teakwood that stood on a low dais beneath an embroidered canopy. The strong worn hands gripped the carved lions' heads of the armrests. Everyone rose, save the black-armored guards who stood motionless before the tapestries, the honed steel edges on the blades of their glaives catching the beams of light from the high round rosette windows.

It glittered too on the carved wood and gold leaf of the coffered ceiling—one of her grandmother Sandra's salvage expeditions had brought it back with much else from a palace on the coast of Westria, California-that-was, built for some forgotten prince of the old Americans generations prior to the Change. Moorish craftsmen had first wrought it for Spanish lords half a thousand years before that, across the eastern sea in Andalusia. Órlaith was suddenly conscious of it; what dramas had it seen in its journey across seas and centuries? What might it behold between now and the time of her grandchildren's grandchildren?

Everyone had knelt save the guards. Except of course Reiko and her followers; she was a reigning monarch in her own right, not a subject of the High Kingdom, and had remained standing after a respectful inclination of the head. Her followers had bowed deeply instead. Her dark kimono with a subtle black-on-black pattern and gray-striped *hakama* and dark gray five-*kamon haori* jacket were crisply perfect but gave a note of sober formality to the occasion—for starters, it was men's formal dress where she came from, apart from the high belting of the *hakama*. It stood out vividly amid the multicolored and wildly-varied splendor of lords and delegates from all of Montival's member-realms. There was even a party of Lakota from the easternmost border marches, in the fringed and beaded leather and the eagle-feather bonnets they kept for special occasions and impressing outsiders.

Todenangst was familiar home ground to Órlaith, but she could tell the Japanese had been impressed by the sheer alien bulk of the great fortress-palace-town, and positively shaken beneath their impassive politesse when they realized it had been built right after the Change when *their* grandparents had been scrambling for bare survival. What castles they had in Japan now were either refurbished survivors from very ancient times or much smaller modern copies.

Of course, Grandfather Norman built this to impress people . . . to intimidate people . . . well, to crush them, really. Nonna Sandra said he'd been drawing plans for it even before the Change. Nobody's ever even tried to besiege it.

The engineers he'd rounded up in his initial coup had picked a suitable hill with a nearby stream, then set to work with girders, rebar, concrete, Fresno scrapers and thousands upon thousands of steel cargo containers brought in over the railway, often by gangs of laborers hauling on ropes. Sometimes she felt a little uneasy remembering the hosts who'd died building the great pile and his other works. There was no getting around the fact that her mother's father had been something close to the Platonic ideal of *merciless tyrant* and possibly . . . almost certainly . . . more than a little mad, in a functional sort of way. And yet nearly all of those people would have died anyway. Hundreds of thousands who *would* have died otherwise had lived because of his ruthless vision.

Reiko had the two swords thrust through her sash and the steel *tessen-*war fan in her hand, and more than one eye among the ranks of watchers turned to the old gold-colored silk cords and sharkskin of *Kusanagi-no-Tsurugi's* hilt. An ancient monk, shaven-headed and saffron-robed among the emissaries of the Monastery of Chenrezi far off eastward across the mountains in the Valley of the Sun took a sharp breath and made a gesture of reverence with his palms pressed together before his face.

The High Queen wore a cotte-hardie in deep forest green that showed her six months' pregnancy rather obviously, and she looked exhausted beneath an iron resolution, her face framed by a pinned-back mourning veil of black gauze held by a silver-and-gold band and a chain of office around her neck, plaques alternating the Lidless Eye of the Armingers and the spread-winged Raven of House Artos. Órlaith was in a kilt of the Mackenzie green-brown-orange tartan, with the plaid pinned back so that the fringe fell nearly to her knees behind; because she preferred that, and because it emphasized that she might be her mother's daughter but she wasn't an Associate. She was also wearing a tight green Montrose jacket with its double row of silver buttons and lace at the throat and cuffs, and a flat Scots bonnet with a spray of Golden Eagle feathers in the clasp—the Eagle was her totem, the creature that had come to her in dreams.

The High Queen's eyes also rested on the hilt of the Grass-Cutting Sword at Reiko's waist for a moment. Órlaith knew her mother felt the reality of flaming power held in check by an intricate pattern of control, as she did; it seemed like called to like. Reiko had told her privately that *she* could sense the Sword of the Lady likewise, now that she bore the Grasscutter.

"The *Tennō Heika* of Dai-Nippon is most welcome at Our court," Mathilda went on, a cool graciousness in her tone. "Our realms share a common enemy and will seek a common retribution for the wrongs done our peoples and the death of our High King and your Emperor. It is a pity that this consultation has been delayed, but We recognize the urgency of the . . . project . . . with respect to Your Majesty's Sacred Treasure."

Reiko's face was unreadable as she made the slightest inclination of her head. Then she blinked as Mathilda repeated it in accentless Japanese, and in the formal, deliberately archaic dialect used by the court on Sado ga-shima at that.

Well, I should have expected that, Órlaith thought. *Mother never liked using the Sword of the Lady . . . nor did Da, really, and I can understand why now. She's always disliked it more . . . but they mingled their blood on its point at the Kingmaking, and it is linked to her as well. And to me through her as well as through Da.*

Reiko's followers were a little shocked at her fluency as well. But Egawa Noboru, the Imperial Guard commander who'd been with her on the journey south to the desert and the lost castle, and her Grand Steward Koyama Akira—who'd been left to wake up to a brief letter explaining why she was gone—both showed well-concealed delight. That statement was a promise of alliance, an alliance that Nippon still desperately needed and that Órlaith simply did not yet have the power to grant.

The Grass-Cutting Sword was a thing of terrible power, and enough to assure that even mighty Montival took Japan seriously. But war still needed fleets and armies, and they were heavily outnumbered. It had always been very likely indeed, virtually certain, that Montival would retaliate for the slaying of the High King, but this made it formal. There was a murmur of agreement from the crowd, and one Powder River rancher even let loose with a *kiy-yip!* of enthusiasm. Sometimes Órlaith thought that the wildly various realms of the High Kingdom were held together by eternal repetitive arguments as much as anything else, but her father's death had brought a wave of unified fury. Sacred blood had been shed, and her folk wanted blood in turn; preferably whole rivers of it.

That happened when you desecrated a people's symbols, unless there was something badly wrong with the people concerned.

"We will confer on these issues, Your Majesty," Mathilda said. "With your advisors and mine. Fortunately the meeting of the Congress of Realms means the whole kingdom can be consulted and informed swiftly."

"This is very good, Your Majesty," Reiko said, her voice soft but carrying clearly. "Yet it is also necessary to inform my homeland of what has occurred."

Mathilda nodded. "As soon as we have the outline of an agreement, I will dispatch a fast frigate to Dai-Nippon, with whoever you wish to bear the news, carrying such instructions as you think best. That will take—"

She turned her head to a square-built woman in a blue uniform and fore-and-aft cocked hat standing not far from the Throne, and they murmured for a moment.

"Sixty-five to ninety days sailing round-trip, depending on the winds," she said when she turned back to Reiko. "Continuous passage and not counting any time spent at the other end."

"I will emphasize the need for haste," Reiko said, and the two monarchs shared a smile as dry as her tone.

Then Mathilda turned her eyes on Órlaith, and her carefully neutral voice quivered with love and anger and pain. Her child wasn't sure that she would have known that quite so certainly before they'd both been bearers of the Sword of the Lady.

"You are Our beloved daughter and heir," she said, and Órlaith winced invisibly at the continued use of the formal Royal plural. "But you are also

under Our displeasure on this day. Her Majesty of Nihon had no obligation of obedience to Us. You *do*. You disobeyed; you suborned others to
disobedience, and placed still others under conflicts of oath and loyalty."

Órlaith considered arguing that she hadn't been specifically forbidden
to assist Reiko on her search for the lost treasure. One hard glance told
her that her mother had seen the impulse almost as soon as it had
occurred to her and that it was wisdom to suppress it. Particularly since
she'd done everything but hide on the bottom of ponds breathing
through a reed to avoid being confronted by servants of the Crown pur-
suing her with a sealed rescript demanding her immediate return.

Still, it had worked. . . .

Her mother seemed to sense that one too: "Even success does not
fully excuse that offense. This is not a tyranny, but a Kingdom under law."

Órlaith blinked. In the time of her mother's father, men had been
beheaded at a nod from the first Lord Protector, some of them in this
very room. When you looked at it that way, her mother had a point. The
High Queen went on:

"There must be due regard for rank and station and respect for authority among the mighty as well as the commons, or that authority becomes
merely the willfulness of vanity sustained by force. You cannot truly or
rightly command obedience until you show that you yourself are obedient to your lawful superiors, and disciplined in your soul. You are forbidden the Court until I inform you otherwise, and you would be well-advised
not to draw Our attention until then. You may go."

Órlaith swallowed and went to one knee again, bowing with right fist
to chest.

"The High Queen commands," she said, backed the precise four steps
that etiquette required before she turned and walked down the strip of
carpet towards the high arched doors.

Some of the delegates stared or very quietly murmured among themselves, the newcomers from distant parts of the kingdom being filled in by
those who were or thought they were more knowledgeable. The courtiers
mostly kept their gazes carefully neutral. Disfavor was contagious, but

Órlaith would be High Queen fairly soon and might remember an open slight. On the other hand her mother would still be Lady Protector of the Association, since she held that title for life in her own right through inheritance from her parents rather than as a temporary regency through marriage.

Mathilda's mouth tightened, and she struck the arm of the throne with one palm. When she spoke it was with the same implacable calm, and to Reiko:

"Your Majesty, we will consult briefly in private with our respective Chancellors, if that is agreeable to you."

"Very much so, Your Majesty," Reiko said, making a graceful gesture of assent with her fan.

"Then this audience is dismissed for the present."

Reiko spared her friend and ally only a single flicker of the eyes as she passed. Órlaith would have been shocked if she'd done otherwise, and inclined to scold her. They'd become comrades and close friends, but Reiko's duty was to her realm and right now that meant her dealings with the High Queen came first. She could tell without looking around when her mother went through the door of the inner chamber; voices began to fill the echoing silence.

Heuradys d'Ath fell in a step behind Órlaith, cat-polite and entirely unconcerned as her long wine-colored cape swung just above the golden spurs on her heels, and her elaborately braided dark-auburn hair brushed her houppelande-clad shoulders beneath her round roll-edged chaperon hat. *She* was Órlaith's personal liege knight as well as a childhood friend, and had no higher loyalty. Her amber-colored eyes didn't stop looking for danger even here.

As they left the audience room the knight's adoptive mother stepped close for a moment, in vivid contrast to those carefully looking elsewhere as they left, or acting as if they wanted to avoid a contagious disease without being rude about it, or fixing their eyes on documents to the exclusion of all else.

"Rusticate, infants," Baroness Tiphaine d'Ath said quietly. "And once you've jumped in the prairie-dog hole pull it in after you. Let her get over it. She can be mad at me in the interim, since I have to be here."

The High Marshal of Montival didn't exactly whisper, and it wasn't necessary for privacy anyway. Even now that she was in her early sixties and there was as much silver-white as white-gold in her bobbed hair most people just moved away from that sword-slim, black-clad form when Lady Death obviously didn't want to be overheard. Heuradys' birth mother, Delia de Stafford, Countess of Campscapell and Tiphaine's Châtelaine for thirty-six years, simply gestured anxious agreement from behind her. The knight nodded briskly to them both without checking her stride, though Órlaith suspected she also winked.

Órlaith sighed as they walked through the gates of the presence chamber and the glaivesmen rapped the butts of their weapons on the floor.

"And the worst of it is I couldn't just be worried for John with Mother," she said. "The last we saw of him was that bloody wave hitting him!"

"We know it didn't kill him," Heuradys said.

"Yet," Órlaith replied. "And that doesn't mean that it didn't *hurt* him, you see. Or that something hasn't."

Heuradys nodded. "You know, I *almost* envy him the experience of living through that wave, since we know he did."

"Well, there's always the feeling of relief you get at not dying," Órlaith said dryly. "But wishing for the experience . . . you might as well hit yourself with a war-hammer because it feels so good when you stop."

"I did say almost, my liege," the knight said. "And anyway, he'll make a nice vivid song of it!"

CHAPTER THREE

Is this what drowning is like? John thought as the wave broke across the *Queen's* stern.

He had time for that, because the whole process was somehow oddly passive from his point of view, given that there was absolutely nothing he could do but endure it. His lungs were burning and cold at the same time. It was black, utterly black, shocking an instant after even the dim storm-cloud light of day. Black and very cold, and the water tore and jerked at him—blows hugely powerful and diffuse at the same time, tumbling and turning him and ramming him against things hard and bruising. Something thumped him in the stomach and he could feel air burst out through his teeth and water come in on the uncontrollable choking reflex.

Weight fell away. Foam surged past him, the rope holding him as he skidded across the deck in the tumbling backwash of the wave, swinging like a pendulum while trying to cough and breathe and vomit at the same time. He settled on a mixture of all three that set him coughing again.

Perfect misery driveth out fear, he thought, as salt water and diluted stomach acids shot out his nose and mouth.

Then he stopped in the very act of retching. He could see a little forward of the south-pointing bow, and the angles and scale of what he was seeing were so alien that for a moment his mind stuttered, trying to picture it. Then it snapped into place as a volley of lightning-bolts gave the darkness a harsh blue-white illumination. They really were sliding backward down a mountain. The *Queen* had ridden up the front side, slammed backward through the crest with water running ten feet deep along the decks, and now the monster wave was running away southward beneath the black clouds.

He forced himself—it was becoming a habit—to look backward. Mostly it was murk and spray driving hard into his squinting eyes, but he thought he saw another wave there that would have utterly horrified him if he hadn't experienced the one that they'd just survived. The surface beneath the keel wasn't smooth either; there was a cross-chop that made the planks beneath him buck and heave.

Evrouin was doggedly crawling towards him, and slumped in relief when John waved feebly at him, staggered erect and wound his arms through the ratlines that ran up to the mizzenmast. Deor and Thora were not far away, and they'd clipped their lines to the shrouds. The *scop* was staring transfixed at the lightning-shot sky and the monster swell racing towards them, and Thora was laughing with her water-darkened hair clinging to the handsome bones of her face.

"That was more fun than I've had with my clothes on all year!" she called to him, just audible through roar and howl and surf-blur.

John suppressed an impulse to scream *shut up, you insane bitch!* back at her and laughed a little himself instead. The grin was forced, but somehow true at the same time.

"Brace for it, brace for it!" Feldman shouted—half croaking—through his megaphone, while he pulled up one of the helmsmen with his free hand; the man went to the aid of his partner, who had a bleeding scalp wound. "The sea-anchor will drag us through the crest!"

The crew on deck were huddled under the break of the quarterdeck; he saw Ishikawa dash down one of the manropes along the deck and do something that involved hitting what-ever-it-was with a mallet while looking over his shoulder. Either option was probably preferable to waiting below, without even the illusion of knowing what was going on, much less having the slightest control over it. The stern rose and rose, until he was looking up at the wheel and the folk behind it. The surface of the wave was white-streaked black, and the crest a tumbling wave of white.

This time he snatched a deep breath and squeezed his eyes shut as the crest fell on the *Tarshish Queen*'s quarterdeck. It still felt like being hit by an enormous padded hammer, then by tentacles that sucked and dragged. But the solid water part—as opposed to the equally unbreathable but lighter froth—didn't rise over his head. And he could feel the way the buoyancy of the ship pushed back against the weight of water on her deck, and how the sea-anchor jerked her backward through the sharp crest. It was a little like that long-ago day when he started *feeling* what the horse he was riding was doing, and why, as if its body and mind were an extension of his.

He opened his eyes in time to dash a palm across his face and catch a blurred glimpse of the white line of the wave running all the way down to the bow across the width of the ship. And then—faintly, like one of the Chinese line-drawings of things seen through mist his grandmother Sandra had collected—the bowsprit corkscrewing upwards as the wave ran away from beneath them.

He looked backward, and for an instant the ship was high enough that he could see a succession of waves marching towards them from the north, each a black whale-monster topped with a bone-white mane of spume. Then they slid back down into the trough. It *felt* as if they were going backward, but they weren't—the ship was traveling before the wind, and quickly, but thanks to the sea-anchor they were going slower than the water they floated in. It wasn't just the wave that was running away from them, the whole *ocean* was sliding forward even as he watched.

John felt a moment of profound vertigo, then shouted aloud with the wonder of it. Something seemed to awake in his soul. It was a line of ancestral seafarers beyond number whose blood lived in his. Warriors

who'd shared snake-headed raiding boats with Thora and Deor's ancestors in the cold North Sea; the little *Dove* that had born the first Arminger
to Maryland in the train of Lord Calvert; a clipper hand named Whittle
who'd beaten around Cape Horn two centuries past and ended his journey in Portland. And through brides of theirs from the potlatch tribes
who'd driven their massive canoes down Montival's coast, Tinglit and
Salish and Maka.

The next wave wasn't as bad; spray broke over the stern, but only a
foot or two of water. Then they seemed to steady, each no better than
the last, but no worse.

Feldman shook himself and gave a prayer of thanksgiving: *"Baruch
Atah Adonai Eloheinu Melech ha'olam, ha-gomel l'hayavim tovot sheg'malani kol tov!"*

"Amen!" John said. "And hear us when we cry to Thee, for those in
peril on the sea!"

Radavindraban came up the companionway, as drenched as they were
and timing his upward steps to the roll of the ship and the rush of water,
sliding his belt line along the manropes.

"We"—he began, then paused as water swirled around their waists.
"We're leaking worse for'ard, Cap'n," he said. "That wrenched the wretch-
edness of the cracked rib, and the stay bars we spiked around the break are
starting to tear loose at the fastenings, yes indeed. We should fother a sail
over it outside, when the weather is better. I ordered the pumps rigged."

"Injuries in the watch below, or our passengers?"

"A broken arm and a collarbone. Some bruises with the soldiers. Not
too bally bad, eh, Cap'n?"

"Except for that, Mr. Radavindraban," Feldman said, and pointed
upward.

The First Mate looked up. *"Anaathai kaluthai!"* he blurted.

John assumed that was something naughty in Tamil, and looked up
himself. Amid the driving spray and rain it was hard to see, but the golden-
brown Douglas fir trunk that made the mizzenmast showed a dark curving
line ten feet up. Then it disappeared, appeared again, disappeared. . . .

It's a split, John realized. Opening and closing as the ship twists.

"Woold her, Cap'n?" Radavindraban said, after a long silent moment.

"That would be very good," Feldman said and grinned, then waited until the next wave passed over the quarterdeck before going on: "I think highly of your shipcraft, Mr. Mate. But if you can think of a way to woold the mizzen in this, I'll think more highly still!"

Radavindraban smiled, a white flash against the blurred darkness of his face. "What then, Cap'n?"

"We need to steady her motion, so that it'll flex less and we can haul in the sea-anchor. A steadying sail. And not on the mizzen!"

"Forestaysail?"

"The jib, I think. Just a scrap of it."

John knew that meant the foremost sail on the line—the stay— running down from the foremast to the bowsprit. He looked south and swallowed, as they bit into the sea and the bow threw plumes of spray twenty feet high on either side.

"I'll see to it, Cap'n."

"No, Mr. Radavindraban, you have the deck; you've done very well with the leak. See to the helm, for the Lord's sake keep her steady, and I'll lead the working party."

"Is there anything I . . . we . . . can do?" John said.

It *had* to be said, though he already knew the answer. John still felt a little silly doing it at the half-shout necessary with the wind this high and rain whipping down like a pump-driven hose at high velocity.

"It's the cobbler to his last, I'm afraid, Your Highness. If we need sword-work, rest assured I'll call on you and yours," Feldman said, as he stripped off his jacket and shirt.

He nodded towards Thora and Deor: "Our friends are good practical sailors after their travels, but I'm not taking them either, nor the Japanese, who are fine seamen one and all. I need hands used to working with each other when they can't talk."

Feldman finished by pulling off his boots and socks and looping a sailor's working knife around his neck on a lanyard; his bare wet torso was wiry with lean muscle, and the abundant body hair showed the white lines of scars unusual for a merchant Captain, even an adventurous one—at some time he'd been flogged, and someone had branded something on his chest in a cursive script John didn't recognize. Then he was away calling for the Bosun, and John spoke:

"I'd better go below and check on the men," he said. "We're a long way from home, and getting farther."

Deor nodded. "I'll help Ruan and the ship's doctor. I've picked up a bit of that trade."

"And then you and I should go to our cubby and dry each other off, Johnnie," Thora said, and winked broadly.

Deor laughed and disappeared down the companionway with a wave, timing his steps as automatically as Radavindraban had done. John cleared his throat.

"Ah . . . *now?*" he said.

And thank . . . well, not God . . . that I didn't squeak, he thought.

Then cursed; he'd headed down the companionway so heedlessly that his head was just at the height of the quarterdeck when a slug of cold seawater sluiced across it and right into the back of his head.

"It'll be a lot more fun than staying here getting soaked," Thora said cheerfully as he stood streaming under the break of the quarterdeck, waiting to open the doorway until the water had abated for a moment. "And who knows, every time may be the last!"

Three days later he watched the woolding of the mizzenmast and thought how fascinating it was. Especially since they were still running before heavy seas and under gray skies that rained now and then. Not anything like the storm-black cover like a cast iron lid on the world, nor the size of the first half-dozen waves that had hit them off Topanga, but still steep enough that every time they went over a crest spray crashed the length of the ship, and the sensation of running down the slope was a lot like skiing on Mount Hood in winter.

And it makes me think how glad I am I'm not a sailor, he added to himself; it was interesting to watch, but he hadn't the slightest interest in doing it himself. *And it would be nice to be really dry and warm for a change.*

No matter how well-found, a wooden ship was always slightly damp below-decks in a blow, and the only really warm place was the galley, where it would have been an abuse of rank to linger. And you couldn't spend *all* your time in the bunk with a nice warm woman, especially when the woman was alarmingly indifferent to hardship even for a Bearkiller. They were all wearing long oilskin jackets and sou'westers, smelling strongly of linseed oil and streaming with the wet, over thick sweaters, and long underwear beneath canvas pants, and sea-boots—even Ruan had given up his kilt for now. It was still fairly miserable, like being on a hunting trip in the Willamette in the Black Months without the fires or the prospect of roast boar.

So it was just as well he had something interesting to watch. The detectable part of the crack where the great wave had wrenched the mast beyond bearing was about four feet long. The crew had taken a dozen of the spare twelve-foot capstan bars and packed them in a ring around the break, slathering them thickly with a melted tarry glue. Next had come three-inch cable wrapped around it in a solid coil two layers deep, stretched taut by a portable winch with offset cranks a bit at a time. And pacing it with the motion of the ship, so that the rope clamped bit by bit when the crack naturally swayed shut.

John watched as the sailor resting against the mast in a harness like that loggers used on tall trees made a final pull at the cranks and the little winch locked with a sharp *clack* sound.

"Done! Tight as she'll go, sir!" he called down.

"Good. Nail it, Vitovski!" Radavindraban said.

The sailor hammered in a row of curved nails with broad leather washers around their flat heads, then slid down to the deck with a thump and unbuckled the crank from his waist. The Captain, the First Mate and the Bosun all took turns climbing up the rope—something they did as casually as a farmer trotting up the barn ladder to the hayloft—to go over the work with minute attention. After they'd thumped back to the deck Captain Ishikawa asked permission and then did likewise, nodding to himself as he returned.

They all do that, John noted privately.

He'd noticed since he first met them months ago that the Nihon-jin carefully examined everything they saw done here in Montival—machines, tools, weapons, buildings, methods, organization. They were intensely proud, but didn't let that get in the way of a relentless pragma-tism; anything useful they saw would be taken to pieces, examined, and if they saw potential advantage in it would be modified, adapted and made their own.

When we get to Dai-Nippon, I think it would be a good idea if we cautioned our officers and engineers and artificers to do likewise, John thought. *Because I don't have the slightest doubt they'll find tricks it would be to our advantage to copy. We've spent the last two generations learning how to do things in the Changed world, but I doubt we've found it all.*

Feldman turned to the Bosun. "Right, Smith, let's finish up."

The Bosun nodded. "Aye aye, skipper."

Finishing up turned out to mean another thick layer of the tarry, chemical-smelling glue applied to the rope, and then a cylinder of rawhide—bull-hide dragged overside a day to soften and stretch it—wound around the woolding and fastened with three rows of the nails from top to bottom. The whole affair looked like a bandage, or the splint on a broken leg, which he supposed was an apt metaphor; he peered intently to fix the image and the form of words away. Everything was grist to the mill. . . .

Deor was grinning at him. "You have the poet's itch, true enough, Prince," he said. "Storing that up, weren't you?"

"I was, fellow-guildsman," he said. "Though it had also occurred to me that this is like nursing along a sick horse!"

Deor chuckled. "More like a machine," he said. "As it was in the an-cient days, a machine and we all depending on it for our lives."

"Now that's a striking image!" John said. "Unusual!"

I knew ships were machines, he thought, musing. *I hadn't appreciated how much sailing was like living in a machine. And we are the way the machine keeps itself alive, like the things inside our bodies that heal wounds and fight off disease.*

They climbed another wave. Feldman trained his telescope to the rear. John did likewise; he was catching the trick of keeping his binoculars steady from a moving surface. The topmost sails on the masts of the pursuer showed for an instant against the dark water and iron-gray sky before they slid down into the trough.

"That Korean is persistent," Feldman said.

Then he looked at the mizzenmast. "I'd prefer to wait for three days of hot dry weather, but only the Lord can deliver that, and He, Blessed be the Name, hasn't seen fit to give us any."

"His judgments are just and righteous altogether," John agreed. "But this storm . . ."

"Isn't natural," Feldman agreed in turn. "It's more like weather in the Roaring Forties than this part of the Pacific. Mr. Mate! We'll see if she'll bear sail. Raise the gaff; six reefs."

Sailors hurried to the winches, and lined the boom for a moment to untie the reefs that held the sail down. The gearing whined, and the gaff began to rise; then they paid out, and the boom swung to starboard. The motion of the ship changed, and the Captain and First Mate spent a long moment staring at the woolding.

"She holds, Cap'n," Radavindraban said. "Tight."

"For now, Mr. Mate, for now. Binnacle!" Feldman said. "How many knots?"

"Twelve even, skipper!"

John did a quick mental calculation; he didn't have any natural aptitude for mathematics, but his parents had seen that he learned the basics, which were essential for a ruler or a commander of warriors both. Sea miles were a little over a tenth longer than the land variety. . . .

He winced mentally. They were making better than two hundred and fifty miles a day, nearly as fast as a hippomotive. That put them a *long* way from home, and farther every hour. . . .

Feldman collapsed his telescope and stood tapping it into his left palm for a moment. "That Korean is hard to shake," he said. "But there's more ways of killing a cat than drowning it in cream."

From the look on his face he had something unpleasant in mind for their pursuer and John heartily approved; he'd already come to hate the lookout's morning call of *sail ho to sternward*!

And it's not natural we can't shake him, too, he thought. *I wish the Sword of the Lady was here. And Órlaith to carry it. It would be a relief to have her being bossy! I wonder what she's been doing?*

CHAPTER FOUR

CASTLE TODENANGST, CROWN DEMESNE
PORTLAND PROTECTIVE ASSOCIATION
(FORMERLY NORTHERN OREGON)
HIGH KINGDOM OF MONTIVAL
(FORMERLY WESTERN NORTH AMERICA)
SEPTEMBER 15TH
CHANGE YEAR 46/2044 AD

The audience chamber gave out onto a D-shaped antechamber occupying part of the north side of this level of the tower, lit by pointed-arch windows through the thickness of the outer tower wall. This high up they could be large, and there was none of the funeral gloom you usually associated with castles. Crossbowmen raised their weapons to the present as Órlaith came through and a stream of Delegates came out behind her. The mild humid warmth of a Willamette summer came in through the open panes, carrying scents of woodsmoke and greenery and flowers, to mingle with the stone and beeswax scents of the building. The silver-gray tile of the wall was divided by thin upright panels of stylized ceramic vines and flowers and birds in blue and crimson and green; niches held the fruits of her maternal grandmother's expeditions and patronage—here a celadon vase made in old China, there a blue-robed, gold-crowned modern Madonna with a soft secret smile as she gazed down at the Child in her arms.

"Phew," Órlaith murmured as they turned left and walked briskly towards the elevators and her waiting followers. "That was bad, Herry. Not as bad as I feared, worse than I hoped."

"Sort of like life that way," Heuradys said dryly. "But look at it like this, my heroic but fretful liege: Reiko got her sword, she's getting the alliance she needs and which in the long run *we* need, John's alive, and in a bit less than five years you're going to be High Queen."

"I'll be a High Queen with a reputation for reckless indiscipline," she said gloomily.

"No, that would have been if we'd screwed up. Right now you're a Crown Princess with a reputation for being smart and daring enough to bring off impossible stuff. Sort of like your dad! Or your mother, before she got all stodgy."

"No, she was always a stickler for rules and procedures, from what I hear. She just loved Da so much she took off after him anyway."

"Ah, I hadn't thought of it that way! Still, while it's not a perfect result, I'd give it a nice solid as-good-as-can-be-reasonably-expected."

Órlaith stopped for a moment and lowered her voice still more. "Remember the beach in Topanga? For John . . . death isn't the worst thing that can happen."

Heuradys winced slightly. Reiko had met *her* brother there, a brother long-lost and thought to be dead for more than half a decade . . . and he'd been a tortured slave of the sorcerer-lords of the enemy who'd broken his soul in captivity. She'd tricked him into taking the Grass-Cutting Sword in his hands and drawing it, and in a single instant it had quite literally burned him to a thin drift of ash before she seized it back and used it to call upon her Ancestress and crush the Korean ships.

That was . . . alarming. It gives me an idea of how it must be for others around the Sword of the Lady.

"There's absolutely nothing we can do about that right now, Orrey. Except win this war we're starting."

"They started it," Órlaith said and made a vexed sound. She shook her head. "It's odd how you can love someone and they you, and the two of you still just can't get along sometimes."

Heuradys mimed clapping for an instant. "My little baby liege is growing up!"

"Says the Wise Crone of twenty-three!" Órlaith replied.

Then she caught the look in Heuradys' eye and knew she was being a little annoying on purpose to jar her liege out of her gloom. It was good to have friends to do things like that for you.

"And she could have done a lot worse," her knight said more seriously. "She let those men-at-arms from the Protector's Guard Sir Aleaume brought with us go back to their posts, for example."

Órlaith nodded. "Mother can be harsh but she isn't vicious," she said. "The problem is she thinks she's going to teach me patience; in fact I'm just going to be wasting time twiddling my thumbs and grinding my teeth when there's *work* to be done."

"Thumb-twiddling and tooth-grinding is what's supposed to teach you the patience, if meditation in Moon School didn't."

"I could never meditate worth a dog's breakfast—you may notice my totem is a bird and a very active one. And if we'd been *patient* we'd still be doing a diplomatic fencing game with Reiko and the enemy might have gotten the Grass-Cutter. Or used Reiko's brother to divide Nihon beyond repair."

"Alternatively we could all have gotten killed. You roll the iron dice."

Her remaining folk were over by the fretted bronzework elevator doors—one of three functioning elevators in all Montival, to her knowledge, and the only one built since the Change. She nodded to them and put on a mostly-genuine smile.

Her greathound Macmaccon was the only one wholly reassured, and came over panting happily with his nails clicking on the marble. He thrust his barrel-shaped shaggy head under one hand while he leant against her, with his tongue lolling over very impressive fangs in a grin of joy. In peacetime Mackenzies used greathounds for guarding herds and homes, and hunting things like boar and tiger.

In war they hunted men.

"Sit, Macmac. At heel!" To the others' anxious expressions: "Not as bad as it might have been. I'm to go contemplate my sins for a bit, some place with few people and many sheep. Finding a magic sword and adding two realms to the High Kingdom seems to count for a wee bit of a something, as opposed to leaving on a Quest without telling her first."

Though misplacing my brother and a ship-full of others . . . ah, that's a different matter. I can't even blame her for blaming me. It's not exactly fair—none of us knew what Kusanagi would do, not even Reiko—but I was in command. It's even a relief to have Mother blame me. It distracts me from blaming me, you might say.

Everyone looked relieved, though; she could have been confined to a fortress somewhere.

"Diarmuid," she went on.

Diarmuid Tennart McClintock nodded, his dark hair curling around his shoulders and brushing the thin wrought-gold neck torc that marked a married man in the Old Faith. He was slim but broad-shouldered and of middling height, which made him an inch shorter than her, and blue curling tattoos on face and arms echoed the sinuous pattern of the jeweled disk that pinned the plaid of his Great Kilt at the shoulder.

"Aye, lass?" he said in the growling accent of the hills and mountains and high valleys beyond the Willamette's southern boundary where his family were tacksmen, sub-chiefs. "Herself herself is nae in the mood for the loppin' off o' heids?"

It was perfectly respectful, by Clan McClintock standards.

"Oh, she's in the mood, sure and she is, but she won't be after the *doing* of it this day, you see," she said, letting her own Mackenzie lilt grow stronger.

They were comrades now, and still warm friends and had been lovers once; he'd been her first man, at a Beltane festival the year she turned sixteen, when he'd been a Fire Squire and she one of the May Queen's Maidens.

"Diarmuid, you followed when I called," she said, resting a hand on his shoulder; the muscle under her fingers was pleasantly like hard living rubber. "And you a newly-handfasted man and Caitlin with a babe on the way. I count that true friendship and worthy of a brave man's honor; the

Morrigú witness, and Lug of the Oaths who loves a warrior's faithfulness."

She pitched it just a little louder so the double-handful of his clansfolk at his back could hear it clearly. They bristled with pride; honor done their leader was done to them also and their kindreds and home-ranges and Clan.

"And folk of yours fell on our faring. Praise they shall have so their names live; and their families their honor-price. Gold and gear cannot give them back to their kin, but what gold and gear can do will be done, so."

"Aye, well, they fell bravely in a guid cause, no' just a scuffle over the reiving of cows or some drunken boast at a feast, and they can say it to the Guardians of the Western Gate," Diarmuid said, though there was sadness in his midnight-blue eyes.

Dryly: "And you'll not see McClintock crofters turning down gold and gear, either."

His followers chuckled; they were a stark people.

"What next, then?" he asked.

"Next you go home," she said, and held up a hand at his protest. "Not for long! I took you from Caitlin at a bad time, for needs must when Anwyn's hounds are at your heels. Go home and see the babe born, which you can do if you hurry; harvest your own fields and hunt your own hills, play with the little one and make some memories to warm your hands at later. There's a fight coming, like none our lifetimes have seen."

"Aye, something tae that," he said. "We missed the grain, but I'll be back in time for the last hay and the grapes and fruit, and for the fall salmon run and the fat elk comin' down from the mountain meadows."

She leaned closer, smiling and whispered in his ear: "And tell Caitlin my reply to her private message, which is this: I *am* after sending you back alive, and I *did* keep my princessly hands off."

"Aye, I'll say that—it may shorten the time I spend sleeping in the hayloft and suppin' on a dish o' want. *Soraidh leibh*, then, and merry part!"

"*Slán leat*: and merry meet again," she replied.

The McClintocks all bowed and trotted off in a flurry of kilts, heading for the stairs they trusted more than the dangerous northern elevator contraption with its moving room, which they thought against nature.

She put her hands on her hips and looked at the rest of them. There were ten Mackenzies led by the Aylward brothers Karl and Mathun; one had died on the journey, and one had gone off with John.

Or more precisely, Ruan went off with Deor because his lover died and they found each other. Joy and luck to them both, and guard my brother!

The Dúnedain Rangers Faramir and Morfind, who were the son and daughter of her father's younger twin half-sisters; and Susan Mika—Clever Raccoon—a small wiry young woman in fringed leathers with a pair of eagle feathers tucked into her raven-hued braids. She was Lakota, more or less an exile and a member of the Crown Courier Corps, or had been up until she volunteered for Órlaith's little conspiracy and used her job as a cover for the messages they needed to keep private.

"So, would any of you be off the now? I'll not grudge it, for it's grand companions you've all been, and this is the end of the venture you joined me for."

Some bothered to say *no;* the rest just snorted or rolled their eyes. Sir Droyn Jones de Molalla threw back his handsome head and laughed outright, teeth white against his light brown skin and tossing black curls; he was three inches taller than she and his wine-red houppelande and tight blue hose showed his tiger build to admiration.

"My liege, I don't think my lord my father is any more pleased with me than Her Majesty is with *you!*" he said, with a sweeping bow. "Since I'm your vassal-at-arms"—he made a slighter bow to Heuradys, acknowledging her senior status in that category—"I claim aid and maintenance and the protection of your arm! I can hope that as a belted knight of twenty I'm too distinguished and too old to *be* belted by my lord my father and then sent to my room without supper, but it's a *faint* hope."

Count Chaka Jones de Molalla *was* inclined to be a bit choleric, though to be sure she'd never yet met a Count who liked being defied. And under the jest were serious matters of honor. Droyn had sworn to her personally, and she'd knighted him with the Sword after the battle on the Bay.

The other three present had come north with them after Topanga, but they weren't exactly her followers, though in a sense she was acting as their patron: Meshek ben-Raanan and his large, hairy, silent brother Dov, and their sister Shulamit bat-Raanan. All three were the children of the *Shofet*—Judge and ruler—of the *bnei Yaakov*, and it showed in a family likeness of wavy black hair, black eyes and long rather boney proud-nosed, full-lipped faces as well as their camel-hair robes and billowy pantaloons tucked into soft goatskin boots. Meshek and his brother were here to investigate the wide and dangerous world of which his desert-dwelling nomad folk knew much less than they now realized was wise or even safe after their long post-Change isolation. Shulamit was seventeen, and she was here because she'd threatened to stow away or walk if they didn't take her. They'd believed it, since she'd absconded from their father's tents without permission in the first place and joined the party heading for Topanga when they were too far along to send her back into the desert alone.

Usually she was a chatterbox; all through Astoria and the trip up the Columbia she'd been a mass of observations and questions—all intelligent ones, if endless. Todenangst had her quiet and wide-eyed, though.

Meshek made that graceful gesture his people used, bowing and at the same time touching the fingers of the right hand to brow, lips and heart and then sweeping it down. The wide sleeve of his robe nearly touched the floor.

"*Nisicah*," he said, which was a title that translated as *woman of high rank* in Ivrit, and was what he'd first called her outside the burning wreck of the cursed castle in the Valley of Death. "My brother will depart now with our first report for our father, if it pleases you. I and Shulamit—"

He tugged at his full, curly black beard; it was a gesture he used when annoyed, which was frequently where his younger sister was concerned.

"—will remain here for a time. To observe, perhaps to negotiate."

Órlaith nodded and reached into her sporran for an order pad and wrote, then tore it off and handed it to him:

"This is a quick letter of introduction to *Rosh* Eyal—"

"Head Eyal?" Dov asked, which was what the word meant in his language.

"Chief, elected leader, of the Confederated Kibbutzim of Degania Dalet, has been for a while, and his grandfather . . . well, he'll tell you. He's here with some of his people for the Congress of Realms, and I think he'll be very helpful in getting Dov home. And helpful in general, *Seren* Meshek. I know him slightly personally and more by reputation and my parents' opinions; he's a shrewd and capable man, and a man of honor."

"Many thanks, *Nisicah,*" Meshek said.

Órlaith smiled. "You got us out of the Mojave alive in high summer, and quickly."

"But he made you ride Ben Zona, Princess," Shualmit said, evidently recovering from her attack of awe.

Her brothers glared at her, and Órlaith suppressed a smile; it was rarely wise to intrude in a family quarrel, and the *bnei Yaakov* were clannish to a fault. Ben Zona—the name meant "Son of a Whore"—hadn't been all that bad. For a camel. Instead she continued to Meshek:

"And without your bola . . . and Shulamit's sling . . . things might have gone otherwise on that beach in Topanga. I owe you and your family a debt, son of the *Shofet.* So does the *Heika.* House Artos doesn't forget an enemy or a friend; neither does the Yamato Dynasty. We'll meet again; until then peace and the blessings of your Lord be upon you, and upon your people and their children, tents and flocks."

"And upon you and yours, woman of valor," Meshek said. "I think my father made the right decision . . . but then, he usually does."

The *bnei Yaakov* might be desert-dwelling herdsmen, but they weren't in the least intimidated by the elevator; Órlaith had been very impressed by the ingenious gadgets and methods they used to squeeze a decent living out of their savagely arid homeland. Shulamit spun the wheel that flicked up an indicator inside it and rang a bell in the treadmill room far below. As the cage sank out of sight she was craning her neck to try and watch the cable connection through the openwork of the ceiling and pointing out details of the mechanism that rang the chimes to her brothers' lively interest.

"Now," Órlaith said, "if we're to get ourselves out of sight like a smacked puppy hiding in a woodshed—"

The rest gave a chorus of realistic whimpers; Macmac put his ears down and glanced around, and Órlaith shook a finger at them before going on:

"—where should we be going? My mother didn't say."

"Which I think is a test too," Heuradys said soberly.

Karl Aylward Mackenzie shrugged as he stood leaning easily on his cased longbow.

"Dun Juniper, surely!" he said, grinning.

Sky-blue eyes and sun-faded flaxen brows stood out the more against skin given a deep ruddy tan by the fierce southern sun. Behind him Gwri Beauregard McKenzie shook her head hard enough to rattle the sapphire beads she'd put on the ends of the many thin braids in which she wore her tight-curled black hair. Then she carefully pulled his queue aside by the end of the old bowstring that bound it and slapped him hard on the back of his head.

"Sure, and for a good bow-captain you're a dolt betimes, Karl-me-lad," the young seeress said. "Politics! Think how Herself streaking for the dúthchas after a quarrel with her mother would look when the clack got about!"

Órlaith nodded as Karl retrieved his bonnet and rubbed his head and his brother Mathun—who looked enough like him to be a twin, though he was nineteen to Karl's twenty—snickered. Gwri was extremely right.

"True enough," Órlaith said. "We can't make this a matter of Clan and Association! That blood-feud needs to lie still in its grave."

The two Dúnedain nodded and sighed regretfully. "The same applies to going to Mithrilwood, I suppose," Faramir said thoughtfully, a trace of a soft musical accent in his English.

He had delicate, snub-nosed features and very slightly tilted eyes; it had made him look a bit naive and childlike when they'd started out. He had a good point, too. Mithrilwood—once Silver Falls State Park—had been the first of the Dúnedain staths. Going there would be just another way to revive the memories of the wars against the Association.

Susan Mika smiled a bit wryly. "I'd invite you all to the *makol*, that's far enough away we didn't lift hair on either side in those old fights, we were too busy with the Square Staters, but I'm not exactly popular at home myself."

With a grin she reached up and tugged at her taller companions' locks in a rough caress: Faramir's were pale gold and loosely curled, his cousin Malfind's straight and as black as her own.

"Though with pretty scalps like this, it woulda been tempting if we'd known you guys existed then!"

"Right you are, cousin," Órlaith said to the Rangers. "In fact, since all the delegates are heading to Dún na Síochána where they'll live in tents or be hot-bunking while they debate at length, somewhere outside the Willamette would be best."

The Citadel of Peace—that was what Dún na Síochána meant—was the new capital of the High Kingdom, under off-and-on construction for some years on the old site of Salem, the pre-Change capital of ancient Oregon, picked because it was long-deserted and on neutral ground.

"Probably best we stay in the Protectorate, at that," Órlaith said thoughtfully. "So as not to look as if we're trying to get out from under Mother's hand, or that we're rejecting the north-realm. But the Association rules a whacking great load of land."

"Not in the Willamette? That rules out my mothers' place at Montinore Manor on Barony Ath. Besides that being where we, ah, left from."

"Ran away from?" Susan Mika filled in helpfully. "Skipped away at night from? What's that word . . . ?"

"Absconded?" Morfind Vogeler said.

Órlaith gave her a quelling glance. Heuradys went on:

"Which would be tactless right now."

"Right; it would be too much like putting a thumb in Mother's eye because I was in a snit. To be sure, I *am* in a snit, but I don't have to act that way," Órlaith said, blinking up at the carved plaster arches of the ceiling.

"A Crown demesne estate would put any castellan I descended on in a difficult position. Not to mention they'd be sending regular reports here."

Heuradys nodded. "How about Barony Harfang out east? Diomede—"

She had two elder brothers: Lioncel de Stafford and Diomede d'Ath.

"—is over at Castle Campscapell visiting my lord dad and Lioncel. And he takes his garrison there to get ready for the autumn war-games after the harvest, so there's room and supplies. Far enough away to be properly submissive-and-repentant-looking but not too hard to get back from in a hurry since there's a rail link. And if anyone asks, I could say I'm visiting my own manors there."

"Right you are, Herry. Any objections? We'll do that, then."

She wrote again on the order pad, then beckoned over one of the castle servants dressed in tabard and brimless flowerpot hat who'd been standing motionless waiting for someone to call, looking rather like an old playing card.

"Goodman"—the name flowed up, probably a fruit of the Sword at her side, and got her an instant of smile in the man's trained gravity—"Faron. Please take this to the Movements division of the Logistics and Transport offices and have them lay on a six-steed hippomotive train and two pas- senger cars, nothing fancy. From here to Athana Manor on Barony Har- fang, and clear it over the heliograph as a second-priority routing, charged to the Household account."

"And have Dame Emilota put up a trunk suitable for a stay in the country; tell her . . ."

She thought quickly; Dame Emilota had doted on her for years, but the lady-in-waiting of the Crown Princess' household here would fill seven trunks with festival finery if Órlaith let her, and insist on bringing herself and a couple of tiring-maids as well. She felt a small guilty stab of pleasure that for once she'd be able to deal with her at second-hand. Emilota had all the loyalty in the world and was good at her job, but she was an excruciatingly skilled bore and never shut up.

". . . tell her it would anger my mother with me further if it was anything but the basics, and likewise no entourage. Provisions for sixteen from the Household kitchens for the journey."

Which meant a lunch, a dinner and a breakfast. A hippomotive could average about twenty miles an hour, so they should cover it in about twenty hours, arriving tomorrow afternoon if they left . . .

"Have it ready for departure in two hours."

Heuradys had been writing herself. "Heliograph this to House Steward Paien at Athana. . . . St. Athana Manor, Goodman. Be a shame to drop in unannounced with sixteen, just when he's getting the domestic staff back from the fields."

The serving-man repeated the instructions, took the discreet tip Heuradys could give where Órlaith couldn't, bowed, and left at a trot. Just then the faint sound of the carillon atop the elevator drifted up the shaft, icy-cool with something like glassy bells. And someone was singing under it, wordlessly but matching the quick trills without effort or strain. Órlaith grinned, and so did some of the Mackenzies. That would be Aunt Fiorbhinn. And if she was here . . .

When the door slid open she spread her arms and cried: *"Céad míle fáilte, a Máthair Chriona!* A hundred thousand welcomes, Grandmother!"

Juniper Mackenzie grinned back, her wrinkled face old and young at the same time, and her leaf-green eyes crackling.

"And a hundred thousand more, child! Merry meet!" she said, and they embraced.

The older woman felt bird-fragile in her arms; the founder of the Clan Mackenzie had always been small and slight, and she was in her mid-seventies now, elderly as the modern world reckoned such things though spry and not stooped; her braided hair had only a few threads of faded fox-red among the silver. She was wearing an arsaid in the Clan's tartan, over a long bag-sleeved linen léine dyed saffron with an embroidery of jet and black silk at the hems and neck. The staff in her hand was topped by a finial in form of the Triple Moon, waxing and full and waning.

The clansfolk present all bowed deeply, with the back of their right hands to their foreheads; Faramir and Morfind did the same with palm to heart; Susan made a gesture with extended arm.

And Droyn is just being polite and probably murmuring prayers in Latin as he bows, poor soul, Órlaith thought, as Juniper raised the staff.

Juniper Mackenzie was a major reason the Old Faith was strong in the High Kingdom, even if she was given to shouting in moments of exasperation: *I am not the Wiccan pope-ess!*

"Blessed be, children," she said.

Then softly to Órlaith: "How you favor your father, my golden girl."

Fingers gnarled by work and age touched her braids. "And his father, save for the hair; a lovely man, he was, in body and in soul, even though I met him in a time as hard and bitter as rue."

Then briskly: "So, Matti has been having a bit of a hissy, then? She always did take herself a trifle too seriously, that girl. I remember her pouting and glaring at me when we first brought her to Dun Juniper. Though since we abducted her on a raid, perhaps that was natural enough."

"She's not over-pleased with me the now, no," Órlaith said dryly; it was always a bit disconcerting to see her mother through another's eyes as a stubborn, willful ten-year-old, back during the old wars of her grandparents' day. "You know what happened? I'd be surprised if you didn't, of course."

"Aye. And I'll be interested to meet your friend Reiko."

Behind her Maude Mackenzie cleared her throat. The current Chief of the Clan and Name sighed and spoke:

"And yes, Mother, I take things too seriously too. But I have you to tell me when I'm doing it, sure and I do."

Aunt Maude had an oval face framed in long loose brown hair; she was in her mid-thirties, and looked older in a sternly handsome way; she *was* a worrier, and had always been grave—her Sept totem was Badger. She and

Talyn Strum Mackenzie of Dun Tàirneanach were in formal Montrose jackets and small-kilts and pinned plaids like Órlaith; Talyn was currently the First Armsman of the Mackenzies, a scar-faced man of middle height in a hard middle age, one who'd fought in the Prophet's War and still wore the shaven head with a long lock at the rear that had been popular with young Clansmen then, as well as a graying mouse-colored mustache. He stepped over to Karl and shook his hand Mackenzie-fashion, gripping on the wrist.

"That's for a job well done, lad," he said. Then he gave him a cuff across the ear.

"What was *that* after being for?"

"For being an insubordinate little shite, so. Your da said to pass it on."

Then he reached out and tweaked his son Tair's nose. "And that's from your mother for running off without telling her."

Tair clapped his hand to the offended member. "What, no clout, Da?" he managed to say as his eyes watered.

The First Armsman grinned. "No, for I've told your brother Cionaodh to keep back somethin' fair nasty in the way of mucking out for your triumphant return to the home-place."

"By way of a present, so?" Tair said.

"Aye, for shouldn't a returning hero have one? That drainage ditch that never seems to keep clear, maybe? Then you can stagger in around dinner for a week or so, covered in high-smelling mud from hair to toe and see how the girls all want to get under your kilt when you tell them of your adventures. You remember it, the twisty one that always turns up rocks?"

Órlaith could tell Tair did unfondly remember that bit of the Strum family croft by the way his face fell.

"The narrow twisty one where you can't get a good swing with a mattock for the hawthorn hedge that leans over it?" the young man said hollowly.

"Just that one! Ah, and Lug Longspear witness it's a wonderful thing how a lad can know his father's mind!"

She could also tell that Aunt Fiorbhinn was taking it all in and storing up bits for a song—John had the same habit, only he was more obvious and obnoxious about it. Fiorbhinn was Juniper's last child, two years after Maude in years but looking six or seven younger, perhaps because she was absolutely *not* a worrier. Fiorbhinn's chin was more pointed and her eyes were bigger than Órlaith's, and they always seemed to have a secret smile in them.

She was in a long white robe belted with silver plaques and a necklace of golden spiral triskelions, and staff of her own topped by the same symbol. That was the dress and mark of a master-fili, a bard, among Mackenzies; Órlaith knew that for a fact, since it was Fiorbhinn who'd decided they were, and proclaimed that this was the ancient custom of the Gael. And who was to say she was wrong, since her fame and her music traveled far beyond the dùthchas? Although she'd gotten the details of dress from a pre-Change book, an illustrated one that seemed to be a guide to a game centered on pretending to be a gang of bandits who wandered about plundering people and looting tombs.

Juniper looked over at Morfind and Faramir. "My granddaughter will be taking all you lot off somewhere else," she said. "I'd be after hoping you realize Mithrilwood is right out of it? Considering how your parents down in Stath Ingolf talked one Edain Aylward Mackenzie out of dragging our golden Princess here back by the ear, as Matti had sent him to do?"

Faramir actually blushed. Morfind gave Juniper a bold stare, unconsciously touching the scar that trailed down across one cheek. An Eater chief's axe had struck there in a skirmish with a hidden band of the foe, one lurking after the little battle that killed the High King. Her brother had died then. Faramir's scars from that fight didn't show, not on the outside at least.

"We'd thought of that, Lady Juniper," he said.

Heuradys stepped in. "We're going to Barony Harfang," she said tactfully.

"Ah, the Palouse," Juniper said, and her eyes went distant for an instant.

"Pretty country, bare but pretty, those hills like the swells of the sea gone solid. I remember driving through there one spring, to perform at the Spokane RenFaire."

Órlaith blinked; she meant driving a *car*, the horseless carriages of the old time. It was a bit of a shock to realize that the living, breathing person in front of you had been an adult when the ancient world fell, when Nature itself changed its contours. There weren't very many left. Fewer still of the giants, the founders and leaders.

Juniper seemed to know the thought, which didn't surprise her granddaughter.

"Back when I was a bard myself, though I didn't go about in a white bedsheet bedecked with tin."

Fiorbhinn rolled her eyes. "This is my fili's robe, Mother," she said, obviously long-suffering.

"As I said, girl."

"And I know you used to wear an arsaid when you performed, the which nobody else between here and Erin did back then!"

"'Twas more of a pleated tartan skirt, really."

Then they grinned at each other. Juniper went on seriously, to Heuradys d'Ath:

"You look after my son's child. You hear, my lady knight?"

"Always, Lady Juniper," she said with casual sincerity and a bow. "With all that I have of wit and will and skill from my patron Athana, and my life's blood if I must."

The others murmured assent.

"And now we'd better go in to be there when Herself comes out, for Matti is stubborn as the White-Horned Bull when she's got a notion, always was."

The Mackenzie party formed up for their entrance to the throne room. Juniper paused and put her hand on Órlaith's forearm for an instant, her grip bony and strong.

"You cannot fight grief with a sword, my darling one, not even with *that* sword," she said softly. "Even the Powers themselves cannot. He was

your father, but my son, my sun-bright beautiful boy running with the
wind in his hair. Take time to weep, where you're going."

Then she stood on tiptoe to kiss her on the cheek, and walked on with
the silver frow on the end of her staff tapping on the floor.

There wasn't much of a send-off, just a squad of glaivesmen under a
squire seeing them out the main gate, bringing their polearms down with
a metallic crack on the granite blocks of the big train station's platform.
Órlaith returned the salute and stepped into the carriage; there was a
shout from the front, a hollow thudding of hooves on the endless belts,
a rumbling whine of gearing, and all the people who'd been kneeling got
up and waved instead. She waved back out the window, since it wasn't
their fault things were wretched right now. The long peace had seen many
stretches of rail line repaired; by now they stretched very far indeed; in
theory and in good weather you could reach the Mississippi. Which was
tempting!

*Lady bless you, Mother, for that you walk in Her power as all mothers do, but I
miss Johnnie too! I did not lose him of my own will!*

The others settled in—not without some squabbling among the
youngsters—and Macmaccon jumped up into the seat beside her and
sprawled. He laid his enormous head in her lap with an even louder sigh
than hers, albeit his was of pure contentment, and went to sleep, for once
not drooling or twitching in his slumbers. The train's two carriages
moved north and west away from Todenangst's soaring multicolored bulk
and out into the green fields and woodlots and hills and towards the tiny
perfect cone of Mount Hood on the far horizon. Her thoughts seemed
to be running on rails too as she absently stroked the dog's ears, and on
a circular track; that loop was going to end up with her thinking about
her father's death again if she didn't watch it.

One reason I'm obsessing about John's fate is that I know he isn't *dead. If Mother
didn't know he wasn't she wouldn't just be angry, she'd* . . .

She literally shivered at the thought, and stroked the dog's ears as a
countercharm. After a few minutes Heuradys nudged Macmaccon's head

off her lap. He woke, sat, turned and stuck his head out the window into the swift wind of their passage with an expression of idiot slit-eyed bliss and his lips flapping back from his fangs. Then her knight nudged her.

"Here," she said, offering a flask. "Mom One got a cask of this from the Dowager Duchess on her last birthday. Don't bother with savoring the piquant bouquet, though, Orrey. You need the effect."

Órlaith took the advice, a brief sniff and then a healthy slug. It was *Poire Guilliame a le Duc*, a pear brandy from the Hood River orchards of the Duchy of Odell, and in this case private stock laid down by the current Duke's father and aged ten years in the barrel. That scar-faced old rogue had known his liquors; cool white fire ran down her throat, followed by an intense pear flavor and scent that flowed up into her sinuses. You couldn't drown anger or grief or even impatience, but you could anesthetize them for a bit, like a surgeon's ether cone.

"Thanks, Herry," she said, feeling the muscles in her neck relax a little as she handed it back. "That bumped me out of my groove and sure, it wasn't a good one to be in."

The others were untying the ribbons of the wicker hampers the kitchens had sent along, the ones labeled *Crn. Prns & pty 1st d. luncheon, 16*, and rummaging inside. Happy Mackenzie whoops were accounted for when someone handed her one of the sandwiches made from a crusty split baguette, which was stuffed with thinly sliced *Westfälischer Schinken*: a darkly pungent strong-tasting ham from half-wild swine fed on acorns, dry-cured with sea-salt, brown sugar, allspice, and pepper and then cold-smoked over beech wood and juniper chips for several weeks before being hung in a cellar for two years. It was one of the exports of the Queen of Angels Commonwealth, ruled by the warrior monks of the Order of the Shield of St. Benedict; her father had liked it too. In this case it was combined with bread not long out of the oven, fresh yellow summer butter from Chehalis, aioli mayonnaise, capers, Walla Walla onions and slivers of a sharp Tillamook cheese.

The screeches of the young clansfolk turned to warbles of joy when several tightly-stoppered stoneware jugs in an insulated container of ice turned out to bear the capering goggle-eyed Mad March Hare mark of Brannigan's Special, a well-known strong ale from Sutterdown in their own dúthchas. Those were soon passed from hand to hand, amid a bellowed version of a song Grandmother Juniper had made in its praise long ago:

"Start seein' things real funny,
And given half a chance—
Hic!
Go swirling around and then tumble down
And the mice on your head will all dance!"

She hadn't thought she was hungry, despite having been too nervous for breakfast; the scent and a bite showed her otherwise, and the impromptu feast made her feel better and less jumpy, along with the bright bitter floral hops and dark malt of the Special. It was vanity to think there was a difference between mind and body. She was on a journey. . . .

What was that saying Da was fond of, the one he heard at Chenrezi Monastery, on the Quest long ago? Yes . . . three set forth seeking fortune. And one found gold; another came on good land, and tilled it. But the third saw sunlight making jewels of the dew. All three went by the same road. Each thought himself the richer.

Heuradys laughed as they unfolded the waxed paper wrapping the dessert that followed: buttery blueberry tarts whose deep amethyst centers were ringed with flaky pastry covered in gold-hued shaved and toasted nuts. Órlaith raised a brow.

"They reminded me of what Mom One said about that low-cut cotte-hardie Countess Stavarov de Chelais wore to the Midsummer masque," Heuradys said in answer to the unspoken question.

Órlaith tried not to show it in public, but she'd never liked House Stavarov. Officially the Stavarovs had headed a freelance troop of men-at-arms before the Change, when her mother's father had recruited them into the nascent Association. Unofficial sources said *mafiya*. Either term meant *gang of bandits*, basically. House Stavarov had taken longer to outgrow the legacy than most.

"Showing off her family's great tracts of land?" Órlaith said a little snidely.

Countess Stavarov had hair of a deep fawn shade, large melting dark eyes with very long lashes, and she was *very* busty.

"Showing off her assets and those new Tanzanite jewels Count Piotr's salvagers dug out of Seattle. Tanzanite centers two inches across *and* gold fretwork *and* diamonds *and* tourmalines in the surrounds."

"Delia said something cutting, no doubt," Órlaith said.

Heuradys' birth mother Countess Delia de Stafford had been a leader of fashion in the Association lands for more than a generation. She also had no time at all for women who were—or far, far worse—pretended to be witless. Which fitted the densely thick Ziaida Dimitrievna Stavarova perfectly since she played kittenish-coquettish as well. By all accounts it had been tiresome when she was a teenager, and now grated horribly even on her toadies and sycophants; Órlaith didn't think she had any actual friends.

Heuradys paused, grinning wider: "Mom One said the look was like a Jersey milker prancing around with a string of blueberry tarts glued to its udder, and Mom Two had just taken a sip of brandy and snarfed it out her nose."

Órlaith choked slightly on her own mouthful of Brannigan's Special, then swallowed and coughed and whooped.

Heuradys waited considerately until she'd recovered before she continued:

"I hear that when someone repeated it to Ziaida she snapped her fan in half and threw it into the punchbowl and slapped a page and she hasn't worn the necklace since."

Órlaith found herself laughing until she hiccupped.

Heuradys licked her fingers and went on: "By Hestia of the Hearth, these are good tarts—split another one? They packed too many for us anyway, this basket's full of them and they won't keep."

"Not with Karl and Mathun eating they didn't pack too many, so let's grab two."

"Right, they're bottomless pits. And little Suzie's capacity is amazing; I don't know where she puts it all."

The Latoka girl overheard the remark, popped her head up over the back of her seat and called:

"Hey, it's usually *guys* who say that!" to a roar of laughter. "Ones with delusions of grandeur!"

They passed the dramatic cliffs and woods and waterfalls and vast views of the Columbia Gorge before dinner, leaving them partly in shadow and partly painted crimson by the setting sun, to the oohs and aahs of those who hadn't been this way before. Traffic was heavy on the road that ran beside the railway, and trains of sailing barges and small ships and once a patrol galley centipede-walking upstream thronged the river in the afternoon light. A heliograph signal snapped from the highest tower of a castle on a promontory, actinic-white as the sun faded.

The long twilight was past and the late summer night fell deep by the time they passed Hood River, the river-port for the Duchy of Odell. After that the habitations of human kind were a thin scatter of yellow lights, passing in the distance amid leagues of emptiness beneath a dense frosting of stars. Cards came out when the lamps were lit, or portable fidchell sets. And everyone played or sang in the improvised céilidh that happened wherever Mackenzies had nothing else to do, to which Heuradys' lute and the Dúnedain flutes were a welcome addition, and Droyn had a wonderful baritone that made the windows rattle to his version of "Across the Broad Columbia." They started with some old favorites:

"I danced at a Beltane with the pole standing tall,
And the ribbons flowing round the dancers all.
I danced in the sunlight at the Midsummer Feast
As the day dawned pink with the Sun Lord's heat!
Dance, dance, wherever you may be—"

Susan had a lot of Lakota tunes and brought out a few they hadn't heard before, including some Órlaith hadn't been exposed to on her visits to the far eastern marches of the kingdom, doubtless because the grave elders of the *tunwan* didn't think them suitable for a young visiting princess.

Particularly the one about the adventures of the buffalo heifer!

Órlaith managed to doze for most of the night. As the light returned they drank cold herb tea, ate hard-boiled eggs and fruit and bread and looked out with interest at the varied lands as they passed and chatted about the details and the crops. They were all countryfolk in one way or another.

"Now, riddle me this," Karl said after a while. "Is it more boring to do this trip afoot, or like this?"

"You've more time for it afoot," Mathun said. "And sure, the country passes more slowly."

"Aye," Boudicca Lopez Mackenzie said from the rear of the car where she was drawing her bow and relaxing it over and over. "But sitting on your arse you notice it more!"

The argument grew lively, and was done entirely for its own sake. Órlaith leaned back and pulled her bonnet over her eyes.

Johnnie, I wish I was with you!

CHAPTER FIVE

"Hunnhh!"

John grunted as he swayed up the companionway to the quarterdeck in the thick darkness. The wind hit him as he came over the break; so did the rain that hadn't stopped much since they'd left Topanga. The awkward weight of the forty-pound piece of steel in a rope sling over his back wasn't helping either, and of course the fact that the *Tarshish Queen* was at forty degrees going up and forty degrees going down as she surged over the waves.

At increasing speed as she emerged from each trough and the wind hit her, then hesitating for a long unpleasant moment on the crest with foam boiling around her, then nosing down for the long swoop with huge rooster-tails of spray to either side and rolling and pitching as she did, then slowing a bit at the bottom, then the whole thing over again . . .

Disassembling tons of catapult in darkness on a violently pitching deck with waves washing over the side at unpredictable intervals, when not one part down to the smallest screw could be lost, and then carrying the whole thing from the bow a hundred and fifty feet to the stern . . .

"Here we go, Your Highness," Fayard said. "That's the right-hand mainspring anchor plate link panel."

Two of the crossbowmen took the weight off his back and John stepped aside to get out of the way; all the Protector's Guard were cross-trained on catapults, enough to be useful in this immensely complex and demanding task. Captain Ishikawa was next, with a big chunk of steel gearing over *his* back.

"Crever, vell . . . *verry clever,*" he gasped as the men took it, almost giggling as he said it.

His grinning face was underlit by the small deadlight lantern hung beneath the tarpaulin that made a sort of improvised tent over the starboard part of the *Queen*'s fantail aft of the wheel and binnacle. Feldman was crouched there with several of his sailors, mostly the crew-captains of the catapults. There was a low muttering among them, a clink of tools on metal that carried even over the moaning hum of the storm in the rigging and the white roar of water. Someone handed John a flask and he drank; it was spiced rum, and powerful. Sweet fire burned its way down to his belly, and pushed back the chill in his hands and the lingering pain of his bruises.

Feldman sank back. "There; just go over the bolts, feel for how tight they are," he said to his crewmen. "We'll hook up the hydraulics at dawn, it won't take long. In the meantime, the rest of you report to the First Mate and help restowing stores. We'll need the trim right."

Then to Ishikawa and John as he sank with his back against the machine:

"I got this idea from the way those Suluk corsairs dogged us back from Hawaii, on the old *Ark*—my first voyage far-foreign, as assistant supercargo to my father. I was interested even then."

"You were?" Thora said. "I remember being terrified, mainly."

She'd been on that voyage, shipping out as an adventurous youngster, and had met Deor at its end, when the crippled *Ark* limped into Albion Cove.

"That memory made me remember how much more time merchant-men spend running from pirates than vice versa. So when we built the *Queen* I had the armorers from Donaldson Foundry make the tracks for the stern chaser suitable for doubling-up. When you add in that it's so difficult to shoot right over the bows but not over the stern . . ."

His grin looked positively demonic in the night, underlit beneath his trimmed black beard.

John looked through a gap in the canvas, northeast towards blackness and a heaving chaos that was visible in glimpses only because the lines of foam caught light from the sterncastle lanterns. They couldn't see the leading Korean in the dark—there had been only a few glimpses of another, or possibly two—but he'd be there when the sun came up behind them. That had happened often enough that they'd taken to using the stern-lanterns again. Dousing them just made life harder for the crew and didn't help shake the pursuit at all.

"Isn't there a risk of being trapped into a broadside action?" he said; someday he'd need to understand war at sea by instinct. "If we take damage that slows us?"

Feldman's chuckle was harsh. "In this storm? The only thing we can do is run with the wind hard on the starboard quarter. If we try to turn . . . or if we lost steering . . . or lost a major sail . . . we'd broach to. In an instant. Same for them."

"Broach?" John said; the word was only vaguely familiar.

"Turn right into the wind and lay over, so we'd be hit broadside on by the next wave and capsize," Feldman said, and Ishikawa nodded vigorously. "And be smashed to kindling and sent to Sheol when the crest fell on us. Carrying this much canvas in seas and winds like this means we're on the edge of it every instant, anyway."

Oh, thank you, Captain. I suspected something like that, but it's so nice to have the details!

Feldman shrugged, his usual broad gesture less visible in the dim light of the lamp and under the foul-weather gear.

"These stern chases can go on forever, across half the world if you're unlucky, or until you run into something solid. This damned wind is pushing us right across the Pacific; I haven't had a good observation for days, but dead reckoning is enough for that."

"They're running us towards Asia and away from Montival," John said.

Ishikawa bowed, his face invisible in the dark beneath the funnel brim of his sou'wester.

"Asia very big pr . . . place, Prince," he said, and John thought he detected irony there—even through the barriers of accent and storm-roar.

Feldman nodded. "It is! Going back, that's another question. This ship is damaged and it's getting worse. Much longer and we couldn't turn back, we'd have to make shore and beach her for repairs or sink. It's worth the risk to break the stalemate."

John swallowed and nodded, looking at the ugly, bulky, angular shape of levers and springs and hydraulic cylinders that crouched before them. The *Queen* had a complete double horseshoe of steel track set into the fantail of the quarterdeck, level with the surface like those of the tramways in a city street; the eighteen-pounder chaser could turn a full hundred and eighty degrees along it.

It also had room for two catapults to sit side-by-side, and they'd spent the night disassembling the big weapon in the bows and carrying it here to put together again beside its sister. Between that and pumping against the growing leak forward nobody had gotten much sleep.

John didn't intend to try now; he just huddled together with Thora and Deor and Ruan, crouching silently amid the roar and wet streaming off—and sometimes under—their oilskins and sou'westers. After a while Rat McGuire, who doubled as the Captain's Steward, brought up a basket of sandwiches; pancake-like flatbread rolled around fried salt beef and hot peppers and onions and potatoes and some of the black pickled olives Feldman had taken on at Topanga, with flasks of hot herbal tea. They followed it with thick wedges of duff, which would have been far worse without the figs and raisins also picked up in Montival's new southernmost realm.

Given how hungry they were it tasted good, and objectively it wasn't nearly as nasty as some of the stories Thora and Deor had told him about shipboard rations they'd had on their travels. He said so, and they both laughed agreement, and added a new one where someone had whiled away the boredom by carving buttons out of the salt meat and passing them off as some rare wood at the next port.

Sometimes I envy the . . . the easiness they have, John thought. *It's like what Dad and Edain had—friends so close they might as well be closest kin. I've always been easy with people, but true friends of that sort . . . well, give me time, I suppose!*

"Dawn soon," Deor said, gently shaking Ruan awake where he'd dozed with his head against the scop's shoulder.

Softly he half-sang as they stood and stretched:

"Morning red, morning red;
Will you shine upon me dead?
Soon the trumpets will be blowing
Then must I to war be going
I and many faithful friends!"

John supposed the sun *was* rising as normal, up above the low racing grayness of the clouds. From what he'd seen flying gliders and from balloons, it was bright and glistening up there; though that was hard to remember now. Instead the dark simply grew gradually less dark over an hour or so, without any moment you could say fiat lux. He'd been expecting the hail from the masthead—

Now, there's a job I don't envy! he thought; they rotated it every two hours, and the one coming down always looked half-dead.

"*Sail ho!* Sail ho, two points to starboard on the stern! It's her, skipper!"

Feldman nodded and started to call a volley of nautical orders, supplemented by details from the First Mate. John gathered it all came to *adjust the sails so we slow down just a little without looking like we're doing it deliberately.*

Despite the stinging high-speed drizzle and spray, many of the sailors were grinning as they went about their work. The Bosun was downright snickering. John wasn't the only one who'd come to resent the way the enemy was hanging on to their tails. Feldman had been getting ready for a voyage very far-foreign indeed when John came to Newport with his sister's offer. To Dhamra, the main port of the great and fabled realm of Hinduraj; on the Bay of Bengal, where no Montivallan ship had ever gone before and few individuals either, though Thora and Deor had. The crew had all been expecting six months away from home, and danger, but this was another matter. They'd been attacked in their own waters and *chased* away from home.

The *Queen* was three quarters of the way up the face of the wave when the Korean appeared cutting the crest opposite, looking chip-tiny and blurred in the darkness and the rain. Radavindraban raised a device to his eyes, a coincidence range finder; it was like a telescope, save that the tube was uniform and the eyepiece was in the middle of one side, with lenses at either end. They were expensive and unusual on a private ship. . . .

But as Captain Feldman remarked, dying is even more costly.

"Four thousand yards!" he said loudly.

"She'll be in range in the next trough, or the one after," Feldman called. "Captain Ishikawa, are you ready?"

Ishikawa made a bow. *"Hai!* This is enemy we fight all our lives, enemy of our people, killers of our families and our *Tennō."*

His eight men listened as he spoke briefly in their tongue, then thrust their arms into the air with a barking scream of:

"Tennō Heika banzai! Banzai! *Banzai!"*

That translated as: *To the Heavenly Sovereign Majesty, Ten thousand years!*

Then they moved with smooth precision to take stations at the starboard catapult. They were professionals, full-time fighting men and an elite at that; they'd been part of the crew of the *Red Dragon*, which their Emperor had chosen to bear him and his heir across the Pacific. The weapons the Imperial Japanese Navy used were basically very similar, and they'd worked hard to familiarize themselves with the Montivallan equivalent. Feldman's crew were tough and well-trained, but a merchant ship fought when it had to, not as their regular trade.

Ishikawa swung into the bicycle-seat-like gunner's position on the left of the weapon and pulled down the sighting frame until it clicked into position in front of his face. One handwheel moved the whole piece in traverse to left or right by trundling it along the steel tracks. The other governed elevation, and a bar under the right foot was the loosing trigger. The members of the crew placed the ammunition in the throwing trough, or adjusted it for the type of projectile, bolt or ball, or manned the hydraulic pump. A slanted steel shield covered the front part of the catapult, with a hole for the trough and another for the sights. The springs were salvage from before the Change or closely modeled on them—great built-up things that had originally been part of leviathan mining trucks in the ancient world, vehicles that weighed as much as a small ship themselves.

Feldman swung into the gunner's saddle of the portside weapon. "Rig for bolt!" he said. "Load cutters!"

The rest of the crew sprang forward; one turned a lever that narrowed the rests in the trough, and the other slapped home a cutter-bolt, a four-foot arrow of forged steel with brass fins and a broad shovel-like head designed to slice through the thick tough rigging of a ship, or wound masts and spars. What it would do to human flesh and bone . . . well, battle wasn't a safe occupation.

The part that concerned John just now was the pump behind the catapult proper, which was a simple enough unskilled-labor job that he could do as well as any of the sailors, which would spare the experts for more difficult work. All the task needed was a strong back and arms and steadiness. There was a rocking beam like the one used to drive inspection cars on the railways, with bars for two workers on either side to grasp. The arched steel beam drove plungers that pressurized water; hoses ran to the two multiton-load bottle jacks built into either side of the frames. Those pushed the throwing arms back and compressed the springs until the locking mechanism caught it.

The whole weapon was a simple enough thing in concept, but only the most skilled engineers and artificers could make one of this size that wouldn't destroy itself when the vast forces within were unleashed. They needed to be precisely balanced and constrained.

He almost spat on his palms as he stepped up to his position, and then caught himself—everything was sopping wet anyway, including the thick callus on his hands. His fingers closed on the polished ashwood of the handle. Thora and Deor and Ruan joined him, almost anonymous in their sou'westers and slickers.

"Cock and lock!" Feldman said.

"Junbi shimasu!" Ishikawa barked in Nihongo.

John pulled down against the soft, yielding resistance of the pump arm, throwing his weight on it as well as the strength of his arms and shoulders when it sank past the level of his waist. Thora called the time with a simple *one-two . . . one-two*. It was hard work, but no more so than running and wrestling and sparring in armor, or hitting a pell-post with a practice blade for hours at a time with a twenty-pound kite shield on his left arm.

A dozen strokes, with a tooth-grating *cring . . . cring . . .* from springs and gears, and then a hard *chunk* as the trigger mechanism locked. The other catapult did the same at an interval so close that the sounds overlapped, almost but not quite perfectly. John waited with his hands resting on the bar at waist-height and turned his head to look. He blinked when he did; a few feet away beyond the stern bulwark was the dark-blue rushing surface of the wave whose face the *Tarshish Queen* skidded down, with the white tumbling crest above them. They must have just come through it, and he hadn't even noticed foam seething around his sea-boots.

Down into the trough, and the dropping note in the wind in the rigging as the crest sheltered them a little from the wind, a slowing of the feeling of rushing speed. The Korean's bow burst through the crest as they reached the bottom, close enough that he could see the odd squared-off look just below the bowsprit. And then the menace of their bow-catapult, as the ship nosed down and began its race after them.

"Two thousand five hundred!" Radavindraban called. "Two thousand two hundred! Closing most fast!"

They started up the forward slope of the next wave, the shriek of the wind rising in pitch again, the taut sails giving a huge creaking groan as the full force of the gale stretched them and threw more strain on the standing rigging that transmitted the force to the hull. It blew more rain and spray into their eyes as they peered southward, too, and harder.

"Ready!" Feldman called.

He and Ishikawa worked the elevation wheels, and the parts of the catapult with the springs and throwing troughs tilted up at the maximum, forty degrees. John ducked his head as the wind battered at his sou'wester, and suddenly realized:

That's why they're not using firebolt or napalm shell, it's not just the rain and spray. The wind would blow them off course. Especially at long range.

The *Queen* raced upwards. John caught a glimpse of the Korean ship down in the trough as they passed the crest and the swirl of foam burst from the bows and raced down the length of the ship. Then the gray-blue wall reared above the stern again, and they sped downward. His hands tightened involuntarily on the pump handle, and he forced himself not to pant.

There!

Shockingly closer this time, close enough to look *big*, not like the model ships he'd played with in the bath as a child anymore. Hundreds of tons of wood and cloth and ropes and metal, probably a hundred or more men. Close enough to see movement from the enemy bow-catapult as it shot, and a blurred streak as the bolt arced out towards them and then disappeared, plunging unnoticed into the wild waters somewhere.

"Twelve hundred!" Radavindraban shouted, his voice a little higher.

Silence, if you could call the tense moment full of the moan and whistle and creak and roar of the ship silence. Then Feldman's foot jammed down on the release lever, and:

Tunnng-WHACK!

Both the eighteen-pounders cut loose within a second of each other. The cutter-bolts vanished as the paired throwing-arms slashed forward through hundred-and-sixty-degree arcs, transmitted the scores of tons of draw-weight through the cables to the bolts and rammed home into their stops of steel lined with hard rubber.

He could feel the quiver through the handle as the recoil began the process of recocking the mechanism, salvaging part of the energy. The four of them flung their strength into the bars in a grunting frenzy. Not until the machine clicked into the locked position did he have a chance to snatch a glance northwards. Now they were down in the trough, for a moment horizontal again, and the Korean was closer still and racing down the slope towards them. Its bowchaser shot again, and this time he could see the blurred streak of the bolt.

It *didn't* miss.

There was a shuddering crash he felt through the soles of his boots, and for one horrific instant he thought it had smashed the rudder and they were all going to die in the next minute. Then Feldman barked:

"Mr. Mate! Take damage control!"

Radavindraban left at a run, throwing the range finder over his shoulder by its strap as he went. The enemy was close enough that the catapults' own sights and Eyeball Mark One would serve.

Tunnng-WHACK!

Both the *Tarshish Queen*'s cutter-bolts hit; one punched a neat slit in the enemy's foremast topsail, and the other took out a chunk of railing not far from the bowchaser. John *thought* it had bisected one of the enemy on the way, but the visibility was too poor and the time too scant and then he was heaving at the bar again. Forty-two strokes, forty-three, forty-four, forty-five and *clack*.

Tunnng-WHACK!

Closer still, and even pumping for all his worth he saw one of their bolts strike the enemy catapult's shield and heard the hard metallic *bang*. The sloping steel bent but didn't crack. It shed the bolt, which broke into two pieces. Each killed men like a flying buzz saw as they pinwheeled across the forecastle and into the waist of the ship. The other bolt ploughed into the deck and sank until only the fins stood out.

And the return shot took the head off one of Ishikawa's sailors at the pump opposite, only six feet away, close enough that the hard wet thump of impact was clear. One instant the man was rising and falling to the rhythm of the pump, and then next body *and* head were sliding down the tossing deck. Two of the Nihonjin sailors who'd been crouching in reserve leapt with tiger speed, one grabbing the body by its jacket and the head by its topknot and dragging them out of the way, the other flinging himself onto the pump-handle so quickly that the reloading was less than a second late.

At least the blasts of spray and spume and rain got rid of the blood quickly. . . .

The bolt went on down the length of the ship, scarcely slowed at all. Ropes whipped free, and the ship began to lurch as a sail turned. A sailor made a reckless flying leap for one severed end, and nearly went over the side before another managed to get her arms around his legs. Two more drew them back, callused hands latched onto the rope and shouted directions from the First Mate and the Bosun directed the swift trim of the sail and spliced a new end onto the line.

"Load roundshot!" Feldman half-screamed. "Point-blank, point-blank!"

Hands slapped the lever to leave the throwing trough at full diameter and shoved the eighteen-pound balls into position, over a spring-loaded retaining clip called *the nose* from its shape. The balls were surprisingly small, less than six inches in diameter, but heavy enough to soak up all the frightful kinetic energy built up in the springs.

Through the crest again, wild wind and tumult and spray enough to make you choke, the beginning of the long swoop downwards. And the Korean on their heels, close enough to see men now, close enough to see one in a plumed peaked helmet pointing a sword at them and screaming something, mouth open and teeth showing below his mustache as he yelled. Yet the sound was lost in the hugeness of the sea.

Feldman's hand spun the elevating wheel and the trough sank. His foot slammed down on the release triggers.

Tunnng-WHACK!

A moment's gap as Ishikawa twisted the handwheel a fraction more and his foot shot out—

Tunnng-WHACK!

At this distance there was less than a second between launch and impact. One ball smashed into the base of the enemy's bowsprit, just where the forestay ran back to the first of her masts. The thick cable curled and cracked like a giant's bullwhip, and the end struck the man with the crested helm. He disappeared into the rain and murk like a rag doll thrown out a window in a child's fit of temper. The mast began to twist instantly, the enormous forces playing on it wringing it like a stick in the hands of a boy playing at swords. Then the second roundshot cracked into the timber of the mast itself, right where the strain was bending it.

The Korean's mast wasn't a single tree; instead it was a composite of interlocked smaller timbers grooved and fitted together and held with shrunk-on steel bands. Normally that was about as strong as the trunk of a big Douglas fir. But when it failed, it failed all at once and catastrophically.

The whole lower half disintegrated into its parts, spinning apart and vanishing or spearing men like lumps of meat on a kebab. The upper forty feet of the mast flew into the air and hit the limits of the cables and hawsers holding it like a gigantic kite that was trying to snatch the hull's hundreds of tons into the air. The bow of the warship slewed around as if yanked by a giant's hand, and the rest of the sails caught the wind broadside-on and slammed downward in a maelstrom of flying ropes and bits of broken spars and human figures pinwheeling off into the storm. The ship spun three-quarters over, showing the white patches of barnacles and long fronds of weed on her bottom. . . .

And then the crest of the great wave curled and broke and came down on her like the Fist of God. The whole fabric shattered as a cheap pine box would under a boot, and then it was gone.

Just . . . gone, John thought, feeling his stomach knot.

The *Queen* was still tearing away at speed; the others were whooping against the scream of the wind and hammering each other and him on the back. The Nihonjin began a chant of:

"Banzai! Banzai! Banzai!" as they pumped their fists into the air and bowed again and again to Ishikawa, their usual gravity forgotten for a moment.

"Two hundred men," John whispered to himself in a tone empty of everything but wonder.

The spot where the Korean had vanished didn't even show any wreckage, and the sight leached everything but a wondering awe.

"My God, two hundred men just *gone*, like a cockroach under a boot!"

Slowly he crossed himself.

Holy Mary, Mother of God, Lady pierced with sorrows. . . . All of them were born of woman. Intercede for them, for us, all of us, foeman and comrade. Now and at the hour of our deaths—Madonna, intercede!

CHAPTER SIX

County Palatine of Walla Walla
To Barony Harfang
County of Campscapell
(Formerly eastern Washington State)
High Kingdom of Montival
(Formerly western North America)
September 16th
Change Year 46/2044 AD

"Thanks, cousin," Órlaith said absently, taking one of the loaded plates Faramir offered.

She'd learned to eat on swaying trains as a child. Lunch was gendarme—also called man-at-arms—sausage, air-cured and fermented links made from equal portions of pork and beef with pepper, cumin, and a little honey. It was named that because it kept well, and was common in military rations and travelers' food generally. She knew from personal experience that this tasted a *lot* better than the mass-produced version handed out to the troops, because her father had started a tradition that in the field commanders ate what came out of the common mess like everyone else.

With it went a sweet-nutty Fol Epi cheese from Barony Gervais or a soft spreadable Tillamook with bits of hot pepper worked in, cracker-like rye flatbread, pickles and some bottles of garlic-cured mushrooms. Last was a maida cake of fine flour, eggs, clarified butter, sugar, petha, marmalade, hazelnuts and walnuts, ginger and fennel, also famous for keeping well, and bottles of fizzy mild cider still fairly chilly though the ice had melted by now.

Macmac sighed loudly, his head moving with every transit of her hand from plate to mouth and deep sadness in his eyes. She relented and tossed him half the sausage, not being all that hungry anyway despite putting in most of the morning on the treadmills with the horses.

The recently-built line they were using as they curved north under the noon sun was modern steel strip on wooden rails. It crossed the broad County Palatine of Walla Walla, which was basically most of the area from the loop of the Snake River southward to the borders of the Pendleton Round-Up, founded long ago to anchor and protect the Association's eastern marchland in her wicked grandfather Norman's time. But they went well west of the great walled city of Walla Walla itself, which was tactful and why she'd done it.

Count Palatine Felipe de Aguirre Smith was a loyal supporter of House Artos, but also a battle-comrade and guest-friend of Baroness Tiphaine d'Ath since an episode in the Prophet's War. Her family visited here fairly often on their way to their estates in the Palouse, and the Count had given her a hunting-lodge in the Blue Mountains as a mark of his esteem. If Órlaith had shown up in the capital city of his County honor would have demanded that he extend her daughter Heuradys— and the daughter's liege—full public hospitality.

And Mother would feel that he was poking at her with a Disapproval Stick, though she'd know better.

The rising sun had lit the rich rolling valley-land west of the city as they passed, with the low massive line of the Blue Mountains on the horizon to the southeast just visible. Fields edged with Lombardy poplars were patterned with strips of reaped yellow grain-stubble or green with alfalfa; vineyards and orchards drew geometries over hillsides; manors and villages could be glimpsed amid gardens and woodlots.

Now and then the great stucco-covered concrete bulk of a baron's castle loomed with banners flying from the witch's-hat peaks of the machicolated towers and a town huddling beneath their shadow, or a monastery or convent stood solid and square amid gardens and almshouse-hospice. The plane-tree-lined macadamized roads smoked white dust as trains of ox-wagons crawled and carriages clipped along, or nobles rode in gaudy brightness. Peasants and peddlers, monks and pilgrims went trudging afoot or pedaling on bicycles between rows of roadside trees showing a hint of tattered autumnal lushness, and under the drowsy warmth somehow came a hint of the coming rain and snows.

At one stop some enterprising soul handed up a basketful of fruit for a silver half-tenth while the teams were being changed: crisp apples and ruby-red late cherries and dripping-ripe pears. For a while the young clansfolk and Susan and the Dúnedain cousins engaged in a cherry-stone-spitting contest out the windows aiming at the trees planted along the right-of-way. Karl had stood on his dignity as bow-captain for about five minutes before crowding forward to take a try.

"Were we ever that young?" Órlaith said softly, as a cheer marked a bull's-eye.

Heuradys chuckled quietly as she strummed her lute, lying back with her boots off, her chaperon hat pushed forward over her eyes and her feet up on the opposite seat. Where Macmac seemed to find them a never-ceasing source of olfactory interest but needed to be poked occasionally to keep him from absently starting to nibble.

"Oh, possibly, just possibly, I say to the girl who had us run away from home on a Quest to find the Super Man in his Castle of Ice beyond Drumheller when she was eight."

"I was impressed by that story Lord Huon told us about his mission to the north, but I wasn't really up to understanding it then."

"I told you it wouldn't work, but noooooo . . ."

"You're never going to let me forget that little slip the now, are you?"

"No, I'm not, my liege. Though now we're the oldest ones in this crowd . . . and it feels very strange."

"Tell me."

Droyn wasn't participating in the pit-spitting, being a belted knight now, but he was watching and grinning.

"Or," Heuradys went on, "possibly you're just still in a bad mood, Orrey. Relax. After all we've been through in the past few months some time lazing around with nothing more strenuous to do than falconry and sparring and music . . . and maybe chatting up some handsome huntsman . . . has some appeal. *Against Necessity, even Gods do not fight.* The *morai* spin, and that's it."

"Yes, Atropos," Órlaith grumbled with a sigh, and laughed unwillingly when her knight made crisp snipping motions with two fingers.

She laid aside her book—it was *The Broken Sword*, a pre-Change historical novel of grim gritty realism by a knight named Sir Béla of Eastmarch, and more accessible to modern tastes than the more fanciful efforts of the time. Then she looked out the window again, the warm wind fluttering wisps of hair that had escaped her braid, a breeze that smelled of dust and straw. It was odd to feel impatient with a journey to someplace you were *supposed* to sit and be bored once you arrived.

The domains of the Counts Palatine ended at Castle Lyon, guarding the bridge across the Snake. Northward the Palouse proper began, barer and higher and far less peopled, mostly within the frontier County of Campscapell that marked the boundary between the Protectorate and the United States of Boise. The hills were like an endless beach of low undulating dunes occasionally rising into a ridge, except that it was all covered in rippling knee-high summer-dry grass, studded here and there with bushes of snowberry and wild rose green against the tawny pelt.

Órlaith reached out and touched the Sword, where it was lashed to the car's wicker inner wall with rawhide ties. There was less of human kind to the feel of the land here, and what there was had an edge like a knife, with an undertone of grimness and old sorrows.

For generations this had been a borderland between the PPA and the United States of Boise, claimed by both and ruled by neither; raid and skirmish had gone back and forth across the marches along with the banditry that always sprang up in debatable lands. In the Prophet's War the wild horsemen from beyond the Rockies had poured through with fire and sword. Peace had found it a wasteland.

A herd of pronghorn stood and watched the train from a ridgeline, then fled like fawn-and-white streaks over the yellow-brown hills. A group of a dozen mounted Nez Perce in red-dyed deerskin shirts and otterskin collars accompanied by a chuck wagon passed them on a broken, potholed ancient road, driving a herd of their prized Appaloosa horses southward. A lobo pack trotted by in the middle distance, dark dots against the grass. Birds swarmed, from clouds of Barrow's Sparrow to hawks hanging in the air above watching for rabbits and ground squirrels. Glimpses showed mule deer and elk, scattered clumps of buffalo, and once a sounder of wild boar grubbing for camas roots in a low patch, ignoring the train with surly indifference. Nothing of human-kind, save here and there the burnt-out snags of an ancient farmhouse or some huge piece of farm machinery that sat rusting as it had since before her parents were born.

Heuradys was smiling slightly and affectionately as she looked out at the lion-colored hills.

"I remember Mom One saying that getting Barony Harfang in fief as a *reward* was like being given a free grant of seventeen million tons of undelivered Arizona sand FOB origin," she said. "Though when I was little I always got sort of excited when we packed up for the yearly trip out here. I can just remember when it meant camping in tents."

Delia had been Tiphaine's official Châtelaine for three decades, and as such general business manager of her estates while Lady d'Ath fulfilled public duties in war and at court. Heuradys went on:

"Mom Two always liked it here—lots of hunting and falconry and best of all *quiet*, like a vacation, she says. Mom One does too, I think, because there's been so much work for her overseeing the development. She also said that at least sand in Arizona wouldn't reach out and swallow all the revenue from your established estates for twenty years."

"A gross exaggeration," Órlaith teased. "You can't hunt or fly falcons on sand."

"Or collect share rents and labor-service from the antelope and prairie chickens. The only thing that's consistently turned a profit here is the wool, and we can't fulfill our baronial obligations with a sheep ranch."

"Speaking of obligations, House Ath never did get around to the castle," Órlaith said, unhelpfully teasing and putting on a mock-monarchic frown. "A barony is scarcely worthy of the name without one!"

Heuradys rolled her amber eyes. "Have you got any idea of what those monsters cost? A castle is a heavily fortified bottomless pit you shovel money into. Diomede can do it when he's baron."

The first sign they were on Harfang was a wooden heliograph relay tower sprouting from a higher-than-usual piece of Palouse; then a mounted patrol of light cavalry armed with sword and recurve bow who raised their hands in salute.

Big flocks of white Corriedale sheep appeared, and herds of red-coated, white-faced cattle, and mare-and-colt clumps of horses, all under the eye of armed and mounted buckaroos. Here and there winding strings of earthen check-dams had been built across swales to turn them into a series of ponds and marshes edged with willows and cottonwoods, and planted woodlots of black locust, fir, lodgepole pine, hybrid poplar and chestnut oak showed on some of the ridges or north-facing slopes and along the banks of streams. Most of the trees were thriving but still spindly with youth, though some had already been coppiced to supply poles and fuel on a regular basis.

Then they could see the four big windmills that served the home-estate where they stood on the nearest hillcrest eastward, slender distance-tiny tapering towers with their great airfoil vanes rotating with majestic deliberation, powering everything from flour-mills to wool-presses. They also pumped at need from deep tube wells into a big concrete-lined tank set at their base, so Athana had running water now, still uncommon in most of Montival outside the cities, and piped sewage delivered to a bio-gas plant for lighting the manor and the public buildings.

Then they were among the tilled land of what was officially *Saint Athana Manor*. The Five Great Fields of the peasant tenants were vast squares edged with neatly trimmed hedges of head-high black hawthorn and tall poplars; within each was a swirling pattern of broad strips laid out along the contours. Two held the dun-gold of reaped grain pimpled with stooked sheaves, two the vibrant green of sweet clover or alfalfa, one the variegated patterns of root crops. Closer to the center were bench-terraced orchards and truck gardens, and off to the south was the demesne, the lord's home-farm.

"That wheat looks better than I'd have expected in a place too dry for forest," Karl said thoughtfully as they passed close enough to estimate the weight of the grain in the ears and he counted the number of sheaves in a section. "What do you get here, Lady?"

"Forty bushels an acre on the demesne in a bad year, better than sixty in a good one, usually," she said. "The tenants the same, unless they all turn up on rent-day beating their breasts and sobbing in heart-rending unison that it's less because they wore themselves out on the demesne, poor lambs."

She shrugged. "We don't fuss if it's close enough for feudal work. Nobody really tries to push the line with Mom One. Not twice."

By now lord and peasant both throughout the Association lands were used to that dance and trod the steps without thinking about it much.

"Sure, and that's not a bad yield, not at all! 'Twould be thought fine even in the dúthchas," Karl said; and the Willamette was a byword for lush fertility.

"The soil here is wonderful and it retains water. We've even got a vine-yard going, on a south-facing slope with good frost drainage. And my brother Diomede has been putting in some sugar beet on the demesne, just small patches on trial, seeing if it goes well enough to justify building a refinery. Dionysus knows there's always a market for sugar."

The gearing hummed as the train swayed and clicked onto the siding by the Athana station. There was a brief metal-on-metal screech of brakes as they stopped, a feeling of surging forward and a falling whine as the treadmills sank back to horizontal. Karl strung his longbow and set the other Mackenzies doing likewise, which was an interesting operation for those sitting down. Heuradys joined him at the door as he twitched back the cover on his quiver, sliding her longsword into the frog-sling at her belt and working her hands to full suppleness with a set of brief exercises that were so automatic she probably wasn't consciously aware of what she was doing.

They opened the door and hopped down together and spread out to either side, and the rest of the party followed. This part of the rail platform was unwalled, a concrete pavement covered with bricks set in a her-ringbone pattern and a tiled roof supported on wooden posts. Órlaith rose and stretched before she buckled on the Sword of the Lady and came out last, save for Macmac at her heels. She'd been accustomed to bodyguards all her life. Though it was disturbing to know that so many people—whether ones you knew and liked or ones you knew only as faces, you passed them braced to attention in front of walls or doors—were ready to throw their bodies between you and a blade to stop that hypothetical enemy. The more so now that she'd seen real battle and some *had* died in her place.

A man she recognized as one of Baroness d'Ath's light horse com-manders waited outside, in half-armor and with his well-trained mount standing motionless behind him over the dropped reins. He had the golden spurs on his heels, a wagon and a few saddled horses standing by, and ten mounted troopers behind him in open-face sallets and short-sleeved mail shirts riveted inside their jerkins, quivers on their backs and four-foot horn-and-sinew bows in the boiled-leather cases before their right knees. Their shoulders had badges in the same black-gold-and-silver arms as he wore on his breastplate, the sigil of House Ath, *sable, a delta or over a V argent.* There was a group of locals in the background gaping and slowing down and stopping in the middle of shifting stacked pallets of boxed Mason jars onto a cart as they recognized her.

Obviously the news of who was visiting hadn't leaked, which was good.

They doffed their hats and fell to one knee anyway when they saw who got off the train and the soldiers saluted fist-to-breast, since she was well-known by sight here. She absently made the gesture—hand out at waist height, then turned palm upward and fingers curled slightly—that meant *you may rise*. She found it all slightly absurd, but custom was king of all.

The knight was a grizzled dark man tanned and windburned to leather with a patch over his left eye, a short stub middle finger on the left hand, and thinning bowl-cut black hair shot with silver like his clipped beard and mustache. She noticed that two of his command were around his age and scarred too, and the rest in their teens and disconcertingly fresh-faced. Including a pair of youngish but tough-looking girls who were shooting glances of adolescent admiration at either Heuradys, herself, or both, or both of them and Suzie and Morfind and some of the Mackenzies too. For women to take up the trade of arms was less uncommon on the d'Ath domains than elsewhere in the Protectorate.

He noticed her noticing the makeup of the horse-archers.

"My lord Diomede has most of the regular garrison and the vassals doing their annual forty days over at Castle Campscapell for the postharvest maneuvers, Your Highness," he said. "These are what's left."

He took a knee for a moment and inclined his head. She extended her right hand for the kiss of homage.

"Rise, Sir Savaric," Órlaith said, when he'd made it.

Then he bowed to his liege's daughter with the leg-forward gesture that involved touching his right-hand fingers to his brow and then sweeping them outward with the bend so that it nearly touched the ground. Faramir and Morfind got a salute and small stiff bow, which did duty for Suzie as well. He nodded casually to Sir Droyn as one equal to another, which made the very-recently-knighted nobleman fight down a grin of pure pleasure. The younger man was the son of a Count and hence much better-born than a landless retainer, but knighthood had its own hierarchies and brotherhoods and he'd just been welcomed into a select company.

"God give you good afternoon, Lady Heuradys," Savaric said. "My lord your brother and his good Lady Ysabeau send their love, and Ygraine and Gussalin and Ismay and young Morgause as well."

"Morgause said that?" Heuradys said. "I knew the little beast was precocious, but . . ."

"Well, she said, 'Wanna see Auntie Herry!'"

Savaric's rather stark single brown eye went gentle for a moment. Then he went on briskly:

"They bid you visit the keep of my lord your father at Campscapell if your duty to your liege permits, since my lord Sir Diomede intends to keep the winter season at Barony Ath in the west with his lady mother and the Baroness. There's word of a muster and he wants to be at hand if . . . when . . ."

"When," Heuradys said flatly to his raised and questioning eyebrow.

"*When* the *ban* of the Association is called to arms."

Órlaith nodded to herself, mentally noting that she *would* see that Heuradys got time to visit.

She enjoys her nieces so!

It had been a while since Ysabeau's difficult last pregnancy, after a close-set series; there would probably be no more.

So Ygraine's the heir of Ath in her generation, and she idolizes Herry and wants to follow in her footsteps to knighthood, too, and her parents sound as if they're reluctantly willing. I can have her attached to my household when this thing with Mother is cleared up, that'll mean her seeing the Kingdom beyond the Protectorate too.

Associate pages were expected to put up with a certain amount of hazing and hardship as part of their training; getting them out of their own privileged family settings and on their own among their peers while still young was part of the reason for the system, as well as forging bonds between families. A page was a very lowly form of life in a noble household, in practice if not theory subordinate to most of the commoner servants and run off their feet between drill, classes and duties. The baboon-troop jostling and bullyragging among the pack of pages in a castle could be quite a bit worse for a girl, though.

Easier to keep a close eye on her in a small menie, which mine will be until I come of Crown age, and Herry will be there to help. Maybe she could be Herry's squire in a few years, or mine if we get on and she shapes well. I'd like to do her family a favor.

She swung into the saddle of the waiting courser with a half-skip and a vault; it was good to be on a horse again after the ordeal of sitting still for a day and night, and feel the lively interaction between rider and mount as the great muscles moved between her knees. The rest of her party did likewise, except for the Mackenzies who slung the gear into the waiting wagon and trotted along on foot. Children who'd been playing in the slightly scruffy soccer field and baseball diamond and tournament track that separated the train station from the village stopped to stare, many running back home as fast as they could accompanied by barking mutts and yelling shrilly themselves.

Athana Manor was bigger and more complex than most, since it was the heart of a barony and provided specialist services for the other settlements on Harfang. In fact, by now it was trembling on the verge of being a town. That was marked by the fact that a second church was under construction behind a maze of scaffolding, and confirmed by the multiple workshops of smiths and carpenters and wheelwrights and leatherworkers and more, and the fact that there were actual full-time stores rather than traveling peddlers on market-days. It was also neater, more uniform and more efficiently laid out than many, because it had been purpose-built on vacant land to a set plan by experts starting well after the Change, rather than cobbled together by fumbling amateurs in a desperate emergency from whatever was to hand and then improved later catch-as-catch-can.

I'm more at home in the dúthchas among Mackenzies, at seventh and last, but this is a good place, Órlaith thought.

A roadway of compacted crushed rock ran from the sheds and stables of the railway station through the village proper on its way to the manor house, lined with copper beeches now casting a welcome shade beneath their reddish-purple leaves on this hot dry summer's day. The whitewashed, tile-roofed, rammed-earth cottages of the peasants and craftsmen were on dusty-brown tree-lined lanes, each steading in its rectangular toft with sheds and gardens and chicken-coops at the rear and flowers or perhaps a trellised rose or honeysuckle in front.

Folk in coarse homespun were busy about the day, the ceaseless chores and working on things like roofs and fences and general tidying-up after the shattering all-hands labor of the Harvest. Most just bobbed their heads, but Boudicca jumped in cat-quick to rescue one basket of eggs dropped when a towhead girl barely old enough for the double tunics, headscarf and wooden clogs of womanhood suddenly recognized the Crown Princess. The air was full of the scents of pickling and canning and bottling and smoking and drying foodstuffs to be packed away in cellars and sheds for the cold season, as well as the inevitable smells of horse and woodsmoke.

They clattered through a stone-paved central square with its church in the Italo-Gothic style still bedecked with sheaves from the Harvest mass, tavern sporting a creaking low-relief sign carved and colored to show a drunken owl lying on its back with a mug in one claw, and shops and worksteads and the long weaving-shed that doubled as town hall and site for dances.

The houses grew larger and the gardens broader and brighter as you went south towards the lord's dwelling, until there were some quite substantial ones built around courtyards for the married gentry staff like Sir Savaric who didn't live in, and a square of barracks set by itself with stables and corrals.

The manor-house proper sat on its own gentle south-facing slope some distance away and a bit higher for the view. They entered through a fretted metal gate; there was a whitewashed wall topped with wrought-iron work and lined with cedars that enclosed lawns and terraced gardens, banks of flowers and clipped shrubberies and scattered trees and a swimming pool behind hedges and windbreaks. A small herd of ornamental white-spotted fallow deer stood in a clump and stared in horror at the Mackenzie greathounds, who in turn covertly looked back as they padded along at heel and let their tongues lap at their noses in interest. A peacock glared with offended aggression, gave its raucous cry and then stalked off past a row of espaliered fruit-trees. Gardeners stood and bowed as they clattered through the gates, busy getting ready for the cold season after the Harvest rush.

The E-shaped Great House was rammed earth too, the more expensive variety with five parts in a hundred of cement mixed in, three stories covered in a warm cream stucco with just a hint of reddish gold, picked out by colored tile arches over the doors and windows. The drive that led to the main entryway curled around a burbling fountain surrounded by elongated leaping bronze greyhounds. A five-story square tower at one corner had an open top floor to accommodate the heliograph, and also had tracks for mounting a nine-pounder usually kept disassembled in the basement.

The whole rather Iberian-Gothic composition was so charming that you took a minute to realize that there was a dry moat disguised by a ha-ha, and the fact that all the exterior windows were too narrow for a man to climb through, and could be slammed closed in moments by loop-holed steel shutters just as strong and fireproof as the yard-thick walls. It wasn't a castle, but it was definitely defensible against anything short of a formal attack with artillery and siege gear.

A fortyish man in a black-and-white tabard holding a white staff of office stood at the front doors, which were high blond oak over a steel core and studded with octagonal bosses of black lacquered iron. He made a knee to Órlaith and bowed deeply to Heuradys as they dismounted and handed off their reins to the grooms, with the heads of the various staff divisions doing the same in the background.

"Your Highness. My lady Heuradys," he said, with a slightly strained smile.

He contemplated a somewhat out-of-favor Princess who nonetheless was heir to the throne, accompanied by more than a dozen rowdy young warriors, mostly pagans from beyond the Association lands with God-knew-what uncouth customs and unreasonable expectations. All this just when he'd expected months of having the place to himself while he put everything in painstaking order.

"Sir Droyn. My . . . ah . . . honored guests of the house."

Heuradys grinned. "Don't worry, Goodman Paein," she said. "This is the last disruption for a while, I promise."

"Shining pearl within the crimson sky
Guide me in the coming night—
Perfect seed within a humble husk
Ground my feet in soil so I may rise—
Patient leaf within the endless pool
Calm me when the torrent falls—
Gentle wind within the slanting grass
Bear me ever on until I rest!"

Órlaith lowered her arms and slid the sheathed Sword of the Lady she'd laid across her palms back to her swordbelt's frog-sling; since her father died she'd taken up his habit of holding it so when she made the Farewell to the setting Sun. Then she turned from the balcony and stepped back into the suite, looking around the bedchamber's expanse of smooth pale tile.

The floor was a geometry of cream squares edged with green vines, and the French doors she'd just used opened onto balconies with their decorative wrought-iron balustrades overlooking the fountain, walkways and gardens in the courtyard below. She sighed happily at the comforting familiarity. This was the suite the Royal family usually got on visits. Like many modern manor houses, it was made up with interior inner-facing windows and glass doors for the light excluded by solid exterior walls. There was a big fireplace with a carved stone surround of owls and vines, swept and garnished with dried wildflowers for summer, but discreet bronze grill vents showed a central heating system, and the frosted globes of the gaslights glowed brightly now that the sun was on the horizon westward.

The large bed had been replaced by two slightly smaller ones, probably last night when the heliograph message came in. She didn't mind sharing with Herry at need, of course. . . .

Despite the fact that she thrashes about and snores and hogs the covers and has cold feet.

But it was nice to be in one place in the Protectorate outside her family's homes that actually understood they weren't lovers. Instead of elaborately pretending they didn't know something that wasn't so in the first place, and which she would have scorned to conceal if it *was* so.

Strange folk, Christians. Though it's wicked of Herry to take advantage of those who think she's a Royal favorite just for giggles.

"Remember the first time we met?" Órlaith said. "That was here, I think."

"Not the first time we *met*," Heuradys said, coming out of the bath suite still combing her damp and slightly frizzy hair.

There was a very nice sunken marble tub, salvaged long ago by one of her Nonni Sandra's programs and stored against the time of some favored noble's need. Norman Arminger had died before she was born, but the Spider of the Silver Tower had always been the brains of the Armingers in her opinion. Certainly the better long-term planner; her schemes were still producing useful things or skills or opportunities long after her death. Norman had been the Brute Squad and the obsessive dream and driving savage will in the first, terrible years of the modern world.

"It was just the first time I thought of you as a potential human being and someone of interest, my liege, not just a snotty little brat with interesting parents."

"Sure, and we were both snotty little brats then, for all your pretensions to the wisdom of age!" Órlaith said, and looked around. "I remember the house was a lot plainer then. In fact I *think* I remember you could still smell the walls curing."

The murals here now were classical-themed mosaics done in tiny squares of iridescent favrile glass, a method invented by the semi-legendary master-craftsman Tiffany in the time of the ancients and redeveloped by artisans under her grandmother Sandra's patronage. The colors glowed in a way that was intense and delicate at the same time, with a surprising sense of depth; one mural showed a trio of dancing Graces in a flowering meadow that suggested Botticelli without imitating. The other had a long view of a white-columned temple on a blue-tinted rocky hill above a wine-colored sea, with a sacrificial procession in the foreground leading a garlanded bull up a narrow path between olive trees and pencil cypress to the music of double-flutes and cymbals.

Órlaith remembered seeing it for the first time about ten years ago. It was Delia de Stafford's taste, but aimed at Tiphaine's interests; like her adopted daughter she followed the Olympians, and Athana in particular. Delia was a witch, more or less of Órlaith's branch of the Old Faith though with less of the Gael.

She grinned as she buttoned her Montrose jacket and watched Heuradys struggling with her hose—it was particolored, of cotton knit and skin-tight, which made it an irritating struggle to get on unwrinkled when your legs were still slightly damp from the baths.

"Sure, and I'm glad I like kilts," she said. "Why not a kirtle?"

Various types of headdress and kirtle over a blouse-shift were what Associate noblewomen wore in casual or semi-formal country settings rather than the formality—and discomfort and difficulty—of the close-fitted court cotte-hardie, which needed skilled help to get you into and out of.

Rather like plate armor, which is a good metaphor, she thought, looking over at the armor-stands that bore their suits and shields, looking rather like the harness of invisible warriors.

The most elaborate versions of Protectorate court dress required on-the-spot sewing to don and pricking-out of seams to take off. They looked pretty when done well and were more varied than the Clan's quasi-uniform and Órlaith had enjoyed wearing them . . . just long enough for a ball or masque.

"I would, except that there's no formal guard here with you, and I'm not going to put on anything that might slow my movements," Heuradys said.

When she'd donned the snowy full-sleeved shirt and brown suede jerkin and rust-colored houppelande coat with its dagged sleeves she opened the leaves of the shrine that stood before the scene of sacrifice; it was much like a big Catholic prie-dieu, except that it was taller and designed for those who prayed standing rather than kneeling. The doors held a round disk of thin hammered gold worked around the edge with olive branches and a silver owl in its center, the design taken from an ancient Athenian drachma.

The wood into which it was set was highly polished olive itself, inlaid with images of the moon and a frieze of feathers patterned on the wings of a harfang, done in mother-of-pearl. When they were opened you saw the carved form of a standing woman, ivory flesh and golden robe. Against her thigh rested a shield painted with a grimacing snake-haired head, and a serpent coiled inside it; one hand held an upright spear, and the palm of the other supported a winged figure of Victory. On her head was a tall triple-crested helm, and her eyes were the shimmering gray of moonstone.

"Athana, great Goddess, ever have I, Heuradys d'Ath, prayed to You foremost of all, and unto You have I made the acceptable offerings. . . ."

Heuradys murmured the formula as she cleansed her hands and face with ritual drops of khernips, lustral water, lit dried olive twigs and incense in the offering bowl on its golden tripod, scattered a little barley in it and passed the owl feather through the smoke and touched it to eyes and lips. Then she poured wine and oil from the libation chalice on the flames, raised her arms with palms upward and softly chanted, her face rapt amid the scented smoke:

"I sing now of Thee;
Blessed and fierce, warlike Pallas, whose Olympian kind,
Bright and clear we ever find:

Thy far-famed altar upon the rocky height,
And olive groves, and shady mountains Thee delight:
In cunning plan rejoicing, who with subtle art and dire
And wild, the souls of mortals does inspire.
Maiden of the awesome mind,
Gorgon's bane, ever-virgin, blessed, kind:
Patron of piercing thought and craft well-understood,
Rage to the wicked, wisdom to the good:
Sprung from the head of Zeus, of splendid mien,
Purger of evils, all-victorious Queen.
Hear me, O Goddess, when to Thee I pray,
With supplicating voice both night and day,
And in my latest hour, give peace and health,
Propitious times, and necessary wealth,
And ever present, be shield and aid,
Much worshipped, art's parent, gray-eyed maid."

After that and a moment of silent prayer she wiped the vessels clean, replaced everything and shut the doors with their shimmering mother-of-pearl inlay. Everyone here knew the split religious allegiances of House Ath—her brothers were Catholics—but sticking a thumb in the majority's eye would have been both unwise and discourteous. There were pagans in the Association and probably more than usual on this barony, but they stayed discreet.

"You know," Órlaith said when they'd both completed their devotions, "after all that happened down south, it's a comfort to think that so many great Powers of the otherworld are inclined to us, and only one to the other side. Granted, it's a formidable One, and it turns out the Prophet was just one string on Its bow, but still . . ."

Heuradys started to nod, then cocked an eye at her. "It would be comfortable if we *knew* that," she said thoughtfully. "Only we don't. We only know what we've met *so far.*"

"Reiko . . ." Órlaith began slowly. "Reiko said that her father once told her he thought the Change was like a hard blow opening a door in the world, one that had been closing slowly for thousands of years. Just a crack at first, and then wider and wider."

"And we don't know what's going to walk through," Heuradys said. "Or what has already walked through, for that matter; Montival is big, but the world is far bigger. Let's leave superstitions like dualism to the Christians, shall we?"

Órlaith blinked. That was true, but profoundly disturbing and there was absolutely nothing she could do about it right now.

"You're such a comfort at times, Herry!"

"Well, it would be even more uncomfortable if I let you blunder confidently into things, my liege. And in the meantime, let's eat," she said.

There was a knock on the door of the chambers even as Heuradys extended her hand towards it. It opened, and Tair looked through; he and his sister Rionach had been standing guard there.

"They've news for Herself, lady," he said.

Órlaith recognized the servant in the tabard behind them. "News, Goodman Seffrid?" she said.

"A gentleman has arrived," he said. "A Boisean gentleman, by the name of Alan Thurston, and a dozen retainers; they came overland."

Órlaith whistled silently, and Heuradys gave her a glance.

"So much for getting away from politics!" Órlaith said. "Shut the door and they climb in the window, that they do!"

Lawrence Thurston had founded the United States of Boise—of *America*, he'd maintained until his death, though it actually governed only most of the old state of Idaho and parts of Nevada and Montana. His son Frederick ruled Boise now as a member-realm of the High Kingdom, duly elected by local custom every seven years against any opponent who wanted to run and didn't mind making a complete waste of their time and being something of a joke.

"So far, so good," Heuradys murmured, echoing her thought.

The problem was that Lawrence Thurston's *eldest* son Martin had killed his own father unbeknownst to most and had ruled Boise during much of the Prophet's War as parricide, usurper, ally and ultimately puppet of the Prophet Sethaz and the Church Universal and Triumphant. It had been a civil strife for that folk, until her father killed him at the Horse Heaven Hills and then took Boise a little later by a personal *coup de main* with Fred.

Martin's wife Juliet had defected to the Montivallan side while he still lived and ruled; not because she disapproved of the murder and usurpation that made her a queen with a prospect of becoming an empress, but because of what Martin had become as the Prophet's Ascended Masters gnawed at his soul. *That* had made her recoil in horror. Her second son— born after her husband's death—was called Alan. He and his mother and sibling had lived quietly on a remote ranch since the war and taken no part in public affairs.

Forgetting, and by the world forgot, Órlaith thought; that was what had made it unnecessary for Fred to kill them, which he'd been reluctant to do in any case. *But apparently Alan's not willing to hide anymore. He'd be about my age. I don't blame him for being restless . . . but it may be a foolish thing.*

"He sent this card, Your Highness," the servant said, holding out a little silver card-tray, a habit the Association ladies had picked up from the perennially popular Austen novels.

She took the paper on it and unfolded it, breaking the daub of wax that held the folded rectangle of cream linen-rag paper together. Within was a visitor's card that read:

Captain Alan Thurston (United States Army, reserve)
Hali Lake Ranch, District of Latah

And beneath it a sign, not one she recognized at all; like a triskele, but as if the central point were a writhing knot and the arms like irregular question-marks, the whole in yellow on a circle of black. It was probably a cattle-brand; most interior Ranchers used theirs as the rough equivalent of an Associate noble's coat-of-arms.

Or a like a Japanese mon, she thought; she'd come to appreciate those for their spare elegance.

Heuradys leaned in to read it, touching the Sword lightly as she did with her hip, which was unusual. Órlaith blinked at a feeling of . . . some-thing. It vanished when she tried to grasp it, and she shrugged and turned back to the message.

The paper itself bore a brief note addressed to *The Lord of this manor, or the senior official in residence*, asking leave to stay for a party on its way to the muster of the realm. Actually there hadn't been a general muster yet, only a specific call-up, but everyone suspected what was coming, and there was a general obligation to help.

"We'll have to invite him and his retainers to dinner, at least," Heu-radys said. "Convey the usual compliments, Seffrid. A seat for him at the high table, of course, and his folk below according to their rank and station."

"It may make things a little awkward," Órlaith said.

Heuradys grinned like a wolf. "What, the fact that *your* father killed *his* father at the Horse Heaven Hills with that magical Sword you're wear-ing right now?" she said. "How could that possibly disturb the succession of courses at dinner? Blood feuds with the soup, epic revenge over the salad, the clash of steel with the entrée and a five-minute skewered-liver dying oratorio with the sweet?"

Órlaith gave her a jaundiced look and then shrugged. "Well, my grandfathers killed each other too," she said. "My parents learned to deal with it, and sure, he'll just have to do the same."

CHAPTER SEVEN

"Kill," Thora Garwood said.

John reeled backward; her wooden practice blade had come in just over the curve of his shield and thumped him behind the ear in the gap between the bevor and the edge of his sallet helmet. It wasn't a dangerous blow from a blunt stick wound with cloth and muffled by the padded coif under the helm, but it hurt like blazes for a moment and made his knees wobble. There were men standing by to make sure nobody went over the side by accident, but by now he was as used to the pitch of the deck as he'd ever been to solid land. Which was fortunate, because besides the risk of drowning the ship had picked up the usual hangers-on common in these waters, and tall stiff triangular fins broke the long low ripples of their wake now and then. The crew amused themselves and provided some fresh food by fishing for them, if you could call hooks as long as your arm reeved through pulleys on the boom and raised by geared winches *fishing*.

He brought his own lath sword up in acknowledgment and knocked up his visor, blinking as the world expanded from the narrow bright slit to a wider field that included Thora's grinning face and Deor leaning against the rail behind her; he had stripped, doused himself with buckets filled overside and was wiping his wiry, muscular torso down with a wet cloth soaked in a small amount of their precious fresh water. Fighting in armor always made you sweat like a steam-bath, and the sun here had a tropic bite not quite like anything he'd felt before, even in south Westria.

"I don't think that would actually have *killed* me," he added, probing at the new bruise with a gauntleted finger and wincing.

"No, but you'd have been frozen for long enough for me to stab you through the eyeslit," she said.

He sighed, handed his shield and wooden sword to Evrouin and moved aside to let his valet strip off the armor. The stiff breeze cut through the sodden clothing beneath like a benediction; it was warm here, but that felt cool as his body shed heat and ached with a good tiredness. He stripped down to the skin too and emptied three buckets over himself; the water was deliciously cool but not cold.

Deor wrung out the towel, dunked it in a bucket and tossed it to him before he went to assist Thora with her gear.

"That was the thing that struck me most when we got south of Gibraltar," he said. "*Warm* seawater."

Ruan came over—he'd been doing the routine Mackenzies did when they couldn't actually shoot, drawing his bow and then slacking off, over and over—and said:

"Bend your head forward, Prince. . . ." He prodded at the mark where the blade had struck with a healer's care. "No, I don't think it's serious. Any dizziness? Pain in the head?"

"Both but just for a moment. I feel fine now."

"Good, but tell me or the ship's physician right away if that comes back, the which it probably won't but might, so."

John nodded. He'd had mild concussions, and it was something you had to take seriously. You also had to practice frequently to keep yourself honed sharp, and they were all quite conscious that two of the enemy ships who'd pursued them all the way from Topanga were still there, doggedly on their tracks. They might be fighting for their lives at any moment.

"You've got an edge on me in speed," John said to his partner, and was surprised to see her shake her head.

Thora Garwood, called Swiftsword, took anything martial very seriously. From sheer love of the craftsmanship of the thing, he thought, as well as the way Bearkillers were raised. She was a warrior born; St. Michael must have blessed her in her cradle.

"No, not as we stand. A few years ago, yes, I was faster than you are now, by a hair. I never had the sort of speed your sister's friend Heuradys does, she's almost freakish that way, and I think Órlaith has a tiny bit on me, even as I was at my peak."

"How'd you get that cut in on me, then?" John said in frustration. "I saw it coming—part of me did—but I just couldn't get anything in its way in time, or me out of it!"

"I moved my sword through a shorter distance," the Bearkiller said. "Mind you, you've probably improved a lot in the last six months. Some real fighting will do that. Training only takes you so far."

He finished with the towel, repeated Deor's wring-and-rinse, and handed it to her as the scop shrugged back into his breeks; he left the long shirt-tunic off for now, in weather so fine and mild. Thora rinsed and wiped down as he had while John dressed; Bearkillers didn't have much in the way of inhibitions about skin and didn't make much of a distinction between men and women that way. Mackenzies even less so, and he'd spent enough time in the dúthchas that he could appreciate the view without it disturbing him. The Guard crossbowmen had spent most of their lives in the Association territories before this venture, and were carefully not staring as they practiced with wooden sword and buckler.

Beyond him came a shout of *disssaaa!* Captain Ishikawa was practicing too; if anything, he was more conscientious than the Montivallans. In his case he was having four of his sailors throw pieces of firewood from the ship's galley at him, and converting them to useful kindling with swift turn-and-strike routines. The wood was light pine, unlikely to damage an edge.

"Besides," Thora said, as she twisted back into her knit-cotton drawers and halter.

Which oddly enough was *more* interesting than nakedness in a way, particularly purely utilitarian nakedness. She went on:

"Unless you're training as a duellist, there's a limit to how much one-on-one like this does you good in a real fight—a melee, I mean, a battle. Yes, it keeps up your speed and endurance and blade placement, but there's too much time to think and make plans and it gets you used to having everything important right in front of you. Bad for your situational awareness."

John nodded as he thought back to the scrambling chaos of the fighting on the Bay, and the night raid in the Chatsworth Lancers' territory down south.

"I can see your point," he said. "But what's to do about it? Something like the melee event at a tournament, I suppose . . ."

She tied the cloth belt of her long-sleeved shirt, which she wore to protect her redhead's skin from the savage equatorial sun, and nodded.

Deor chuckled softly. "Oh, you may regret asking that, brother bard," he said. "You just made a suggestion for more arms-play to Thora Swift-sword. I've had her beating on me the world around. . . ."

"Keeping you alive the world around," she retorted with a smile.

Then: "What we'll do about it is have our own miniature melee. You and me and Deor. Two against one, and so on. That'll be fun, and useful too."

"Yes, lots of fun," John said hollowly, and Deor laughed aloud.

"Sort of like an orgy, but with swords," the scop said.

"I wouldn't know," John said, trying to summon Christian rectitude. "Never been to an orgy."

"It's overrated," Deor said. "Two is company, three is choreography and while I'm fond of dancing I prefer to do it upright."

John found he *could* blush, tropical tan or no.

Thora snapped her fingers. "We'll get Ishikawa in on it too. Completely different style, that will be useful; the katana's a bit like a *kriegs-messer*, but faster. It doesn't do to teach your reflexes as if you'll always be up against people who fight like your sparring-partners. And Ruan and some of the crossbowmen, a couple at a time. And Ishikawa's sailors use the *naginata*, defense against polearms is good. . . ."

John nodded; that *would* also make the whole process more interesting, like a jam session with a strange musician. Fighting drill was an acquired taste for him, but he'd long ago decided that since he had to do it and quite often, he might as well like it.

"I'd better go up and see what's happening with our enemies," he said, settling his real sword in the frog of his arming belt.

The *Tarshish Queen* was a merchantman, not a naval vessel, but he still went up the starboard gangway to the quarterdeck, and saluted the Crowned Mountain and Sword flying from the gaff at the stern. Ashore the position of honor for a flag was a matter of height, but at sea it was the rearmost that took precedence; hence Benny the Beaver, Corvallis' national ensign, was at the mizzen, and the Feldman & Sons house flag of a stylized schooner slanting upwards was on the main.

"Your Highness," Captain Feldman said gravely.

"They're still there, I see, Captain," John said with a sigh.

The two hard-to-see dots to stern were about a mile apart from each other and a mile and a bit behind their ship; their hulls were blue and the sails a neutral faded gray, hard to pick out. He hadn't expected the two *Chosŏn* ships to be gone, though it would have been a profound relief not to have three or four hundred cannibal savages and disconcertingly civilized diabolists—who were also savage cannibals—on his tail.

He said so, and Moishe Feldman shook his head. "Closer to two hundred by now," he said. "They couldn't have had enough rations in store to feed crews that size, not when they'd already just crossed the Pacific east-to-west, and probably not enough water either, even with full tanks to start with. What's that Mackenzie story, about the cats trapped on the island with nothing to eat . . . ?"

"The Kilkenny Cats," John said hollowly.

In a way it was reassuring to have enemies who were just unambiguously evil. On the other hand, it was obscurely disgusting—it made you feel hating them was a sort of loathsome intimacy. It was even more upsetting when you realized that basically it was sheer luck who'd ended up like them and who hadn't. There was nothing about Koreans or the former inhabitants of Los Angeles that naturally inclined them to become puppets of the Adversary. It might just as well have been him, if things had gone differently in Montival. . . .

"That still gives them an edge of four to one. I take it they're not going to give up," he said.

"Not while they have enough hands left to tend the sails," Captain Feldman said, then added casually: "I hate stern chases."

There was a crack-tung sound, faint over the distance. A finned bolt splashed into the cerulean blue of the waves several hundred yards behind his ship. He gave an ironic wave.

"Fire away and waste your ammunition, you overoptimistic *mamzrim*. . . . But I don't dislike the chase nearly as much as getting caught."

John nodded, looking around at the *Tarshish Queen*. The weeks since the unnatural storm abated had seen her transformed from a near-wreck to something much more like the taut ship who'd dropped out of Newport several months ago. If you looked closely you could see evidence of the long hard grind of skilled effort that had repaired the storm's damage, or much of it. The mizzenmast above their head creaked ominously every once in a while beneath the woolding. . . .

"What about the *Stormrider*?"

Feldman shrugged eloquently, ending with a gesture that flipped his hands palm-upright.

"Your Highness, the only thing we *know* about where she is, is *not here*. If she came through the first blow she might have run back to Topanga— we told Captain Russ that the Princess was there—or he might have tried to follow what he thought might be our course. Since *we* didn't know what that was for a couple of days, how could he? Could be anywhere from Hawaii to Cairns by now, or show up in an hour . . . but I wouldn't bet on it. Not anything I couldn't afford to lose, at least."

The Bosun padded up and knuckled her brow, blue eyes worried in her weathered pug face and her striped cotton shirt and pantaloons sopping and clinging to her stocky, knotty frame. On this merchantman she doubled as master-wright, in charge of under-way repairs under the ship's officers.

"Cap'n, Mr. Radavindraban's compliments, survey complete, and we've done everything we can with that leak from the sprung strake for'ard."

"Details?" Feldman said.

John recalled that they'd taken an enemy roundshot at the waterline back in the Bay and the storm had worsened the damage. Beyond the fact that it was the reason they were leaking he hadn't paid overmuch attention, except to do what the experts said he should, which was mostly pull a spell on the pumps every day.

"If we tighten the jacks any more on the stick she'll crack out, right through the hull. Isn't just bashed in anymore, it's flexing both ways with every pitch, you can hear the sodding thing crunch and the planks creaking, spewing oakum. And it's no good spiking bars across the gap, that's just chewing at the parts as aren't busted. We need to beach her and come at it with some of the planking off, scarf in a join and peg it, then re-plank and caulk, if we can't get at a shipyard. Otherwise it'll get worse as she works. If it comes to another blow . . ."

She shrugged less elegantly than her Captain but just as eloquently; she wasn't telling the owner-commander of the *Queen* anything he didn't know, but evidently she felt it bore repeating.

"Water in the hold?"

"Gaining on the pumps now, but slow, skipper. A couple of inches in the last day, more or less. But we're a little down by the head, I'd say. It's going to get worse every bloody day until we fix her. Or we sink."

Water was jetting over the side, pushed by the pumps rigged in the hold. John flexed his hands, which were more callused than sword-drill had made them; everyone took their turn. Though that continuous telltale jet itself was information to the enemy. Every inch of sail was set, and the wind was steady but light, the sails just taut and making the ship a thing of geometric grace as it went forward with a roll that took the bowsprit in a slow hypnotic rise and fall against deep-blue ocean and pale-blue sky. There was very little pitch, since they were running only a little off the wind and the swells were long and smooth with only an occasional whitecap.

The First Mate came on deck, stripped to a twisted loincloth and beads of water glistening on his lean dark body; he'd been leading the team working on the leak personally and hands-on.

"Cap'n!" he called. "Permission to move stores aft to dress her trim!"

"Make it so, Mr. Mate," Feldman replied and gave him a wave.

He nodded and disappeared back into the hold with a casually agile hop. Orders sounded down there, and after a while thumps and the rumbling sound of barrels being rolled.

"They're going to catch us, Captain, aren't they?" John said, looking aft and raising his binoculars.

The two Korean ships didn't look as tidy as the *Tarshish Queen*. There were rattails and loose lines in their rigging, and one of them canted visibly. They'd been damaged in the howling storm that blew them south and west from Westria too, and hadn't done as much to repair it.

Or possibly they just don't care about appearances. We haven't been able to shake them, after all.

"With this much water in the hold, and if they don't founder before we do, yes," Feldman said, stroking his beard. "In about three days, give or take, if this wind holds. Unless we do something about it."

"And not what Captain Ishikawa proposed, either," John said.

They smiled at each other. The Nihonjin sailor had said they could do a quick turn and let him and his Imperial Navy sailors board one of the enemy ships to smash incendiaries on the deck and fight off the crew until the flames had taken hold. He'd been perfectly serious, too, though he hadn't fought very hard when they turned him down.

"This is becoming . . . monotonous," the Captain went on, as the First Mate reappeared and paced slowly from bow to stern, checking the waterline's tilt against the ship's Plimsoll line and hence their trim.

John snorted slightly. That was one way to put it. They'd tried dodging the pursuers before but the two of them were enough to bracket the course of the *Queen*. If the Montivallan schooner turned either way, one of them could cut the cord of the course and overtake them, and if they tried to fight past the other one would come to its aid before they could sink it; the *Queen* had heavier broadsides, but wooden ships were very difficult to destroy except by fire. There wasn't much between the three vessels in speed; the only safe course was to continue directly away, with the wind on the starboard quarter, which was their best point of sailing.

That meant continuously heading south and west; they'd crossed the equator some time ago, and hadn't been able to make the waters that were occasionally patrolled by the friendly Kingdom of Hawaii.

"Or they could run out of food and water," John said hopefully.

"Water, possibly. With them, they only run out of food when the last man finishes gnawing the bones of the second-to-last," Feldman said.

John winced. That was only a slight exaggeration. He'd seen things through the binoculars that he *really* would rather have not added to the images in his mind.

"And I think they topped their water tanks just before we left," the merchant skipper added. "While they were hiding amid the wrecks in San Pedro."

"We could try and turn in the night again," John said.

Feldman shook his head. "The sky's clear, the moon is full, and the weather in this part of the Pacific is pretty consistent this time of year. We lost distance the last time we tried and we haven't made most of it up."

There was a gap in the rear railing not far from the stern chaser catapult where a six-pound roundshot had come home that night and left a deep dent in the catapult's shield before it went off into the dark amid a sound like a hammer in God's smithy. If it had cut a backstay or hit the mast, or even crippled the wheel and made it impossible to maneuver quickly for a crucial few minutes . . .

He looked around, and John could see the maps in his head. "If we could shed them for a day or two, we could make landfall. Mind you, it's best to be careful in this neighborhood even with a fast well-found ship, much less beached and doing repairs. Very careful; put up a palisade, remount the catapults ashore to cover it, the lot."

"Pirate waters?" John said.

"Yes, and bad ones. This whole part of the world fell apart like a pot dropped on a rock after the Change and it hasn't got any better. Worse, because the knack for building modern ships has spread."

"Not to the Death Zones?" John said.

Feldman shook his head. "No, Java was wrecked like California, and most of Sumatra and big chunks everywhere around the major ports; you don't put in to those places, unless you're a salvager working the dead cities. And you're insane, which is why most of them are from Australia. The rest is a crazy-quilt, apart from a few places like New Singapore, and Bali and its possessions, and Capricornia. Those are as civilized as home is, in their way. Elsewhere one little stretch may have palaces and scholars and artists and dance festivals, and a day's sail away it's jungle and swamps with dugout canoes festooned in skulls trying to swarm you at midnight, bones through the nose, knives in their teeth and showers of poisoned darts from *sumpitan*."

John made an enquiring noise, and Feldman translated:

"*Sumpitan*, blowguns. And everything in between. There's enough trade to sustain a lot of pirates, and enough ordinary fishermen and farmers for longshore raiding for slaves and loot, but nobody strong enough to keep order. The Sulu Sea and south Mindanao just northwest of here are very bad, corsair nests. Nobody honest goes there, though *somebody* is selling them catapults. Then there's the Bugi men. . . ."

"Bogymen?" John said, blinking.

Then he crossed himself. *Ships decorated with skulls . . . warm seas . . . this is starting to remind me of that dream I had. Maybe next it'll be that old man shouting. Not good, John, not good! Órlaith and Reiko had prophetic dreams and look what it got them into! They got out again, but that's no guarantee I would.*

Feldman went on, answering his last word rather than the thought:

"Bogymen? The Bugis are where that word comes from! Sea-nomads, some reasonable enough, some reasonable as long as you look heavily armed and alert, some very dangerous even then; and there are the Iban too, the Sea Dyaks, and then just all-round pirate sons of bitches from no place in particular. So those Koreans on our tails aren't the only potential problem. If it's any consolation, the local lowlife would attack *them*, too. For their catapults, mainly; those are worth more than gold out here."

"Not much consolation. What's right ahead?"

"Maluku and then North Sulawesi. But there are islands close, this area has them like a teenager does pimples, and we could sail reach across this wind easily enough."

His eyes narrowed a little. "Now, if these Koreans were ordinary pirates—we've been using our navigation lights every night, there's a little trick you can play—put a raft astern with lights rigged so that they look the same, douse our own, and then cut it loose to draw them while we sail off darkened. It's surprisingly convincing, if you're used to seeing the real lights."

Suddenly Feldman stiffened, dropping the abstracted air of someone speculating.

"Wait a minute!"

He leveled his telescope again. *"Beshum ofen lo!* They're shooting, broadsides, and at each other!"

"Yes, they do that!" Radavindraban said in glee, running up and using his own glass. "Bloody fool, bloody fool!"

Feldman kept the telescope steady for a long moment. "No . . . one of them's firing into the water and the one to the southward is firing in the general direction of the one to the north!"

John used his binoculars again. The two Korean warships had changed course, slanting towards each other, and they were shooting their broadside catapults at something between them, something he couldn't see. They were shooting rapidly, too, one discharge after another. Water fountained upward, white against blue, as roundshot struck. Then a streak of yellow fire and black smoke as flames played across the water; a napalm shell. Sharper splashes as they switched to bolt that zipped into the sea like needles.

And then one of the ships staggered in the water. He could see cables snap and writhe, and the foremast went over, beginning slowly and then gathering speed until it crashed into the bowsprit with a crunching, tearing sound audible even here.

Feldman nodded crisply.

"They ran into something. All hands on deck, action stations, fighting sail only. Helm, come about!" he barked and followed it with a volley of nautical jargon whose gist was *turn right around and head for them.* "Catapult crews, load firebolt!"

Sailors ran past him and flung themselves on the stern chaser catapult. John hopped down from the quarterdeck, taking the four-foot drop directly so as not to get in the way on the companionways. More sailors, including Ishikawa and his Nihonjin, were tearing the covers off the broadside catapults and the bowchaser, unlimbering the pump-handles that powered the hydraulic jacks to cock the weapons. More tallied on to the windlasses and deck lines that controlled the fore-and-aft gaffs, or ran up the ratlines to furl the square sails on the main and foremast tops.

Dodging the working parties on the main deck wasn't easy either, as the ship heeled sharply to starboard and then steadied on its new course. John filled in the others as they edged forward to the space in front of the foremast, which was the nearest the ship had to clear when everyone was in action. It also gave them a better view, though Radavindraban pushed by supervising the opening of the arms chests and the racking of gear where it was easy to hand. The sailors slipped the scabbards of their bell-hilted cutlasses through the loops on their belts as they had the opportunity and they always wore at least one knife as a working tool, but the rest was clipped where it could be grabbed easily—boarding pikes and crossbows, bucklers and helms and reinforced walrus-leather cuirasses.

John felt the situation catch up with him, a combination of excitement quickening his pulse and a twist in the stomach at the thought of edged metal and strangers with murderous intent. He understood Feldman's actions perfectly; anything that altered the balance like this gave them a chance to settle with the pursuers. Then they could repair the ship at leisure—or labor, rather—and go home.

Fayard had his crossbowmen formed up—crowded together, in fact—and looked a question. John replied, to him and Evrouin who had the sack with his suit of plate.

"Just helmets and weapons now," he said. "We'll let the situation develop."

They could get into half-armor quickly, helping each other, and with luck the action wouldn't come to boarding. If it did, the protection would be worth the risk of ending up in the water with steel strapped to you. If it didn't . . . well, every naval weapon that had a range of more than a hundred yards would go through ordinary armor as if it were cloth; they were designed to injure the massive fabric of ships. Fayard looked slightly dismayed, since the doctrine of the Protector's Guard called for armor in all combat situations, but he obeyed.

"Different rules at sea, Sergeant," John said; his parents had always said you should tell the *why* of an order if you had time. "We know Captain Feldman isn't going to get into a boarding action if he can help it; those enemy ships have around three times our total numbers. Each."

Plus, he thought but didn't say, we have no earthly idea what's going on there.

"I have an ill feeling," Deor said quietly, touching the triple triangles of the *valknut* hanging at his throat, the mark of Woden. "There's something at work here, but it doesn't . . . taste or feel of anything I've felt before. And Thora and I have sailed these seas. If these were northern waters I'd be thinking of etins or trolls."

John crossed himself and touched his crucifix to his lips, wishing he'd had time to be confessed and take the Bread and Wine much, much more recently than many weeks ago.

The distance between the ships closed with that shocking suddenness that came after intervals when nothing seemed to happen at all. Soon the clanging thumps of the catapults were clear, and so were screams—war-cries and plain raw terror. Whatever it was, they were fighting something.

"Fighting and losing, I think," he murmured to himself.

Radavindraban came by, hopped up onto the rail with his binoculars to his eyes, then blanched. That wasn't easy for someone of his shade of very dark brown, but his skin turned muddy gray in spots.

"Bujang senang!" he screamed as he let the glasses fall and pointed, in no language John knew.

But not his native Tamil either from the sound.

"Bujang senang—Bujang senang raja!"

John felt like screaming himself, as they closed rapidly on the action. The first Korean ship lurched again, as if it had struck a rock, and it was farther down by the bows now. Something shot out of the water as if propelled by an invisible trebuchet, spray exploding forward with it. Scores of feet of scute-armored muscle, tons of weight crushing down on splintering wood as it sprawled across the forecastle of the ship, jaws the length of a man lined with serrated ivory knives. They gaped and clamped down on something that rolled sprattling and down the slanting deck towards it, ignoring the double-headed axe he cut it with. Then it tossed the man up like a gobbet and swallowed him whole save for the arm holding the axe. That fell down on the deck, a tidbit ignored.

A bristle of long spears pointed towards it, which was remarkable discipline when you imagined this *thing* exploding out onto the deck you were standing on. It turned and the tail swept sideways like a flexing war-hammer. Pike-shafts broke like straws, and bodies went tumbling through the air like leaves. The beast turned and clamped its jaws shut on the edge of the deck as it threw itself into the water, spinning. Wood parted with shrieks louder than the voices of the damned, and the water flowed in as it disappeared beneath the surface again. What had been a warship was now a stationary hulk, sinking by the bows and heeling far over as the sea unbalanced her.

Crewmen fled wailing up the lines to the mastheads, clinging in struggling clumps that dipped further and further towards the surface as the ship bent. Then it rolled on its side. But before they could strike the sea the beast came out again like a projectile launched from the deeps, its jaws closing on the mass of struggling humanity and disappearing with a cataclysmic impact that sent water higher than fountains, incongruously beautiful as the bright sunlight turned the drops to a thousand sparkling jewels. Some of them were ruby-red.

"Saltwater crocodile," Deor said, his voice oddly flat with awe. "We heard of them, *lm liczba mnoga* they say in Bali. In Darwin . . . There they call them *salties*."

"We saw their hides and bones," Thora said. "They said they could grow to twenty feet long or more. But by Almighty Thor! That's *forty* feet if it's an inch, it must weigh . . . tons. Njord, stand by us!"

Feldman's voice came through his speaking trumpet; the *Tarshish Queen* heeled until it was running at ninety degrees to its previous course, but it slowed as sail was reefed. John's head whipped around to look at the quarterdeck as he heard *that* order; so did Radavindraban's. Feldman's voice had an edge of strain in it, but only an edge.

"We can't outrun that thing, not with the wind this light, shipmates. If it comes at us all we can do is try to fight it. Stand ready all!"

The second Korean ship loosed a broadside at the ripple of water streaking towards it, and spray exploded upward again as the creature writhed. Then it dove, into the crimsoned water that rose in pink froth. Silence fell for an instant, save for the shrieks of the men swimming. The waiting fins were closing in from every direction. The Korean apparently thought this was a good time to leave and paid off to the north, the booms of its sails swinging as it went into a reach across the wind.

Then it lurched, bow dipping down and stern rising. The monstrous paddle-like tail rose up and smashed sideways into the warship's rudder, and the metal-bound wood splintered and cracked and pieces of it fell away while the bulk of it sagged, useless. Instantly the ship started to slow and fall off before the wind again without the leverage that held its bow pointing up, the sails slatting and thuttering.

"Broadside catapult-captains, fire on the Korean's stern as you bear!" Feldman's voice cracked out. "Reload will be with solid bolt!"

There was an eightfold chorus of *TUNG-WHACK*, earsplitting loud, and then another two even louder as the eighteen-pounder chasers at bow and stern cut loose. The firebolts arced out over the three hundred yards, seeming to slow as they approached the target. Three missed, ending in puffs of steam as they struck the surface and the warheads ignited their thermite filling. Seven struck the Korean, from the waterline alongside the broken rudder to the quarterdeck, and two disappeared through the sterncastle windows.

Instantly white-hot bursts of incandescence lit, and then the yellow flame and black smoke of burning wood. Captain Feldman had gotten the less useful firebolt . . .

Less useful against an insane aquatic behemoth! Some distant rational part of John's brain gibbered.

. . . out of the catapults, replaced it with solid bolts that *might* retain sufficient force through several feet of water, and made sure the Korean wouldn't be a problem if they survived the monster. It was an impressive display of quick thought under pressure, or perhaps of lunatic optimism.

Nobody on the Korean warship seemed to be paying attention to damage control, either. Firebolts had to be cut out and quenched in the crucial moments after impact, before it was too late.

The *Queen's* crews didn't even pause to cheer as they flung themselves into the rhythm of reloading, though the Nihonjin managed a breathless *Tennō Heika Banzai!*

Extra sailors leapt to grab on to the pump-handles that powered the hydraulic jacks and bent the throwing arms back against the massive coil springs. The *chunk* of the mechanisms locking was overridden by the metallic clatter of the four-foot bolts of forged, finned steel being slapped into the troughs.

"Here it comes!" Radavindraban shouted. "Boarding party to me, pikes, pikes!"

A score of crewmen, those whose battle station was repelling boarders or swarming onto another vessel, ran along the deck to the First Mate's side. He snatched one of the half-pikes from the rack beside him, not trying to take enough time to fit the bottom section into the metal sleeve; that left him with seven foot of Montivallan mountain ash and a foot of heavy double-edged steel blade. He poised it, leaning over and ready to thrust downward.

John could see from his face that he was just as terrified as he'd been at the first glimpse of the massive creature, and realized the First Mate wasn't the sort of man who lost himself in the heat of battle and the rush of adrenaline in the blood so that reflex took over and spared mind and heart. He was doing this cold, purely as an act of disciplined will, and even at that moment the prince dipped his head in a little gesture of acknowledgment, fixing it in his memory as the image of an act of chosen, deliberate courage. If John lived to make the song, unlikely as that seemed at the moment, at least Radavindraban's name would survive. Perhaps someday his kin might hear it and know he had died with honor.

A long ripple in the water, across the swell. Something was breaking the surface and leaving a narrow frothing wake; the broken stub of a catapult bolt lodged in that mass of hide armor and bone and gristle. It didn't seem to be slowing the creature down.

"You will be aiming at that wake, catapult fellows!" Radavindraban called, his voice high but tightly contained with the liquid singsong accent much stronger. "As you bear, *fire!*"

The catapults went off one after another, in a close-spaced ripple but not all at once. It was a testament to the *Queen's* picked crew that each catapult-captain waited until his best shot despite what was bearing down on them. At this close range—less than a hundred yards now, down to twenty before the bow-chaser loosed last of all—the bolts were only flashes, flattened streaks through the air. Each pitched into the water *close* to the onrushing streak with its black core, but it was impossible to see of any hit.

Then they were out of time. The *Tarshish Queen* slammed backward in the water and John would have fallen if he hadn't grabbed a line; several did fall, skidding on their backs across the deck. The king crocodile burst out of the water again, throwing a storm-surge of water at them that battered and stung. The Korean catapult bolt stood out of one shoulder, and another from the *Queen* had sunk half its length in the monster's flank, but the pain had put it in a fimbul-cold rage. The pink gape of the mouth came at them, shreds of flesh hanging from the great curved daggers of its teeth. It bellowed as it came, a huge guttural sound in a wind that stank like old wet death.

Radavindraban shouted: *"Adi kollu!"*

And lunged, aiming the knife-edged steel at the hinge of the thing's jaw. The head of the beast alone looked longer than the half-pike, and gaped impossibly broad. The spear seemed no bigger than a twig, but it flexed without breaking in Radavindraban's grip as the crocodile tossed its head and threw him high into the air. At the top of the arc the steel slid free of the joint in a spray of blood-drops red against the white frothing water. Radavindraban struck the surface and disappeared; so did the crocodile. An instant later the ship shuddered again, more faintly this time, as something massive brushed against the keel.

"Plenty of slack, and be ready on the winch!" John shouted to the Bosun, who seemed to be one of the few not transfixed and frozen.

That was what he was shouting aloud; some distant portion of him was silently screaming *nonononononono!* Several of his companions were shouting at him too as they realized what he was about to do, but there was no time to stop him.

He vaulted to the rail, grabbed the shark-fishing line just behind the heavy steel hook—more steel wire was wound around the wrist-thick cable for a yard above—and hit the water in a creditable dive, given his burdens.

Salt stung his eyes, and the light upper waters faded quickly to a darker blue; John was conscious of two more bodies hitting the water seconds after his, but he had no time to spare for more than the hope neither of them was Evrouin, since the man couldn't swim well at all. He spotted Radavindraban's limp form sinking rapidly, still clutching the half-pike in a death grip; the brightness of the steel was really what caught his eye. He dove, kicking powerfully in the stroke his parents had taught him, and caught the sailor around the waist. Deor and Thora were suddenly with him; they helped him slip the hook through a loop on the man's belt and tug strongly on the cable to signal the deck-crew to spin the windlass.

Something brought him around as they did, something that made him ignore the burning in his lungs. He could see the hull of the Queen above them, slowly passing. And from beneath it a shape, sculling its tail sideways and back like an oar, driving at them like an arrow. Despite the growing absolute need for air the three of them hung motionless for an instant, until they realized in the same moment and all together that the creature was going for the moving target, for Radavindraban's limp body shooting upward with the speed the high-geared winch made possible.

John kicked out strongly. Thora was beside him, her knife in her teeth. What she thought *that* was going to accomplish only her Gods knew, but if the crocodile had gulped her whole she'd probably have stabbed it on the way down. Deor was an eel-swift form on his other side. They reached the side of the ship just in time to seize ropes and see the crocodile rise half its impossible length out of the sea with its jaws agape beneath the dangling form of First Mate Radavindraban.

They slammed shut, and just as they did the half-pike fell from his hands. Fell with malignant precision into the beast's maw, and jaws that could crush teak drove it through its own lower mandible. The beast bellowed again, even louder, and on a different note.

It was about time they had a stroke of luck.

A dozen crewmen were thrusting their long pikes at the white, softer skin of its throat and chest, and Fayard gave a crisp order and his men volleyed. Ruan was shooting his longbow in a steady ripple, bodkin-heads designed to punch through steel armor, and the Japanese leaned recklessly over the rail to thrust with their *naginatas*, screaming their warcry:

"Banzai! Banzai!"

Another bellow and the monster crashed backward into the water . . . and vanished, diving deep, even as the wave of its passage thumped the three of them heavily against the sheet-metal covering of the ship's hull.

John clung; his mind felt like an eye that had stared too long at the sun. But he *had* seen what he had seen: a metal armband around the thing's forelimb. And graven on it a sigil, a three-armed thing like writhing, curving tentacles, in yellow gold on the black surface of the band.

Thora's hand slapped on his bare shoulder, painful enough to jar him back to the world of common day.

"On deck before the sharks arrive, lover," she said; he was aware of himself enough to recognize the look in her eyes, and be warmed by it. "You're either very brave or very crazy."

"Or both," Deor added with a slightly crazed grin. "Well, you're a maker of songs, so it's probably both."

Many hands pulling made climbing back on deck easy enough. John slumped down, letting Evrouin pour a slug of rum down his throat and begin to rub at him with a towel, perhaps a little harder than necessary to express an anger he couldn't put in words. Several experts were pressing the liquid from Radavindraban's lungs and breathing into his mouth with his nose pinched shut. He coughed seawater, retched more and began to revive.

Everyone else kept their eyes on the water around them; the first Korean warship had vanished, and the second was a smear of smoke several miles away. Azure silence broken by the creak of wood and cordage reigned, until Feldman's voice came sharp, giving the helm directions and setting the deck crew to the ropes and rigging. The motion of the ship picked up as more sail sheeted home and caught at what wind there was; he was vaguely aware of Ruan scolding Deor, and of Thora sitting quietly by his feet with her arms around her knees looking at him and smiling.

John came fully out of his shivering stupor when he saw Feldman's seaboots standing beside him. He looked up at the bearded face; the Captain had his thumbs hooked in his belt again.

"That was . . . interesting," the merchant skipper said. "Thank you for saving Mr. Radavindraban; he's the best First Mate I've ever had. We're going to need him on the repairs, too."

"Where are we headed?" John asked.

"The closest dry land we can find. The leak's much worse; that *thing* rammed us as hard as a ship could have done. I appreciate irony as much as the next man, but just sinking and getting eaten by ordinary common sharks after all that would be . . . excessive."

John managed a small chuckle, then sank back again and closed his eyes, enjoying the warmth. He felt bone-chilled as he hadn't since a memorable bear-hunt in County Dawson by the Peace River February last. And a weariness as deep as a day spent fighting in armor might have brought. He waved aside the flask of rum.

Still and all, I'd rather be here than back home in Orrey's shoes, explaining to Mother why I'm not there.

Behind his eyelids, the yellow sigil turned.

I should mention it, he thought as thought slipped away.

CHAPTER EIGHT

BARONY HARFANG

COUNTY OF CAMPSCAPELL

(FORMERLY EASTERN WASHINGTON STATE)

HIGH KINGDOM OF MONTIVAL

(FORMERLY WESTERN NORTH AMERICA)

SEPTEMBER 16TH

CHANGE YEAR 46/2044 AD

The Great Hall of the manor held most of the central arm of the building's E-shaped layout. Archways on either side were filled with French doors now open to the cooling evening breeze and the musky scent of roses and the lemony tang of verbena, and wet stone from the fountains. A gallery ran all around it at second-floor level, shadowy now but lively in the winter months.

Órlaith looked up at it and grinned for a moment; on one memorable occasion she and Herry had hidden up there and eavesdropped on their elders discussing matters of weight . . . including whether one Heuradys d'Ath should be allowed to take the first steps on the path of knighthood. The smile died quickly; John had been along on that visit, a four-year-old running about with a gap-toothed smile that could melt even a sister's heart.

Above that were the great man-thick ponderosa-pine timbers of the hammer-beam ceiling, whence hung wrought-metal chandeliers on long chains and captured banners stirring among shadows that obscured the rips and narrow holes and faded crusty red-brown stains. The yellow-and-red sunburst of the CUT was prominent among them, trophies of the great charge that broke the Prophet's guardsmen at the Horse Heaven Hills.

Heuradys' eyes were on the banners too, and apparently her thoughts followed the same track.

"I've been told that after the charge Mom Two found a bunch of the Prophet's men eyeing her, when everything was mixed up and she and her menie were between them and the way out," the knight said, love and pride in her voice. "She drew her sword and looked at them and then said: I am Grand Constable Tiphaine d'Ath. And you are *in my way.*"

It was a multipurpose room, in many ways the heart of the estate; the Court Baron met here, and it was where dances and masques happened when they weren't out in the gardens, where ceremonies were held and public announcements made. This evening it was put to the most common use, though. This was where everyone who slept under the manor roof from nobles to garden-boys and laundresses would take the main evening meal, save only the actual kitchen-staff; that was old Association custom, with the ceremonial golden saltcellar marking the transition from the gentry on the dais at the upper table before the hearth to the commons at the trestle tables below. With the Baroness and her Châtelaine on their other estate in the West and her heir Diomede and his lady and their principal fighting tail and personal attendants all gone, even the guests didn't make it look fully occupied. Not even including the extra dozen who'd just arrived.

Alan Thurston was waiting in a circle of space, since nobody quite knew what to make of him, leaning one shoulder against the wall and reading a small book bound in sandy-buff-colored leather. He looked up and smiled as Órlaith and her knight came through the doors at the base of the Hall, closing the book and slipping it into a pocket in his jacket. She caught part of the title as he did: *-rial Dynasty of America*—

That didn't make much of an impact, because Alan Thurston was possibly the most beautiful man she'd ever seen, discounting her father.

Enough that looking at him made her feel a little winded for a moment. He was just a hair above her own height, perhaps six feet, broad in the shoulders but tapering to lean hips and long trimly muscular legs shown off by the tight blue linen jeans and the tooled riding boots that were de rigueur for a Boisean rancher. The hair that curled past his ears was a shade of dark honey-brown sun-streaked with something on the verge of gold, and his eyes were large and a sage green rimmed with a darker color, seeming to flicker with some secret jest. His features were very regular but not aquiline, nose straight and slightly flared, high cheekbones tapering down to a square chin with a cleft, full lips smiling and showing very white, even teeth.

His father had probably looked a lot like Sir Droyn—his uncle Frederick Thurston certainly did, with thirty years added—but Alan evidently favored his mother, and his complexion had a creamy olive tint just on the pale side of very light brown, a little darker with sun on his face than on his neck where a neatly folded silk bandana rested. His short blue jacket had copper studs and worked silver buttons and was open to reveal how his shirt of imported cotton clung to the lean sculpted muscle of chest and stomach. There was a plain gold ring in his left earlobe.

There was someone at home there, too, you could see that. Thought flickered in his eyes, and a feeling that laughter did too.

Beside her, Heuradys made a small quiet wordless *oooooh* sound, which Órlaith understood perfectly.

And he moves well. Graceful, and trained to the sword. Sure, and he probably dances well too. And he doesn't wear that ugly short crop most Boisean men do; I do like a man with nice hair. The sort that feels like living silk when you run your fingers . . . stop that!

"Your Highness," he said, his voice holding a slight eastern twang under an educated man's diction. "Such a pleasure, and pardon the imposition. My lady Heuradys, my thanks and that of my men for your hospitality."

"Though it isn't actually the first time we've met, Your Highness," he said, following her lead towards the dais.

Órlaith lost half a step as she racked the Sword in the stand behind the chairs on the dais. That was true . . . or at least the man believed it.

"It isn't?" she said.

"So my mother tells me. You were about a year old at the time, and your mother Her Majesty was carrying you in her arms, and my mother the same with me. It was during the tail-end of the war, of course. Just before she and my brother, ah, retired to Hali Lake Ranch. As a matter of fact, that was when she got the name for our land-grant; from some things she found in the libraries at Todenangst. She said your grand-mother . . . the Lady Regent Sandra, the Queen Mother . . . was quite a collector."

"That she was, to be sure," Órlaith said.

"She and my mother corresponded occasionally, and the Queen Mother loaned her books."

The which must have been a comfort in that remote place, Órlaith thought; Juliet Thurston had grown up in Boise, a major city with an active cul-tural life. *But it's more compassion than I'd have expected from Nonni.*

Her grandmother Sandra had shocked her once by remarking that pity was how suffering became a communicable disease, quoting some ancient philosopher she'd liked.

She put him on her right at the high table, with Heuradys cheerfully moving a seat farther away; he *was* royalty, of a sort, if of a fallen line. As they sat her liege knight caught her eye behind the man's back, cocked an eyebrow and made a gesture with thumb and forefinger, as if flipping a coin to decide who got a prize. Órlaith answered with a gesture of her own, involving the middle finger, and they grinned at each other for an instant before gravely assuming their seats.

Droyn was on her left in Associate dress, beyond him were the Dúne-dain cousins, in the long loose-sleeved robe that Rangers wore for social occasions; his was black silk with cable-work in bullion around the hems and in two bands down the front, hers dark indigo linen worked with silver thread and turquoise beads in the forms of fantastic birds. Between them Susan Clever Raccoon wore a bleached deerskin tunic with a blue-

and-red yoke of beadwork and elk teeth over the shoulders and beadwork elsewhere, fringes along the seams, and leggings likewise fringed above strap-up moccasins decorated with colored porcupine quills. Two eagle feathers were thrust in the long braids on either side of her head.

The plump, jolly-looking House chaplain in his cassock rose and said the Catholic grace, ending by crossing himself as those of his faith in the room did likewise and murmured along with him:

"Bless us, O Lord, and these Thy gifts, which we receive from Thy bounty, though Christ our Lord, Amen."

Heuradys made her small offering to Hestia the hearth-Goddess, and Órlaith and the Mackenzies drew the Pentagram over their plates and the invocation that ended with . . . *their hands helping Earth bring forth life.* Faramir and Morfind put their hands to their hearts and bent their heads to the westward; in the silence of their minds the form of words would be:

To Númenor that was, and beyond to Elvenhome that is, and to that which is beyond Elvenhome and will ever be.

Susan Mika murmured something that started with: *Ate Wankantanka, Mitawa ki;* thanks to the Sword Órlaith spoke fluent Lakota—several dialects of it, in fact—but as usual when she was at a social occasion she made a slight practiced effort and didn't mentally translate that and tried not to focus on the truthfulness of what anyone was saying.

You had to be cautious about the Sword's gifts; her father had said that if you didn't restrain yourself you'd become impossible for ordinary people to be around with any degree of comfort or even liking.

When you could say to someone *how do you feel about me* and know exactly how true the answer was, for instance. There were reasons her parents laughed bitterly when they heard of someone envying them the right to bear the Lady's gift. And it explained why they'd trained themselves to be extremely honest with each other without allowing it to hurt.

"One thing I'm looking forward to when I get to the coast is tasting fresh seafood," Alan said lightly. "We're not much for fish on our home-range."

She'd notice that he just bent his head while the others said their various thank-prayers, rather than joining in or hammer-signing his plate. The main branch of the Thurstons offered to the Aesir, which was a major reason that branch of the Old Faith had spread widely in Boise's domains these last decades; they were popular rulers, both from the war and from Fred's firm and just hand since. A substantial majority were still Christian though, many of them Latter-day Saints, and Protestants out-numbered Catholics among the remainder, in vivid contrast to the near-monopoly of the Church in the Association lands.

She was curious, but didn't ask. By Boisean standards that would be rude if he didn't bring up the subject first. Their tradition was that reli-gion wasn't a matter strangers had any right to ask about. And that those in power should be strictly neutral, as far as their public acts went; they were like that in Corvallis too.

"Apart from trout," he qualified. "We've got plenty of trout, and bass. Smoked and salted ocean-fish we see occasionally, and potted shrimp or canned salmon or sardines, but it isn't the same. Or so my grandmother said when she visited."

"No, it isn't," Órlaith answered, smiling at the fondness in his voice and eyes as he mentioned her.

Yes, Cecile would have visited there, even if she didn't mention it. He and his brother are her grandchildren, even if she repudiated his father and never liked Juliet.

"She said fresh oysters were like kissing the ocean on the lips," he chuckled. "Which she says my grandfather Lawrence said to her while they were courting—dating, they said in the old days, didn't they?"

She'd met Cecile Thurston, and liked her, though there was a deep well of sadness in her that left her wholly only when she was with her grandchildren and great-grandchildren. After the war she'd busied her-self with good works, too; most notably in the chaos and despair of Nakamtu, where the fall of the Church Universal and Triumphant had left a gaping void in the hearts and souls of the folk as well as hunger in their bellies. Órlaith's parents had been glad of that, and had funneled a good deal of the Kingdom's aid through her. As her father said, they remembered *him* there with a sword in his hand against a background lit by burning roof-trees. He'd added that some wounds healed faster if you didn't poke at them.

"Well, there's seafood in plenty in Portland and Astoria," Heuradys said. "If we're out there the same time I can point you to some good places; or we could ask you over to the d'Ath townhouse. Nancy, she's our cook there, can do things with lobster you wouldn't believe."

I'd invite him myself, but that wouldn't be politic. Not without consulting Mother, Órlaith thought. *And she still grinds her teeth whenever the subject of Martin Thurston comes up. Sigh . . .*

"I'll hold you to that, Lady Heuradys," he said genially, not seeming to notice that Órlaith hadn't issued any invitation.

Then he leaned a little closer and murmured to Órlaith: "I understand perfectly, Your Highness."

Oh, sweet Brigid, he even smells nice, she thought in exasperation. *And he's perceptive and sensitive, too.*

Aloud he added:

"Though this looks very fine," as the food was borne in.

Everyone in an Associate lord's household ate in the same room, but of course not on the same fare. Down below the salt they were getting baskets of still-warm maslin loaves—half wheat, half barley—set beside butter and rounds of cheese. There were crocks of white bean and ham soup, roasts of pork and mutton with gravy, steamed cabbage and carrots and peas and green beans and heaps of fried potato, along with locally-made catsup and pickles. For after there were pies put out to cool on a sideboard, apple and cherry and rhubarb and peach. It was good plain food and plenty of it, much like what a minor knight would have daily or a well-to-do peasant on Sunday. Plus there was a cask of small beer in its carved X-shaped wooden stand from which anyone could draw.

And a noble's staff saw far less of the hard grind of labor that went with a peasant or craftsman's life. Positions in a great household were sought-after, as long as the master and his kin didn't have a reputation for bad temper.

Karl and Mathun could have made a good case for seats at the high table, since their father was Bow-Captain of the High King's Archers, the premier guard regiment. Like the other Mackenzies, they looked perfectly content where they were, talking and chaffing with the manor staff and retainers and sampling the beer with the air of experts. Some other parts of Montival found the Protectorate's system of ranks childish—she inclined to that view herself sometimes—and some considered it intensely annoying, while a few held to the view that it was active wickedness.

Which in our grandparents' day it sometimes was, she thought. *More to the point it often was when my mother's father was Lord Protector. But those were harder times, very hard indeed.*

In their own more modern day most Mackenzies treated it as an amusing game, with which they would play along indulgently if it wasn't too much trouble. The more touchy-proud Associates found that provoking in a way that hatred wasn't. When someone hated you they were at least taking you seriously.

The food above the golden cellar wasn't the formal dishes you found at a High Court function either, for which she was thankful. Her father had said he'd had more success beating hostile armies than getting the palace cooks in Portland and Todenangst to stop putting so much of their efforts into making their dishes look like anything but what the makings actually were, from whipped-cream swans with goldenberry eyes to forcemeat pastries like oceangoing ships.

And the pity of it is that the Protectorate sets fashions in food; though it's good when they don't go berserk.

She knew that apart from a passion for asparagus in season Baroness d'Ath liked simple hearty fare, and would have been perfectly content with what the commons were getting here, but also didn't care enough about the matter to spend much thought on it. Countess Delia had always seen to the kitchen appointments, and *her* tastes tended to an elegant simplicity largely copied from Sandra Arminger, her original political patron.

They started with little half-moon-shaped fried dumplings of translucent dough filled with a mixture of scallions and minced lamb spiced with garlic and rosemary, and a sauce of hot chilies spooned over it to taste. The soup was a clear beef broth with noodles, several varieties of mushrooms and small veal meatballs made with ricotta, and followed by a green salad garnished with walnuts and dressed with local oil and fruit vinegar. After that came Hungarian pheasant—they thrived on the rangelands and stubblefields around here—done in the Norman style with gently cooked apples, sweet onions, cider and cream until it was tender enough to come off the bone on the point of a fork. Their fried potatoes were elegantly cut in long shoestrings rather than chunks, and there were baked tomatoes stuffed with sweet peppers, mint, dill, and a little sharp sheep's-milk cheese, along with tender steamed brussels sprouts in a tart lemony butter sauce.

"Is this a local vintage?" Alan asked as the butler poured for the pheasant course and set out the tall gracefully-shaped decanters.

"By Dionysus Oeneus, no!" Heuradys said, sniffing and sipping. "Our vineyard here's still experimental. We donate most of it to the Church for communion wine, or for the lord's portion in village festivals on the estate. This is from Montinore Manor back on Barony Ath in the Tualatin. Most of our demesne there is vineyards."

Órlaith took the scent: freshly-caramelized pear and a pleasant overtone of herbs, like walking through a spring hillside. She ate a forkful of the pheasant, then drank some of the wine. It had a hint of green apple and butterscotch and lime, which went well with the rich sweet savor of the bird, but there was a dry mineral quality that left the palate clear after a moment and ready for more.

"That's your 'forty-three Pinot Gris Reserve, isn't it?" she said; she recognized it well enough without a label.

"Yup, my liege. This one can stand quite a bit of aging. Well, quite a bit for a white, and it's a little tight right out of the bottle. Better decanted."

Droyn poured himself another glass. "My lord my father is rather bitter about the Montinore vineyards, Rancher Thurston. They were famous before the Change, and are now. Even abroad."

"They like our wines in Hawaii," Heuradys agreed. "We have a contract with Feldman and Sons for three thousand cases a year for that market. Though the Goat Killer alone knows what they do with it at blood temperature among the palm-trees and pineapples and breadfruit on Maui. Some of our reds would go well with pit-roasted pig, I suppose."

Droyn finished his glass. "We've good vineyards in Molalla now, but it's a slow business."

Heuradys winked at him. "Unless you poach a master-vintner from our winery with showers of gold," she said.

"No, even then," Droyn replied, and everyone laughed.

Alan broke one of the dinner rolls—fine crusty white manchet bread here—took a bite to clear his palate and sipped again.

"Very nice," he said. "But truly, at Hali Lake we were mostly a beer-cider-and-whiskey ranch. Wine was for Sunday dinner, and from the co-ops around the capital . . . Boise City . . . at that."

Heuradys laughed. "You haven't lived until you've drunken wine made by Mormons," she said.

The Latter-day Saints didn't drink anything with alcohol, and there were a lot of them in Boise. For that matter they didn't drink coffee or tea, either, though that mattered much less in the modern world where both were exotic luxuries.

"Oh, that's not quite fair," Órlaith said; not coming from a family with vineyards, she had no dog in that fight. "A lot of the Boisean wines are quite drinkable, whoever makes it."

Suzie leaned forward from between her two taller companions. "Yeah, I hear you, Alan. Out on the *makol* we really didn't see wine very often at all. And that was from Iowa as often as not. I can taste that this is a lot better, but that's about it."

Heuradys shuddered with deliberate theatricality. Órlaith laughed; that was a little bit of Montivallan chauvinism. True, Iowa was never going to rival the West Coast of the continent for wine. Their fat black earth was better for grain and livestock, which it produced in quantities both amazing and needful, given Iowa's enormous population and vast teeming cities. Des Moines alone had a hundred and fifty thousand people, twice the size of the largest urban center in Montival and far and away bigger than any other in the stretch between Panama and Hudson's Bay. Iowa as a whole had as many people as it had before the Change or possibly even a little more, something very rare in the modern world.

She'd been there herself, as part of a Royal diplomatic visit a few years ago. And her mother and the Dowager Bosswoman there were friends from the time of the Quest.

"Mind you, back home a lot of the older big shots don't like anyone drinking firewater at all, not that that stops people, you know?" Suzie went on. "Sour old killjoys with their mouths pursed up like a cat's asshole, the way they talk you'd think White Buffalo Woman was whispering in their ears every damn day. Yeah, I hear it was a bad problem for our people before the Change, but that was then and most nowadays can handle it OK. Though what we drink for day-to-day is *airag*. I miss that, you just can't get it anywhere else."

Faramir and Morfind looked interested. Órlaith and Heuradys kept their faces politely blank as they nodded. Órlaith had enjoyed her long stay with the Lakota in her seventeenth year immensely, for its own sake and because it had been one of the first where her parents had left her on her own.

Not that I didn't miss them, but it was . . . like growing up. Which back then I was wild to do.

Fermented mare's milk had *not* been one of the high points, though, even when served with superb grilled buffalo-hump steak after a hard day's ride; and it wasn't even a local tradition. A young Mongol had been studying range management at South Dakota State University when the Change struck, and had already been a close friend of Suzie's grandfather John Red Leaf. Red Leaf became one of the leaders of the renascent Lakota *tunwan*, and his friend Ulagan Chinua had become his right-hand man, married into the family and introduced quite a few of *his* native customs, which had worked well because they were so suited to tent-dwelling herders on a high cold steppe. *Airag* had been one of them, giving a nourishing and very mildly alcoholic drink to nomads many of whom couldn't digest ordinary raw milk anyway. Órlaith had gotten used to it, more or less. Heuradys had simply refused to try it more than once.

"I envy you all," Alan said. "I've always wanted to travel. Hali is beautiful, but . . ."

There was a slight silence; the reasons he and his mother and brother had been planted in the backlands and encouraged to stay there were political, and at a level that was still sensitive a full generation after his father's treason. Órlaith thought she detected a fair degree of sympathy for Alan among her friends, precisely because he'd been born after his father died. They'd all found themselves unwillingly entangled in their parents' feuds now and then.

"Oh, we've just started traveling too," Faramir said. "Morfind and I were born in the Willamette, but we moved south when we were small, when our parents founded Stath Ingolf, and stayed there. It's beautiful and there's plenty to do, but it is the same old round of place and people."

Which was how most people lived all their lives; without ever going more than a day or two's journey from their birthplace. Unless war or disaster struck, of course. But the well-born and warriors, often the same thing, moved around a good deal more in ordinary times.

"I've heard from Rangers—some pass through Hali—"

"Yes, there's a Stath in the Bitterroot country in Nakamtu these days," Faramir said. "And we have an exchange program with the Scouts in the Mountains of Golden Stone. We've learned from them, and they from us."

Alan nodded. "The ones I met say that it's customary for young Dúnedain to move around between Staths."

"Oh, yes. The *Mincolasira*, we call it. The . . . time between, time of the gap, in the Common Tongue; the gap between being old enough to travel and fight, and settling down. You move around between Staths, and help with whatever they do and hone your skills, especially at places like Tawar-in-Mithril . . . Mithrilwood, where our rulers live. And you join expeditions—salvagers, caravan guards, explorers—or reinforce Staths that have fighting to do or need help getting established. We, Morfind and I, ah, we weren't quite ready."

Morfind was usually more taciturn than her cousin, and blunter when she did speak: "Our parents didn't think we were old enough yet."

"Our mothers weren't much older when they went on the Quest of the Lady's Sword," Faramir said.

"And my father—Hîr Ingolf the Wanderer—left home when he was younger than us," Morfind added. "He crossed the whole continent *three times*."

That seemed to be a sore point, and she finished her wine at a gulp. Faramir was more philosophical, and smiled as he said:

"Uncle Ingolf's always saying he wants to imitate a barnacle on a rock, and that travel is overrated, mostly being uncomfortable and bored when you're not being chased by people trying to kill you, but he's *done* it."

"Same here," Suzie said. "Always wanted to travel, never got the chance until I, ah, sorta had to leave."

Everyone knew her folk were nomads; she went on at their look of surprise:

"Yeah, we live in tents . . . *ger*, actually, some people call 'em yurts. Tipis are sorta for official stuff. And we move camp every couple of weeks in summer. But we move to the *same places*, mostly. Spring pasture, summer pasture, fall pasture, winter quarters . . . There's the buffalo hunts, and that's when the *guys* get to hunt and *we* butcher and scrape hides and make pemmican."

"I thought you hunted?" Faramir said.

"Yeah, but I had to kick up a fuss and everyone looks at you funny. The festivals when everyone gets together for the ceremonies and meetings and dances are fun but it's the *same* everyone you met last time, except for some traders trying to sell you stuff. A lot of the time it's almost as boring as farming. Except for horse-stealing, *that's* fucking exciting but mostly girls don't get to do that either, which sucks, frankly. When the High King got me into the Crown Courier Corps I was happy as a colt in clover. Couriers get to go everywhere and see *everything*."

She gave an elbow to the Dúnedain on each side of her. "And you meet people!"

The dessert was a tribute to Lady Delia's sweet tooth; layers of dense chocolate cake soaked in a clear light cherry brandy that had a faint overtaste of almonds, separated by layers of sweetened whipped cream and brandied cherries, frosted on the sides with chocolate and topped with more of the cherries and cream and chocolate shavings. Heuradys took a substantial wedge of it and began to chuckle again. When Droyn looked at her:

"My lady mother Mom One absolutely loves this stuff. Because, well, *Schwarzwälder Kirschtorte*."

Órlaith forced herself not to choke on her piece. Heuradys had once told her that when they were both in their cups her birth mother had confessed with a giggle that she'd had her first experience of this cake when Tiphaine gave her one as a present on her nineteenth birthday. The cake had been presented when they were in bed, and ever since she'd associated it with piling one pleasure on another.

"So we have it fairly often," Heuradys said, smiling fondly as you did at a pleasant family memory. "And she takes this little tiny piece, looks at it, pats her waistline, and eats it one teensy particle at a time. The rest of us around the table, Mom Two and Lioncel and Diomede and me and Evil Small Sis would have big slices and be scarfing it down and she looks like she's going to cry, and Mom Two says she can always spend two or three hours a day running up and down stairs in armor or hunting boar and then Mom One just *glares* at us."

Everyone laughed, though Sir Droyn looked as if he was feeling a little shocked too, or at least thought he should be.

"Your lady mother the Countess has a most uncommonly genteel figure," he said. "Spectacular, even, for a lady of her years."

"Sure she does, Droyn. She's as disciplined as a knight. But she has to work at it. And not in the way most people do."

Which for the overwhelming majority meant long hours of sweating-hard labor nearly every day. For that matter, given what chocolate and sugar cost, nobody but a noble or a very wealthy merchant could afford to have this sort of dish often enough to be a problem. That reminded Órlaith of an early memory.

"I remember something Grandmother Juniper said once, that half the people in her coven had *weight problems* before the Change—I think that's how they said *were fat* back then—but that none of the ones still alive did a year later. She said it was a case of *be as you wish to seem.*"

Somehow that led to talking about being and seeming and that to the theatre season in Portland, which Alan Thurston had heard of and was eager to hear compared to its competitors in Boise and Corvallis.

"I've only read plays, really," he said wistfully. "Though I'd love to see professionals stage them."

"You don't get strolling companies, or even tinerants?" Droyn asked; both were common in the Willamette and up the Columbia.

Alan's smile turned a little sour. "At our ranch, we visit neighbors maybe once a month, and we see real outsiders . . . oh, three times a year. One to buy our wool and steers, one to deliver a pack-train of what we need to buy, and once to collect the taxes. And we go to the county Ready Reserve militia musters, at the same time as the County Fair. Hali's . . . remote. Nobody had used that land since before the Change, and not much then."

More cheerfully: "I used to go outside past the horse barn where nobody could hear and do the parts myself:

"Along the shore the cloud waves break,
The twin suns sink behind the lake,
The shadows lenathen in Carcosa—"

"Taking in some shows ought to be possible, even off-season. They say you can find anything in Portland," Heuradys said.

Alan's smile turned slightly bitter again. "Then maybe I can find . . . someone who repairs reputations."

He nodded upward at the captured banners; in the dark space beneath the rafters you could somehow sense the tatters and the old dark-brown stains where warriors had fought over them savagely, hand-to-hand, and where the vanquished had fallen bleeding to death on the cloth at the last.

"God, how I hate those people . . . those *things* behind the people. They're the ones who *really* killed my father. He was an ambitious man and maybe a ruthless one, but he *was* a man, and a great one, before they got their hooks into him."

Then he collected himself, rose and bowed. "Many thanks for your hospitality again, Lady Heuradys, and for a delightful evening, Your Highness."

"The Steward can find you a room, Rancher Thurston," Heuradys said. "We're not crowded!"

"I appreciate the offer, but it might be better if I don't sleep beneath your rooftree, my lady. Causing you trouble would be poor repayment for your generosity. I'll camp with my troop; if I'm to lead them in battle, I should share their hardships."

That was, of course, unanswerable; even if sleeping in a hayloft on a summer night after a good dinner wasn't *much* of a hardship. When he had gone, Heuradys cocked an eyebrow and glanced after him and then at the Sword where it stood on the polished, carved ashwood of the rack behind them. She knew it and its powers and limitations as well as anyone outside the Royal kindred, and she knew that the truth-sensing remained when it wasn't underhand, fading and blurring with distance.

"He was certainly sincere about hating the CUT," Órlaith said.

"Well, he'd be the heir of Boise, but for them," Heuradys said.

"And sincere in general. But . . . unspoken reservations."

Her knight nodded. "Well, who doesn't have those? Do you think your mother will let him fight? He *has* gone around his uncle President Fred. Gone over his head, in a sense. If he does well in the field it'll be impossible to keep him out watching the grass grow and the cows shit for the rest of his life."

"Possibly he's gone around Fred by prior arrangement with people in Boise. Probably Fred himself, even if nobody spelled it out."

"Hints and machinations," Heuradys agreed.

"He's his father's son, but he's Fred's nephew, and Fred's the sort of man who'll remember that. Doing it under the table, maybe? So Victoria won't know until it's too late."

Heuradys shuddered slightly. Victoria Thurston was a Rancher's daughter from the Powder River south and east of the old Montana border. The CUT had killed her father and run her off her family's land during the war, which was how she'd met the Questers, and she had a ferociously straightforward view of what was best done with enemies . . . or their heirs.

"You saw Alan's retainers?" Órlaith went on.

"I did, briefly, and they were doing a little target practice to keep their hands in. Quite good of their kind for cow-country horse archers, from what I could see, and well mounted and armed. Maybe I'll go take a closer look after dinner."

"Then I think Mother will let him. Another troop of good light cavalry is always welcome. She'll hope he gets heroically and conveniently killed down fighting the Eaters in Westria or across the sea, but she won't put him in the way of it. Fighting's a dangerous occupation all on its own, without any of that . . . what's that story the Christians tell? From the Jewish part of their Bible?"

"Uriah the Hittite," Heuradys supplied.

"Just so, without any funny business of that not-very-funny kind, so to say. And that may occur to Victoria too, after a while, that it might. She's a bit bloodthirsty, but no fool. Sharp as Fred, sharper possibly."

Heuradys yawned. "We should turn in. We need to make an early start on doing nothing tomorrow. We could take some falcons out, for example. Or see if there's a polo match going . . . No, not until the autumn maneuvers are over. Maybe hunt some antelope?"

"It's a hard job but, sure, someone must slog through, and it's up to us," Órlaith paused. "I wonder what in Anwyn's name *Johnnie's* up to?"

"And with who?" Heuradys said, watching as Faramir and Suzie and Morfind sauntered off, hand in hand, and the Mackenzies and the house retainers and the Boisean horse-soldiers started to sing.

"Let's just hope it involves more fornication than decapitation," Órlaith said. "We'll be feeling the consequences fairly soon, I think."

"See you later, then," Heuradys said.

I'm awake, she thought, several hours later.

Heuradys had shown up a while ago smiling a revoltingly smug smile and with bits of hay in her hair. She was snoring slightly in the other bed, sleeping turned on her left side with one hand under the pillow, resting on the hilt of her knife. Órlaith swung her feet to the floor, feeling oddly reluctant to look back, and walked over to the French doors on tile that felt cool to her feet. They'd been left slightly ajar for the night breezes, and she walked out onto the balcony. Nobody was about in the courtyard below, though there would be two of her party on guard at the foot of the stairs under the arcade below. Moonlight played on the water splashing from a fountain in the middle of the long narrow pool that ran down the center of the rectangular space.

She looked up. The black of the stars moved against the sky, in patterns obscurely meaningful. A tower rose in a field of dark flowers, and huge blurred columnar shapes with the heads of bats or twisted dogs floated around it, slowly turning so that their blank yellow eyes glared in her direction. They started to drift towards her. The moon was huge and full beyond the wall southward, and *behind* it were the spires of a city. . . .

"Whoa!" she said.

She jerked upright in bed and pressed her hands to the sides of her head. Macmac whimpered and twitched in his basket by the door.

"Wazzat?" Heuradys said, opening her eyes without moving her head.

"Nothing, just a dream . . . Can't even remember the details."

She sank back and closed her eyes. Soft music fell down the stairs of sleep with her, past long terraces of pink stone to a cerulean sea where Johnnie's ship ghosted along with all sails set.

CHAPTER NINE

John's fingers moved on the lute as he sang softly in the darkness, leaning against one of the catapults; Thora was lying on the deck nearby, fingers laced behind her head. Deor had his harp Golden Singer out, and Ruan his flute, and they were letting the tune wander between them as they worked their hands supple again after a spell on the pumps.

Night and mist enclosed the *Tarshish Queen*, lit only by gleams from the stern lanterns that sparkled on the drops hanging from the star-tracery of rope and rigging, amid quiet creaks and a faint chuckle from beneath the bows and a gentle whisper of the wind. The words shaped themselves to the sounds:

"Willows whiten, aspens quiver,
Little breezes dusk and shiver
Through the wave that runs forever
By the island in the river,
Down to towered Todenangst.
Sometimes a troop of damsels glad,
An abbot on an ambling pad,

Sometimes a laughing shepherd-lad,
Or long-haired page in crimson clad,
Goes by to towered Todenangst;
And sometimes by the river blue
The knights come riding, two and two . . ."

"Ah, now that is music," Deor said, when they'd stopped, and Thora sighed wordlessly. "That's your grandparents' dream turned to air and song."

"Not my lyrics, mostly," John said. "An old poet of the ancients, singing of King Arthur's court. I just reshaped it a bit. And I had a hint on the tune; my aunt Fiorbhinn said someone had sung a bit of it from memory— badly—when she was a child, and she'd always wanted to make something of it but never had the time. She gave me the little fragment she had."

"All honor to her as a maker, and she taught me much. But by Woden who sends the mead of poetry to men, you made *this*," Deor said.

Ruan spoke up unexpectedly. "It's the Prince's grandparents' dream— his mother's parents. But it's the best of it. The beauty and the gallantry beneath. And that's why they built better than they knew with their waking minds, or even intended. That's what has lasted when the rest was burned away by time and war."

Deor nodded soberly and carefully wiped down the harp with a special cloth before he snapped it into its padded leather case. John did the same before he put Azalaïs into the case Evrouin held out. He'd let the valet handle it a few times, which he'd done quite competently, but found himself reluctant to do that when Deor was around.

He sets a high standard, as a troubadour, John thought whimsically. *And when you're around a man like that, you . . . just don't want to let the side down.*

The First Mate went by, pulling on his long shirt as he did, his feet still wet from the hold. They all glanced at each other and waited in silence; they were just under the break of the quarterdeck, and they could hear a conversation by the wheel.

"She's gained another foot overnight, Cap'n," Radavindraban said. "The pumps are indeed going flat-out, but they cannot keep pace."

John rose, as if casually, and went up the quarterdeck ladder himself; he had that privilege, as Prince or perhaps just as the one who'd chartered the ship, as long as he kept out of the way. Thora and Deor did too, as very old friends of the Captain.

Feldman gave them a glance and then nodded to his first officer.

"Then we're beaching her today, like it or not," he said. A grim smile. "On the bottom, if nowhere else."

There was a thick mist, curling around the *Tarshish Queen* like darker tendrils in the gray light of predawn, and John was glad of his arming doublet. There was a damp chill to the air now, despite the tropic heat he knew was coming. The ship was silent save for its eternal creak and groan, and the rhythmic thumping of the pumps and the splash of water jetting overside. The motion beneath their feet was perceptibly different from the big schooner's usual light dance with the waters, a sluggish check to the roll as the liquid weight surged through the hold and ran inches deep on its planking. It would have been worse if the ship had been carrying cargo there as usual, rather than just people and their supplies.

"I'd really rather not go for a swim around here, Captain," John said lightly. "Considering the sort of thing they have in the water."

A few within hearing smiled, but only Thora Garwood's chuckle was heartfelt. There hadn't been any sign of the monster saltie, but none of them had forgotten it. In a few months it would be a valuable prop in tales told in longshore bars provided that they ever saw one again, but right now the memory was entirely too fresh. Deor was at least as courageous, but he'd obviously sensed something about the animal that wasn't of the world of common day. So had John, but he didn't want to think about it. It was hard not to, drifting over a dark ghost sea through the mist, as if they were on some voyage in Limbo that would never end. In fact they had less time than that; the sail they'd fothered over the leak was pressed away from the hull whenever they made any progress forward. The winds had been faint and irregular, but a flat calm wouldn't save them, just make sinking slower. Those triangular fins were still out there.

"There's land nearby," Feldman said. "I can smell it, even if we're not sure on the charts."

John breathed in deeply. There were the usual smells of wood and tarred cordage and the breakfast hash frying, crumbled ship's biscuit and salt beef, and the slightly stale brine of the bilges—much cleaner because of the flow-through between leak and pumps. Perhaps there *was* a hint of something else, something between rotting fish and hot sand and compost, but it was nothing like the cool fir-sap scent you mostly got off Montival's coasts, or the dry rock and fennel of the far southern reaches they'd left. Or it could be his imagination.

"Aye, Cap'n, maybe," Radavindraban said doubtfully. "The islands don't move, but the shoals do, and the reefs grow fast this past while. Bad sightings these last few days, too."

"That's why we'll have soundings, Mr. Mate."

Silence fell again, broken every few minutes by the cry of the leadsman in the bows: "No bottom! No bottom at forty fathom!"

Then another cry came from the lookout at the masthead. "Light! A light!"

John's breath caught. That brought every head up, and the Captain's speaking-trumpet. "What light, and where away?"

"Burning yellow, skipper! Hard on the port beam. A fixed light!"

"Mr. Mate, come about, thus," Feldman said, and pointed. "We'll close her. Keep the soundings coming. And have the crew stand to; it might be wreckers."

The watch below had come on deck at the call, their feet wet from the water sloshing beneath their hammocks, and there was a little crowding and the sound of the Bosun's voice cursing and the thump of a bare foot on a backside as the lines were trimmed and the ship's head came slowly about to the northeast.

"Bottom!" the leadsman cried, her voice cracking. "Bottom at thirty fathom!"

"What bottom?" Feldman called, and there was a delay as the sailor examined the soft tallow on the bottom of the cone-shaped lead by the light of a shuttered lamp.

"Shell and coral sand, skipper!"

Another spell of silence, and then a gust of wind and they all saw the light, a low yellow flicker ahead. Feldman looked up at the sails, where they disappeared into the darkness and the fog.

"Wind's quickening," he said, as if speaking to himself. "And it's on the port quarter; morning wind, from the land. It'll shift this fog soon enough and the sun will burn off what's left."

"By the mark . . . twenty-six! Twenty-six fathom even!"

Then they all saw it, a steady yellow spot on the horizon. The mist closed in again, parted again, as they crept forward. Their progress was a faint chuckle of bow-wave under the schooner's sharp prow.

"By the mark . . . ten fathoms! By the mark . . . eight! Shelving!"

"What bottom?"

"Sharp sand and coral rag, skipper!"

"Back topsails," Feldman said. "Starboard your helm. Mr. Mate, anchor when she's stopped. We'll wait for dawn. The reefs *do* grow fast around here."

The *Tarshish Queen*'s head came into the gentle wind from the northeast and she slowed to a halt. The forward anchor went in with a rumble and splash.

"She holds, skipper!"

"Strike all sail," Feldman said. "Now we'll wait."

They did, and the world turned from shades of black and gray to pale gray and white; then the mist began to lift in earnest.

"Mr. Mate, tell the hands off for breakfast," Feldman said; unspoken was the thought that it might well be their last meal if they didn't find a good place to careen. "And then double the stays, preventers fore and aft. We may be trying the masts hard soon, and the mizzen's already wounded. Pull them taut, if you will."

"Aye aye, Cap'n."

Thump . . . thump . . . thump went the pumps, and the water jetted. Gangs

of sailors went aloft with heavy cables over their shoulders, like the legs of
a long narrow climbing centipede. John split his attention between them—
it was always fascinating watching experts do something difficult—and the
sights to northward as the mist burned away and the sun came up.

The eastern horizon flashed green as the burning arch cleared the
horizon, with crimson the color of molten copper on the fringe of clouds.
The stars showed as the mist cleared and then were gone in the greater
light, fading away to a few scattered in the midnight blue of the western
horizon for a moment. Ruan's young voice rose from the bows as he
greeted the sun with the Dawn Chant.

Even after weeks in these waters, John was still rapt for a moment.

"Dawns like thunder," Feldman said softly, with the air of a man quoting.

Deor smiled and spoke:

"Between the pedestals of Night and Morning
Between red Death, and radiant Desire
With not one sound of triumph or of warning
Stands the great sentry on the Bridge of Fire . . ."

The Captain nodded and they shared a smile, as old friends do over
a common memory.

"I loaned you that volume, a long time ago," he said, and turned his
telescope northward. "While you and Thora were staying in Newport
that first time, at my father's house.

"There's the light," he went on to John. "See, on the headland of that
sandspit?"

John used his own binoculars. The light was on a small platform atop
a tall rickety-looking triangular framework of poles—Deor supplied the
word *mangroves* when he asked what the material was; in Montival the
equivalent would probably have been made from two-by-fours of milled
timber. As he watched a bucket swung down at the end of a lever and a
cap smothered the flame in its glass enclosure.

"Clever," Feldman said. "A water-clock arrangement. Probably palm-oil for the light, and someone comes by to reset things every evening. All you'd need to do is pour the water in at the top again and fill up the lamp now and then."

The last of the fog cleared with a rush, and heads all over the ship turned towards the land that was revealed. They were anchored off the western end of it, with a long slope of mountainous forested interior fading off to the eastward in rippled blue-green reaches. Closer to the shore was a white road, running through groves of coconut and other palms, stirring in the breeze coming down from the mountains. John turned his binoculars to the east, and saw the green of tilled fields and what looked like thatched roofs and walls. There was a slight sighing, as the crew knew they weren't in danger of being cast adrift in small craft far from land. They could reach that shore easily in the ship's boats. Of course, what lay on it might be just as dangerous as the sea and its dwellers.

"Mr. Mate, we'll raise the anchor, if you please, and keep course at this distance from the surf-line," Feldman said. "I don't like the look of it right inshore. And regular soundings."

A volley of orders followed, and the long capstan bars were fitted into the drum on the forecastle. John trotted forward and joined them; there weren't many things he could usefully do on a ship, but pushing hard on a stick was one. Just to add joy to the occasion, the Bosun was looking over the side to see how raising the anchor affected the makeshift sail patch over their leak, which hadn't been helped *at all* by the encounter with the giant crocodile.

John braced his palms against the smooth ash surface of the capstan bar; he was barefoot, and he crooked his knees and worked his toes on the holystoned fir planks of the deck to get a firm grip.

"Annnnnnnd . . . *heave!*" a bosun's mate cried. "Break her loose, buckos!"

They heaved, putting their weight into it, faces growing contorted and red as they groaned. There was a long moment of strain as the leverage of bars and gears fought against the anchor's weight and the catch of the wedge-shaped flukes on the rocky sand below. The ship heeled slightly, and pivoted slowly around the rigid bar of the chain. Then it came free and they all lurched forward a step. The mechanism below-decks gave a single sharp metallic *clunk!* as the ratchet caught the pawl that prevented it running backward.

"*Heave* and go! *Stamp* and go! Heave her 'round and make her *go!*"

It was still hard work, but not quite such a strain. Thora was beside him, and Ruan, but Deor had hopped up on the drum of the capstan and held a long note before plunging into a song with a strong steady beat, stamping to emphasize it, and those at the capstan with enough breath took it up too:

"*It's a damn tough life full of toil and strife*
We sailormen undergo—
And we don't give a damn when the gale is done
How hard the winds did blow—
We're homeward bound from the Arctic ground
With a good ship taut and free—
And we won't give a damn when we drink our dram
With the girls of Old Maui!"

The song came to an end and the labor did, after a remarkable catalogue of what the sailors intended to do with the alcohol, girls, boys and sheep of Maui. They all rested for an instant while the forward anchor was pinned home, and then the capstan bars seemed to vanish as if by magic—his slid through his hands almost quick enough to burn when someone snatched it away—and a volley of commands came from the quarterdeck:

"Loose heads'ls there! Hands aloft to loose tops'ls, on the fore, on the main! Lively, we haven't got all day!"

Some of the sailors running up the ratlines and making the rigging thrum like a guitar chuckled grimly at the graveyard humor—they wouldn't be *floating* at the end of the day, one way or another, and they all knew it. The staysails at the bow blossomed above their heads and brought the bows around eastward, parallel with the shore.

"Hard a'starboard the wheel! Let fall! Haul away and sheet her home!"

The big gaff mainsails ran up the masts as the windlasses whined, then swung to starboard and cracked taut in long white curves. Now the *Tar-shish Queen* heeled that way too, and the water began to chuckle at her prow as she gained way. The square sails caught with booming sounds and added a little more roll to the pitch.

"Thus, thus, very well, thus! Sheet her home, hands to braces!"

They were sailing at a bit less than right-angles to the wind, easy enough for a schooner, and with the advantage that it slowed the leak by leaning the ship over so that some of the damage was raised a bit above the surface of the waves. From the conversation that passed back and forth he gathered that the pumps were closer to keeping pace . . . but not gaining on the water. The break in the frames was working at the planks further and further from the original round-shot wound, made much worse by the elephantine bulk of the creature that had struck them.

They were a little closer to the shore now, though far enough out to avoid the patches of white where the waves caught on offshore rock or reef. Low combers were breaking in azure and cream on wide white sand beaches, but everything was intensely green beyond, coconut palms and trees he didn't recognize even from pictures, with patches of forest on higher land or abandoned fields starred with clumps of great vivid flowers, red or white or blue. Birds even gaudier flew upward now and then in clumps, strange creatures with huge beaks or trailing tailfeathers bright as a hummingbird's breast.

Beyond was a stretch of rice fields covering about half the flat ground, paddies separated into rectangles by the bunds that controlled the water and spotted with low bits in reeds and swampy bushes and higher areas covered with trees. The tall stalks of the rice were still vividly green, but here and there a tawny streak showed that the heads of grain would turn dry and golden soon. Now and then he saw a windmill, different in detail and made of laminated bamboo from the great feathery clumps that served for woodlots, but doing the same work he was accustomed to. He walked slowly back to the quarterdeck. Captain Feldman was examining the shore himself with his telescope, and speaking to Deor and Thora—who'd also sailed in these waters. Ruan was there, looking on with fascination.

"A lot of that land was abandoned, and then some of it's been reclaimed lately," John said.

"You're right," Feldman replied. A moment later: "More of it under the plow as we move east. That's where the resettlement started."

"My great-grandfather's parents came from hereabouts," Ruan said.

John looked at him with surprise. "I thought he was from China?"

"No and yes, so to say," he said; his green-hazel eyes sparkled, and the sun had put reddish highlights in the long black hair that fell down his back in a queue bound with an old bowstring.

"You're a Mackenzie for certain!" Deor said. "Paradox on contradiction!" To the others: "Get him to explain."

"That from a bard?" John said with a smile.

Ruan turned to John: "It's simple, so it is, Prince: my great-grandfather's *ancestors* were from China, and they always thought of themselves as Han, but their families had moved to these southern isles long ago. Then he and his wife fled some great upheaval or war here, a generation before the Change, and my grandfather was born near Astoria. When he was of a man's years he married a woman of the Gael, which displeased his kin, so my grandparents moved to Eugene, where my father was born, and his sisters. After the old world fell things went hard for all of them, but they joined the Clan the next year. There's not much else in my father's stories—his mother and father died in the second Change year, and he was fostered when he was only five. That story and our midname Chu was all of the tale we had."

He turned eagerly to his lover. "Now you can show me the wonders you told of, and we can see them together!"

Deor smiled and put an arm around his shoulders. "See how the houses are mostly inside compounds?" he said, pointing. "And how the compounds all face the same direction? That's how the folk of Bali build their homes; they're called *karang*, and many generations of a family may have houses within."

John focused his glasses. Apart from the smallest and simplest thatched huts the houses of the dwellers—presumably mostly peasants—were indeed within walled enclosures, grouped into long rectangular villages, always with mixed orchards and leafy gardens around them. All were neatly aligned towards a mountain he could see very faintly on the horizon to the northeast.

"And those little buildings in front of the gateways?" Ruan asked, borrowing the glasses for a moment.

"Shrines, where offerings are made to the wights. The entrance is always narrow—it's called an *angkul-angku*. Within is a wall facing the gate, to bar hostile spirits."

"Sure, and it would be useful for those of human kind entering with ill intent," Ruan observed shrewdly. "Like a Dun in little."

Thora laughed and clapped him on the back. "Wit as well as looks, youngster," she said. "I thought exactly the same the first time I saw them. The compounds can be forts at need. Put a few score together and the whole village is a fort."

"Indeed," Deor said. "But to the dwellers they're the universe writ small, as the human body is. The head for goodness, the feet for evil, and the middle the mixed ream of human kind."

The walls and the sides of the buildings within were of some thick-looking substance brightly whitewashed; possibly plastered mud-brick, or rammed earth, or compacted coral rag limestone, topped with curved tile. Each compound had a single gateway flanked by pillars, its ornament and size varying with those of the compound as a whole. The roofs that showed over the walls were steep-pitched in their upper sections and then hipped out below, sometimes of clay tile, sometimes of golden thatch or a darker coarse-looking material. It was just too far away to see details of the people except for the odd fisherman casting nets at the water's edge, though there were plenty about, and now and then an outrigger canoe or double-hulled vessel with an inverted pyramid for a sail kept its distance.

"They know we're here," John said.

He thought some of the horsemen on the road were cantering along and matching the ship's passage, and doubtless others had galloped ahead to bear the news. When they got a bit closer he could see that many other folk were stopping and pointing. Here and there a spearhead twinkled.

"It has a Balinese look, right enough," the Captain said. "I've done good business in Bali, though they're not the most welcoming of folk until you've proven yourself honest."

John frowned. He'd studied the geography of this part of the world, albeit briefly.

"We're a long way from Bali, aren't we?" he asked.

"About a thousand miles, but that's not all that far in sailing terms. Four to twelve days, with reasonable winds," Feldman said. "Plenty of places to stop for water along the way, too."

"Even so, what would they be doing here?"

The three experienced voyagers in their thirties looked at each other. Deor was the one who spoke; he was the maker of tales, after all, the wordsmith.

"There was war in Bali after the Change."

John shrugged mentally; there had been war nearly everywhere, after the Change. Ranging from minor, structured conflicts more like rough peace-officer work to frenzied mass many-million-fold struggles of all against all as the doomed death-zones perished in fire and blood, famine and plague.

And everything in between.

It was a time of legends to him, of villains and heroes and giants, the saviors of peoples and the builders of nations. And of fell, stark warlords carving out realms at the edge of the sword. Who was which often depended on where the question was asked, or in his case how they felt about his respective grandfathers.

Deor went on: "First there was war against the . . . outsiders there. The Javanese, mostly—Java was the ruling part of a great empire of these islands then, its people the masters overall, and some of them had settled on Bali to enforce their rule; about one in ten of the total or a little more. The Javanese had different Gods and customs, and neither much liked the other. Also, to Balinese good comes from inland—from the heights, from *Gunung Agung*, the mountain that is the abode of their Gods and to them the navel of the world. Kaja, goodness and fertility and right order, flows down with the water. Evil comes from below, from the sea—*kelod*, chaos and destruction and demons. The Javanese came from oversea and were mostly city-dwellers on Bali, so . . ."

Thora was blunter, as usual. "So, this," she said, and made a slicing gesture across her throat with one thumb.

John wasn't surprised at that either. If there just wasn't enough to go around, you'd naturally see that what there was went to your own folk, those you were bound to by belief and blood, and you'd drive out strangers who added more mouths. Kill them like rats if you had to, when it was a choice of their children starving or yours. That was how human beings were made; like wolves they were creatures of the tribe, of the pack. They could be more than that, but that was the foundation without which nothing could be built.

From the tone of Deor's words, he suspected that the *scop* had fond memories of his time there, and wanted to think well of the folk.

"They didn't kill all of the other outsiders," he added a little defensively. "The ones who were few and not a threat or great burden, or had useful knowledge."

Feldman smiled with a wry twist of the mouth, as if mentally thinking back through the long history of his people. He spoke matter-of-factly:

"There were also about three million people on Bali in the year of the Change, and it's half the size of the Willamette Valley. And it's pretty hilly. Fertile, rich soil and well watered, they have terraces going up the mountains like green staircases, but even with the *outsiders* gone there just wasn't enough."

"Three million in a place that size?" John blurted, and Ruan whistled.

Usually the numbers of the ancient world were just that, meaninglessly huge strings of numerals, but sometimes they hit home. "And they weren't ruined completely? The whole of Montival has, what, five million people?"

Deor sighed. "The Balinese are true landsmen, skilled and hardy for toil and very good at working together, and quick to come to a good understanding with the wights."

"The *aes dana*," Ruan said, using the Mackenzie term for the spirits of place.

"And they had many fine makers, craftsmen and not machine-tenders, back before the Change, smiths and potters and weavers. But even so, there was cruel hunger, and death stalked the villages."

"Exactly," Feldman said, his voice coolly unsentimental. "They had a strong king right from the start, one who seized power almost at once by whipping folk up against the outsiders, and *he* was no fool and saw the implications."

John nodded again. *That* was thoroughly familiar too. Besides luck and strong will and wits, a willingness to see and accept what the Change would bring had been a common trait of many who'd risen to power then. All four of his grandparents, for starters.

"It's a small enough place that men on foot or on bicycles could keep them acting together when the ancients' machines for talking at a distance failed. Most of the other islands around *were* ruined utterly, with fighting and chaos so bad they kept the next crop from being planted or harvested."

"Ah," John said. "So the Balinese were very hungry by then, but not quite so bad that they couldn't do anything but claw at each other and perish. A borderline case where what the leaders did was crucial. I've studied such."

He carefully didn't mention that his grandfather Norman Arminger had *been* one such leader, and the choices *he'd* made. Most of them had involved killing people in very large numbers. People who'd have died anyway, but . . .

Feldman nodded: "So by the second year they set out to conquer more land and settle colonists there, the people they couldn't feed at home."

Deor nodded soberly as well. "That's hard for Balinese, to uproot themselves. They sink deep roots in a place, and the family shrines where they worship their ancestors are dear to them. They drew lots to see who must go, I was told; two families in three, over the next few years. They've made poems of the bitterness of it."

Feldman supplied the bare facts: "The eastern edge of Java and Lombok are close to west and east of Bali—almost close enough to swim, in easy reach for any sort of little fishing boat, and they had many sailing vessels . . . yachts, they called them then."

Thora's right hand closed unconsciously where the hilt of her backsword would have been. "It's a king's duty to find his people fields to plow if they lack them, to work the land and feed their children," she said. "So the first Bear Lord of my folk did, by the sword when he had to."

"Rajadharma, they say here," Deor said. "As Hengist and Hrosa led my people, in the very ancient days:

"Engle and Seaxe upp becomon,
ofer brad brimu Britene sohton,
wlance wig-smithas, Wealas ofercomon,
eorlas ar-hwaete eard begeaton!"

He thought for a moment, then said: "Or in the modern tongue:

"—since from the east Angles and Saxons came up
Over the broad sea. Britain they sought,
Proud war-smiths who overcame the Welsh,
Glorious warriors, they took hold of the land."

Everyone nodded, and Feldman went on: "Raja Oka rules east Java and the whole of Lombok as well as Bali proper these days, and bits and pieces elsewhere. He's the grandson of the first, Oka the Great, and there are Balinese colonies all over. They just headed out to anyplace they thought might be doable—they even tried New Guinea, though not twice."

"Desperate and fierce and ruthless as so many were in the terrible years," Deor said. "Sometimes taking land spear-won, sometimes being pushed back into the sea and dying with their families, either way sparing the food-stocks back home so that their kinfolk might live."

"It looks like this is one of the places they fought their way ashore," Feldman said.

Then he frowned. "Though I've never heard of it, specifically. Probably it has its own ruler and he doesn't want to attract Oka's attention or pay tribute. We'll see."

John nodded, feeling his heart swell suddenly as the wind brought a strange spicy waft and the palms swayed in the distance, the light of dawn flickering and flashing on their fronds.

We will see, he thought. *And I'll have a chance to see. We'll go back as soon as we can*—duty prompted that—*but until then . . . we'll see things strange and wild!*

"Christ have mercy!" he said later that day, as the sun was just an hour above the western horizon.

When he crossed himself there was pure awe in the gesture. The harbor was broad, shaped like an irregular C pointing southwest. Most of the shoreline was farmland or forest or gardens—he thought he could see glimpses of what must be villas, with pools and artificial streams and very beautiful gardens. Otherwise it was as if it was in two different places at once, or two profoundly different countries whose capitals were close enough to see in a single sweeping glance.

One was to the west, their left-hand side, or port-side as sailors said. There rose a spread-out walled city of palace and temple, pagoda-like structures towering up in narrow pyramids of one roof after another, each smaller than the last. Or triple rows like steep triangular hills carved from white rock in fantastically intricate patterns, patterns that blazed with light from gilt and stucco and metal and glass. Open spaces full of trees or busy roads separated them, and he thought he saw leaping fountains. Farther inland were compounds like those they'd seen in the countryside, but jammed together to front on dusty streets that thronged with people. The whole was very substantial but not huge; there were probably at least twenty thousand people, possibly thirty, not quite half what a really big city like Portland or Corvallis held.

On the eastward side of the bay to their right was a structure just as huge, but . . .

"That looks sort of like a Classical building," John said.

Music was his favored art, but he'd looked into architecture too since he was bound to be a patron of all of them someday. After a closer look he went on:

"Not quite, though—maybe Venetian, or Byzantine? And not as big as Todenangst, say, unless there's a lot more on the other side of that crest, but still pretty damned big. And not anything you'd expect to see in this part of the world!"

He thought it must have been built into and over the side of a substantial hill, sculpting away the bulk of the earth. Most of it was made of some stone that ranged from white with a slight hint of pink through rose to deep dusky scarlet.

"Coral block," Feldman said, identifying it. "Pretty, and easy to work. Maybe blocks over a core of pounded coral fragments. But it doesn't make that . . . whatever it is . . . as lighthearted as I'd expect just from hearing *built of pink stone.*"

No indeed, John thought.

Wall and terrace and rising stair, tall slender round towers with bulbous tips, narrow slit windows much taller than a man in blank surfaces that would be easy to defend even if it wasn't strictly a castle, flanked by engaged pillars twisted like spirals. And on the topmost tier columns and domes, eerily elongated and . . . somehow subtly twisted. As if they were notes in the harmonies of songs he'd never heard. He blinked his eyes. There had been a shimmer before them, as if he was seeing *through* the scene before him. Folk were crowded on the walls, watching, ant-tiny at this distance. A black and yellow flag flew in many places, though it was impossible to see the details of it. Looking closer, he had the impression that there were many enclosed courtyards, possibly very large.

Captain Ishikawa had come up and was standing with one hand on his katana and the thumb on the guard, ready to flick it out as his right hand reached for it—that seemed almost instinctive in Nihonjin entitled to wear the twin swords. Ishikawa was also a naval officer, and an engineer, a man of varied accomplishments for his thirty or so years. He looked narrowly at both sets of buildings.

"These are new," he said.

In English which was still strongly accented—he pronounced *these* as *zese*—but now fully fluent and understandable, unlike the third-hand book-learned variety he'd spoken when he arrived on Montival's shore that spring.

"Both the city to the west, and that structure to the east. Built since the Change; I think that one may incorporate ruins"—he nodded to the mass of rose coral—"but neither existed before the ancient world fell."

A rueful shake of the head. "It is humbling, to see others building so, in so many different countries, when in Nihon we strive to keep the old in repair."

John inclined his head slightly. The Japanese—or the ones he'd met in the past six months—were an impeccably polite people, but also intensely proud. Ishikawa was more approachable than the others around Reiko, which made him only extremely reserved and taciturn by Monti-vallan standards.

"Your people have had their war to fight, Captain Ishikawa, against terrible odds. That consumes all the energy they have to spare."

Feldman and his First Mate had been scanning the harbor as well. "Now, here's the question: where do we head? Because we have to beach her, and soon. Unless they have a drydock free here."

Under the ramparts of the coral-built palace-city were docks and wharves, also solidly built of stone, and a breakwater. Anchored a bit off from them was a very large ship, a long sleek shape with flush decks and four towering masts and a hull painted some neutral blue-gray color. Smaller ships were at the wharves, some of types he was familiar with, others the odd-looking ones called prau in these seas.

Feldman examined the giant. "That's a pre-Change ship, by the Lord of the Universe! Two thousand tons, or even more. I've heard they built ships for sail, sometimes, right before the end."

"The displacement would depend on her lines underwater," Ishikawa said, and Radavindraban made a wordless sound of agreement as he used his binoculars.

"Steel hull, then," Feldman said enviously. "She'll be fast, from the look of her spars and the amount of canvas she could spread. Not very nimble, though; she's ship-rigged, all square except a gaff on the mizzen and the staysails and jibs. And she'd draw deep—thirty feet, maybe more. I don't like the look of this bay, see the mottled color of the water, shading to green and back to blue? Shallow spots, reefs or mudbanks or both. I wouldn't care to exchange broadsides with that monster either, though."

John nodded; the steel sides would make her relatively immune to fire, and nearly so to catapult shot and bolts.

"And the ancients built it for . . . amusement?"

"Not one damned thing amusing about her now," the Captain said. "She's got a full broadside, probably modifications since then. Fifteen firing ports a side, and more on her deck. That's a specialist warship, and a very strong one. Stronger than any single ship in the Royal Navy."

He peered closely, his lips moving. "I can make out her name. H . . . A . . . S . . . T . . . U . . . R . . . *Hastur*."

He turned his glass to the westward. "Now, they've got much less in the way of dockage and wharfage over there. I'm not very surprised; Balinese don't really take to the sea well. Praus, plenty of fishing boats, and very little else . . . except that barquentine. Smallish, two hundred tons, maybe two-fifty. Looks fast though . . . catapults too, some sort of light sea-scorpion."

"Aussie, Cap'n?" Radavindraban said.

"Yes, from her lines. And they like that rig, square on the fore and fore-and-aft on the main and mizzen except for a main top'sle. Darwin, maybe. Or maybe Townsville, or Cairns. And she's got a shark-mouth painted on her waterline."

His brows went up. "And they're weighing anchor and making sail. Making sail right away, they tied a float to their anchor-cable and threw it overside. They're anxious to make our acquaintance, it seems. Mr. Mate, all hands to battle stations."

The crew already was, but they stood to in anxious tense silence when Radavindraban conveyed the message; Ishikawa nodded and trotted down to the catapult he and his men crewed. John frowned. Something was bothering him. . . .

Something besides being on a sinking ship and having multitudes trying to kill me. The things I do!

"Captain," he said. Feldman glanced aside at him, frowning the way a man did when his concentration was upset. "This island doesn't do much trade, right?"

"None, from what I've heard," Feldman said flatly. "It might as well have sunk right after the Change. Which is a bit odd; it's fair-sized, and obviously well-peopled."

"But those people there"—John pointed eastward—"have that bloody great ship, the *Hastur*! And a bunch of others. And that building is something you'd talk about if you ever saw it. Why hasn't any word of this got out? Why hasn't someone like you put in here to see if there *was* any trade? And brought out news?"

"Not worth my while, but you're right in principle. Someone would . . . like that little Aussie barquentine. In the last decade or two with trade picking up the way it has . . . it's become harder to be entirely out of the way than it used to be."

He snapped his fingers. "Unless you're *trying* to stay out of sight! I should have thought . . . well, busy. Those ships are all colored blue-gray. Camouflage, yes; pirates and warships. Honest merchantmen usually don't try that hard not to be seen!"

Just then the masthead hailed: "Small craft putting out from the quays to eastward below the pink castle, skipper! Dozens of them, crammed with men! I can see spearheads, and some of 'em are galleys with catapults in the bows!"

A moment later. "More small craft from the westward harbor setting out towards us as well, skipper! Same sort, but not as many!"

"Any sign of movement from the big ship?" Feldman called back.

"No, skipper. She'd take a while, that 'un. Anchored fore and aft, too.

Wait. . . . Some of the small boats are putting alongside her, men going aboard, lots of 'em."

"Thank you, Your Highness," Feldman said. "We'll head west towards the Balinese, and hope we get there before those galleys do. This may well come to a close-quarter action, and I don't like fighting galleys in confined waters where you can't dodge about to make them exhaust their rowers. They can come at you right out of the eye of the wind."

John nodded wordlessly and vaulted over the railing and down to the main deck. Evrouin was moving towards him with the canvas sack and his shield over his back, and he took a deep breath and nodded.

"Full gear, Sergeant Fayard," he called to the underofficer of cross-bowmen. "This looks . . . serious."

Out of the frying pan, into the fucking fire, he added silently, and saw the thought echoed in the underofficer's eyes.

John had expected to feel better when he had a chance to do something he was properly trained at. Right now, he'd have settled for being a supernumerary idler again. The valet-bodyguard started pulling things out of the bag; Deor wiggled into his mail shirt, then started helping Thora, as Ruan shrugged into his Mackenzie brigandine and buckled the straps under his right arm and stepped through his longbow to string it with his thigh braced over the riser. John's mouth was suddenly very dry and he wanted a drink very badly, but you didn't want a full bladder in a suit of plate before you had to.

What in the name of all the Saints and the Virgin is going on here?

He didn't know. He didn't even know if anyone else knew, either. Maybe the Australian ship could tell him, if *they* weren't coming to attack him too. He considered that as he bent and twisted to let the plates and pieces settle and they were buckled and fitted and strapped.

I wonder how they got here?

CHAPTER TEN

"**O**h, for fuck's *sake*, Pete!" Lady Fiona Holder said. "Wake up!"

The accents of the vanished American West were still strong in her voice, despite forty-six years in and around and across post-Blackout Australia and all the seas that bordered it; she'd been born in a trailer park in what was then the dry eastern part of Oregon.

She supposed it was still dry and still had cows, though it was part of the High Kingdom of Montival now, which was an absolute kick in the head on the infrequent occasions she thought about it. Outsiders often mistook her range-country twang for faded Southern Gothic, and for sure when her temper frayed, you could still hear an echo of the conga line of deadbeat stepdads who'd passed through her mom's trailer all those years ago. Years, decades, whole worlds ago. They'd spoken a uniform dialect of genuine Toothless Cracker Appalachio-Methhead, though by now she supposed there weren't many left who knew or cared about the regional variations. She'd taken off at sixteen and never looked back. As best she knew, her mom, a onetime *Hustler* model, had sucked the big one a couple of years later in the great die-off after the Blackout. The Change they called it back there.

Not back home. This was home now. Had been for the longest time.

Sir Peter jerked his head up in the bamboo lounger and closed his mouth, reaching for the tall cool glass of Saltie Bites Lager at his elbow.

"Not sleeping. Just thinking," he said, but his voice was thick with the granddad nap she'd caught him at. "Worried about Pip. She's all we have left of Jules now."

"You were on the nod, Pete. Don't shit a shitter," she said, conscious that her own worry was making her snap.

Lady Fiona—universally known as Fifi, though only the favored few called her that to her face—was in her sixties, with just a few streaks of golden corn-silk color left in her shoulder-length white hair. Her figure, still very trim for her age, worked well in the national dress of Capricornia— khaki shorts, slip-on leather sandals and the blue sleeveless vest favored by the kingdom's iconic sheep shearers. Her face had the leathery reddish tan of a blonde who'd spent much of her life on the tropical oceans and her hands were covered in thick calluses that would never go away. Neither she nor her husband favored the broad-brimmed hats with dangling corks you saw everywhere on the streets of the capital. Instead they made do with the Capricornian Salute, a hand waved in front of the face to move the flies along. An act performed so often it became as natural as breathing.

Her husband was at least a decade older, with thick white chest-hair showing over the top of his vest. More hair than he could boast of up top. Pete had gone egg-bald some time ago, a hard thing for a man as quietly vain as him. He had so enjoyed his earlier, virile legend as Cap'n Pete, greatest of all the mighty Salvagers. Fifi knew he was "at least" a decade older, but other than that, Pete could not say. He'd always been vague about exactly when he'd been born. Not that he was reluctant to specify, but the years were never the same twice. He was adamant though that he was a born and bred Tasmanian, which made of him a natural republican. He was forever teasing the King about it.

"Hmmmph," Fifi said, and took another pull at her gin-and-tonic.

The umbrella-set rooftop terrace was part of the city palace of the Birmingham dynasty of the Kings of Darwin; currently the residence of the first of that name, generally known as JB to the peasantry, whose interests he routinely favored over those of the gentry. At least according to the gentry. JB was pretty much their friend, certainly their patron in the older, wilder days, and definitely an ally now. He was also older and balder and even more wrinkly than Pete. In Fifi's opinion that was all just camouflage, though. She had never met a man who put her more in mind of a crocodile drifting along with only the eyes and nostrils showing. Not that she took Pete's act too seriously either. He might present these days as a harmless-granddad-sitting-in-the-shade, but together he and his old mate the King were the richest, most powerful old bastards in this part of the world. They were far from fucking harmless.

Nor was she.

Fifi freshened up her drink from the fixings on a small occasional table next to her lounger. The ice was fresh, as it always was at the City Palace and she wondered, as she always did, what mad bastard adventurer had been dispatched to some snow-capped mountain far, far away to retrieve it for her drinking pleasure. She walked to the balustrade, resisting the urge to ask Pete if she thought Pip would be okay. Despite his protests he really was half asleep in the late afternoon heat and, besides, she knew she would just be flapping her gums to stop her fears and her guilt running wild off her tongue. After all, were it not for "Aunt" Fifi, Lady Pip would be ensconced at the Court of St. James under the wing of the current King-Emperor. In Winchester, on that cold rainy patch on the other side of the planet, safely bored out of her pretty head, not tear-assing around the islands east of Java and north of Lombok.

At least Fifi hoped she was still tear-assing around the . . .

"She'll be fine, darlin'. She is her mother's daughter."

Pete had come up behind her, surprising her when he put his hands around her waist. He had always been able to do that—sneak up on her. There was a reason he had been the designated back tracker when they'd run salvage under the Royal Warrant. She placed her free hand over his and squeezed, sipping at the drink again. Not trusting herself to speak.

From here you could look out over Stokes Hill wharf and the busy port, a forest of masts from fishing smacks to the tall spars of warships and oceangoing merchantmen, stacked with their bowsprits stretching in over the pavement and the inset tracks of the freight trams.

A fair share of the hulls worked for their Darwin & East Indies Trading Company, sailing from Hobart to Patagonia, Hainan to Zanzibar. Trading in wheat and wool and wine, sandalwood and copra, salvage steel and fresh-cut teak, rubber and gear-trains and swords and rice and rum, coffee and tea, hides and . . .

And once we shipped a dozen baby elephants to the Raja of Bali, and we had to catch them first. And then the fucking ship just disappeared and we had to do it all over again!

It was sundown, and just slightly cooler; they'd had a thunderstorm earlier, washing the air, the sign that the Wet was coming soon. Lightning flickered in the black clouds on the horizon, over the azure surface of the Arafura Sea. There was still a clamor of voices and a ratcheting of cranes and more and more bright lanterns, and a distance-softened surf-roar of voices and wheels from the streets beyond where *late* didn't begin until well after midnight.

The silty wet smell, sometimes fetid with fish-guts or perfumed with spices and always seasoned with eucalyptus woodsmoke, made her think of voyages gone by. Back when it had been just her and Pete and Jules on the old *Diamantina*, the most successful salvagers and smugglers and all-around fortune-and-glory rogues afloat in the chaos of the years after the Blackout. Back then, this time of day, they'd have been down in the dockside pubs, the sort of place where you sat on your sheathed knife with the hilt coming out from under your right butt-cheek. So you wouldn't forget it was there and could draw without bringing your hand across to your belt. Sitting amid caterwauling music and a fug of smoke that just started with tobacco, knocking it back and pretending to play cards and sniffing after the scent of an opportunity like sharks in waters full of tempting, juicy, bleeding toes paddling temptingly into range.

She'd seen this city recover from the terrible years, seen it change and grow and flourish like some brawling, bawdy child; a mutant mix of old and new, and she'd been part of that. Her children and grandchildren had grown up in and with it, grown into its bone and blood. The kids were even respectable, in a raffish here's-the-deal-and-here's-my-catapult sort of way.

But there are times I miss the old days. Even if there was a lot less lounging on teak decks surrounded by potted palms and bougainvillea. Though Jules did always love a G&T with ice when she could get it; I wouldn't ever have drunk one except for her.

"Nostalgia's a bitch, isn't it?" Pete said.

She sipped at her drink, but couldn't keep back a grin. It would have been surprising if they didn't know each other well after forty-six years in each other's pockets, plus Pete had always been smart. And one of those rare men who really knew how women thought, too, without letting his own—enormous—macho legend get in the way.

"I miss Jules," she said. "And I worry is all. I promised her, Pete. I said we'd look out for Pip."

"And we did. That's why her father won't talk to us anymore."

Fifi sighed. The Colonel-designate of Townsville Armory had a serious pickle up the ass, but he had a point too. . . .

"Did I do the wrong thing?"

He tugged gently on her elbow, turned her around. She was struck again by how much she was still attracted to him. After all of those years. And wrinkles. He was still such a good-looking man, as he never tired of reminding her. In his younger days he'd looked a bit like his fellow-Tasmanian Errol Flynn, though an increasingly scarred and battered version as time went on. Flynn might have played piratical swashbuckling adventurers in the old movies. But Pete had *done* it for real, starting well before the Change too, and those days had left their marks.

He grinned.

"You know who I miss?"

"Your younger, prettier self?"

She pronounced it "purdier"—exaggerating her accent, as she did when they were playing.

"No. I'm still pretty. But no, I kinda miss Shoeless Dan."

Fifi snorted a mouthful of gin and tonic through her nose.

"Yeah, right. That's why you let the sharks have him."

"No, no. I let the sharks have him because the treacherous bastard tried to arsefuck us on that Sydney run for JB. That was just business. He fed us to the Biters, I returned the favor."

"And? Now you miss him?"

"I miss the fun we had because of him. In spite of him. The man was a perfidious arseclown, but he did put us onto some of our best scores."

"So he could rip us off . . ."

"So he could *try*. And fail. He always failed. Because we were better than him. You, me and Julesy. Especially Jules. Remember when he thought he finally had us? And she just carved through his boys with those choppers of hers?"

The memory was both horrific and satisfying. Fifi shuddered and smiled, faintly.

"Well, as good as Julesy was, she raised Pip, and Pip is better. A natural. She'd have died a thousand fucking deaths at Court back in the Old Country, Fifi. But out there"—he waved at the slate gray sea under the dark wall of thunderheads—"you just know she won't even get a scratch."

Two burly guards in helmets and water-buffalo-hide cuirasses with the white-gray-orange Desert Rose of seven petals on their chests lounged outside the notional door to the dining room, with heavy Golok-knife choppers at their waists and the handles of asymmetrical war-boomerangs showing over their shoulders. They had identically tall rangy muscled builds and might have been brothers except that one was blue-eyed and weathered red and the other extremely black; both had their round shields hanging from the shoulder-straps and leaned casually on broad-bladed spears—the Capricornian military didn't go in for standing to attention—but their eyes never stopped roving. They had the knack of good Palace guards though—making Fifi feel as though they purposely did not see her, which was good, given the enthusiastic groping she was receiving from her husband.

The door to the room was open wrought iron, and the whole space was really just a tall louvered roof supported on drum-shaped pillars of the same blocks of compressed and stabilized laterite that made up the palace. Bamboo screens between the pillars were overgrown with floribunda vines whose clusters of white flowers scented the air passing through.

One of the palace staff leaned her head out the doorway and jerked a thumb over a bare tattooed shoulder.

"Come on, your feed's ready!" she announced cheerfully. "Better get a move on before JB scoffs the lot."

Pete gave Fifi a pat on the ass to get her moving towards the chamber every crony of JB knew well; it held a long table suitable for dinner for twelve guests but it was set for seven tonight, wicker chairs, and a slow-moving overhead fan driven from a windmill on the roof. When the breeze failed, wallah-boys were sent up to pedal stationary bikes hooked into the drive train. Globes of frosted glass lit by gaslights were suspended from the center-beam of the exposed roof trusses. The floor was the same openwork teak as the deck, and there was a mill-and-swill area fronting a fully stocked bar. A normal visitor would have marveled at the genuine antique bottles of wine and spirits on display. Fifi did not. She had salvaged at least half of them from the dead cities.

The open space in front of the bar was occupied now by sawhorses, and on them was . . .

"Fuck me purple," Pete said reverently, and fished his bent spectacles out of a pocket in his shorts, putting them on and peering intently.

"Holy shit," Fifi said, almost in the same breath.

The skull of the saltie was clean but still raw, smelling very faintly of seawater and decay. They both recognized it instantly—anyone who spent much time at sea in this part of the world would—also anyone who hung around the banks of the big tidal rivers, where the saltwater crocodiles were wont to lurk, erupting out to grab anything even vaguely edible . . . and it wasn't uncommon for them drag full-grown water buffalo back in for a snack. The biggest ones had been getting bigger all her lifetime since the Blackout because it was so damned difficult to kill them nowadays. She'd seen one hung up in Port Moresby about ten years ago that was twenty-four feet long, and it had weighed nearly three tons. This one though . . .

Fifi had gotten very good at estimating sizes in a long career both larcenous and commercial. This skull was about four feet, maybe four feet and a hair. Nine times that to get the total length. The hide was draped over another set of sawhorses, and it was looking a bit moth-eaten. Shark-eaten might be a better way to put it, big semicircular bites taken out of the thinner belly-skin and almost certainly done postmortem, but the overall length bore out her estimate: more than thirty-five feet, less than thirty-six.

"Glad I didn't meet this one before someone turned him into handbag meat," Pete said, awed delight in his tone; he'd always loved marvels, the stranger and more dangerous the better.

More than ten feet longer than the one we saw in New Guinea, and the mass goes up as the cube of the increase in length, so—

"It must have weighed . . ." she said, hesitating because the deduction was perfectly logical but made the thing the same bulk as a fair-sized elephant.

"About five tons, Lady Fiona," another voice said.

Fifi wheeled at the thump of spearbutts on wood, and JB was there by the inner doors, grinning like an ancient baboon. He wasn't the one who'd spoken, however. That was a stranger in an unfamiliar white linen uniform with a sort of naval look to it; tanned and fit, thirtyish, brown-haired and sharp-faced and unremarkable . . . except that his English was unmistakably North American, which you didn't hear every day even now with trade picking up again.

So that's who the visiting frigate was, she thought.

It had vanished into the Capricornian naval docks when it arrived two days ago, and the security had clamped down harder than she'd ever seen before.

"Captain Richard Russ, Royal Montivallan Navy, officer commanding

Her Majesty's frigate *Stormrider*, my lady," he said, with a slight bow and another to Pete. "Sir Peter."

"*Her* Majesty?" Pete said sharply.

Russ looked grim. "The High King was killed this spring. High Queen Mathilda is Queen-Regent until the heir comes of age."

He indicated the woman beside him, who wore the same getup down to the fore-and-aft cocked hat under one arm. "My executive officer, Lieutenant-Commander Annette Chong."

She looked a bit younger, also clever and tautly fit, and as if at least one of her grandparents had been Chinese despite her blue eyes—very much like the eldest of Fifi's daughters-in-law, in fact. They were accompanied by another man, a bit younger and built like a really dangerous rugby forward. She felt her brows go up at the way *he* was dressed.

Like a playing card, she thought.

Tight sienna-colored pants almost like panty hose, tooled ankle boots with upturned toes and golden prick spurs, a loose blue coat whose open dagged sleeves dangled past his waist, a black jerkin of suede leather with a heraldic device of a burning phoenix-like bird, and what she thought of as a pirate shirt all white billowy sleeves and fastened at cuffs and neck with black silk ties. When he swept off his hat as part of a formal-looking bow—the hat was a round blue silk cowflop with a rolled circle around the edges and a dangling tail—she saw that his head was shaved except for a long black scalplock over his right ear, bound with golden rings.

"And Sir Boleslav Pavlovitch Kedov de Vashon, of the Protector's Guard."

She stuck out her hand. The two naval types shook it; Sir Boleslav bowed and kissed it with an authority which suggested he was used to doing it. That was an interesting experience, the more so as he took a quick look at her cleavage in passing—discreetly, but you could always tell.

Beside them JB looked like an old, disreputable devil; he'd been a heavy-boned muscular man, and now the bones were plain behind his spotted, parchment-thin skin and the scars that knotted it. Beside him stood Prince Thomas, very obviously his son and in his fifties, with his usual colored bandana around his rather long graying blond hair. He gave the Holders a careful nod; he'd known them all his life, of course, but now that he was grown he was a little cautious of the sort of buccaneering reprobate his father had always swum with. And he'd realized most of the stories they'd told him as a kid were *true*.

"Let's get the roadkill out before it spoils dinner," JB said cheerfully; he'd always liked a feed, even before the Blackout reputedly.

Living through that nightmare had made a lot of folks who'd managed it crazy where food was concerned, especially the ones who'd escaped the cities on foot during the collapse. Come Blackout Day not everyone was lucky enough to find themselves working on a survivalist super nerd billionaire's yacht in San Francisco Bay as a sous-chef (as she had), or safely out at sea on an old wooden sailboat beating south towards Sydney (as Pete had, on the *Diamantina*). And those who'd been in the air—well they were pretty much fucked, weren't they? Except for her friend, her comrade, her murderous soul sister Lady Julianne Balwyn, who'd survived when her flying boat came down hard on the Great Barrier Reef and crawled out on the beach already looking ahead and planning survival with style.

For that matter, making himself king and founding Capricornia wasn't much more amazing than JB's feat in simply getting himself and his young family out of Brisbane alive. There had been two million people in the city in nineteen ninety-eight, almost as many as there were on this whole continent now, and damned few had managed it. Much less getting to the seething chaos of Darwin within a year, seeing what the place needed and providing it. Hordes of suburban refugees ended up as indentured laborers on some outback station all over the shattered continent, knuckling their foreheads to the stationmasters. Only one got to be King.

The staff took the remains out, and everyone sat. Fifi hid a smile at the Montivallans who very obviously looked to her and Pete to give them the lead. They'd probably been briefed on the unusually relaxed protocols in

Capricornia but it was still doubtless a little unsettling to see the King grab a platter of barbecued Bangkok chicken thighs from a serving girl with a wink and start handing them around himself.

At that point Sir Boleslav took off his coat and tossed it to the staffer who already held his sword-belt and a severely plain sheathed hand-and-a-half longsword whose guard had the battering and filed-out nicks of serious use. Then he undid the ties at the neck of his shirt, letting it fall open to reveal more of the corded muscle there and a scar that looked as if someone had tried to slit his throat and come remarkably close to success.

"Da," he said, in English that had a slight guttural accent. "In County Chehalis, we have a saying: among friends, wear the collar open, drink deep and speak truth."

"In this climate, you don't need a collar at all," JB said genially. "Get on the end of these bad boys. You got me this recipe book, didn't you, Pete? From that joint I used to like back on the old Sunshine Coast."

Pete smiled and held up the back of hand to show off a thin, white scar; she wondered if he'd be pulling up his vest to show the one below his belly-button next.

"Got you the recipe book, samples from the herb garden, and sixteen stitches for my trouble when we ran into a scavenger band on the Noosa River coming out."

"Pfft," scoffed Fifi, snagging one of the bright yellow nubbins of meat. It was crisscrossed by caramelized scorch marks from the grill and dripping with sweet chili sauce. "It was barely six stitches and Julesy grabbed the herb samples because Pete's botanically illiterate. He watered a plastic fern on our boat for three months before we told him what he was doing. If you'd trusted him to salvage your barbecue herbs he'd probably have brought you back a toilet deodorizer shaped like a plastic pinecone. We have to keep him off that Station we bought because the grass goes brown if he steps on the place."

Captain Russ and Commander Chong shared a brief uncertain exchange of glances until both Pete and JB roared with laughter; Sir Boleslav joined in, booming as if his usual venue was under a bridge waiting for billy-goats Gruff.

"That fucking plastic fern." Her husband chuckled. "Man, I was so proud when that thing didn't die."

The King used a linen napkin to wipe grease from his fingers and most of the smile from his face. Only a trace remained, but it did linger for a while.

"I reckon Julianne told me that story half a dozen times, and we laughed longer and louder with each telling," he said, sighing out the last few words.

"To absent friends," Captain Russ said, raising his glass.

"Absent friends," they all replied.

Pete and JB clinked their enormous beer bottles lightly together. Boleslav killed his and reached for another from the bucket of ice; it nearly disappeared in his spade-shaped paw.

"So," Fifi said, pointing her fork at the label—it showed a crudely-drawn saltie biting a fishing smack in half. "Does this have anything to do with that monster? And anything to do with Pip?"

More staff, who were never referred to as servants in this most unusual of Realms, arrived with the main course. Silver platters—salvaged from the reliquary of Melbourne Library, again by the crew of *Diamantina*—were piled high with seafood. Enormous, bright orange lobsters, freshly shucked oysters as big as your fist (which, frankly, made Fifi want to gag), sashimi-grade tuna, beer-battered reef fish, garlic prawns, spicy mussels, long golden chains of flash-fried octopus rings and—wonder of wonders—salt and pepper Dungeness crab; this last, a small miracle performed entirely for the benefit of their visitors.

Captain Russ blinked at the crab, deftly winkled some of the meat out and ate it.

"Wonderful," he said. "My mother used to make it like this."

The Montivallan knight was digging in with a blissful expression, casually cracking lobster-claws in his fist.

"Like a feast on my family's estates on Vashon Island, Your Majesty!" he said to JB. "Only with new types of fish."

Fifi had no idea how the Royal kitchens had sourced the Dungeness crab. They sure as shit hadn't Fedexed an aquarium overnight from the Pacific Northwest.

Just the King of Darwin working his mojo, isn't it? she thought. *Keeping the world guessing.*

"It *may* have something to do with your young protégé," Russ said to Fifi and Pete. "It *certainly* has a lot to do with that . . . crocodile thing." He looked at the crab again. "Extraordinary."

Oh, you hazarded the cruel seas and high adventure for six months to join us? Here, have a little reminder of home.

If there was one thing that you could rely on at the Palace here in Darwin, it was a good meal and a gentle reminder that they were walking with the King.

His Majesty started in directly as he tore open a crab claw and worked out the meat, stuffing it into a freshly baked baguette slathered with avocado butter:

"Captain Russ got the saltie up in the Ceram Sea," he said. "He was following a Montivallan ship, the *Tarshish Queen*, Moishe Feldman's boat. Feldman was being naughty."

Fifi and Pete looked at each other. The Ceram Sea was where Pip had been heading, and had vanished off the face of the earth a length of time ago that was making them both profoundly nervous.

"We've dealt with him, and his dad too. Feldman senior was the first American . . . pardon me, Montivallan . . . in here since the Blackout. Moishe's a chip off the old block; hard enough to crack fleas on and the devil's own bargainer, but honest," Pete said cautiously. "Likes seeing somewhere new as much as he likes a profit, and he *really likes* a profit. Bit of a blood desperado, when you come right down to it."

JB laughed raspingly, almost coughing up a chunk of crab meat. "Takes one, eh, Pete?"

The Montivallan naval officer blinked at the exchange and went on: "We were actually chasing the two Korean warships. Who were chasing Captain Feldman," he said. "He hadn't actually done anything illegal. Not *technically* illegal."

"We are bloody *experts* on being not technically illegal," Pete said; which was true and a good placeholder too. "Koreans, eh?"

The Holders exchanged another look and JB nodded soberly to it. The gaslight danced on his liver-spotted pate, which was shining with sweat in the humidity. Post-Blackout Korea was a black hole; nothing that went in came out, and sometimes it stuck out a pseudopod and absorbed passers-by. That was a major reason nobody much went that far north, not even when tempted by the prospect of salvage in Tokyo.

Also while the surviving Japanese weren't exactly utterly hostile—ships of the Darwin & East Indies Trading Company had touched there briefly a couple of times—the locals certainly didn't like *gaijin* making free with their ruins, and they and the Koreans were mixing it in all the time. The three of them had discussed a salvage run amongst themselves more than once in the old days, and always managed to talk each other out of it. Their eyes went wider as Captain Russ explained what had been happening in Montival and how the Koreans had been involved.

"Montival isn't going to let the killing of our High King go unpunished," Russ said. "And we'll have allies."

"Kim Il Fuckwit is certainly getting big eyes, not just raiding the Japanese and the Chinese coasts anymore," Prince Thomas said. "We got complaints about that from the Luzon people at the Regional Security Conference. And more and more ships are going missing up in the Ceram Sea, beyond what the Suluk were always up to. The Timorese were on about it; we thought it was just their old blood-feud talking, but . . . I don't know if there's a connection but I don't like coincidences."

His father nodded vigorously and swallowed an oyster with a squeeze of lime, looking at the Montivallans as Russ went on:

"We'd found a couple of empty barrels floating with the Feldman & Sons mark and thought we were close on their track, just between North

Sulawesi and Malaku," Russ said. "Then we saw a little smoke. It was one of the Korean ships, burned to the waterline and breaking up. Firebolt, I'd say; the *Queen* has eighteen-pounder bow and stern chasers, and an eight-catapult broadside of nine-pounders and knows how to use it."

The Holders both nodded, knowing what thermite could do to wood if you placed it well and the receiving ship's damage-control wasn't on their toes.

"The other one had foundered and turned turtle, but it was still floating even though the keel was awash."

Wooden ships were extremely hard to really sink, as long as any air remained trapped in them at all. The material they were made of was inherently buoyant, after all. It took a full hold of water to pull them down.

"We took a prisoner, one of the Eaters they'd picked up in the ruins of Los Angeles, who was lying on the keel. He was the last one, and he'd gnawed most of the meat off his left forearm."

Fifi thought for a moment before remembering the term Eater; in Australia they were usually called *zed* or *Biters*.

"He was mad . . . well, probably mad even before what happened, and dying. We gave him a little water and asked him some questions . . . they speak English, of a sort. All we could get was *teeth, teeth,* teeth *in water*. I thought he was talking about the sharks at first, there were plenty of those about."

Chong, his second-in-command, spoke: "I was looking at the hulk, trying to see what had taken her out. There was a chunk on the starboard bow that looked as if it had been ripped loose, deck stringers snapped and pulled out from the ribs and hanging knees. Not round-shot damage, I know what that looks like. This wasn't anything I'd seen before. And we found this stuck in the wood."

She drew a curved tooth out of a pocket; it was thick as paired thumbs at the base, and as long as her palm was broad. Fifi had no doubt at all it would fit right into the gap in the big skull's grin.

"From the look of it, that damned animal *bit* a great big chunk out of the ship. Probably tried to get aboard—"

Fifi thought about the image that put in her mind and her eyes went still for a moment. Adventure was all very well, but . . .

"They can jump half their length out of the water like someone shot them out with springs," she said softly. "Half of thirty-six feet . . . that would be enough to get right on the deck. And five fucking tons dropping on it wouldn't help at all. Like a randy elephant trying to mate with the bows. They'd be fucked for sure."

Pete waved a bottle of the beer. "This label's based on something that really happened, too. Those jaws can shear wood like a hydraulic saw."

The Montivallan nodded. "Then the weight on the deck forced it down enough that the water flooded her forward, maybe her ballast shifted and then she capsized. It wasn't a very well-built ship and it had probably taken storm damage before then."

Her Captain took up the tale. "So that was when we decided to investigate the place all the gulls were circling. The crocodile . . . saltie, you say . . . was floating belly-up, bloated with gas. We were lucky, a few hours more and it would probably have sunk for good, the sharks were at it. We weighed it when we winched it up on a boom; just under five tons."

Boleslav laughed harshly. "The ancient stories say knights slew dragons with sword and lance. That one, even if I were a bogatyr of old like Dobrynya Nikitich, I would be glad to use a catapult. From a castle tower, hey?"

Pete closed his eyes; for a moment she was worried the dinner and the wine had sent him off to sleep again. Then he frowned in a way she recognized; he'd been watching a movie of alternatives behind his eyelids.

"The Koreans were chasing them; Moishe wouldn't have run if he thought he had a chance in a sea-fight," he said. "So something happened to change the odds."

"The saltie happened, to one of the Koreans at least," Fifi added.

"Right. So Moishe whipped around fast and gave the other one a broadside, maybe it was damaged already too, and set it afire. It's what I would have done in his shoes. Then he shot the saltie and ran for it, which he could do on a different course since they weren't bracketing him anymore. Which was why you lost him, Captain. He's a tricky bastard, and he couldn't be sure that the two after him were the only problem. Lot of places to hide, up in the Ceram."

Captain Russ spread his hands. "We *hope* that's what happened. I would really rather not have to go home and tell the High Queen that her eldest son was eaten by a giant crocodile eight thousand miles from home."

"While we were cruising about nearby," Chong added.

"Giant accursed crocodile," Captain Russ qualified.

"Accursed?" Pete asked. "You getting technical there?"

Fifi tensed. Over the years, they'd both met things that couldn't be explained by the pre-Blackout logic they'd grown up with. JB snapped his fingers, and called out over his shoulder:

"Hey, bring in those bolts, wouldja? And the bracelet."

Two of the staff came in. One held a pair of catapult bolts, and the other a covered tray. Fifi looked at the bolts with interest and Pete put his glasses back on. Both were the sort launched by a medium-weight military or shipboard catapult; one was broken off, and had a thick hardwood shaft with a hand-forged head, a three-sided pyramidal one heat-shrunk onto the oak. The other was solid forged steel, swelling to a four-sided point and with three brass fins brazed on the base and subtly curved to spin the projectile in flight. She'd killed a Biter in Sydney with a bolt like that once. Literally blew him to pieces.

Yeah, good times.

"The steel one is Montivallan made to our Navy specifications, and we think it was what killed the beast eventually. Manufactured in Corvallis, Donaldson Foundry and Machine marks. Almost certainly from the *Tarshish Queen*; Feldman and Sons buy from them exclusively. The other's unfamiliar but we assume it's Korean."

He licked his lips, obviously reluctant. "And this was around the crocodile's . . . arm. Forelimb. Whatever. Very close to where the Korean catapult bolt hit, it may have struck it in passing."

The cloth was drawn aside, and instead of the macadamia and chocolate tarts they'd been promised for dessert, it held what was obviously an armband.

"Our chaplain advised us not to touch it if we could avoid it, Sir Peter," Russ said quietly.

He crossed himself; so did Sir Boleslav, though from right to left rather than vice versa; Lieutenant-Commander Chong touched a small amulet, nephrite jade carved into a mandala. JB rolled his eyes; he was an old-fashioned atheist. But nor did he reach for the thing, Fifi noted. She had an aversion to the tub-thumping Christianity that had afflicted her childhood, but apart from that had never wasted much time worrying on such things. She had a child's faith in the Lord, and a lifelong conviction that He didn't bother meddling in the business of anyone so far beneath Him as her.

The Royal family—and the rest of the Holders—were Buddhists, which was common enough in Darwin, if not the rest of Capricornia. And Pete had always declared himself a Buddhist so lazy that he intended to pursue enlightenment when he got around to it in the next life . . . or three.

"I have to assume . . . very reluctantly . . . that the crocodile attacking the ships wasn't an accident," the Montivallan said gravely. "I have tried to think of some normal explanation for a five-ton carnivorous reptile engaging in a fight to the death with three armed ships. I cannot. Can anyone here?"

None of them spoke, or moved to touch the armband, and she noted the servant—sorry, the staffer—wore thick leather gloves entirely inappropriate for the local climate. The band seemed composed of some ruddy metal, probably aluminum-bronze cast from salvage. On it was a broad circle of some glossy black material, and inlaid on that was a three-armed triskele, with curved writhing arms coming from a central knot. The material was almost certainly fairly high-carat gold, but she thought she wouldn't have tried to pry it out even when she'd been working salvage herself, rather than running the largest salvage company with Warrants to the dead cities of the Australian coast. The impact of the bolt had scored right across it, for which she was obscurely glad.

"There's one good thing," Prince Thomas said thoughtfully. Everyone looked at him, and he went on: "It attacked the *Korean* ships. Which means our enchanted saltie isn't enchanted with Kim Il."

"A point, Your Highness," Russ said. "We also spoke with some local small craft, those long double-hulled things with the odd sail plan. . . ."

"Prau," Pete replied automatically. "Or proas."

"They hadn't seen the *Tarshish Queen*, or at least couldn't describe her—I was surprised that any of them spoke English at all."

The Capricornians all chuckled. "Lot of traffic through here," JB said. "We're the big entrepôt now. And our ships get all over. There's ships from the rest of Oz too, come to that, and the Kiwis. From New Singapore too, and they speak English . . . well, Singlish."

Russ nodded. "Ah, a lingua franca. They did say several ships of conventional pattern had passed through within the last few months; one of them was a three-master with a shark-mouth painted on the waterline—"

"Holy *shit!*" Fifi blurted; that was the *Silver Surfer*, Pip's ship.

"They were quite cooperative . . . well, they were looking at our broadside . . . until we showed them the crocodile's skull and the armband. Then they screamed—quite literally—something like *Pulau Bintang Hitam!*"

"And then *Pulau Satem!*" the other officer said.

"After they'd run around screeching and slapping one another for a while they hoisted their sails and made off southward as fast as they could, ignoring our hails," Russ finished.

"Ignoring a twenty-four-pounder warning from our bow-chaser, too," Chong added. "Just kept right on, still screaming and gibbering."

"*Pulau Bintang Hitam*," Pete said, and rolled his eyes up in thought.

They both had a nodding acquaintance with the many varieties of Malay current in the islands.

"Island of Black Stars," he translated.

"*Pulau Satem*," Fifi said. "That's . . . *Island of Devils*, sorta."

"Then we headed south," Russ said. "We'd taken storm damage back in Westria . . . California . . . we had no current charts of the area, and we were almost out of water."

"Battle damage also," Sir Boleslav said; he'd been punishing the beer as well as eating heroically, without noticeable effect, but a smoky look came into his eyes. "In San Francisco Bay we fought these Koreans, together with Haida devil-pirates and Eaters in league with them. At Topanga, we were ready to fight them again except for the enchanted storm. I have not taken my share of the blood due for the High King's murder. But I am young, there are years of the sword left to me yet."

Captain Russ nodded, his expression similar for a moment: "We headed for Darwin as the nearest friendly port where we could get quick repairs, and information in our own language."

Pete sighed. "We . . . the Darwin and East Indies Trading Company . . . do trade up that way. Some of the islands are civilized and you can do business; some are uncivilized and you can do business if you're heavily armed. Some are just . . . not visited much. A few months ago, our niece Pip . . . Lady Philippa Balwyn-Abercrombie, well, sort of an informal niece, the daughter of the co-founder of our company, Lady Julianna Balwyn-Abercrombie . . . she took a small barque up that way, the *Silver Surfer*. To try some of the places nobody else bothered—high risk, high reward."

Fifi was sure Captain Russ and Lieutenant-Commander Chong caught the fact that much wasn't being spoken.

"She's very badly overdue. We'd be happy to give you all our commercial intelligence on the area, and any help our agents there can furnish; supplies, too . . . perhaps a supply ship to go with you."

JB nodded. "The *Stormrider*'s being refitted in the Navy dockyards, triple shifts, double time for overtime. I'll be sending some of my blokes along when she leaves. Wish I could send a ship, but we haven't any to spare right now."

Not now that you turned up some expendable, heavily armed foreigners to do it for you, JB, she thought. *If you fell out the window dead-drunk into a shitheap, you'd come up smelling of hibiscus with a gold brick in your teeth.*

"We are sending a fast courier to Hawaii," JB added. "With dispatches and the *Stormrider*'s reports."

The discussion went on for some time.

"God, Pete, I wish we could go ourselves!" Fifi said as they left the Palace gates and climbed into their open-bodied coach; green-and-black butterflies with six-inch wingspans were fluttering around the lanterns.

"Pip will be fine," Pete said. "She's as crazy as we were, but smarter with it. And she's got her mum's lucky choppers."

They looked at each other again. *And look how many times we came within a thin hair of getting killed in spite of all that,* they both thought, and knew they shared the thought.

CHAPTER ELEVEN

"Oh, bugger, she's sinking," Lady Philippa Balwyn-Abercrombie said, lowering the telescope from her eye as she stood beside the wheel of the *Silver Surfer.* "That would be a bit disappointing."

She spoke in the precise clipped tones she'd learned from her mother, who'd graduated from Cheltenham Ladies College not long before being stranded off Queensland by the Blackout. Hers was a very ancient family in Britain, stretching back to William the Conqueror's time through a long line of barons, crusaders, Cavaliers, enclosers of commons, colonial plunderers, flint-hearted oppressors of the poor, honorary members of corporate boards and general ne'er-do-wells, and she was some sort of distant cousin of the current King-Emperor.

It was an accent that exuded arrogant self-confidence even to people who didn't know the background, and she found it useful in convincing herself too. Those dulcet syllables announced for all the world to hear that a thoroughly English God, Fate and the Natural Order of Things had a thumb firmly planted on your side of the scales and that resistance was useless.

Though from what Mummy said, she had to leave England one step ahead of the

court bailiffs when she was younger than I am now, after Granddad was caught out in
some financial roguery or another. I suppose they would have been glad enough to see
me in Winchester now, though. Like a bloody thoroughbred mare turning up, to help
with their dream of Deep England!

She'd avoided finding out by carrying on the family tradition: the grab for valuables, the inspired dive out the window and then running for the horizon herself, and now . . .

The strange ship running with all sail set into the harbor was moving far too sluggishly, given the amount of canvas on her three masts and the fine turn of her cutwater and flanks. And lying too low, with the water well above where her Plimsoll line would be if they had them where she came from. It would be a complete anticlimax if they slid beneath the surface now. Leaving nothing but survivors clinging to the mastheads by the time her ship, her variegated band of thirty bloodthirsty buccaneers, rogues, and quasi-reformed pirates and the hundred guardsmen lent by His Dithering Majesty Raja Dalem Seganing arrived to be slaughtered by the enraged Carcosans.

"Mebbe she's just heavy-laden, Pip," Toa said, in a voice like gravel shifting in a bucket.

"Not with her pumps going like that. We'll have to get between her and the Carcosan galleys. The Raja's trebuchets won't keep those off."

"Right, too many of them, small targets," Toa said.

They'd already seen that, since they arrived and found themselves on the Raja's side of the local feud willy-nilly. His artillery would keep the . . . big ship . . . from getting out into the middle of the harbor, but that was about it.

She looked up at the sails; everything was set, but the land-breeze was light, just enough to fill the beige manila canvas, and the deck was nearly as steady and level as a dinner table. The motion of the ship was almost completely smooth, leaving a low creamy wake from her sharp bows. The *Silver Surfer* was about as small as a three-master could be, two hundred and fifty tons of sleek speed and longshore versatility. Unfortunately, this was one of the occasions when something with oars or paddles had an advantage.

"Tally-ho! Helm, thus. Hands to sheets!"

She used her cane to point and saw the helmsmen spin the spokes in obedience, and bare feet thundered on the deck. She tapped one end of it on her hat to seat it more firmly and twirled it idly between her fingers. The speed gradually increased until it made a whir of cloven air. Then she released it to spin unsupported for an instant, and let one end smack into her right palm. It stung, but the show was worth it.

Kombagle at the wheel grinned like a shark at the sight, which was alarming given the boar's-tusk ornaments that curled up from his pierced nose and the vast mop of frizzy hair. The rest of the crew and the Raja's men were festooned with assorted cutlery and focused on their work, hauling on ropes to keep the sails precisely trimmed, giving the pintle-mounted prang-prangs a last check, or just crouched on the deck waiting, and giving kris and parang a last going-over with a hone. Or chewing betel . . . though the locals had at least grasped that they had to spit overside and not on her deck.

She *could* have gotten a Darwin & East Indies Trading Company crew, who'd never have dared to say boo to Pete and Fifi's honorary niece . . . but she'd preferred to find her own desperadoes, save for Toa. After she'd told them all where they were going and heard the cries of fear and rage, the two stupidest of the recruits she'd signed on before they left Darwin had taken her up on an offer of a blowie, five hundred in cash and a discharge to anyone who could shove her off the quarterdeck.

It had been a fine distraction to give the rest the chance to cheer and yell at one another as they laid side-bets, though Fool Number Two had to be pushed bodily forward by the rest after Imbecile Number One was dragged off screaming and trying to press his kneecap back together with bloodied hands. She hadn't specified any rules, except no edged weapons. Both would probably live, but not as sailors, since their legs would never work well enough again.

The rest had decided that the little rich girl should be taken seriously when she gave them an impassioned speech on how much they stood to make on shares. Drops of blood had flicked off the head of her cane as she stood on the edge of the poop deck looking down at their hungry upraised faces and waving it as a visual aid to the rhetoric.

Good advice on how to handle a lot like this, though, Mummy.

She flipped the cane again, upwards this time, and raised her hand to snap it out of the air without looking. It was of ireng wood, dense and immensely strong, an ebony the color of a moonless night sky, and just long enough to lean on with her hand down by her waist; there were grooved pear-shaped nobs on both ends cast from fourteen-carat gold, alloyed with silver and zinc, with a slogan cast into the metal in very small type: ***thus I refute him.*** The bowler-style hat had a low steel cap inside it. For the rest, on her mother's advice she preferred to rely on speed rather than armor and wore white cotton shorts and shirt, though there were steel toecaps on her strap-up sandals and knee and elbow pads adapted from her school's Extreme Field Hockey kit.

There were also two kukri knives hanging from the back of her belt with the handles jutting out conveniently to either side where she could whip both out simultaneously—her mother had taught her that trick too, and the knives were an inheritance. A variety of other useful and lethal devices were clipped to the belt and her suspenders, including a military slingshot with a forearm-brace and a bag of balls for it.

Everything ready, she thought. *Except . . .*

The greasepaint stick made a quick circle around her left eye, as close to mascara as she could get, and very like the striking image of some imaginary English hooligan she'd noticed in one of her mother's magazines long ago.

"So, how does that look?" she asked, blinking it at her second-in-command.

"Bloody silly, if you ask me," Toa said. "But there's no talking to you, any more than there was with your bloody mum, both of you always up yourselves, you Pākehā are like that."

"What, like *your* mum?" Pip said, and smiled, more a narrowing of the eyes than anything else.

"Half my mum, and anyway plain and simple's better than that makeup nonsense."

This time she snorted. Toa was very big—a full foot on her five-six— and very broad and very brown, including his stiff roach of hair drawn back through a bone ring, his eyes and his skin. That pleasant toasty-brown skin was extremely visible since he was wearing nothing but two feathers thrust into his topknot, a broad belt of patterned flax to hold his loincloth and knives, and a sort of short string apron before and behind. Almost all the rest of him was covered with a swirling pattern of tattoos including the ones that turned his otherwise amiable coarse-featured face into a thing of brutish menace when he scowled, which was doing now. The spear he was leaning on was seven feet of the same ireng as her cane with a great palm-broad steel head polished silver-bright that made another foot of height . . . which added to the effect.

"Run up a hoist, *coming to your assistance* and *conform to my movements*. And show them the Pickled Fish," she said.

A flag ran up the mizzen and broke out at the masthead above the colored signal pennants; a solid blue field with a white disk in the center and a fighting marlin picked out in blue in the circle, curled in an arching leap around a stylized crown. That was the compromise that had eventually been worked out, not without a little skirmishing, between the Colonelcy of Townsville and the Commonwealth of Cairns after both claimed the old Queensland state flag.

Or as I prefer to think of it, between the noble, enlightened, disciplined and civilized folk of Townsville and the brainless bogan horde of His Degenerate Idiocy Joh the Third, the you-know-what of Cairns.

She'd actually taken the banner from home, along with her mother's kukris from over the drawing-room fireplace. Usually it was run up the flagpole in front of the Station's main house every morning when the Balwyn-Abercrombies were in residence. She'd taken supplies and the six best long-range racing camels, too, but that had been strictly practical and she firmly intended to remit their sale price when she found the time.

And the money.

And when her father stopped mucking about with technicalities about her age and forwarded the shares in the Darwin & East India Trading Company she'd inherited from her mother.

I don't actually hate Daddy, whatever I said. He just monumentally *pissed me off. He's gotten utterly impossible since Mummy died. Grief, I suppose, but that's no excuse. I miss her too, but it hasn't driven me bonkers.*

Though considering where she was now, and that she could have been sitting on the verandah at Tanumgera Station drinking a cold G&T and watching the stationhands pretend to work . . .

Pip wasn't even angry now as she watched the Carcosan praus and galleys, and her mind reeled off distances and numbers as they grew from tiny dots to centipede-walking shapes against the blue-green water. The galleys were about as long as her ship, but much more lightly built, with an open framework between the hold and the deck. You could see the slaves heaving at the oars, and the marines waiting under a thicket of spearheads and long bamboo bowstaves, and the single heavy catapult crouching on its turntable in the bows.

Also the rows of skulls along the edge of the deck.

Before she'd encountered danger she'd wondered how it would take her; being the daughter of a legendary adventurer like her mother and granddaughter of the first Colonel of Townsville put a lot of pressure on you. Mostly she found there wasn't much time for actual fear, because she was too busy and too much depended on her. She suspected this would be much harder if she was just waiting rather than in charge. Her gaze flicked the hundred or so feet of the *Silver Surfer*'s deck, conscious of the looks she was getting.

The wind stirred her bobbed hair; it was tawny, since she took after her father in that respect. He'd also contributed her gray eyes and skin that took a sort of blond tan. The rest, the sharp features and wiry ferret quickness, were her mother's.

Now let's see what I am by myself, she thought. *Or possibly what I can convincingly put on for this bunch. Be what you want to seem, eh?*

Toa blew out his cheeks in relief. "Schooner's making for us," he said.

The big foreigner *was* heading towards them, which was essential . . . but rather slowly. Pip looked behind her; the shore was over a mile that way, though part of that was because this was nearly high tide and it was shallow water all the way. Good firm sand and gently sloping, though. So if the stranger was in danger of foundering, that would be the right place to beach her . . . though it was uncomfortably close to Carcosa and the causeway. On the other hand, as she'd discovered since her arrival months ago, everything in Baru Denpasar was far too close to Carcosa. Everything on this bloody island was, for that matter. It was also all far too close to Uncle Pete's preferred type of pre-Change adventure tales as well, which had mostly featured brawny Men with Swords and toadlike Things with Tentacles.

"There we go," Toa said quietly.

A faint *tung-whap* came over the water. Something arced out from the bows of the closest Carcosan galley, something barely visible. It landed about fifty yards short of the foreign schooner and a brief spout of white foam announced its kind.

"Roundshot," Toa said. "Tryin' to batter 'nd dismast her."

"They must really want that ship badly," Pip observed.

The schooner put her nose a little further north of west for an instant, and the hard cracking sounds of catapults echoed over the calm water in a single quick ripple. They would have a slight advantage, with the sun low in the west behind them and the target to the east. Pip raised the telescope again, and the foreign schooner leapt close—they were within a thousand yards now. Close enough to see her jerk in the water slightly under the savage recoil of the weapons. They were a little higher off the water and the range had closed. . . .

"Ten," Toa said, cocking his head. "Two heavies, bow and stern chasers, eight on the broadside."

"I'll take your word for it. Oh, jolly good show!"

"Roundshot back at 'em," Toa agreed.

The cast-steel balls had mostly struck the galley, which was prow-on to the schooner's broadside; two jets of foam showed misses. The iron TACK-*whinngggg* of high-velocity metal striking metal was clear as the galley's bow-piece was dismounted and pitched over on its side. The distance mercifully hid the precise consequences of the fragments scything through the packed ranks on the forecastle. Six more hammered into the galley's bow, punching ragged holes through the light planking or plunging through the gap between deck and hull.

The long sweeps instantly lost their mechanical unison. A few kept trying to stroke and fouled the ones that went limp. Others jerked upright; one flew out the side of the ship like a giant arrow as a roundshot shattered it in a freakishly precise way.

She winced slightly at the thought of what the high-speed weights of steel were doing as they bounced and ricocheted down that packed stinking darkness.

"You know, Toa, if I'd wanted to do this sort of thing for a living, I'd have joined the bloody Navy."

He grunted. "Too right. Just a bit of a risk, maybe a skirmish now and then, a big score and away again home, that's what you told me."

"And you believed me," she replied dryly, and they both chuckled.

"Believed your Mum, too," he said. "When I was no older than you are now."

"Exactly. So who's the fool there?"

Another broadside; three shots missed, though narrowly. Seven more smacked into the galley's quarterdeck in a group far too tightly placed to be accidental, sending the wheel up in a spray of splinters and leaving mangled flesh scattered across planks running red out the scuppers.

"Nice to know you're not trying to rescue incompetents," Pip said thoughtfully. "And forty-five seconds, that's very good practice with standard throwers. They must have a full crew to pump the jacks that fast."

The motionless galley began to list and go down by the bows; the remaining crew leapt overboard. There were fins in the water, but most of them would probably be picked up by the praus following, or even just swim to shallow enough water to stand up in. The rowers chained to the benches probably wouldn't, though a few were staggering up through the hatchways with broken fetters dangling from their ankles and following their masters into the water.

"Heavy metal for a trader, pricey stuff!" Toa said thoughtfully. "Not a warship, though. She'd have 'em on a gundeck below if she was. Merchantman-privateer, mebbe."

"Like us, but bigger," Pip confirmed.

The schooner turned back towards her. Pip focused on the name in black-and-gold letters beneath her sharp but figure-head-less prow:

"*Tarshish Queen*," she read. That brought her spyglass up to look at the gaff top again. "Blow a bit, little windie. . . . Yes, a Crowned Mountain and Sword, green and silver-white—Montivallans!"

That was interesting. She'd never actually met any, since there hadn't been any in Townsville lately, and none in Darwin on the times she'd gone along on one of her mother's visits. She'd heard a fair bit about the weirdly varied kingdom on North America's west coast, though. There was a house flag flying from the foremast, a stylized schooner soaring upwards. That prompted a memory of a visit to Darwin; it was recorded in the Company's books as a firm they did business with now and then.

"It'll be interesting to meet them," she said. "If they're not dead by then, of course."

"Never did much fancy conversations with deaders," Toa agreed. "One-sided. Straight-up dull."

Pip nodded. "We'll come due north of them, so we don't mask their broadside," she said, giving Kombagle the direction. "Then come about and hold station off their bow and rake the galleys and praus until they're safe and the Raja's boats arrive."

She cast an exasperated glance westward. "If they ever do!"

"Well, if they don't, we're most likely going to die," Toa said, with a sort of gloomy relish. "We'll have to mix it in then, unless we let the Pallid Mask take the ship an' her catapults."

She swung her telescope towards the delicate towers of the citadel of Carcosa for a moment. Was that a hint of tattered yellow robes in the tall twisted minaret?

"I think it's not just the Pallid Mask," she said quietly. "The *Raja Kuning* is watching himself."

"Three feet of water in the hold and gaining fast, Cap'n!" Radavindraban called, his head just out of the hatchway. "The pump crews cannot work down here very much longer, no indeed!"

"Keep them going as long as you can, Mr. Mate," Feldman called crisply, not taking his telescope from his eye. "It's a little crowded on deck and likely to be busy. Tell them help is on the way—I see a signal reading *coming to your assistance* on the Aussie."

He laughed, honestly and easily. "And *conform to our movements*. Not likely to do anything else, am I? Until our keel touches bottom, at least."

John shrugged his shoulder to settle the shield on its guige strap. The hot humid air made his skin feel still more swampy than usual beneath the plate and padding. He nodded to Fayard; the Protector's Guard crossbowmen were in their half-armor, waiting kneeling on the deck to stay out of the way until they could rise and shoot at close range. A few of them were telling their rosaries. One of them laid his crossbow on the planks as John watched, drew his sword and used a ceramic sharpening-stick for a moment, then sheathed it and went back to the port-arms position. They had come a long way from their home villages to die, but the stolid yokel faces were impassive, gleaming with sweat beneath the brows of the flared sallet helms.

I suppose if I end up in the drink, I'll be cool while I drown, he thought, as he walked down the line and gave each a hand on the shoulder and a word. *And the thing is, they really appreciate it. That and having me here and not looking afraid.*

"I wonder if there are fountains in Purgatory?" he said aloud. "Nice cool fountains with shady arbors?"

Privately he doubted it. His mother had had a vision of *her* father in

Purgatory while she was at the Kingmaking at Lost Lake, and while his fate there hadn't been torture, it had been a hard penance for his deeds.

I hope I'm not as great a sinner as Grandfather was. On the other hand, only God knows that one for sure. And at that, Grandfather was shriven just before he died. He must have made an honest confession, too. God's forgiveness is infinite, or he'd be roasting.

Thora was beside him. "Cooler still in Hella's hall," she said, and they grinned at each other.

Deor had the nose-guarded, boar-crested helm of his folk pushed back on his head, and the raven shield of Hraefnbeorg on his arm. His other hand whipped his Saxon broadsword in a figure-eight to loosen his wrist. As he did he chanted, a deep rolling poetry that worked by a wave-like rhythm in each stanza:

"Næs hie ðære fylle gefean hæfdon,
manfordædlan, þæt hie me þegon—"

Then he repeated it in the modern tongue:

Those fell creatures—shall have no fill
Of rejoicing—that they consume me,
Assembled at feast—at the sea bottom
But in the morning—wounded by blades
They will lie on the shore—put to sleep by swords
So that never after—will they hinder sailors
In their course on the sea.
The light from the east,
Bright beacon of Woden!

John let the words roll through him; they were oddly soothing.

Not exactly calm, he thought. *But as calm as can be expected! Father, I'm your son . . . and Mother, if I can't spare you more grief, at least I won't make you ashamed.*

There were six of the galleys, not counting the one they'd just battered into a hulk; all of them had slowed down to come on in a line, bypassing their sinking friend. None of them had masts up or sails set, but they did have poles for their flags, and the prahus behind them had their odd upside-down triangular sails deployed. Banners and sails alike bore the same image, a yellow disk with a mask on it in white—the sketched outline of an oval face, features barely suggested, but the elongated eyes blankly golden and a dot he couldn't make out between the brows.

"Catapults, we'll start on the bow of the third galley from the left!" Feldman called crisply. "One broadside per ship, on my command!"

John realized it was slightly larger than the others; possibly that meant it was a flagship. And much more sensible than trying to hit them all. *Captain Feldman isn't just smart, he's smart when people around him are losing their heads—literally.*

There was a saying both his parents were fond of, that trying to be strong everywhere meant you were weak everywhere. He'd *understood* it, but it was only now that he realized just how powerful the temptation to try to cover everything could be, as the impulse to scream *sink them all, now now now!* washed through him.

The bow-chaser gave its massive *whack-tunng* and the others followed at intervals of about a second, he could feel the deck heel backward a little under his feet amid the deafening giant's-anvil chorus. He wasn't nervous about the way the slides of the catapults pistoned backward as they cut loose, part-cocking the mechanism. He'd been around war-machines all his life, but it was different somehow now that they were throwing real metal at real people, not earthen mounds or piles of bailed hay.

Like the thought going through his head, something visible only as a blurred streak went by. It was four feet over his helmet, but he could feel the wind of its passage on his sweating face, and he was already ducking when a massive crunching *CRACK* sound as the roundshot hit the boom of the mizzen mainsail. The six-inch thickness of Sitka spruce leapt and vibrated all along the lower edge of the sail and then cracked where the steel had gouged it and the leverage of wind and sail still bent it like a bow. Splinters flew; one foot-long wooden spear took the Bosun in midstride, lancing through her thigh. Ruan pounced, whipping out a spare bowstring to use as a tourniquet, then dusting antiseptic and bandaging and administering a syringe of morphine. Two other crewfolk dragged the semiconscious form over to where the ship's doctor was frantically busy with patients brought up from the half-flooded lazarette and the steady trickle of gruesome casualities from the enemy projectiles and the splinters and whip-cracking rope-ends they produced.

John suppressed an impulse to lower his visor—a nine- or ten-pound ball of steel like that would just take his head off if it hit him, helm and all—but promptly went to one knee, which put all of him below the fourfoot height of the bulwarks if he ducked a little, and the others did likewise. If it was good enough for Fayard and the crossbowmen, it was good enough for him, and there was nothing to do—the catapults all had a full set of hands on their cocking pumps, and what the rest of what the crew did was skilled teamwork with no room for outsiders.

I can pray a bit, he thought, and did. To St. Michael, for courage and strength; and then to God.

Give my people victory, O Lord, and rescue them from the fury of their enemies. Let me be their shield, as is the duty laid upon me by You at my birth.

He disliked that, sometimes, and God certainly knew that, but like or dislike didn't really matter if you *did* it. Though complaining about it was comforting now and then. He could do that with Órlaith; Mother got . . . stroppy about it. He forced his mind to concentrate on the prayer again:

Yet let Thy will be done, not mine, and give me that which is best for me, though it be that which I most fear.

"Amen," he murmured, kissed the crucifix and tucked it away.

The *Tarshish Queen's* broadside cut loose again, and he popped his head up. The galleys were shockingly close now, close enough that he could see the bunched roundshot hammer into the bows of another, planks shattering in a cloud of splinters. This time it didn't dismount the catapult, but all ten shot hit between deck and waterline. The stempost broke, a broad gap opened in the bows, and the forward motion of the long sweeps immediately rammed a huge slug of water into the oar-deck. They were only a few hundred yards away now, and he could clearly hear the screaming as the sea swept in and the long slender hull reared up at the stern and slid slowly downward.

And I think they're chained in there, he thought.

That made him feel strange, as if his stomach was running a fever and the back of his neck was hot and cold at once. His father had once told him that in every battle in the Prophet's War he'd felt sick to his stomach for a little while, thinking of all the men on the other side who'd just been levied from their homes and farms, serving evil unwillingly, often enough simply thinking they were defending their households and kin. It had seemed a little fanciful then, and not all like a *chanson*. At least those had been enemies with weapons in their hands. The rowers on those galleys hadn't just been levied, they'd been abducted and then shackled to be parts in an engine. Now they were dying in the dark, terrified and despairing.

He was almost glad for the interruption when a roundshot struck the bulwark not far from his head. The timber cracked, and pieces and splinters scythed across the deck. One struck his shield with a sharp slapping sound, driving him back on his heel as if it had been a war-hammer. Another tinged off his helmet, wrenching at his neck. That turned his gaze just enough to see a sailor leaping for a severed rope hit by another of the steel balls, and *shatter* in a cloud of pink mist.

His name had been Brian—John had recognized the twin-raven tattoo on his back—and he came from Boise, wandering westward to the coast because he wanted to see the world and because he was fourth child on a farm none too large, and he'd been saving to buy his own fishing smack and settle down. He had a fiancée in Newport, too.

Parts thumped down wetly. Other sailors grabbed the body . . . the main chunks . . . and pitched them over the side to clear a passage. More of them ran into the rigging with their knives in their teeth as shot whistled through and heavy rigging-lines parted with sounds like giant unturned lutes popping a string.

"One more broadside on the northernmost galley!" Feldman called, cutting through the clangor with his speaking-trumpet. "Then load canister!"

That meant tubes full of palm-length finned darts. The tube stopped at the end of the catapult's throwing-trough, and the darts went on like a spreading cloud of lethal wasps. It was a short-range weapon, just not quite as short-range as grapeshot. Feldman didn't think the catapults were going to stop all the galleys, and if they didn't they'd get boarders over the rail and stop the sailors tending the lines, and then the ship would stop. And the question would be if they sank first or were overrun.

Thora hadn't been looking at the approaching galleys or the praus behind them. She hissed, staring *northward*.

"That Aussie ship is close," she said. "Very close, boring right in. They've got guts, by almighty Thor!"

John nodded, hopefully coolly, and looked that way himself, over the *Queen's* bow. The smaller ship was bowsprit-on to them, green water purling back around the shark-mouth painted at her waterline, as if the savage teeth had foam on them. There were a surprising number of warriors on board, mostly squatting with only their heads and the shafts of spears showing. There were weapons along the side too, catapults of some sort, light things about the size of a man lying down, set on pintle mounts, the sloped steel shields on either side of the throwing-trough concealing any details.

"Nice to know we won't die alone," Thora said cheerfully, and Deor thumped her on the back of her lobster-tail helmet with the edge of his shield.

"When you get a dinner invitation from the High One, you say . . ."

". . . perhaps another day?" Thora answered, and they both laughed.

John joined in the chuckle. He felt warmed by it and a little excluded at the same time.

"Your Highness!" Feldman's voice came, still brisk and taut. "You and your party to the bows, please. They'll be coming over the starboard foc'sle."

In a slightly different tone: "And the hand of the Lord of Hosts be with you and shelter you, my Prince."

John flushed again. Once past his first childhood, he'd spent a good deal of his life wondering about the motives of people who tried to be friendly, even though his parents were harsh on flatterers and would-be sycophants and had the Sword to read the truth of men's words. Now he was in a situation where he was *feeling* somehow genuinely flattered simply to receive respect.

They went forward in an almost-duckwalk to keep their heads below the bulwark. More roundshot went by overhead, or twice thumped into the thick wood with crunching sounds. Thora cast an experienced eye upward.

"They're shooting for our rigging and masts," she said. "Trying to cripple us so they can board at leisure."

Ruan joined them, longbow in hand, and snuck a glance over the bulwark. "Close enough for bow work soon," he said, his voice tight.

Deor put a hand on his shoulder. "All men fear, in battle," he said gently. "Even if Victory-Father lifts their hearts."

"I'm not afraid!" the young man blurted. Then: "Well, yes, by the Threefold Morrigú, I am! But it's not that, mostly."

A hesitation: "The last time I went into battle with a lover . . . I lost him."

Deor hugged him for a moment and kissed him gently. "I've been in many a fight, dear heart. It's not my proper trade—"

Thora snorted and rolled her eyes.

"—but I've done it full often. It's part of life. And I'm not feasting with Woden yet! The more often you walk away from this table, the less likely you are to be carried off, like any other skill."

Unspoken went the command: *so don't you die on me now!*

Ruan's face went from pale to flushed to almost normal in a few heartbeats, as the hard clang of the bow-chaser overrode speech and thought for an instant. Thora took a more direct approach.

"Care to try a few shafts?" she said. "I'd like to see how this new bow does at real work."

She was wearing a quiver slung over her armored back, and the scabbard designed for a saddlebow and usually buckled before a rider's right knee. She pulled the weapon out as she spoke. Most of the short, powerful killing tools used from horseback were built up of layers of horn, sinew and wood glued together and then lacquered and varnished against the wet, but this was one she'd acquired recently.

The *bnei Yaakov* of the Mojave Desert they'd met and allied with on their way to the cursed castle in the Valley of Death had a different solution to the same technical challenge of making a bow with a long powerful draw short enough to use mounted. They took the great scimitar-shaped horns of the dryland antelope known as *gemsbok*, trimmed them, softened them by steam, then put them in a set of sinuous clamps in the hard dry heat of the desert to set in the double-curve shape. The riser joining them was carved from mesquite root, immensely hard and durable, and the whole was just about as waterproof as simple staves of varnished yew. Ruan looked at it with interest. The Clan Mackenzie were a people of the bow, whatever else they did.

"What's the draw?" he asked.

"Eight-five," she said, waggling a thumb to show she hadn't had the time to put it on a tillering frame to check, and meant more-or-less. "Yours?"

"A hundred and three," Ruan said; he was a slender young man, but had the broad shoulders, thick wrists and corded arms that came of training to the longbow all your life. "Broadheads?"

"Didn't see much armor," Thora agreed. "Just some helmets and shields. Let's take the catapult crew on the nearest galley . . . you left, me right."

They pulled shafts from their quivers and set them through the centerline cutouts in the risers of their bows and the nocks to the string. The triangular heads glittered a little ruddy along their razor-honed edges, with the lowering sunlight from the west catching on metal from salvaged stainless-steel spoons hammered and cut to a vicious point.

"On the count," Thora said; they'd both pop up at the same time to spread the risk. "One . . . two . . . *three!*"

They both came smoothly to their feet, drew, shot upward at forty degrees and crouched again in a single movement without pausing to aim; aiming was for beginners and amateurs. Ruan was a little grim but steady; Thora was grinning broadly.

She doesn't enjoy killing, John thought. *But she does enjoy fighting and the killing doesn't bother her much as long as it's armed fighters trying to kill her. Which is a sensible attitude but it isn't the way it hits me. Or Deor, come to that.*

Shrieks of rage came from the galley, faint but audible even over the two-hundred-odd yards of distance and through the clamor of battle.

"In the eye?" she chaffed. "Showing away, Ruan! That's a field-day shot at this distance, and it can jam in the bone with a broadhead. For the center of the chest, that's the mark when you're doing real work."

He shook his head, relaxing a little. "I *was* trying for his chest," he said. "The eye was what I *hit* when he looked up at the sound. *You* hit exactly what you wanted."

"That's a Mackenzie for you, acting thunderstruck when someone else knows how to shoot," she said easily. "Let's displace and try again."

They duckwalked a few feet and popped up again. John turned to Fayard. The underofficer nodded, signed to his men, and they rose kneeling above the bulwark, leveled their crossbows, shot and ducked down to pump the levers in the forestock, came back up, shot. . . .

John chanced a look himself. The remaining galleys were shockingly close now, only a little over two hundred yards. Several of them looked battered and one was listing, but they were still coming. Men were raising tall bows from their decks, unencumbered by masts or rigging, and the first flight of arrows fell only a few yards short of the *Tarshish Queen,* dimpling the water like a sudden flurry of very hard rain. It went on for quite some time because the four remaining galleys were still twenty yards or so apart and the shooting wasn't quite in unison. But there were a lot of arrows, and that meant—

"Down!" he shouted.

Everyone who could ducked or rolled into the shadow of the slight inward tumblehome of the bulwarks, or both; Thora and Deor put their round shields up over Ruan where the three knelt together, and John raised his kite-shield and put his shoulder under the curve, knocking his visor down as he did. That left nothing but the vision-slit vulnerable, which meant that only sheer bad luck could kill him. He didn't think any local archers were a menace to one of the finest suits of plate in Montival, and they certainly weren't going to get through the shield.

The arrows sleeted down, mostly standing quivering in the deck or impaling ropes. Some struck flesh.

He looked back at the quarterdeck, and his blood froze for a moment until he saw Captain Feldman stand again; he had an arrow through the fleshy part of his left arm, but he was still shouting orders briskly. The ship's healer dashed up, examined it, snipped the shaft across with a pair of odd-looking clippers evidently intended for just that, pulled the stub through, slapped on a dressing and jumped back to his station on the main deck in a single flurry of movement. One of the crossbowmen pitched backward with an arrow sunk through the bridge of his nose, thrashing like a pithed frog until he went limp, and John felt a brief flash of guilt that he couldn't remember his name until he imagined the written roster and *Bors* came to his mind.

"Fire canister!"

The sound of the catapults discharging had a whining bee-like undertone now. John raised his head to look, the narrow slit in his visor focusing his gaze. An arrow shattered as it struck the brow of his helmet, knocking his head backward like a punch with a grunt of shock and pain. He still saw the massed darts sweep across the decks, hundreds of them, and wished he hadn't. You couldn't really *see* them, not moving so fast that they were barely streaks, but you could see where they hit—red splashed, and the sheer impact of a tenth of a pound of steel traveling at hundreds of feet per second made men flex like whips when they struck. Some killed three men in a row.

The sound of them striking the decks and hulls was like hail on a shake roof. Except that the roofs didn't scream.

"Load grapeshot!" Feldman shouted. Then as he swept out his cutlass: "Lash the wheel! *Here they come!*"

The last of the sailors aloft thumped down on deck, wounded or fill-ing in the gaps in the catapult crews. Save for a brace at the maintops with telescope-sighted crossbows, who were carefully and methodically tar-geting anyone who looked like an officer.

The killing machines shot one last time, and the crews snatched up boarding axes and half-pikes and cutlasses. The sound was different, a great *shrrrusshh* as the steel ball-bearings cut the air and then almost immediately a hail-patter as they struck. Or a sound very much like a ball-peen hammer in the hand of a maniac hitting a dead chicken.

Fayard and his remaining men were shooting stolidly at the Guard's steady bolt every six seconds.

"Into the brown!" the underofficer yelled as he worked his own weapon. "You can't miss, just fucking *shoot* and shoot fast!"

Ruan and Thora where drawing and loosing continuously now. The darts and grapeshot sweeping the enemy decks had broken their massed volleys of arrows, but the long bamboo shafts were coming over in a sustained flicker. Two hit the Montivallan archers in the chest almost simultaneously; they both took a step back and grunted. The one striking Thora's articulated breastplate shattered; the other hung for a second in young Ruan's brigandine, stopped by the little steel plates riveted between the twin thicknesses of leather.

John could see the young man—he was a little older but John *felt* more mature—turn red and gulp for wind. Then he forced himself back into action by sheer willpower, doubtless feeling as if he'd been punched in the gut.

Time, the Prince of Montival thought, and surged erect with his shield up. His sword flared free, up in the knight's position, hilt-forward above his head. It was simple steel, and he was simply a man, one who would have been a musician first if his fate had been otherwise. But he would *do* what he could.

"Haro, Portland!" he shouted, his voice hollow from within the helm and visor and bevor. *"Holy Mary for Portland!"*

CHAPTER TWELVE

"Shoot!" Pip called.

They'd crossed the bow of the new ship and lay broadside-on to the galleys attacking under the banner of the Pallid Mask.

She grimaced a little. Nobody knew exactly what the Pallid Mask was, except that he, or possibly *it*, worked for the Yellow Raja—prisoners from the Carcosan side of the harbor had called him the *fore-bringer* or the *emissary*. Sometimes before biting their own tongues off and inhaling the blood. There were also rumors that the Mask actually *was* the Yellow King, somehow.

But he's not invincible. Here's evidence of that!

Even then she blinked in astonishment at the sheer amount of damage the Montivallan broadsides had wrought, ships sinking or turning turtle, bodies thick in water turned red, glutted sharks striking over and over again in a frenzy. The three survivors were boring in though, the long boarding gangways rising up and ready to topple over on the foreign ship and their oars backing water to avoid a hull-crushing impact.

And all I wanted to do was make a really smashing deal in nutmeg and mordant and show Daddy I wasn't born to be a deb in Winchester. And live up to Mummy's legend, she thought. *Well, I may manage that, perhaps! Because here I'm marooned on an island that has a genuine Eldritch Horror running half of it and turning people into . . . things that aren't really people.*

Then aloud, loud but carefully not screeching:

"Maximum fire!"

Her prang-prangs opened up. They were basically huge crossbows with a set of leaf-springs at the front like a massive bowstave, but the devil was in the details and the engineers of Townsville Armory had come up with something quite devilish. Each had a simple hydraulic cocking mechanism that pulled a traveler back against the half-ton resistance of the springs and then released it if the triggers were held down. A hopper above fed six-inch steel darts machine-cut from rebar, given a crude point and spiral grooving to make it spin and provide some stability, letting one drop into the slot each time the traveler came back.

The power was provided by pairs of men sitting on the deck to either side of the weapon below the level of the bulwark, the soles of their feet against each other and their hands on the bars of a rocking pump as they surged back and forth. Prang-prangs didn't have the range or ship-killing battering power of conventional catapults. What they did have was speed.

Prang. Prang. Prang—

The whole cycle took about as long as it took to say *one hundred and one.* Sixty darts a minute or a little better, and there were four of the prang-prangs able to bear, each with two men slapping new bundles of darts into the hoppers.

A ripple of pointed steel rods sprayed towards the Yellow Raja's ships . . . and his men . . . at the rate of four or five a second, into the boarding parties packed ready to swarm forward. Most of them were naked except for loincloths or sarongs. A few carried hide shields and rather more wore helmets; even fewer had torso armor of steel plates joined together by patches of chain mail. None of that had the slightest effect when the darts struck except to produce a spark and *ping* sound on impact, and the *Silver Surfer*'s weapons were aimed across the front of the formation, if you could call the three crowded mob-blobs that. Military types called it defilade fire; basically it meant targets in depth, so that if a bolt missed one man it was much more likely to hit another.

The wind was pushing them towards their enemies broadside-on, as the boarding ramps fell and locked the whole mass together in the shark-swarming sea. When her ship touched, the fight would be at knife-length.

Toa jumped down from the quarterdeck and gave a huge guttural cry as the deck boomed beneath his weight:

> *"Ke ma-te! Ke ma-te!*
> *It is death! It is death!*
> *Ka-ora! Ka-ora!*
> *I may live! I may live!"*

He danced as he sang, astonishingly agile on the crowded deck—not simply agile for a man of his size, but moving through the packed space like a ghost, the huge muscles rippling beneath his tattoos like mating pythons in a jungle. Stamping straddle-legged, kneeling, springing back into the air, his tattooed face a horror of lolling tongue and glaring rolling eyes as he whirled the great spear about himself or held it out rigid and trembling as he slapped chest and thighs and belly and screamed rhythmically in the tongue of his ancestors:

> *"This is the hairy man*
> *Who brought the sun and made it shine!*
> *It is death! It is death!"*

The crew of the *Silver Surfer* looked at him with a mixture of fear and respect—not much of a difference, with most of the sort willing to ship on a venture like this. The Raja's soldiers had no idea what was going on, but they knew Toa wasn't in the least afraid of the Pallid Mask—you'd have to be a lizard or dead not to hear the brutal strength and arrogant menace in the war-haka.

Certainly when Toa does it. Mummy said she nearly wet herself, that time they first heard it outside the ruins of Auckland.

Pip looked quickly westward. The wind was from the south, favoring neither side, and the Raja's boats were straggling towards her in no particular order. That would get *some* of them here before the more disciplined Carcosans arrived en masse. It would be very close. . . .

"Ready, all!" she called.

Prang-prang-prang . . .

CHAPTER THIRTEEN

BARONY HARFANG
COUNTY OF CAMPSCAPELL
(FORMERLY EASTERN WASHINGTON STATE)
HIGH KINGDOM OF MONTIVAL
(FORMERLY WESTERN NORTH AMERICA)
SEPTEMBER 20TH
CHANGE YEAR 46/2044 AD

"Oh, stop *smiling* like that," Órlaith said, half-serious in her irritation.

Heuradys extended her face forward, slitted her eyes and smiled again, this time in self-caricature as if she were a cat basking in the mellow golden afternoon sunlight of a long autumn day.

The Harris's hawk on her gauntlet bated slightly, extending its wings and turning its hooded head with an air of *what-are-you-doing?* The courser she was riding shifted slightly too.

Órlaith felt the talons of her own hawk tighten through the thick supple leather of the gauntlet.

"Looks aren't everything," she replied. "And pay attention to your hawk. Macmac, *stay.*"

The weather had broken; it was fall now, days in the seventies, nights crisp. The first rains had fallen, harbinger of the wet months of winter, and a ghost of green went over the yellow-brown hills around them. It was perfectly comfortable, even warm with a coat, but you could *smell* the cold coming somehow. An odor like damp leaves and the taste of spring-water. Macmacon sat obediently, his eyes on the brush and his nose wrinkling. The breeze was from their backs, which wouldn't matter much since the quarry they were after were birds and didn't have a sense of scent to speak of.

"Looks *aren't* everything," Heuradys said. "But combined with charm and wit and being a good dancer and having a nice sense of humor . . . then good cheekbones and shoulders and a nice tight butt don't hurt at all. Help quite a bit, in fact."

"Oh, that's right, rub it in," Órlaith said gloomily.

Dust smoked off the fields southward, tiny plumes in the distance. Teams of big draught horses were drawing the three-furrow riding plows and disk-harrows and seed-drills along the curving contour-strips, turning under the previous year's close-mown alfalfa or sweet clover to plant the winter wheat and barley; the massive and costly equipment was owned jointly with the demesne and used on each peasant's strips in turns drawn by lot. Birds followed the plowmen, attracted by the insects thrown up— or the seed grain in other spots, but children with slingshots and noise-makers deterred them there, as well as scarecrows. It was hard work, but not quite the round-the-clock scramble of harvest, since the planting would go on for a month yet.

Heuradys sent her an apologetic glance. "Sorry, Orrey. I tease too much sometimes."

"That you do, and I your liege, the black shame and disgrace of the world it is."

The hunting-party were well outside the fenced and hedged inner core of the manor, though this area was part of the stinted commons and regularly grazed. A long snaking swale ran between the hills, and a generation ago horse-drawn scrapers had shaped the light soil to turn it into a series of earth dams and ponds; ponds for about two thirds of the year, and thicker patches of green grass and reeds the rest, and some water was showing through the vegetation now from last night's rain, like little glints of silver in moving green. Willow-trees and cottonwoods lined it, dense with bushy undergrowth of black hawthorn, wild rose, wax currant and bright-crimson smooth sumac and more, with purple-flowered thistle tight beneath. It was designed to provide food and shelter for game, among other things.

"It helps not being Crown Princess, too," Órlaith said a bit sourly.

She was trying not to let it spoil a lovely day.

"Even a roll in the hay is political for me, much less anything serious. Oh, Anwyn take it."

Ironically, it would have been easier if Alan Thurston *wasn't* born to a family of high estate, except that then she'd have been unlikely to find him as attractive. It wouldn't matter and she wouldn't care in many places, but here in the Association territories she'd never liked dalliance with people far down the pole of rank; it gave her an odd and disagreeable feeling, no matter how enthusiastic they were.

That had never bothered Heuradys, but then she was an Associate. And Sir Droyn had begged off the hunt today. Officially he was indisposed; unofficially it was a girl, she thought. The tall, handsome, dashing and well-spoken young son of a Count back from a fabulous adventure of magic and battle at the side of the Crown Princess (who had knighted him personally with the Sword of the Lady) wasn't likely to lack for company.

"That does suck, Orrey," Heuradys said sympathetically. "Not fair at all."

"I can't ask you to be like a Christian nun just because of that," Órlaith sighed. "It wouldn't help me, now would it?"

Heuradys winced. "Look, he's going to be gone in a day or two anyway—"

Then Órlaith cut in sharply: "There!"

The Mackenzies and their greathounds were working the brush towards them, and not making much noise about it save now and then a happy *yuuurrp* from a greathound making close acquaintance with a rabbit. Songbirds rose, yellow-breasted meadowlarks and goldfinches complaining liquidly, bluebirds and many more. Those weren't proper prey;

unless they were a threat to people or crops most Montivallans didn't kill animals that weren't eaten, or at least found useful for fur and hides. The reasons given for that differed from place to place—Órlaith thought of it as not angering Lady Flidais and the Horned Lord—but the attitude was fairly general.

Then something flickered along the edge of the scrub, amid a patch of yellow tansy.

"There!" Órlaith said softly, feeling that hot focus that was the hunter's mind take over, and feeling much better for it. "Fine fat gobblers, to be sure!"

The wild turkeys broke cover and came scuttling out, ready to take to the air—they weren't great fliers, but they could get off the ground. These were the yellow-legged variety, young males plump with rich autumn feeding on stubble and among the berry-bushes.

"No need to take turns! All at once, then!" Órlaith called to her companions, and raised her right fist in its gauntlet.

The hawk gave its harsh, prolonged, almost whistling *irrrrr-irrrrr* call in earnest this time, hungrily certain that she was about to be flown at quarry. That was answered by the others, on Heuradys' wrist and the gauntlets of Morfind and Faramir. They were all female Harris's hawks, and hers was a big one of about three and a half pounds, two feet long and well over forty inches of wingspan. They were handsome birds with golden legs, dark-brown plumage that shaded to chestnut-red on the shoulders and with white at the tip and base of their tails.

Susan Clever Raccoon had her bow out instead, and besides his recurve Alan had a hunting spear in a tube scabbard on his saddle just in case something bigger than a turkey showed up. Everybody except a few townsmen or clerics hunted, for the pot and sport and to keep the animals off the farms, but Boisean ranchers rarely practiced falconry. Probably that was because it had been so linked to the Protectorate gentry in the old days, but the habit stuck. And it was one of the Mongol customs that Ulagan Chinua *hadn't* been able to get his adopted people to take up.

More of the turkeys flushed, and their attention was all behind them, which ought to overcome their impulse to head into cover for a few crucial instants at least. Órlaith reached across and gently removed the hawk's hood. Its head whipped around to follow the turkeys in a moment of utter focus, and the wind of its first strong wingbeat buffeted her face as she pushed up sharply—*letting slip*, in the jargon of falconry. It felt more like throwing a living thunderbolt.

Órlaith's bird overflew the turkeys and came in behind them with a loud raucous cry, and they swayed away from her like tall grass before a wind. The other three hawks spread out smoothly, their wings beating to give them extra speed as they swooped down the slope in curves as graceful as an arrow's flight, if an arrow had had a mind of its own. Most raptors hunted as individuals; Harris's hawks were more like wolves of the air, intelligent social beasts who cooperated by instinct. Working with humans came easily for them, and they were even affectionate to their handlers.

A mews-bred group like this reared and trained together acted with the killing unison of a pod of orcas closing in on tunny.

The turkeys panicked, churned about on the ground and in the air, then exploded outward in a starburst with a chorus of frantic *cuk-cuk-cuk-cuk* sounds. The hawks closed in, flared up and then folded their wings and plunged downward in near unison. There were a series of heavy thumps as they struck their prey in flight with stunning force, bound and tumbled to the ground below.

The turkeys were twenty pounds or better, at the upper limit of size for a Harris to take. One managed to break free in a shower of tailfeathers and the hawk twisted in a complete loop to dive and drive its talons into another, quick and deadly and remorseless as a wasp.

"Now that was beautiful," Órlaith said as she clucked and tightened her legs to put her horse moving.

"And Mom Two says Harris's hawks aren't really falconry!" Heuradys agreed. "I call that Puritanical Peregrine Purism."

The hunt servant walked from bird to bird snapping necks to put the creatures out of pain, then opened them to drain and removed hearts and other morsels for the estate falconer. That highly-regarded expert swung his lure to bring the hawks in, hooded them and put them on the perches—crossbars on sticks driven into the ground—and went from one to the other feeding them from his hand while he smiled fondly at his charges and crooned soft words.

Órlaith swung down, pulled off her gauntlet, put a finger to the blood and marked her forehead, then took a clod of earth and touched it to her lips. To live was to kill, for human-kind as much as the wolves. But to kill was to acknowledge your own mortality, the Mystery which all who breathed on the ridge of the world were ultimately initiates, whether human-kind or the other Kindreds. Then she murmured the prayer that started by thanking the prey for their gift of life and ended:

"Lord Cernunnos, Horned Master of the Beasts, witness that we take of Your bounty from need, not wantonness, knowing that to us also the Hour of the Hunter comes at last. For Earth must be fed, and we but borrow our bodies from Her for a little while."

Morfind and her cousin put hand to heart and faced the west to thank Oromë the Huntsman, and Heuradys spilled a libation from her canteen and softly invoked Artemis:

". . . fleet archer, deer-shooting Goddess, O You of the Golden Bow . . ."

"When Mathun and the others join up, let's camp," Órlaith suggested. "Looks like it'll be a clear night, and there's nothing better than turkey roasted over a campfire."

The call of the horn sounded just as she was putting her foot into the stirrup. She looked up sharply; it was a Mackenzie horn, which meant it must be Mathun's, and it was using the simple three-note pattern.

Alarm, alarm, danger. Alarm, alarm, danger . . .

She continued the motion of swinging into the saddle, on the theory that whatever the danger was it would probably be easier to deal with on horseback.

Her right foot was just reaching for that stirrup when the tigers broke cover. Behind them came the frantic voices of the Mackenzies and the snarling brabble of the greathounds. There were two of the beasts, both young but adult males—unusual among the generally solitary predators, but not entirely unknown. Then the wind shifted, just as one of the animals gave a racking snarl. Her courser was a good-natured beast, but it wasn't one she'd worked with for years and there were limits to what you could expect of horse-kind. It *knew* that was the sound and smell of something that wanted to eat it, and it reared, came down with a jarring thump that slammed her teeth together hard, bucked, twisted, kicked its heels high in the air in squealing panic, and bolted as she came loose.

Órlaith felt a moment's gratitude as her left foot came free of the stirrup rather than twisting in it and dragging her behind the horse, and then the ground came up and hit her like a war-hammer. She'd been curling in the air automatically, with a lifetime's training in how to fall, but it still knocked the wind out of her, and the pommel of the Sword thumped her under the left armpit with savage force and her head rang as the metallic-salt taste of blood flooded her mouth. The Lady's gift wouldn't cut a member of House Artos—she could run her hand down the preternaturally sharp blade as if it were a wooden ruler—but it remained a physical object. More or less.

"*Streak!*" someone shouted, the hunter's call for more than one of the big cats. "'Ware streak!"

Wheezing on the ground, Órlaith had an excellent view of the two animals as they slunk into the open.

Objectively considered they were beautiful, pale red-brown shapes covered in narrow black stripes, shading to cream on their necks and bellies, moving with a grace like water from a fountain. She'd read somewhere in her studies—probably at the university in Corvallis, the course called *Post-Change Ecological Transitions*—that most of the tigers in the world on the day of the Change had been on this continent, essentially kept as pets or trophies by people with more resources than sense. Thousands had escaped or been released, and enough had survived and adapted and bred very rapidly that they were ubiquitous everywhere except the treeless parts of the Great Plains and the deserts of the south, where lions were doing likewise a bit more slowly. Their ancestors had been a mélange of every sub-breed, but the genes of the Siberians among them had prevailed a little more each year, being better adapted to a climate with cold winters.

Unfortunately the first generation had survived mainly by eating humans, a habit never entirely lost even after other game became common again, and *Siberian* meant *big*.

This pair were just under four feet at the shoulder and weighed as much as a smallish pony or three large men each. Seen from ground level as they came rapidly forward they looked even bigger, their massive wedge-shaped heads low, bellies to the ground and tails lashing. One snarled, and she had an excellent view of the inches of white fang and the pink-and-crimson gape of the mouth.

Órlaith managed to take a quick glance to either side. Her friends were spread out in exactly the wrong way—a semicircle so the tigers couldn't get past without charging directly at a human; and with the best of motives the Mackenzies were keeping up their shouts and horn-blowing and crashing through the brush as they came on at speed, ensuring that the animals wouldn't be turning back.

Órlaith managed to suck in a whooping breath and started to shout *everyone together!*

The tigers were running from a threat, not hunting. They wouldn't try to hunt an alert group of humans in the open anyway unless they were utterly starved, and these were glossy with health; just to start with they were usually perfectly well aware of what bows could do. If she could get everyone in one clump shouting and waving things, they were likely to dash past and then go looking for somewhere to hide.

No time.

Even a tiger moving away from a threat was very dangerous; they didn't like being frightened, and they had top-predator reflexes towards anything that got between them and where they wanted to go. The big cats' tails stopped lashing and went rigid. They were staring at her with fixed glares, and she was on the ground and looking vulnerable. That was . . .

Bad sign.

Then the claws on the tigers' forepaws came out and retracted again, and they worked their hips to settle their hind feet into the earth.

Oh, very bad sign.

Once while she was hunting in a swamp near the ruins of Eugene she'd seen a tiger leap fifteen feet up into a big oak . . . with the body of a fair-sized yearling boar in its mouth. Ground-to-ground they could cover thirty feet in a bound. And these two were only about fifty or sixty yards away, albeit downhill.

Heuradys spent a moment fighting the terror of her horse out of the reflex of someone virtually reared in the saddle, then flung herself off and landed crouching, her sword coming out in a silver flash as she dashed towards her liege. It was very swift, but it seemed to take forever. There were only . . .

Seconds, Órlaith thought. *Seconds before they reach me.*

She shoulder-rolled, sprang to her feet and drew. The shock of holding the Sword of the Lady ran through her; everything was *there*, balance and breath and muscle in cool harmony. She fell into the *nebenhut* position: knees crooked, left foot forward, blade back and point down and edge angled for a rising strike, with the right hand just at the guard and the left on the lower lobe of the hilt firmly up against the pommel.

She knew she was very accurate and very quick; yet nothing human could out-quick a tiger. But cats could be predictable—

Motion slowed. Her own with it, but she could *see* it all with crystal clarity, as if she was watching everything including herself from a distance through a powerful telescope. The cat-brothers leapt almost in unison but not quite, long low arcs like the stave of a strung longbow, landing with all four paws together and back curled in a horseshoe shape and then springing off the hind legs again. Dust and fragments of grass and dirt spurted back explosively as they launched into the second leap.

The third began the same, but both animals spread their forepaws in the air, and the dagger-length claws slid out as their mouths opened for the killing bite.

Órlaith stepped forward *into* the leap just as the lead tiger left the ground towards her. Her right boot slid forward, gliding sure-footed over the tussocky grass. The Sword came up in the long diagonal cut with the same motion, rising and then sweeping across with a snapping twist that put the strength of gut and back as well as arms and shoulders into swinging the not-steel.

The Sword of the Lady could do many things; her father had thought it wasn't matter at all, really, but instead a thought in the mind of the Goddess made material enough to touch. Órlaith believed it—when it had passed to her she'd noticed with a prickle of awe that it unobtrusively became the ideal length and weight of a longsword made for *her*.

When you wielded the Sword *as a sword*, as a thing meant to cut and stab, three things were important and very different from ordinary steel, however fine. It was sharp as an obsidian scalpel, able to cut a drifting hair that merely touched it, far sharper than battle swords were ever made or even *could* be made. The blade was a thin-sectioned and utterly rigid shape invulnerable to all harm, unlike the surprisingly fragile nature of a war-sword. And it was completely frictionless, smoother than wet ice, incapable of jamming or binding in anything whatsoever.

The rising blade moved in a blurring arc and struck the tiger's right forelimb just above the elbow-joint. It was thicker than her own thigh; she felt the jarring thud of impact, and then a harder cracking shock through her wrists as the edge met bone. Then something struck her and sent her spinning to the ground again, harder this time, and the Sword flew out of her fingers as her elbow rammed down and numbed her right arm.

The tiger was five yards away, thrashing and biting frantically at itself and giving an earsplitting and piteous high-pitched squeal. The limb hung by a tiny shred of hide . . . and then came free. For an instant the glass-smooth surface of the wound simply glistened meat-red and bone-white and gristle-yellow, and then disappeared in a gout of blood as the momentary shock that squeezed the veins shut vanished. The copper-salt odor was overwhelming, vanquishing the musky-sour-vinegar tomcat stink of the beast itself.

The second tiger landed with an audible thump where she would have been; no matter how broad and soft the paws and resilient the legs, it *did* weigh something like six hundred pounds and it had been expecting to land on her, not the ground. Even lying stunned before it, some remote corner of Órlaith's mind still felt a mad impulse to giggle at the I-meant-to-do-that look that flickered across its face for an instant, exactly the same as that a household moggie wore when it missed a leap from a sofa to a windowsill.

Sure, and it's more sympathetic to mice I'm becoming, by the moment!

Then the tiger whirled in a way that ought to have been impossible for something so big, a twisting S-curve through space that left it towering over her with its paws raised to pin and rend. She tried to reach for the hilt of the Sword; it was only about a foot away. For a moment she was chiefly conscious of an agonizing frustration as her right arm refused to do what she told it. Then something gray shot by in a galloping blur; Macmaccon, leaping in a frenzy of silent effort for the tiger's belly with his jaws gaping. The tiger hop-jumped backward, drawing in its stomach and batting with one immense paw; there was a thud and yelp and the greathound pinwheeled away.

Two arrows flickered over her head, amid a rippling hammer of hooves. Susan Mika had managed to get her horse under control and rode by shooting. The shafts thudded into the animal's breast and shoulder, but only sank in a handspan or so, which meant they'd struck bone. The Lakota girl's bow was too light in the draw for the sort of smashing power that could crack armor, or ribs and shoulder blades. But the tiger felt it, giving a coughing roar and shaking itself and looking around with a bewildered rage as attack piled on attack and things stung and hurt it. The smell of its littermate's blood would be priming it for battle too.

Órlaith's hand closed on the black staghorn hilt of the Sword, and she was in command of her body once again. She rolled up to one knee, but Alan Thurston was between her and the tiger now, the hunting spear braced in his hands. The head was a twelve-inch blade with a crossbar welded at the base, but the shaft was only seven feet long. That meant getting within range of murderous paws that could gouge you open like so many flensing knives, or break a bison's neck. Alan's face was gray-pale beneath his natural tanned olive, but there was no hesitation as he ducked in crabwise and jabbed the point forward with hard precision.

"Yaahhhhhhh!" he shouted. "Heee! Yaaaaahhh!"

The tiger snarled again, batted at the spearpoint, backed a little and then lunged. Alan went to a knee and frantically butted the spear into the ground. It held for a moment, the point sinking into the beast's shoulder, but then the tiger bit the shaft and shook it savagely. It snapped across and Alan went tumbling, his hundred and eighty pounds lifted off the ground and tossed by the tiger's neck-muscles and his own death-grip on the ashwood shaft. As he did Heuradys d'Ath darted in behind the beast and swung her longsword down two-handed across the animal's spine in a shining arc of speed, just behind the shoulders.

The tiger screamed, a high-pitched sound, and whirled on her in a blur. But its hindquarters went limp and it collapsed for a moment as it tried to charge. She backed carefully, a little crouched with her sword up in the Ox, the two-handed guard position. Locking eyes with the dying beast and leading it away from Órlaith as it dragged itself along on its front paws, moaning and snarling at the same time. Her face was pale beneath its tan, but set in a mask of concentration.

Morfind and Faramir ran up swearing, their recurve bows drawn as they fanned out to either side of her. Two arrows slammed into the big cat's neck and chest and sank deep, deep enough to touch the white gull-feather fletchings to its hide; the tiger moaned, sank down and bit at the ground for a moment as blood flowed out its nose and mouth, then went limp save for a little twitching.

"Enough!" Órlaith wheezed, but loud enough for her voice to carry in the sudden quiet.

None of them was inclined to babble just because their hearts were pumping.

"It's good as dead, leave it! Check for who's hurt."

A quick glance around showed that none of the humans seemed injured, beyond bleeding grazes and bruises and wrenching. The falconer and his assistant were in front of the hawks, which was very creditable considering that they were armed with nothing but the hunting knives in their hands. She clashed the Sword back into its scabbard—blood simply fell off it, and it never needed to be sharpened or checked for nicks. A brief nod and sign of the Horns to the tigers acknowledged their courage, and that they had a right to fight for their lives just as she did for hers.

Then she ran over to Macmaccon. Her heart lurched for a second as the greathound lay so still. Then she saw he was still breathing, and knelt to examine him. There were four deep gouges down one flank, bleeding freely, and the left shoulder and forelimb were canted in ways they shouldn't be. The brown eyes rolled towards her as she touched him gently, but the tongue lay limp out of the fanged mouth.

"There, Macmac, my faithful one, hero of a thousand. *Beidh lá eile ag an b'paorach.* We'll live to fight another day."

Then a little louder. "Fetch the kit! Quickly!"

"Here," Heuradys said, and handed it to her; it was of stiff black leather, with an embossed golden winged staff circled by a serpent on the top.

Órlaith opened it, pulled out a hypodermic of morphine, and adjusted the dose—Macmac was easily as heavy as most men, but dogs were more vulnerable to opiates. He sighed deeply as the needle took effect and lost a tension that hadn't been obvious before.

"The leg's broken and the shoulder . . . no, it's dislocated but the bone's whole," Órlaith said after a moment. "Hold him, Herry. And by the way, thanks."

Heuradys shook her head as she took Macmac's muzzle in the crook of one arm and braced the other against his chest.

"I wasted a good thirty seconds trying to get that slug of a horse under control," she said. "I didn't *think.*"

"Don't second-guess yourself, knight," Órlaith said sharply. "I'm here and not in bite-sized gobbets because you cut a bloody great tiger's spine with a sword, and not a magic sword at that! The result answers for the act, so."

She pulled sharply and twisted slightly, careful to keep her grip well above the break and not stress it; besides formal instruction she'd been helping with injuries in the hunting field and elsewhere since she'd been old enough to go along, and that was over a decade ago. The joint clicked back into position and moved naturally when she manipulated it.

"That's got it," Heuradys said, and shook her head again. "We *never* get tigers this early. In a month or two, yes. They follow the game down from the mountains, dodging around ranches and settlements and then sometimes start sniffing around the herds on the common here. But never this close to the manor and village!"

"These two decided to get an early start," Órlaith said.

Then they swabbed and stitched the cuts, shaved and splinted the simple greenstick fracture in the dog's forelimb, and wound on bandages that would also serve to keep the joint immobilized. There were only a few whimpers, and she thought it likely that somehow the greathound knew they were tending his hurts. There was a slight difference in the size of the pupils in his eyes, and she took his head in her lap to keep it elevated. On balance it was probably for the best that he'd been dazed.

She was conscious of snarling in the background, then sharp calls to heel in Mackenzie voices. When she looked up Karl Aylward Mackenzie was there twisting his bonnet in his big hands, swallowing and visibly making himself not look away.

Heuradys stood in a single graceful motion. Her face was white around the lips with fury and her voice tightly controlled.

"Thank you so very much, master-bowman, for near as Hades getting the Princess killed. You drove them right onto us!"

"It's most sorry I am, Lady Heuradys," he said, with a hitch in his voice. "We stumbled across them—they were laying up on a deer carcass and they just took to their heels—we ran after—"

"Which was just the worst possible thing to do!" she snapped.

Morfind and Faramir were there too, and also shaken by what might have happened.

"And blowing your horn as if this was fucking Helm's Deep," Faramir snarled, in a voice very unlike his usual pleasant tone, while Morfind muttered liquid Sindarin scatology.

Órlaith held up a hand. "Enough, all of you. Done's done, and we were all taken by surprise, just somewhat! Karl, cut some poles out of the brush and make a stretcher, and get something to keep his head up. I think you've some dog-nursing in your future, as Macmac took these hurts in my service, and he knows you well enough to obey."

He nodded silently and trotted off, happy to escape so easily. Susan was coming back leading several horses by their reins.

"Thanks, Suzie. Would you run over to the manor the now, to tell them we need a wagon? And to have the healer ready to check people, that'd be best."

Alan Thurston limped up as she heeled her horse off and up to a hand gallop, gingerly touching his face where it had plowed into the dirt and was bleeding freely.

"Here, let me see to that," Órlaith said, signing him to lie down.

Karl returned with horse-blankets, and she folded several under Macmac's head and spread another over him for warmth against shock. Alan lay down not far from the semi-comatose greathound.

"Sorry," he said, as she swabbed at the grazed area.

The pain had to be fairly intense—skin was hanging from the edge in shreds, and she had to get all the bits of dirt out of the raw flesh lest it fester—but he only blinked as she swabbed and used the tweezers and trimmed the edges with the razor.

"I saw you jump between me and a tiger with a spear," she said dryly.

"The which you did when I was lying flat with the wind knocked out of me and a nasty belt to the elbow making my arm buzz. Not much cause for apology, I'd say."

He smiled a little as she applied iodine and a pad and wound fabric tape to keep it in place. "I . . . ah, I sort of prayed that I'd have an . . . opportunity to show my loyalty to you, Princess. That's the problem with asking for something—you may get it. And in spades! So this is, umm, sort of my fault."

Órlaith raised a brow. *He means that, too,* she thought; the sincerity had an unmistakable tone, when you bore the Sword. Of course, that only meant *he* believed it, and he'd just had a hard thump on the noggin. Her own was aching a bit, and she took one of the twists of willow-bark extract and washed it down with a gulp from her canteen, then offered one to each of them.

Heuradys chuckled. "You can petition, but the Powers dispose, Alan," she said, declining the medication. "No thanks, Orrey. I was just scared witless, not thrown by a horse or tossed about by tigers."

Then she took a deep breath as he swallowed his portion. Órlaith suspected she was about to say she had to go visit her own manors, or her brothers and father over at Castle Campscapell.

Which is noble self-sacrifice, Órlaith thought. *The which I will not forbid at all, at all. Though Alan and I both need a day or two to recover, lest we end up rubbing wounds on wounds!*

Approaching hooves brought their heads around. Someone was riding out from Athana Manor, someone with a remuda of two remounts on a leading rein, and Susan Mika was coming back with him. When he drew rein and saluted she saw that it was a small wiry man in brown leathers and a broad-brimmed hat hanging down his back. The sigil of House Artos was on his jacket beneath a stylized galloping horse, and his mounts were rough-coated garrons of quarter horse stock, not showy or even more than middling fast in a sprint, but bred for toughness and endurance. He might have been any age between thirty and forty, with skin tanned to the color and consistency of leather, bright blue eyes and tow hair sun-faded to a white color.

Crown Courier Corps, she thought, rising. *Well, well, well. 'Tis the story of the three wells!*

Barony Harfang was tied into the heliograph net and had been for years; you could put a message through from here to Portland in a few hours, day or night. Or to Corvallis on the south in scarcely a little more. Using a Courier meant . . .

The man confirmed her suspicion by swinging down and going to one knee; as he did he reached into the flat pouch that hung by a shoulder-strap over his left hip and produced a tube of tooled boiled leather, whose cap was bound by a knotted ribbon and a blob of red wax stamped with the Royal seal.

"Your Highness," he said in a round-voweled New Deseret accent that turned each *s* to *sh.*

He bowed and kissed the hand she extended. The Couriers were a body sworn directly to the Crown, which meant to her as well as her mother.

"Thank you, Courier," she said, taking the message tube and touching it to her lips. "Your task is performed."

He grinned, showing a gap where a tooth had probably met a fist, or a horse's hoof, or a fall. "Not until I have your reply, Your Highness," he said.

She broke the seal and read. While she did she heard the Courier say casually:

"Hi, Suzie. Good to see you again."

"Han, mis eya, Charlie," she replied, which meant much the same thing. "Life treating you OK?"

"Could be worse," he replied, looking around and his eyes settling on the two very dead tigers, now buzzing with flies that lifted in a cloud as the falconers and the clansfolk began skinning. "Not bad. At least nothing's tried to eat me. Just lately, not since that fucking grizzly down by the San Luis last year."

Órlaith chuckled as she rolled up the Chancery writ and the short personal note inside it.

"The response is: The High Queen's will shall be done in every particular."

Then aloud to the group: "Friends, it looks like our exile here is short-lived. We're to make tracks back the way we came. From the sound of it, I'd say Reiko made plain she wanted me involved in this war that's brewing. Probably arguing that the Sword is needed, and I come with it."

She looked at Alan Thurston. "And you're welcome to come along, my friend, if you don't mind trailing in my fighting-tail. It could be that there'll be ways to show your loyalty that don't require fighting big cats with a knife on the end of a stick."

He smiled—gingerly, given how sore his face must be—and bowed. It was extraordinary how well he looked, even rolled in dirt and with a stained bandage over one cheek.

CHAPTER FOURTEEN

*P*rang-prang-prang . . .
The nearest of the galleys was frantically trying to get its bow-catapult trained around on the *Silver Surfer*, but the carriage wouldn't bear easily with the long narrow ship pinned to the Montivallan merchantman by its own boarding-ramp. Many of the archers on its deck were shifting around to shoot at her, though the prang-prangs had cut swaths through them. Pip looked down towards the Raja's men on deck and slashed the air with her cane towards the target. Their officer in his engraved spired helm glanced back at her, a scar-faced local grandee named Anak Agung.

"*Tembak, Tuan Anak!*" she shouted. "Shoot!"

He echoed her and the archers drew. The local Balinese used a recurve made of laminated bamboo, and they often shot while sitting cross-legged. It looked odd to her, but it worked and it took up remarkably little room. Forty or so of the Royal guardsmen immediately began pumping arrows towards the Carcosans. The Carcosans shot back, which had the advantage of directing their black-fletched arrows away from her and her crew. The spearmen squatted and leaned forward on their left hands, a position that would have tied her in knots but left them mostly sheltered and ready to spring into action. As she watched they began to slap their hands on the deck and chant, at first a few and then all of them, the whole body of men presenting a sea of mostly naked and leanly muscular backs rippling in unison to the sound of:

"Amok! Amok!"

The tone rose, shriller, hysterical, edging up into the blood squeal:

"Amok! Amok!—"

And the prang-prangs went *prang-prang-prang* . . .

The last bursts shredded the crew around the galley's bow-catapult and left a dozen bodies blocking the boarding-gangway that had dropped on the Montivallan's forecastle; then they tilted the weapons up to rake the other two galleys beyond this one. Pip looked over her shoulder to the westward; the rest of the Raja's men were *finally* making some progress towards the spot where the action was, and shouting and waving their weapons as the oars flashed.

Pip took another deep breath, ignoring the rank stinks, flipped the cane over her shoulder into the loop sewn to her suspenders and flicked open the forearm brace of her pistol-grip slingshot. Three steel balls from the bag went into the pouch and she took up enough tension to just stretch the rubber a little. Soon, very soon, pump air into your lungs, make them hold it, don't let the muscles in your back and neck tense up, stay loose but alert—

"Ready, all!" she shouted.

The grapnels flashed across the gap—some crunching into the deck of the Carcosan galley, some into the Montivallan's bow-netting. Winches spun and hauled the *Silver Surfer* into a hard contact that made the deck lurch beneath her feet, their stern tucked against the other ship's bow and their bow midway along the galley's flank, with a triangle of water full of wreckage and bodies between. The sea right here was literally pink with blood, and it flowed out of the galley's scuppers in long red streams. Raja Dalem Seganing's men rose up with a final united scream of:

"Amok!"

They threw themselves in unison across the rail of the galley. The archers dropped their weapons, drew their parangs and followed.

The Carcosans still on their feet met them, with a shout of: *"Untuk Raja Kuning!"*

That was brave, or at least sensible; the alternative was to jump into the water with the sharks and hope they were stuffed to the gills already and not in a mood to nibble.

Pip shouted herself: "Tally-ho! For the roast wallaby of Old Townsville! *Silver Surfers, attack!"*

Toa was first across to the Montivallan's forecastle, making a huge leap into the rear of the Carcosan boarding party with his great spear flashing as he gripped it near the base and swung it in a circle like the propeller of a legendary helicopter of the ancient times, or a reaper using a scythe. Three of the Carcosans who'd just stormed onto the deck there died; only one had time to scream before blood choked his throat. The scream was overridden by Toa's lion roar, shocking even in the tremendous brabbling noise of the battle. Quite literally a lion roar, something she could recall vividly; the beasts haunted the hills at the edges of Tanumgera Station and she'd heard them after dinner often enough, not to mention hunting them.

The spear darted out like a frog's tongue flicking, and withdrew leaving a huge wound beneath a man's ribs. Toa grabbed another by the throat with his left hand, crushing his windpipe as he jerked him up off his feet and into the path of a Carcosan parang like a shield, then dropped him and used the steel-shod butt of the weapon to crush the parang-wielder's skull. For an instant the Carcosans recoiled, stunned and horrified.

She leapt after him, and the rest of the crew who weren't working the prang-prangs followed—by now she was pretty confident they would, if only because they knew she'd gotten them into a situation where they had to win or die, and they were pretty well all self-starters anyway. She pulled the slingshot across her body and released just as her feet touched the planks, and three Carcosans toppled backward from the rail into the water and the waiting jaws.

No bloody problem hitting something with so many targets! Or this close.

Then she went to one knee and switched to single shots, draw-spot-loose as fast as she could from a few paces behind her second-in-command and concentrating on the ones he didn't have time for. One punched into the eye of an archer drawing a bead on Toa, the next broke a kneecap, the third thumped into the side of the head of a spearman in the soft spot just up and forward of the ear, and the fourth went *crack* into the breast-bone of a half-naked man running screaming at her with a wave-bladed keris in hand.

He stopped and looked down at his own chest. Then his eyes rolled up and he fell to the red-running deck with a sort of boneless splat as his heart was shocked into stillness. Her mother had been very fond of this slingshot. . . .

She snapped it shut and pulled the cane out of its sling, suddenly conscious of how the Carcosans were retreating from this part of the ship. Then her eyes went wide as she saw why.

A steel man was fighting his way towards her. His armor glittered like fire in the afternoon sun, painful to the eyes, from feet in articulated metal shoes to the tall ostrich-feather plume on top of his helmet. A long double-edged sword was in one hand, and a big shield like an elongated round-edged triangle was on the other arm, marked with the Crowned Mountain and Sword. His face was a blank curve of steel with only the shadowed horizontal eyeslit breaking the line of the visor.

Arrows stood in the shield; they splintered on the surface of the body-armor as she watched. He moved as if the harness was no heavier than cloth, smacked the shield into a face with an impetus that knocked the victim backward like a rag doll, stabbed, chopped, a swift economical piston-like succession of moves.

"At 'em!" Pip shouted again, and pulled the cane into her right hand and a kukri into her left.

Now, there's a girl of parts! John thought. *Or at least, she leaves a trail of parts.*

The view through the vision slit of his visor was necessarily limited to the barely necessary, and concentrating on the men trying to kill him was the first priority—a good suit of plate made that process very difficult but didn't make him invulnerable, a fact teachers had made painfully clear to him years ago. But he could see the figure in the white shorts and shirt moving through the chaos of the deck-fight like a dancer who was never still for an instant; one of the more lively dances, a volta or a leaping and twisting galliard.

She sank nearly to a knee and smashed a foot with the knob on the end of her cane, blocked a downward cut with the odd back-curving knife in her other hand, flicked the cane straight up into the man's chin, cut sideways and took off most of a hand, twirled in a three-quarter circle and smacked the end of the cane into the angle of a jaw in passing with a force that left a spray of blood and teeth in the air as the man fell backward.

The huge man beside her had more tattoos than a McClintock and was using his spear—enormous even for his size—as a combination stabbing and cutting and clubbing weapon, one with immense leverage at the end of his long thick arms and the long shaft.

John went forward, with Thora and Deor on one side of him and the Fayard and his surviving half-armored crossbowmen on the other with sword and buckler, and the point of Evrouin's glaive poised at his liege's sword-arm shoulder ready to stab and hook and cut. The slightly-built and lightly-armed locals were terribly vulnerable to that ironclad violence. And Ruan was barely a step behind the foremost trio, shooting with deadly skill so close to them that sometimes the fletching brushed his friends as the arrows went by—not one of the enemy archers managed to live long enough to raise a bow behind their own hand-to-hand fighters.

"Keep at 'em!" Thora wheezed past the three-bar visor of her Bear-killer helm. "They're back on their heels, I can feel it. Don't let 'em get set!"

She's right, John thought, and cut a man across the neck and chest as he tried to dodge backward and couldn't because his comrades were too close behind. *They had their peckers up but the Aussie shocked 'em.*

Thora went in under the point of a spear, levering it up with the edge of her shield as she slammed into the man bearing it body-to-body and then cracked the basket hilt of her backsword into his face in a quick hard jab while he was off-balance.

"By the Aesir, it's nice to be bigger than average for a change," she grunted as she recovered into guard.

Another tried to stab her in the side with a *kris* while her sword-hand was busy and had just enough time to see the point skid off the steel surface of her cuirass before Deor's broadsword slammed down and cut three-quarters of the way through his arm.

"Woden! Ha, *Woden!*"

The enemy fighters surged back from the wedge of Montivallans, some trying to crowd back down the nearest boarding ramp; he realized he didn't even know what to call them, apart from these-people-trying-to-kill-us. It was time to charge them, turn them into a mob trying to escape and too tightly packed to use their weapons or even run.

John tucked his armored shoulder into his shield and sprang . . .

. . . and bounced back from the tall figure that stood before the place where the ramp's spikes had crunched deep into the *Tarshish Queen's* bulwark. A white robe covered him from shoulders to feet, but there was armor underneath it, and a sword much like a Montivallan knight's weapon in his gauntleted hand. A helm covered his head, but the front of it was a mask. John couldn't tell exactly what it was made of; ceramic or ivory, at a guess. Certainly it was pale—not white, but some indefinable off-white color that gave the impression of being like flesh, but not living flesh. A three-armed sigil rested between the brows.

The features of a face were there in the mask, but smoothed and flattened, more suggested than shown. The eyes were empty sockets. . . .

And there aren't any eyes behind there either. It's just . . . yellow.

He couldn't move his gaze from those golden pits. He was on the deck of the *Queen*, but he was also somewhere else, as if two places and times had merged. More *there* than *here* with every breath.

His armored feet rang on flags as he walked between shuttered buildings of pastel-colored stone, beneath a pale sky and paler moon and black stars. A child looked at him between the convoluted bars of a balcony, a face elfin and huge-eyed framed in pale hair, then turned and flowed away like a snake on its belly. A tall structure like a church glowed from within like a furnace. Its stained-glass windows cast shadows that danced and capered across the square before it, making a play where stick-thin mantis figures whirled around another tied to a stake, one that burned and screamed silently.

Beyond the not-church, broad stairs led down to a blue-black lake, where waves like pale mist beat on the stone. A boat waited there, a slender double-ended thing with curling stem and sternposts and a hooded boatman holding a tall pole.

His shadow went before him, more terrible with every step as it showed the shape of his soul. Then it turned to look him in the eyes . . .

Thock.

Something hard struck the man in the mask on the side of his helm—a ball-bearing from a slingshot—and John was back on the deck of the *Tarshish Queen.* Evrouin lunged with the point of his glaive; the masked man swayed aside and seized it just below the head. The valet-bodyguard dropped it with a yell as his opponent yanked it forward, nearly throwing him off the deck. The longsword moved *before* Ruan loosed, and the bodkin point went *ting* off the watered steel and shattered. Then it went up with smooth menace.

"St. Michael with me! Holy Mary for Portland!" John bayed as his sword went up, his shield raised to just below his eyes.

A sword I can deal with.

He took a step forward, feeling a transport of anger born of fear. Thora and Deor were at his side, she calling on Almighty Thor, he on Victory-Father. The three swords cut air as the Pallid Mask leapt backward with tigerish agility, onto the boarding ramp and back down it. The boarding parties had fled behind him, all but the ones twitching on the deck as the sailors finished them or tipped their bodies overboard.

The young woman in white, now liberally splashed with sticky red, nodded to him when they finally stood separated only by a few feet of deck covered in bodies. She also wore an odd-looking round hat with a stiff brim, and knee and elbow pads, and a circle of some sort of black makeup around one pale gray eye. Wisps of tawny hair escaped from under the brim of her hat, sticking to the sweat-slick skin of her face and neck.

"Good show!" she said briskly, in a drawl that reminded him of how some Dúnedain in Mithrilwood spoke, taking after Hiril Loring's dulcet tones. "Now let's get this cleared up."

Feldman was shouting orders from the quarterdeck through his speaking-trumpet; a quick glance showed John that the Captain was still on his feet, though his left arm was in a sling and a broken cutlass lay at his feet. Radavindraban led a party down the rail with come-alongs and pry bars and axes, loosening the grapnels and boarding ramps.

"Cover them!" John called to Fayard, and the crossbowmen sheathed their swords and unslung the weapons across their backs.

The woman in white turned and shouted orders herself to someone named Kombagle. The little barquentine cast free, turned, and crept alongside the *Tarshish Queen*. A cable was passed and rigged—Captain Ishikawa seemed to have taken charge of that—and the *Queen* turned her bow north again, and then further west of north as the thick rope came taut and rose out of the water, with spurting little jets of water as the ship's hundreds of tons bore on it.

The *Queen* responded sluggishly. As it did praus and rowboats and things he couldn't name except that they floated and had armed men on them and were coming from the western part of the bay streamed past them, falling on the drifting galleys. The flood of small boats streaming out from the pink whatever-it-was to the east moved forward likewise, and in a few moments they were exchanging flights of arrows and flung spears, then crashing together in knots of screaming hacking ferocity on the blood-tinged water.

John looked northward towards the shore. Troops were moving there from both sides, glittering blocks of spearheads and . . .

"Are those *elephants?*" he blurted.

CHAPTER FIFTEEN

"Well, this is a pleasant contrast, what?" Pip said, beaming and lying back in the recliner.

She was enjoying feeling clean and the fresh clothes and the smell of dinner; also having all the leaders of the strangers here where she could appraise them and get a feeling for what was going on. They had been appropriately, though not effusively, grateful when the battle ended in the usual inconclusive withdrawal by both sides to lick wounds. Now there was time to talk.

The night was dark with a thick frosting of stars and a quarter-moon just risen, but the lamps on the poles above and the fire-pits and the bigger lanterns around the grounded *Tarshish Queen* a few hundred yards away gave plenty of light. Palms rustled overhead, and there was a heavy sweet scent from a nearby frangipani tree; she had some of the cream-and-gold blossoms tucked into her hair.

She lay back carefully, to avoid too much pressure on her bruises or the bandages covering a few cuts; fortunately the batik *kain sarung* and light lacy *uden* blouse she was wearing were very comfortable, as well as being extremely fetching in her opinion. None of the hurts were serious, and only one had required a couple of stitches.

She was feeling a bit of a glow of satisfaction too, one that had only a little to do with the tall glass of fruit-enhanced rum in her hand; it had a little pink paper umbrella in it, which seemed to be a Balinese tradition. Or at least to be what they assumed outsiders would like, for some reason. There was a platter of mango and pineapple cubes and bits of spicy grilled chicken on little bamboo skewers on the other arm of the lounger, by way of an appetizer. Fortunately nobody had managed to hit her in the face, so eating wasn't uncomfortable.

Captain Feldman wasn't as happy, which was understandable given the state of his ship. From this camp on the shore her sailors had set up—with spars and sails for shady pavilions—there was an excellent view of the *Tarshish Queen*. It was even dramatic, in the flickering light of the torches and lanterns, glints on metal and on the surface of the water, the masts looming up into the darkness, and beyond that the yellow lights of the city. She didn't look east to Carcosa; you didn't, unless it was really necessary. Looking too much seemed to give them a grip on you, with consequences that varied but were never good. And you could never tell how much was *too* much until it was too late.

The elephants had managed to get the Montivallan ship well above the low-tide mark when they took over the tow from her ship; it was amazing how much force a half-dozen of the big animals could exert. Then they'd brought up timbers in their trunks as the mahouts shouted and waved their goads so that the crew could prop her upright on her keel when the tide went out, and pump her dry. Tomorrow they could get her stores and catapults and ballast off, then float her farther in on the next tide, and do thorough repairs on the hull damage before running her over to the rather rudimentary *Baru Denpasar* docks for fitting out.

Speaking of which . . .

"What's your ballast?" Pip asked Captain Feldman.

Even though she gathered he was on a government charter—they'd been a little evasive about that and she sensed dissension where they came from—the ballast was probably something he was planning to sell if he could. There was always rock to replace it. Sand would do at a pinch.

"Metals," the merchant skipper from Newport said. "Mostly rebar in bundles wound with copper wire. Some brass or lead or PVC pipe, some aluminum sheet."

He had a good poker face, but his ears were pricking up a bit in a reflex Pip was very familiar with, someone scenting an opportunity. She'd grown up around salvagers and merchant-adventurers and listening to their stories, the sort who'd follow the scent of a score across broken glass. And probably sell the glass, too, just for the giggles and the principle of the thing. She liked and admired them, or she wouldn't have ended up on this harebrained venture; they were certainly more fun than the stodgy burghers and smug bankers . . .

Bankers! Avert the omen, she thought, and took another sip of the rum. *Buccaneers, only with lower morals and less style.*

. . . and pompous Stationmasters who were the other parts of the tip of the modern social pyramid in Australia's fragments once you got above the level of—she shuddered—*honest toil.*

The bits lower down could be fun too, particularly if you avoided the solid, stolid yeomen and worthy artisans, but only to dip into occasionally. Her mother had been fond of saying that she'd known riches and poverty both, and riches were much, much better. Daddy, of course, had been born heir to the Colonelcy.

"Metals? Oh, jolly good," she said. "Just between me and thee, Captain, bargain hard. They're very short of steel here and they need every spearhead they can make. If it had been spring steel alloys you could write your own ticket, they want that very badly indeed."

He shifted in his rattan recliner, winced as it put stress on his wounded left arm in its sling, and sipped again at his drink.

"The Raja is honest?" he said. "He wouldn't just take it? Monarchs tend to do that, in time of war."

"He's *reasonably* honest. I'd worry if you announced you were planning on sailing off with that load, since he needs it badly, but if you're willing to sell, he'll pay."

"So he'll be as honest as his sense of duty lets him?" Feldman asked, with a crook of one eyebrow.

Pip crooked one eyebrow back at him, and they smiled in mutual recognition.

Really, no flies on this one at all! Remember that being bright doesn't mean you're always the smartest person in the room, as Mummy said.

"That's a very good way to put it, Captain," she said with respect.

Besides the arrow wound Feldman had a couple of bandaged cuts and stabs, nothing serious either but enough to hurt. Pip suspected that he was also restless because he couldn't be up and about supervising the stripping-down of his ship, though his First Mate seemed entirely competent and they'd shut down for the night anyway. He'd commendably seen to the arrangements for the wounded; there was an infirmary tent, and his physician had confirmed that the local doctors knew their business before pitching in to help them.

Feldman said something in a language she recognized as ancient Greek, but didn't speak herself despite the best efforts of Rockhampton Girls Grammar School, though she could puzzle out a written sentence if she had to and handle Latin rather better.

Though I managed to score top marks in surreptitious drinking and covert shagging, she thought mordantly.

At her look he quoted in English:

"'So I will never waste my lifespan on the vain unprofitable search for a perfect man; if you find him, send me word. But that one I will love and honor who does nothing base from free will. Against Necessity, even Gods do not fight.' A poet named Simonides of Keos said that, very long ago. But some things do not change, even after the Change."

Prince John frowned.

Which doesn't make him look any less ducky, she thought.

In fact he looked the way a Prince should, rather than like a harassed bureaucrat, cunning politician or chinless wastrel, which in her experience were more typical of the breed. And he'd been strumming that lute-thing quite skillfully as background music. She had a weakness for handsome, square-chinned, broad-shouldered, long-limbed young men with nice hair who could play the guitar and had big soulful greenish-brown eyes. His charms were showing to advantage, since he'd switched to a sarong too; athletic, but not blocky, and not *too* much body hair.

Wouldn't be like wrestling with a sheepskin. Some is good, too much is a bother.

If they could use a sword with dashing authority, so much the better. And he had an intriguing accent, almost French; she knew what that sounded like, because her nanny had been from the Republic of Noumea, over on New Caledonia, a refugee from one of the incessant kanak-colon fights there.

The frown gave way to a charming smile directed at her; she hadn't been wrong about feeling his interest.

"I thought that there's been an awful lot of building here, if they're short of tools," he said. "But perhaps they used up their reserves, Lady Balwyn-Abercrombie?"

"He's not just a pretty face," Thora Garwood said, smiling a little wryly at her. "Lady Balwyn-Abercrombie."

"Oh, do call me Pip, all of you," she said, smiling back. "Everyone does."

Now that's complex, Pip thought.

She mentally shifted her gaze between Thora and John; she prided herself on being able to read body language.

They are so getting it off together, but if it weren't for that I'd have sworn she was with that other musician, Deor . . . except that he's queer as a two-headed calf. Pity, and even more about his boyfriend; he's quite ducky in a sensitive, earnest youngish way. Nice backside, too.

She stuck to business, something that was becoming dismally familiar. Socializing on shipboard had been very limited, because she was in more or less a lion-tamer's position, and whatever you did with lions if you had any sense you didn't take them to bed. Which was all very well for the month or two she'd anticipated this trip taking, or even three or four months, but it was going on *six* months now, which was ridiculous for a red-blooded Townsville lass. Landing here hadn't made much difference; she didn't dare let any of the courtiers get too close, or show what local custom would see as vulnerability. And an adolescence spent largely at Rockhampton Girls Grammar School had taught her that while girls could be a lot of fun and often had fewer complications, she basically preferred men.

Back to economics, she thought, and went on aloud:

"There's a big pre-Blackout . . . pre-Change . . . wreck on the north coast that drifted hard aground; there's the ship, and its cargo was structural steel. Plenty for a very long time."

Everyone nodded in understanding. There were a few places where they mined gold or gems, but she'd never even heard of anywhere that bothered with smelting iron or copper or any other base metal from ore. Even the most advanced countries only used a few pounds of metal per head every year; back before what the Montivallans called the Change, they'd used *tons* per head and there had been ten or twenty times more people. Even leaving aside things that could be reused directly, the world's blacksmiths and foundries weren't going to run out of salvage metal anytime in the next millennium. She recalled vaguely that it wasn't even possible to get aluminum out of bauxite since the Blackout, but there was so much to salvage that didn't matter either.

The distribution was the problem, which was another way of saying opportunity; she'd had a cargo of metals and tools on board when she arrived here, and had done very well with it in return for the spices and artwork and so forth. A massive score, just the thing to prove herself, enough to pay for the ship and the running costs and a good bit left over.

Or would have, if I hadn't been sodding stuck here! It'd all be gone by now if I hadn't managed to hit up His Clutchfisted Majesty for a good retainer for helping him with the Carcosans, and that was like pulling teeth because I was stuck and pretty much had to do it anyway; and only the fact that there's nowhere to go has kept the crew from deserting. Hmmm. But from what Captain Feldman says, the cargo would be worth three times as much where he comes from. Farther from the tropics . . .

"With that sort of resource on hand, why do they want to import, Captain?" Feldman asked curiously.

"It's rather a point-failure source," Pip said. "Which means everyone wants to control it. No real alternative, you see."

This part of the world hadn't had many of the big population centers where salvage was concentrated, and the dead cities were dangerous environments anyway. A quick and dirty in-and-out for gold or watch-maker's tools was one thing; her mother and her Uncle Pete and Aunt Fifi had made their initial bundle of boodle that way. But even blood desper-adoes like them had put their pile into safer investments later. Working big-city ruins for ordinary metals was the sort of thing only a nearby government or the equivalent could run, because of the scale needed and because kings were best placed to fight off predators.

"Even overland across the mountains it's only a week or so . . . except for the history."

Deor Godulfson sighed and settled back with his drink; he and Ruan were holding hands between their couches, and they'd both switched to local sarongs too, since their own clothes were mostly soaked with blood and needed attention. He seemed to regard the whole thing as raw mate-rial for epics, which showed commendable professional dedication in a way, except that they were caught in the middle of it. Which was much less comfortable than the part afterwards when you basked in fame, for-tune and glory.

"To be brief, the Balinese and the good ship *South Sea Adventure*—"

She pointed eastward towards what she had taught herself to think of as *the big steel ship anchored by the pink coral fort*. Feldman raised a brow.

"You mean the—"

"Don't say the H-word! Really. For one thing the locals get very upset and for another . . . just don't, Captain. Please?"

Captain Ishikawa spoke up. "This is evil, but it is not the same evil as the *kangshinmu*," he said. At her look of enquiry: "Korean . . . magicians, I think? Sol . . . Sorcerer."

"Remember the crocodile, Moishe," Deor said quietly.

Good advice. My sense of the possible is getting stretched, she thought. *And Korea does have a very bad reputation, though I hadn't known that sorcerers were running about the place. As opposed to Japan, which has very little reputation one way or another these days. It's so reassuring to know there are many different varieties of eldritch evil abroad in the world, what?*

He nodded, and she went on:

"The ship formerly known as the *South Sea Adventure* arrived on these shores at about the same time as the Balinese. The Balinese were hungry and desperate and had had to leave their home for the homeland's good— they were drawing straws for that. The *Adventure* had been pirating about for a year or so to survive, picking up the skills as they went along; they had a big crew including the ones who'd been on board for the fun of it and found they'd landed in a *real* South Sea Adventure instead of just playing at it. Tubby Yanks to start with, mostly . . . no offense."

"None taken," Feldman said, and the others chuckled.

All the shattered kaleidoscope of varied weirdnesses that Australia had become still had a slowly-fading sense that they were Australians, and though it didn't stop them quarreling with each other they closed ranks against outsiders. Evidently the same wasn't the case over across the Pacific, but then they were a lot more isolated.

"Well, the current Raja's daddy, like most dynastic founders a lucky general, made a deal with the *Adventure* when it turned up at the same time as his invasion. Things weren't going very well for him, because the local people had a fair number of ships—boats and whatever—back then, but that applied to both sides."

"Nothing like that four-master, though," Feldman said thoughtfully.

"Exactly, and they had a machine shop aboard and had already made up catapults. So they swore rapacious brotherhood . . ."

Thora nodded. "The Balinese had the army, and the *Adventure* had the sea power."

"Just so. And they fell upon the locals in cahoots, as it were, with the ship smashing up the defending fleet so the Balinese could—and did—

swarm ashore and slaughter everything in sight that didn't run for the hills very fast indeed. They don't talk about it much but apparently it was quite thoroughly bloody even by the standards of the time. And then they divvied up the spoils. The Balinese got most of the land, being your sturdy-honest-yeoman types who'd come here to till the soil and eat rice in the sweat of their brows, but the Adventurers got the surviving people because they weren't interested in farming rice with their own hands but perfectly willing to eat in the sweat of someone *else's* brows. Then the *Adventure* disposed of the ships from the Raja of Bali looking to collect tribute from their new colony ready or not . . ."

Prince John spoke thoughtfully: "And the colonists wouldn't be blamed. Plausible deniability of the best kind: denying that you even exist. All they'd know was that ships sent this way didn't come back, so they'd assume the colony failed and was massacred instead of vice versa."

"Right-O, Your Highness!"

"Oh, John, Pip. We're a long way from Montival."

"John, then. And the *Adventure* ferried metal back from the wreck on the north shore in big job-lots, and they pirated around for things they traded to the Balinese settlers or used themselves, in between lolling in their hammocks like lords and being served on bended knee by the surviving locals who couldn't object because otherwise the Balinese would have cut their throats one and all on the general principle that corpses can't plot revenge and neither can the children they don't have."

"There's an old saying from a country where my ancestors lived for a while," Feldman said. "When people cause you a problem . . . remember that death solves all problems."

"Bloody-minded lot," Pip said.

"Or just frank about it. My ancestors left, you'll notice."

Pip nodded and resumed: "The *South Sea Adventure* set up their own little kingdom: the Captain on top, then the Officers, the Crew, and the Passengers in that order, and then the locals doing all the work down at the bottom."

"There was a famous article in *Tournaments Illuminated* . . . a magazine published in Portland . . . titled 'Feudalism: God's Will or Just Common Sense?'" Prince John said dryly. "This all sounds . . . cozy."

"Very, I imagine. If that had been the whole story I might have been able to do business with them when I arrived back in February. Unless they'd gotten lazy and been massacred by the staff."

"But then they fell out with the Balinese settlers?"

"Well . . . more on the order of, *but then Captain Wilde went on a little trip into the interior.* A few years later, chasing bandits or freedom fighters depending on your point of view. And he found something there. When he came back he was . . . different. So were the people who'd been with him. Pretty soon, a lot of the people over there were . . . different. The ones that didn't run fast enough. And they built that thing, the place they call Carcosa, and they renamed their ship."

"With the H-word," Prince John said.

"Exactly. And since then, things have been going downhill, you might say. Or getting . . . stranger. Strange and bad."

She could tell they all agreed with that. Prince John looked as if he'd bitten down on something sour for a moment. At least they weren't showing the sort of skepticism she'd have expected back in Townsville.

"They've cut the island off from the outside world quite thoroughly, as I found out once we got here. It's not just their wanting to take over, not the usual I-want-it-because-it's-there thing."

"Then what *do* they want?"

"We don't know. I think it *starts* with taking over the island and turning everybody here more or less . . . strange . . . too."

"Why did you stay here once you realized what was going on?" Feldman said bluntly. "It's foreign territory to you too, and you said they paid well for your cargo."

Pip grinned raffishly. "Perhaps I'm committed to the cause of the suffering people of Baru Denpasar. Or perhaps I just can't get out—between that bloody great steel ship, the other craft they've got, and . . . well, there was a Timorese ship here for a while. They snuck out one moonless night, thinking they could get far enough away that the you-know-what couldn't find them."

"What happened to them?" Thora asked.

"We're not sure, though after what you've told me I suspect a very large aquatic lizard happened to them to start with. A fishing boat picked up a survivor. He was clinging to a baulk of timber. He lived for about a week and didn't say a word while he was awake. Just huddled and shivered."

John picked up on the clue, she was glad to observe. "And when he slept?"

"Then he mostly screamed. When he babbled . . . nobody who could speak Timorese would stay around him after that. Or talk about it."

"Died of shock, I suppose," Feldman said compassionately.

"Not really," Pip said.

This time she finished her drink and signed for another from the white-coated steward. Rum helped with some things.

"As far as we can tell, he was strangled," she said.

"By who?" Prince John asked.

"Either by himself . . ."

Toa spoke up for the first time. "Or by his own shadow, maybe. It looked like that. Didn't have a good view, though. Couple of other bastards got in my way. Nearly ran right over me trying to get away from him. Straight up."

There was an echoing silence for a moment, and then Pip clapped her hands:

"Well, the feed's ready! The Raja sent me some of his own cooks, and they know their way about a kitchen."

The attendants brought in a low table and set it with platters with conical pyramids of rice—several colors of it, steamed or fried or boiled—and dozens of other dishes. Ishikawa exclaimed with delight when he saw the rice, and that was the first word she'd heard him say besides his comment about Korea. His sailors were two fires over, and were much noisier in their approval; they were also punishing the *brem*, a thickly sweet, dark and potent rice wine. It might not be what they were used to, since one of the terms for *sake* literally meant *clear spirit*, but they weren't letting that stop them. Throw in some friendly local ladies, or at least commercially acute ones, and they were content.

She knew some Hindus were vegetarians, but she was thankful the Balinese generally weren't, having been raised in a thoroughly carnivorous part of the world herself. The centerpiece of the feast for the officers and leaders was a suckling pig in scarlet glory, rubbed with turmeric and then stuffed with coriander seeds, lemongrass, lime leaves and salam leaves, chilies, black pepper, garlic, red shallots, and something gingery called kencur that crinkled the tongue; then the whole was spit-roasted over coconut husks.

Feldman made a sign to the attendants not to serve him any of that, but there were also tempe—fermented bean cake—in sweet soy sauce, chicken in coconut curry, snake bean and coconut salad, vegetables in peanut sauce, tuna steamed in banana leaves, tender slow-cooked duck rubbed with tamarind puree and salt and stuffed with eggs, cassava leaves and a spice mix called *bumbu rajang*, and a good many other things worth tasting.

They all had healthy appetites, since it had been a very long strenuous day without much time to stop until now; she thought Toa was going to demolish the pig by himself. Dessert was coffee and coconut pancakes and pineapple preserves, plus an array of fruit—durian was something she loved, though some found the strong odor off-putting.

Deor wiped his mouth on a napkin. "For people who came here because they were starving, they've done well for themselves!" he said, patting his lean ridged stomach, now slightly bulging. "It's not that the lords are eating and the rest going hungry, either, from what I could see."

"Oh, they're excellent cooks," Pip said. "Good farmers with plenty of land, too; and God knows they fight well, or the survivors would all be worshipping the Yellow Raja by now. The real problem is engineering."

Toa belched and then grunted. "Or monsters from the bloody beyond," he said. "But right, it starts with engineering."

"No sharks?" John said dubiously two days later.

He stood shading his eyes with a hand and looking down over the blinding white sand of the beach and the low white surf beating on it and hissing upward in foam. There were about twenty yards between the surf and the line of coconut palms, with the tide in, and a big raft made of bamboo sections as thick as his thigh was anchored within easy swimming distance of the beach.

"No crocodiles?" he added as an afterthought.

"No ghoulies or ghosties or sharp-toothed beasties inside the reef," Pip replied, pointing.

Her finger indicated a streak of white foam a thousand yards out where the fangs of the coral lay just below the high-tide surface now.

"Generous of the Raja," John said. "To let you . . . us . . . have this place."

This beachfront house was a possession of Raja Dalem Seganing, made available to his guest-allies as a gesture of goodwill. It was hardly a building at all, to Montivallan eyes. More a matter of pillars of rough coral limestone rising from waist-high walls of the same and holding up a high steep roof of shining black-streaked borassus timbers covered in neat palm-thatch, with internal partitions of woven bamboo and rolls of rattan matting that could be let down or raised to mark the exterior. The floors were smooth cool cream-colored marble, and the foundation below was probably a concrete slab.

"Not as generous as you might think, since *they* think that upstream is good and downstream is bad, and the ocean is the source of *kelod* . . . the domain of Yama, Lord of Hell. So they're not much on beach culture, especially compared to us in Townsville, or even those bogan degenerates in Cairns. Who may not bathe or brush their teeth, but by God at least they surf!"

She paused for a moment, and then went on coolly: "My face is up here, John. Just look up over the collarbones and above the neck."

He flushed, and she winked to take the sting out of it; she was wearing sandals, a sarong and flowers in her hair and around her neck. Just about what he was, though . . .

She's more distracting. At least, more distracting to me, if that makes any sense . . . my blood supply isn't concentrating on my brain right now . . .

The light construction certainly went with this climate; the breeze blowing in off the sea made it comfortable enough, but it was *as* warm as an inland August noon back home, and much more humid than the lands over the Cascades ever got. The closest he could come to it was a memory of a visit to Iowa long ago with his parents. That had been in August, but apparently it was like this pretty much year round here, with the main seasonal difference being the amount of rain. Despite being insubstantial the house was fairly large—several big bedrooms, a dining room that could seat a dozen. And there was a helpful staff of six who also knew when to keep out of the way. None of them were in sight right now, for example.

Having grown up in palaces and castles, John knew that was rarer than simple skill at the official job description, though he also didn't doubt they'd have the exact details of everything that went on in real time; that went without saying. He was only conscious of the fact that some thought the lack of privacy attendant on servants irksome because he'd been outside the Association territories and in the rest of Montival fairly often.

Pip continued: "Just be careful where you put your feet anywhere near the coral. It's sharp, and there are sea-urchins . . . think of them as poisonous underwater hedgehogs."

What is it with me and masterful women? he wondered.

To change the subject he turned his head to look at the house. "This doesn't seem much like the rest of Baru Denpasar. Or even the palace."

"It's pre-Blackout . . . pre-Change . . . and built for foreign visitors then, I rather think. Tourists, they called them, didn't they? Though the rest of the compound is more recent. Now, about that swim?"

He hesitated as she gestured towards the water, and she chuckled.

"Why be such a baby, John?"

"Well, to tell the truth, milady, I haven't been *in* the ocean more than a few times in all my life. And the last time, a forty-foot crocodile tried to eat me."

From a few remarks and a little discreet pumping of her henchman

Toa, he'd gathered that Lady Balwyn-Abercrombie was of very distinguished ancestry indeed. As daughter to the heir to the Colonelcy of
Townsville she was for all practical purposes the child of a monarch, as
he was, and through her mother related to the Windsors and of many
quarterings. He wasn't a snob about birth, or hoped he wasn't, but it did
give them something in common.

*Though Father once said you should keep in mind that the first of a dynasty is
usually just a warrior with a ready sword and a serious run of luck.*

"Which didn't stop you jumping in to save your ship's First Mate," she
said, giving him an admiring glance; she'd gotten the details out of the
others.

*I must admit, having a beautiful woman wearing very little look at me with admi-
ration is pleasant.*

He shrugged, with an it-needed-doing expression. "It was an impulse.
But back home salt water is bloody *cold*. Most places if you fall in you'll
die if you're not pulled out in time, and it isn't *much* time. There's an arctic
current all down our coast. People swim in ponds or rivers . . . a few
pools built for it . . ."

He could see her astonishment. "That's . . . that's bloody awful!" Then
more cheerfully, "You're in for a treat, then. Last one in is a Tasmanian!
Nothing dangerous in the water except *me!*"

She threw her sarong onto the lounger beneath the beach umbrella
and ran down the white sand, diving cleanly into the swell of a waist-high
wave and sleeking outward like a seal, a white streak in the ultramarine
clarity of the water.

John sighed, rolled his eyes upward, and muttered: "But you know
what a weak sinner I am, Lord."

Then he followed her in. Even knowing that the water was warm, and
even after his experience on the *Tarshish Queen* in these seas—granted,
the one time that he'd gone over the side on her had been a near-death
experience—it was still at some level a shock to find the wave no more
than slightly, pleasantly cool on a hot day.

He *wasn't* used to swimming in the ocean, but he had a good powerful crawl stroke. Pip seemed to be part sea-otter, though. By the time he'd reached the raft anchored a few hundred yards offshore he couldn't see her at all.

Until a hand clamped around his ankle and pulled him underwater with a strong backward jerk. It released him almost immediately, and he surfaced coughing and snorting bitter seawater and looking wildly about. Pip surfaced a few yards away, grinning, her hair darkened and sleeked down by the water.

"If only you could see your face," she laughed.

"Son of a *bitch!*" he swore, coughing.

"Bitch, rather. Care to try for revenge?" she said.

She backed slowly as he swam towards her, then dove and turned in a fluid curve and what was probably a deliberate flaunting of a very shapely backside.

Well, that's enough to drive out visions of giant crocodiles, he thought, and dove after her.

CHAPTER SIXTEEN

Thora Garwood looked up. Prince John was standing not far from where she and Deor sat. He was in local dress, and despite that sweating more than the mild humid warmth of the night in the Raja's palace required. His brown eyes were anxious but determined, yet she'd seen less fear in them on a deck that ran like rainwater with blood, or even when he leapt into the sea with the monster . . .

By almighty Thor, he did do that, when nobody would have thought the less of him for staying where he was. I'll go a little easier on him for it.

"Ah . . . milady Thora . . . I think we need to talk, but . . ." he began, his quiet tone hidden by the rustle and low voices of the rest of the audience taking their places in the amphitheater.

Thora let one eyebrow rise and glanced past him to where Lady Philippa Balwyn-Abercrombie sat with the cool regal self-satisfaction of a tawny cat.

"Johnnie, I hope we'll be talking in the future. But there's really no need for words about *that*. You're a free man and I'm a free woman. You might have told me in words *first*, though."

"Ah . . . later then . . . Thora, Deor," he said with a nod, and talked away.

He wasn't dragging his feet or hanging his head, but you could see that it was an effort. Thora grinned for a moment, wryly reminded herself that he hadn't quite seen twenty years yet—there were times you could forget that about him, and others when it was all too obvious. She hadn't wanted to hurt him, much, but that had been a body-blow anyway, and she didn't particularly regret it. Deor made a questioning sound.

"No. It's a bit sad, but I'm not angry, my friend," Thora Garwood said, very quietly. "We never pledged troth, just companionship, and I didn't expect us to be lovers for long—not as long as happened, given how unexpected that storm and this voyage were! We'll still be good friends, I think, in the end."

"You were right. He might have told you first," Deor grumbled.

Thora's shrug was rueful. "He did, just not with words, and yes, he should have spoken the words. But John's always going to be putty in the hands of a woman who wants him. He was for me! Though it would be different if he were married; he'd sweat blood resisting temptation, but he'd try and I think he'd manage it. And I saw that one stalking him like a wolf-bitch who's seen her mate. What we had was good, but we're too unalike, not to mention the gap in our ages. It wouldn't have lasted as long as it did, if we hadn't been on the *Queen* and cut off from the world."

She breathed out through her nose, long and slow. "Let's pay attention here. We may never see this again—I didn't think we would, when we left Bali."

That argument moved him; his appreciation of beauty was keener than hers, but that wasn't to say she lacked it altogether.

The Cendrawasih dance was to be performed in a sort of amphitheater in Raja Dalem Seganing's palace, lit by lanterns in bamboo cages around the upper tier and over the split gateway—through which the dancers would come—shaped like a temple entrance into fantastically-shaped gods and monsters and curl-tusked, club-wielding guardian *raksasa* spirits on either side, with stairs descending to the coral-block floor. Stone benches surrounded it on three sides; the local folk mostly sat on mats with their legs crossed. Prince John was a few yards away to her left now, with Captain Pip sitting next to him; Thora thought it was her imagination that a clear quivering barrier separated them from her and Deor. Both were wearing local clothes which the Raja's tailors had run up for them. They were wearing daggers as well—perfectly acceptable here, since no male Balinese went beyond his own threshold without his keris tucked into his sash, and for that matter half the women did too.

Deor looked at her dubiously, and she put a hand to her stomach. "Besides which . . . remember what we discussed? You might say I've gotten what I wanted."

"How did—" he began.

Then he cut himself off and glanced around. Ruan had been quiet, probably out of embarrassment; now his gossip-loving Mackenzie ears pricked up visibly. Thora leaned close and whispered in Deor's ear, and the younger man was too mannerly to do anything but look away. His folk knew that two could be *anamchara*, siblings of the soul, whether or not they were lovers in the conventional sense.

"The usual way, and by happenstance; precautions don't always work, you know. Which relieved me of the weight of deciding! And right now . . . well, I don't even feel I'm obliged to talk it over with the Prince, all things concerned. Later, maybe."

Deor looked slightly panicked. "Don't worry," she said. "We've months before things get urgent."

"How many months?"

"Oh, about eight, I think. Though it'll be a nuisance a bit before that."

John sat and smiled weakly as Thora nodded to him, and swallowed. Her answering smile seemed genuine, if a bit pawky.

I should have remembered that I can't get away from this. But I wasn't thinking, not with the head on the end of my neck, was I? I like Thora. On the other hand, I like Pip, a lot—we're more comfortable together, and despite her not being from Montival we have more in common. Except that right now, I'm extremely uncomfortable. Maybe I wasn't born to be a Prince or a musician. I should look into a career as a worm instead.

"It's not fair," he murmured. "We Catholics get to feel everyone else's guilt too."

"Well, I'm Anglican Rite," Pip said.

The Anglicans over in Greater Britain had rejoined the Church en masse back before he was born, not long after his grandfathers killed each other and the Association lands found there was still a Pope in Italy. It had been a matter of politics, mostly, and he supposed the ones in Australia had eventually done likewise; though thus was the will of God fulfilled. It was through men and their works that He brought to be that which must.

"We don't do guilt," she went on. "Such a grubby little emotion, and such a handicap to empire-building."

He glanced at her in startlement and she smiled fondly and went on:

"As Mummy explained it, we'd land somewhere and plant the banner and claim it in the name of the current enthroned wastrel, and if a native of the place ran up gibbering in protest we'd look at him like this—"

Her drawl grew more pronounced, and she mimicked an icy, condescending stare down her short straight nose:

"—and we'd say just before we kicked him out of the way: *Do you have a flaaag? No? Can't have a country without a* flaaag, *old boy*. As Mummy told me, keep this basic attitude firmly at the forefront of your mind and life becomes much simpler. And that's why there are people speaking English all over the world."

He glanced at her again out of the corner of his eyes, unsure of how serious she was. Instead of asking for details he gave her hand a quick pat.

She'd given him a rundown on local etiquette; *don't show people the soles of your feet* was part of it, and while hugging and hand-holding were common, they had a stiff sense of propriety here in their own way. And this was a court occasion, so reasonably formal.

There was a very quiet murmur of conversation in the liquid local language; for once he felt a pang of envy for his elder sister and the instant comprehension the Sword gave her. Huge colorful moths flew around the lanterns, and bats swooped through occasionally to harvest them. The night smelled of damp stone and the sea not far away, and of the palm-oil burning in the lamps; very little of the city not too far distant apart from the smoke of fires, for these seemed to be a very cleanly people, and ones who wasted nothing.

The orchestra filed in and struck up and dead silence fell among the watchers. The instruments were only very roughly similar to those he knew, and the musicians sat crosslegged or kneeling on woven bamboo mats to play them—flutes, long drums held across the lap and slapped with the hands, a zither-like piece, and an amazing array of xylophone-like things played with hammers over bamboo sounding tubes, or suspended gongs struck with mallets. Just looking at them was a pleasure. He could recognize fine workmanship when he saw it even in another idiom, and the golden winged gryphons . . . more or less gryphons . . . that held them and carved and inlaid teak and bronze of the frames was as good as any he'd ever seen back in Montival.

The music made him close his eyes with a frown of concentration. Nothing was familiar, but . . .

Ah, a five-octave range or better. My God, but that's a complex background rhythm! As complex as a chamber orchestra doing Bach, and at a faster tempo. This particular piece is sprightly, too. I can feel colors in it.

He relaxed his mind, and felt movement in the music as well. It was for a dance, after all.

Pip touched him and he opened his eyes with a slight jerk. Deor was looking at him; the other musician raised a brow and nodded slightly, sharing this at least.

I hope I haven't lost his friendship. That would be a pity, after we've made music together and fought side-by-side.

Pip murmured very softly in his ear. "This is the *tari Cendrawasih*. It's supposed to be the mating dance of the Bird of Paradise. The Bird of the Gods, they call it here."

The doors on the other side of the amphitheater opened. Two men stepped out carrying fringed parasols of red silk very like the four who surrounded the Raja on the other side of the enclosure, and stood stock-still.

A woman danced down the steps after them—and the dance was as alien as the music, and like the music held him spellbound. She was dressed in a tall golden headdress plumed with impossibly colorful feathers and a sheath-like red dress that left arms and shoulders bare save for a fretted golden necklace and armbands, with deep pleats in the skirt that swirled around her bare feet. From the rear of the dress hung two long swaths of golden silk; when she grasped them and raised her arms high they trailed behind her like wings.

There's a whole language of step and gesture here I don't know, he thought with fascination. *But even the glimpses are lovely.*

The side-to-side motion of the head, the curling spread-fingered movements of hands and arms, the eloquent darting glances of her eyes, the quick bobbing movements of the whole body, all suggested a bird— and also longing. Then the music rose to a crescendo and a second figure arrived, her costume subtly different but just as flamboyantly colorful. They faced each other with the yellow wings outstretched, bobbing and circling, then danced apart . . .

You know, John thought, *there's nothing here that you couldn't put in front of a convocation of abbots and abbesses, but that's an* extremely *sexy dance.*

He stopped himself on the verge of applauding when he noticed nobody else was; evidently you showed appreciation by intense focus and approving looks. The performers didn't bow to the audience either, just circled still dancing as they exited up the staircase they'd entered by.

Did she wink at me? That was the first one, the dance leader. She did wink at me, I think! What a remarkably accomplished girl. And very pretty, too.

Pip chuckled softly. "I think Sulastri wants an introduction. She's not as standoffish with outsiders as most people here, I found."

My God, I'm transparent!

At his look of alarm she tucked a hand into his arm and went on: "And I have *no* intention of introducing you."

The look of teasing mockery died down. "This dance is sort of unusual here; it isn't really religious . . . not part of a ceremony, at least."

"Most of their dances are?"

Pip frowned in thought. "More a matter of nearly everything being part of their religion here, and religion being part of everything else."

Sounds like Mackenzies! he thought.

She paused for a moment and went on: "Well, not absolutely every-thing, and putting it on for us with the best performers in town is a ges-ture of honor. It's also a way of saying that the Raja is willing to do serious business . . . in a day or two."

"Aren't they in a hurry?" John said.

"For them, this *is* hurrying. They've got dances that go on for *twelve hours*, more like ballet combined with a mystery play. Anything less than what we're getting would be mutually insulting."

John ran a hand over his hair. "And I thought we Associates were obsessed with ceremony!"

"Oh, you have no idea. It doesn't hurt that you're a Prince, too, and not just some weird foreigner. Weird foreign *woman*, at that," she added dryly, an edge in her voice.

"Weird foreign male Prince," John said, and glanced over at Raja Dalem Seganing. "They should count themselves fortunate they didn't get my elder sister."

The ruler of Baru Denpasar was in his sixties, and like most of his people he was lean and slightly-built. And short by Montivallan standards; about four inches below John's five-foot-ten, which made him tall for his folk, with thick white hair that still held a few streaks of black, cropped closer than the shoulder-length or more which seemed standard for men here. The Montivallan thought there was a profound weariness in his eyes, under a smooth mask of calm good nature and a costume which, despite its darker colors, made the dancers seem positively restrained—it included a crown of leaves made of gold, for starters, and a jacket that showed patches of black between riots of embroidery in threads of pre-cious metal and jewels.

Countess de Stafford would be entranced, John thought.

It gave him a momentary glow of nostalgia. Delia de Stafford had been by way of an unofficial tutor for him in Associate court etiquette and ceremony and fashion. He still remembered her endless kindness when he was petrified that others were laughing at the pimply fourteen-year-old Prince. Not openly, but behind his back, which would have been worse, and it wasn't something you could discuss with your parents—the very thought of doing *that* made him cringe, even in retrospect.

John felt slightly more at ease as the Raja made a minimal gesture that Pip's nudge indicated was a summons. The faces around the Raja weren't nearly as alien as the gamelan music or the dance. Not nearly as beautiful or interesting either, to be sure, but he recognized bureaucrats and generals and the sort of senior clerics who were involved with Court business when he saw them, whatever sort of clothes they were wearing.

The Raja gave a very slight smile as John made a Court bow—the precise inclination and sweep of the hand that went from *non-inheriting child of a monarch* to *foreign ruler sovereign in his own right while meeting in his kingdom*. The detail of the movement wouldn't matter here and had been completely useless even at home until recently, but that he was obviously taking care probably would.

"As son to High King Artos and High Queen Mathilda, I greet Your Majesty with gratitude for Your hospitality and succor. House Artos and the High Kingdom of Montival are in Your Majesty's debt, nor will the debt be forgotten."

"You are welcome, and you have already fought our enemies, Your Highness. And . . . so interesting, so unexpected," the Raja said, in rusty but fluent English. "This modern world of ours is full of surprises, but how America has turned out is not the least of them."

He smiled, obviously seeing how startled John was at his command of the language:

"My mother the late Queen was an official of the Bali Tourism Association before the Wrath of Indera . . . the Change, you call it. And it was useful in dealing with the *South Sea Adventure* people before they . . . became what they are. I hope Your Highness was pleased with our small entertainment?"

John made a graceful gesture. "Your Majesty is most gracious. The music and dancing were surpassingly lovely. My only regret is that I am too ignorant of the . . . background and conventions . . . of this form of art to fully understand it. I wish that I could take the time necessary to appreciate it as it deserves."

It was pleasant when complete honesty was the best policy; John thought of it as storing up credit for times when it was necessary to be more . . .

Creative, he thought.

There was a murmur as someone else who spoke English translated for the nobles, and they probably heard the sincerity in the tone. The suspicious looks faded a little. It was a little disturbing; being a patron of the arts was all very well, but these people evidently took it *very* seriously.

"Tomorrow we will consult further," the Raja said, and added something in his own language.

"That went very well," Pip said, when they were alone again. "He used the . . . well, he addressed you as an almost-equal, I'm pretty sure. It's that sort of language, it's easy to be unintentionally rude because everything changes according to the relative status of who's talking to whom. Not just the titles or pronouns, the vocabulary too. I get by because nobody expects a foreigner to know the subtle parts."

CHAPTER SEVENTEEN

"*B*akayaro!"

"*Naskleng Japon!*"

Captain Ishikawa and the chief artificer of the Raja's armory were yelling at each other again; the local was much louder as he grew more frustrated, and probably also somewhat deaf from years of exposure to the clangor of his trade. John could hear them over the wall that enclosed the buildings, warehouses and workshops despite the smithy-loud background and from somewhere the howling whine as someone put hard timber to a power-driven band saw.

The only thing he learned from the exchange was confirmation that Nihongo cursing sounded explosive and ripping and the Balinese equivalent shrill and high-pitched.

"*Oh, God,*" Pip said, as the mechanical scream died down and the human equivalent continued. "Experts at war, at war."

John hesitated for a moment, then laughed; he liked her talent for wordplay, almost as much as her sense of humor, wits and looks. In fact he liked her more than any girl he'd ever been involved with, despite or possibly because she scared him a little in several different ways. Or was it that she tempted him severely? Or possibly she tempted *and* scared him and the fright was part of the allure. Some Associate noblemen preferred demure and deferential females, or at least ones who acted that way, but he'd always thought that would be too much like making love to a cow. Also he'd noticed that men like that ended up being led around by the nose a lot of the time, or by some other part of their anatomy, and not even realizing it was happening.

The problem is that I'm not sure I should like Pip as much as I do, he thought. *Someone might have designed her to tempt me. And the problem with temptations like that is that they're so bloody hard to resist.*

"I don't *think* they'll kill each other," he agreed aloud, as they stopped under the shade of a jacaranda tree dropping its purple flowers in a carpet on the brick sidewalk not far from the gate. Then he took a deep breath before going in.

He was joking about the Japanese and the locals coming to blows, but not altogether. That was why he crossed himself and murmured:

"*O Blessed Archangel Gabriel, who stood by Michael's side when the hosts of Heaven cast down Lucifer, you who brought the Good News to the Blessed Virgin Mary and are patron of all who must persuade and bring men to agreement, I beseech thee, do thou intercede for me, a miserable sinner, at the throne of divine Mercy, that I may fulfill my duties and do battle with these my friends and followers against our enemy and the enemy of the Most High. Amen.*"

Gabriel was God's messenger, and the Saint who watched over diplomats.

"Amen," Pip echoed. "We're going to need all the help we can get . . ."

". . . to keep this bunch together," John said.

Nihonjin samurai had a low tolerance for disrespect from those they considered inferiors; among their own people an elaborate code of ritualized deference controlled everything. It wasn't altogether different from the way Protectorate knights and nobles behaved back in the PPA territories, but the edge of danger was stronger—rather the way it had been at home in John's grandfather's day, he suspected. Ishikawa was easy-going and even a little democratic by those standards, but only by those standards.

And the locals were also a very polite people . . . until something snapped. That was when the word *amok* came into play. They could induce the state deliberately and en masse; he'd seen that in the battle on the harbor. From what Pip and Toa said and from a little he'd seen, it could also simply seize on individuals or small groups who'd been pushed too far by others or by circumstance.

I think that's a major reason *they're so polite most of the time. They don't dare* not *be polite if the person they disrespect may start screaming and frothing and hacking.*

He relaxed as the voices died down. "Ishikawa's quite in love with your prang-prangs," he said. "*Very clever,* was what he called them, and it's a term of art he doesn't use lightly. I think he's been working on some engineering drawings to take home."

Pip preened a little. "Townsville Armory is second to none," she said. "They're the very latest thing in conclusive argumentation."

"I wonder why nobody else has come up with the idea?" he said.

"Well . . . they're about as hard to make and only a bit smaller and lighter than the usual catapults and just as easy to spot and target. And while they're bloody wonderful little devices for mowing down a pack of screaming gits with cutty-choppy-throwy things from farther out than their bows and blowguns and spears and cleavers can reach . . . if the gits have conventional field catapults, which alas the Carcosans *do* have, they'll pound you to scrap from out of range. Which is why we haven't tried this expedition against the fortress before you got here. Despite our hosts being so desperate."

"I don't blame them," John said. "Seizing their water supply by building a fort on it . . . well, the Yellow Raja has his hand around a sensitive spot, right?"

"No fear!" she said, which was apparently Townsvillian for *damned* right. "The next rice harvest is in about a month. They let the fields lie fallow and dry for a month after that to keep blights and bugs down, and then it's back to plowing and flooding and transplanting; it hardly ever stops, really. Two rice crops a year and veggies in between and they use the paddies for fish, too. But it all needs a lot of water and that fort the

Carcosans have built means the Baru Denpasarans would lose a third of their acreage."

"Starvation?" John said; nobody in the Changed world took that lightly.

"Disaster, at least. They keep a year's famine reserve but there are limits."

"I *thought* that was what the Raja said," he said; the court language had been notably opaque.

"Well, to be fair, no monarch I've met would be happy about publicly singing that song."

At his enquiring look she trilled: "*The bastards have us/By the bloody throat today/*Tra-la, tra-la."

"Ah," he replied; there was a lot of truth in that.

She shrugged. "When the authorities say *the situation is grave but don't panic,* it means *everyone, panic right now!*"

He hesitated and then spoke: "How did you get your hands on the prang-prangs, Pip? I gather you and your father didn't part on the best of terms. I sympathize given that I had to run out on Mother, but . . ."

"Well, ummmm . . ."

Her eyes went up slightly and she pursed her lips. When she'd arranged her thoughts she continued in a tone of innocent sweetness several years too young for her . . . and she was young anyway, at least in years:

"Well, actually, one reason for my abrupt departure on the racing camel was that a few forms and invoices and tiresome clerkish things like that may have gone missing from Daddy's study, you see, before the prang-prangs were crated up and shipped out . . . on one of Aunt Fifi and Uncle Pete's ships . . . because he was being an absolute *beast* about my plans and his absurd scheme to send me to court off in Winchester."

"Why Winchester?" John asked.

Granted that the King-Emperors of Greater Britain were the senior monarchs of Christendom, not least in their own estimation, it was still the other side of the world.

*That meant months of sailing either way even on a fast ship making a direct passage,
and leaving aside storms still not a very safe journey unless you did it on a warship.*

"The Windsors have been breeding like rabbits and I think Daddy
wanted me to nab some minor Royal, one looking for a soft job as an
antipodean consort and stud-bull among the koalas and kookaburras. To
give Townsville's new little hereditary Colonelcy even more genetic pol-
ish than Mummy did and trump his ghastly set of nephews, eh? What a
fate! So really, I didn't have any alternative. Tempting to do it just to dish
my cousins, but . . . no."

"Ah," he said; that seemed to happen a lot when he was talking to Pip.
"Well, lucky for me you did, right? The prang-prangs certainly came in
handy in that fight."

"Righty-O. I knew it would all work out for the best! And the Darwin
and East Indies Trading Company *paid* for them, all very regular, but what
with the confused paperwork the initial *sale* may not have been quite
quite-quite, if you know what I mean, and then it turned out JB in
Darwin—King Birmo of Capricornia—had gotten one long enough for
his own military to take apart and do a complete set of drawings so they
could copy it later. Spot of bother, that, but fortunately I'd left by the
time the details came out. It'll all blow over eventually; Townsville and
Darwin *are* friends and allies after all. Usually."

"Have they ever fought?"

"Not *fought*, not really, just a few scuffles over absurd old lines on the
ground in the outback where only lizards live. Capricornia is the shield of
Oz, as JB is very, very fond of saying. And JB's people would have dupli-
cated the prang-prangs anyway once they knew about them, there's nothing mysterious about the concept, I just saved them a little time and
removed a cause of Capricornian-Townsvillian friction . . . rather altruistic
of me in fact, if you look at it properly. Blessed are the peacemakers, what?"

"Ah," John said expressionlessly as they passed a two-wheeled oxcart
bearing a load of rusty steel bars he recognized as part of Captain Feldman's ballast.

Then: "You like to travel, Pip. What do you say to taking a trip to Montival after this is all over? Assuming we're not killed or possessed by demons or whatever."

"Smashing idea!" she said, with a brilliant smile, squeezing his arm. "For all sorts of reasons."

There were guards by the heavy timber gate; it was plain massive wood and steel strapping, unusual among this decoration-happy folk. They didn't do snapping to attention here, but the local equivalent involved a bow and calling them *Putra* and *Putri*, which were both personal names and titles roughly meaning *of royal rank*. He suspected that years of study would be required to really understand the system of honorifics, and Pip had casually remarked that she had only the basics *and* they also used titles borrowed from Malay in some contexts . . .

By the time they walked through the gate, Ishikawa and the Raja's engineer were bowing—in rather different ways—and smiling at each other with patent insincerity.

Thora and Deor were there, probably to help with the translation; it would be from Ishikawa's uncertain newly-learned English to Deor's uncertain, rusty and limited Balinese eked out with some Malay, which in turn was a second language the chief artificer had a little of; it was related to his native Balinese tongue but not mutually comprehensible with it.

He strongly suspected they'd also probably kept things from escalating dangerously by shading the *ignorant savage* and *arrogant young pup of a foreigner* bits out of the exchange.

The Raja's man was about sixty, hair untypically cut to a gray bristle and hands and arms scarred from burns and sparks and dealing with sharp moving metal and heavy weights.

Both the Montivallans nodded to John politely, and he smiled back and winced inwardly as he stepped closer with Pip at his side. Another thing he hadn't thought of was that he was going to have to go right on working with Thora after shifting to Pip . . . although he hadn't been thinking much at the time at all.

This section of the complex was a big walled compound, part of it covered by a tiled roof supported on tall wooden pillars in turn supporting cranes and lifting devices, part open, and all paved in flagstones. Heat rippled from half a dozen charcoal hearths of various sizes and shapes. Even in simple hose and shirt, the way it combined with the walls cutting off any breath of air and the natural muggy warmth to make him envy the local workers stripped to their loincloths and some protective gear. Though in Portland or Walla Walla the metalworker's guild councils would have hit the roof screaming at how skimpy that gear was.

Some held metal on the various anvils with tongs and pounded on it themselves or angled it while others hammered it, or put it back in the hearths to heat again or plunged it dragon-hissing into the quenching baths of water or oil. More were laboring with file and peening hammer and other tools at long benches. The familiar rasp of files and *tinka-tinka-tinka* of metalworkers' hammers and *punk-punk-punk* of punches and occasional scream of a grinding wheel sounded amid the hard stink of hot metal and hot oil and fire.

Things more advanced than tongs and sledges included a number of lathes and drill-presses, hydraulic hammers and heavier machine-tools, all pre-Change salvage converted to modern power sources but well-maintained and capable of making all their own replacement parts, and it was reassuring to see a set of neatly-kept gauges and measuring instruments hung from a pegboard against one wall. In fact, judging by the gearwork and hydraulic cylinders being crated up, and even if this was the only such facility in Baru Denpasar . . .

"You know," John said to Pip, "it strikes me as odd that they can't make their own field and naval catapults. Something along those lines, at least, now that they've seen modern examples. They've got the foundry equipment and machine-tools and skilled labor they need, I'd say."

Pip nodded. "If they had the materials to work with they could, they've been building their capacity since you-know-who went to the bad—"

She jerked her thumb towards Carcosa, without looking in that direction.

"—but the alloy steels for springs aren't that common here; remember what I told Captain Feldman."

That was reasonable. Those mostly came from vehicle suspensions and they were much, much less common than ordinary metal.

"And the . . . people across the bay . . . were careful to keep it out of their hands both before and after their . . . alteration. They've got the trebuchets, but it's not the same."

"No, they're not," John agreed; trebuchets could throw enormous weights, but they were bulky and immobile.

A large pipe made from spiral strips of the bamboo which was the local ubiquitous material came in over one wall, pouring water into the funnel intake of a small Francis turbine. There must be dry periods, because an alternative power source was a huge post with nearly-as-huge padded levers on either side, where two elephants could put their heads and push and supply power via leather belts to the main shaft and its massive flywheel. Pip looked at it and began to laugh. Deor raised an eyebrow, and she spoke through a last gurgling chuckle:

"My family were responsible for that. More or less and without knowing it. Long before I was born, they captured eleven cow elephants and a young bull—there weren't the swarms you have now but even then the zoo escapers were breeding in the outback in Oz—for the Raja of Bali. Some sort of status thing, in Bali, having elephants to ride on."

John nodded; to his relief, both Thora and her companion seemed genuinely amused. On the one hand he felt ashamed that everyone was being so civilized about things; a screaming match would be a relief. On the other hand, he was ashamed of his own craven relief that there *wouldn't* be any screaming.

And on yet another hand, I can't imagine Thora screaming and crying. Bashing and beating, yes, screaming and crying . . . no.

He wrenched his mind back to what Pip was saying. Evidently Australia was even more of a mess than his home continent with introduced animals spreading chaotically. Eventually things would balance out, God willing.

"JB gave them some help because he was looking into taming them too and wanted to be good mates with Bali. To hear Mummy and Auntie Fifi describe it, catching them was an epic and getting a ship rigged to carry them was even worse . . . And then it just disappeared off the face of the sea and they had to do the whole thing again to meet the contract, which ate the profit to the last penny."

"The beasts ended up here?" John said. "That's where the ship went?"

Pip nodded. "So they tell me. The *South Sea Adventure* caught them and brought them here, and then handed them over to His Majesty's dad because they couldn't figure out anything else to do with them except eat them. They made that sort of goodwill gesture occasionally before they . . . altered. And the climate here suited them."

John chuckled, but he was more interested in the weapons laid out in the open workspace. Six of them were from the *Tarshish Queen*, the bow and stern chasers and a half broadside, and six were prang-prangs from Pip's *Silver Surfer*. Ishikawa stamped over for one more inspection of the field carriages whose construction he'd supervised.

He'd been put in charge of that project on John's recommendation, since the Imperial Japanese Navy designed their shipboard weapons so that they could be transferred to knockdown field carriages in a few minutes. And he was an engineer with experience in the construction of war machines of all sorts and field entrenchments and sieges, all things Japan did to a high standard and the *Kerajaan*—that meant roughly "kingdom"—of Baru Denpasar did not.

John had done his best to get Ishikawa to be tactful. Apart from suspecting outsiders in general, the locals retained specific, lively and unpleasant memories of campaigns the Empire of Dai-Nippon had waged in this neighborhood about a century ago, two generations back before the Change. There had been fingering of keris knives amid mutters that included the words *Orang Japon* and spitting on the ground.

Even without knowing a word of the local language he was pretty sure that absolutely nothing in those comments was a compliment or an expression of comradeship. He'd talked a little with Reiko and her countrymen about the history while they were traveling together back in Montival, and *their* version of that period was that Japan had been attempting to bring peace and prosperity to Asia as an act of selfless generosity when jealous, malicious outsiders viciously attacked them. They'd been tactful enough to say *outsiders* rather than just *Americans*.

All depends on your perspective, I suppose, he thought. *It's history, emphasis very much on story part.*

"These dancing barbarian monkeys!" the Japanese officer said as he walked up beside John with his left hand on his katana.

He was rather obviously doing a breathing routine to control his temper. Ishikawa was sort of spontaneous compared to his compatriots John had met, and he was still self-disciplined enough to make the Montivallan prince feel like an impulse-ridden slob.

"Your Highness, I would not trust them to build a treadle pump. Or dig a privy properly!"

I'm glad he said it softly. I don't think the Raja is the only one here who speaks English. And it's interesting the way we've been promoted from barbarian monkey status in Captain Ishikawa's eyes. Not that the Nihonjin ever came right out and said it to our faces in our own language, but you could tell back in the beginning that they were surprised we took baths and didn't fart and scratch our backsides at the dinner table or smash our faces down into the food like dogs. I like them, but they're a bit . . . insular. Maybe because they haven't seen or dealt with foreigners except at the sword's edge for generations, and at home all their people do things pretty much the same way.

Feldman was looking at his catapults impassively. As he did he worked the fingers in his injured arm in a set of exercises Ruan and the healer on the *Queen* had agreed would help the return of strength and flexibility.

"Full recompense for any combat damage, Captain, and repairs for the *Queen* at the locals' expense, as well as a full cargo for your metals," John said. "The Raja agreed."

The merchant smiled and shrugged, carefully because his left arm was still in its sling. There didn't seem to be much damage to nerves or tendons or any infection, but you didn't recover from an arrow through a limb in a week, or two.

"Thank you, Your Highness. Though even if there's no financial risk I don't really like loaning weapons in a longshore quarrel. Fully justified in this case . . . but I don't *like* it. I'm not a man of war by natural inclination. Trade benefits all parties; politics, not so much."

"I don't like what they may do with 'em, skipper," his Bosun said. "*To* 'em, more like. They need tending, these beauties. They're more delicate than they look."

She was in a wheelchair, with her bandaged thigh propped up on a folding rest, and her rather lumpy weather-reddened face was wrinkled in a knot of worry.

And maybe when we're gone they can get her to stay in the hospital, he thought.

Ruan was pushing the wheelchair; he looked up at John and he knew the young Mackenzie shared the thought. They had quite a good house of healing here. This wasn't a backward country.

The Captain of the *Tarshish Queen* sighed and spoke: "It's makeshift, but it'll do."

Ishikawa sucked air between his teeth. "Captain-san, your *weapons* are excellent. But these carriages . . . there is too much wood and not enough high-quality steel, just this hand-shaped rebar. They weigh twice what ours do and are much less strong."

"The trial firing went well enough," Feldman said.

Ishikawa shook his head. "For a few rounds, yes. But hard use could shake them to pieces in the field."

"They'll do for the one mission," John said. "It's not as if this were the Prophet's War."

At Ishikawa's slight look of enquiry he specified: "It's not as if we were going to haul them a thousand miles from Portland to Corwin and gallop them cross-country in battles and fight for years at a time."

Instead of saying: *You, my friend, are a perfectionist, but* The Best *can be the enemy of* Good Enough. *This is what we've got, and the Raja is contributing the best he has.*

Ishikawa *was* a perfectionist, a hard intelligent man of unbending duty. Feldman was knowledgeable and decisive and deeply thoughtful; Pip was ruthlessly opportunistic and fearless; Thora had a natural aptitude for the details of war honed by experience all over the world starting when his voice hadn't begun to break; Deor was good at understanding and communicating and could do . . . things. All of that was actually very reassuring.

Because he suddenly seemed to be in charge of all the outsider contingent, due to his birth and local expectations about it. It was deeply comforting that there were people he could consult who actually knew what they were doing.

Remember, John—project confidence. Even if you don't feel it. Especially if you don't.

They set out at dawn of the next day when there was still a faint breath of coolness, though he was sweating heavily in his half-armor already and as always here the sweat just *stayed* there, marinating. There were crowds, cheering and making bowing gestures with their palms together and throwing flowers behind rows of the Raja's soldiers acting as crowd-control with their spears held horizontally, and he waved back.

An enemy they fear and hate with very good reason has taken something they need for their very lives, and we're going out to get it back. No wonder they're cheering! Though I suspect they're cheering their own people more than us. Which is entirely natural; you love your own more than even the friendliest strangers, that stands to reason, there would be something wrong with anyone who didn't.

There were fifty mounted lancers with helmets and round shields and light torso armor of small plates and mail in their party, and several times that number of footmen with spears and bows marching in good order, everyone who could be spared from keeping watch on . . .

You-know-what, John thought uneasily, carefully not looking eastward.

. . . across the bay; the plan was that the reserves here would march out and keep the Carcosans from sending reinforcements inland.

All had their keris knives, and a slightly curved hook-hilted sword-like chopping thing with a broad blade about thirty inches long called a parang, worn in a horizontal sling. There were also six elephants with huge pack-saddles and nets of cargo in boxes and bales, each with a

mahout astride its neck. The great gray beasts loomed over the cavalcade, all at least ten or eleven feet at the shoulder, and the ground shook
a little as each immense padded round foot came down with five or so
carefully placed tons behind it.

*And that crocodile was about the same weight. This is a very pretty part of the
world but it's too interesting for comfort! I prefer it where there are only tigers and grizzly bears to worry about.*

Various servants, laborers, ox-carts and hangers-on ate the dust behind, but not too many given the size of the operation. Beneath infinite
differences of detail, it wasn't altogether unlike a similar movement in
Montival.

Pip handed him her canteen, which was ancient aluminum covered in
modern cuirboilli worked in odd angular animal-shapes and full of well-
water cut with lemon and lime juice. He drank deeply, savoring the way
the slightly acid bite cut through the feeling of gummy thickness in his
mouth and throat even when it was lukewarm.

*I'm not exactly hungover, but then, I'm not exactly not hungover, either. And she
and I didn't get much sleep last night, even after the feast ended. My God, how does Pip
do it? She looks as fresh as a . . . well, not a daisy. Hibiscus, maybe, she grew up in
tropical Townsville. I wonder how she'd like the Black Months back home? Maybe I
can arrange it so we get there in spring. April and May in the Willamette are lovely,
and it's blossom season in the Duchy then.*

"You're going to have to watch that you drink enough water, darling,"
she said solicitously. "You look quite yummy when your skin's wet with
sweat, but it's really pouring off you already in those steel-crawfish togs."

John nodded, thankful he was on horseback—though he'd spent
hours getting acquainted with the little horse he'd been given, which was
used to different signals.

"Unless you're standing still in the shade you get hot and tired quickly
in plate. Even if you're very fit," he said. "You can get actual deaths from
heatstroke if you're not careful. And it's a lot worse here than anywhere
I've ever been before."

"That's probably why we don't go in for it in this part of the world," she said. "Mind you, it was extremely Lancelot-ish back in the battle in the harbor. Very impressive!"

He grinned. "You were even more so, given that you weren't wearing anything but street clothes and other people's blood."

"These aren't just my clothes. This is a *costume*. It's a statement, rather! Very Old Country, very *droogish*, you know."

A chuckle, and she looked at him with a charming sidelong glance. "I got the look from an ancient magazine that Mummy had in her collection. About a . . . film? Movie? Whatever they called them."

Fayard and the Guard crossbowmen looked hot in their armor too, and glad that they were riding to the fight instead of marching; everyone in the Protector's Guard had to be a good horseman even if they went into action on foot. There were parties from the crews of both the *Silver Surfer* and the *Tarshish Queen* to handle the catapults and prang-prangs and Captain Ishikawa's half-dozen sailors marched behind his horse, striding along in a rolling toes-out pace with their *naginatas* and bows over their shoulders.

All the commoners were also looking a bit crapulous and worse for wear to start with if you paid close attention; the lower-class feast laid on to send the troops and sailors on their way had been a lot less decorous than the court version for the officers, and that had been lively enough. The sun was coming up eastward, but he spared only a single glance at the way it turned the coral limestone of Carcosa a deeper, more bloody red. He suspected few people contemplated the beauty of sunrise here.

"Who are those?" he asked quietly, nodding to the seventh elephant riding near the head of the procession.

That one had a howdah framed in intricately carved and inlaid teak and ebony, shaped like a small one-room cottage. The sides were curtains of gauzy cloth, but he could see the pair within—a man and a woman, both aged and distinguishable mostly by the man's thin white beard, both wearing fantastic jewelry over shimmering pale clothing and drum-like hats covered in wrought-gold plaques.

The commander of the lancers was in overall charge of the expedition, but he'd been very deferential indeed to that pair. Anak Agung was a blunt-featured man in his thirties with a wispy close-cut beard and mustache, universally addressed as *Tuan*, lord. He'd lost the tip of his nose sometime in the past, and his hand rested on the use-smoothed ivory and gold hilt of the parang slung horizontally across his armored stomach as if that was the only place for it; his bare arms were corded with muscle and showed thin scars. When he drew the weapon to gesture his troops forward the blade had a swirling pattern in the steel, layer-forged and then acid-etched. It was as fine an example of the bladesmith's art as John had ever seen, but you could see where nicks had been filed out of the edge.

Highborn warrior in his prime, he thought. *Knows his work, tough, experienced, intelligent; his weakness would be arrogance. If he's that elaborately polite to the old lord and lady, they're movers and shakers of some sort.*

"A Pedanda," Pip said in answer to his question. "A High Priest of the local faith. And his consort, the High Priestess. Very high-powered, by local lights; too holy to speak much to foreigners like us. They take their religion seriously in Baru Denpasar, which with some the things going on here . . . well, I don't blame them. I've been praying more lately myself."

John crossed himself in agreement. And they were trapped here, unless they could help the Baru Denpasarans. The *Tarshish Queen* needed repairs, and both it and the *Silver Surfer* needed their full help to make it out of the harbor. Quite understandably, they wouldn't do that without receiving help in return. The Raja had to think of his own people first.

Outside the palace district the city was neatly laid out on a gridwork of streets roughly north-south and east-west, with an occasional irregular opening for public use and frequent temples of all sizes, a couple as large as cathedrals and a riot of painted sculpture. From the smell, or comparative lack of it, there was a good sewage and water system.

The encircling wall was quite respectable as a piece of military engineering, large blocks of cut limestone on the inner and outer face and a core of pounded rubble and mortar, with octagonal towers spaced along it. The gates weren't metal-faced in the way he was used to, save for savage-looking triangular spikes, but they were made of thick baulks of dense tropical hardwoods, and there were portcullis and murder-holes in the covered gateways between the inner and outer portals. Heavy walled platforms towards the harbor southward held trebuchets on turntables. The counterweight-lever machines were less flexible that torsion cata- pults but simple to make and good for covering a known range of targets from a fixed position.

It was the decoration of the wall that made him give a low whistle. The stone arches and surrounds about the gates were carved in low relief and painted or picked out in stones of different colors, a luxuriant visual explo- sion of foliage and figures human and divine and—he hoped—imaginary, demons and dragons with bulging eyes and curling fangs and long claws, acting out stories whose meanings he did not know. Some of the stretches still blank were covered in bamboo scaffolding, with artisans arriving and setting up for the day's work. Nothing about it interfered with the func- tion of the fortifications, but the impact was overwhelming, like walking into the pages of an extravagantly illustrated book.

Pity, he thought with an admiring look. *I can appreciate the workmanship, but I'd have to know the context for the full effect. It's a song in a language I don't speak.*

He voiced the thought aloud, and Deor snorted. "Thora and I jour- neyed the world around, and that was my greatest grief amid the joy of it," he said. "I'm a man who makes words and music—and words vary so much. Music too, more than you might think. You have to learn a new way of listening for that, too."

Thora patted the hilt of her sword. "Universal," she said dryly.

Deor grinned at her. "Yes, and your sword has sung me many a gallant song, but you can only have one conversation that way," he said.

As they left the city's outskirts everyone got out of the way of the Raja's men with deferential speed, something else perfectly familiar to an Associate. The roadway leading north was about thirty feet across and from the fragments of asphalt had been paved once; now it was graded dirt and gravel, but well-kept, and lined by ditches and then biggish straight-trunked trees that cast welcome shade.

John looked at them with an approving nod. There were dozens of ways of ordering a realm, and he knew most of them by personal acquaintance. Montival had nearly every one you could think of in one spot or another, from the Association's ordinary feudalism to New Deseret's exotic democratic theocracy. All of them could work well, or badly. The best rule-of-thumb signs for which of those was happening in any given time or place was whether the common people had enough to eat and whether there were bandits, but how competently things like roads were managed came a close third.

Here near the coast the land was flat and largely open, though mountains reared blue-green in the distance all along the northern horizon, and the highest was directly ahead.

Where we're going to fight, John thought. Unless they run away . . . no, that's wishful thinking. Don't worry about it, John: that doesn't help. Particularly don't think about the Pallid Mask . . .

He really didn't want to think about those lambent yellow eyes, and the place they'd taken him.

Near the city were orchards and patches of things like spices and breadfruit-trees, and the type of sugarcane they chewed raw like candy here. He looked at those with interest. Breakfast had been one of the globular breadfruits, cored and stuffed with sweetened pineapple and banana and durian chunks and shaved coconut and spices, then covered and baked and presented to be eaten with a spoon, still steaming and about the consistency of a moist fruity brioche.

Wish I'd been in better shape to appreciate it, he thought.

Beyond was the open countryside, the peasant's world of rice-paddies each with a little pyramidal shrine at one corner, much like the calvaires you found in Catholic areas back home. The villages were long irregular rectangles of joined compounds, embowered with fruit and banana and coconut trees and clumps of carefully managed bamboo. Each had three substantial public temples—one at the northern entrance where an S-curve in the road foiled evil spirits, one in an open square in the middle and another at the southern end with the cemetery.

"What are those?" he asked Pip, pointing to fields that weren't in the waving knee-high green of rice.

She gave the fields a flick of the eye. "Plantains . . . manioc . . . those are sarda melons, we grow them at home . . . those leafy things are *loba*, they make a mordant for dyeing cloth that works better than alum, I wish I could get a cargo of it . . . that strip is cardamom, and those are cinnamon bushes, and the one beyond is indigo," she said. "The row of little trees with the multiple stems is nutmeg."

Then she gave him a glance. "You've never seen those before, have you?"

He shook his head; the list of names just meant *green, bushy or leafy* as far as he could see. "They don't go with having a winter. Live and learn!"

It all *smelled* green, in a rank way unfamiliar to him, a hot scent of growth and mud and rot and an underlying tang of compost and manure from the paddies.

And it all looks like gardens as much as farms, he thought.

There were colorful flowers in plenty too, on tree and vine and even moving towards the city by the cartload along with baskets of grain and fruit and heaps of nameless roots and trussed chickens and pigs and bundled firewood.

My God, how they must work *to keep all this up!*

A throbbing drum-like sound echoed from each village, one after another taking it up, running on ahead of them.

"What's that?" he said, cocking an ear at the low percussive beat; each would be audible for miles, and together they made a sound like the heartbeat of the Earth.

"*Kulkul,*" Deor said; he'd been getting more communicative again, apparently taking his cue from Thora, and John was glad of it.

Though it makes me feel guilty. But then, right now what doesn't make me feel guilty? I'm not exactly looking forward to a fight, but I am going to welcome the distraction *of it.*

"Sort of a hollow-log drum with a slit in the side, and they've got one in every village, in a little tower arrangement they call the *Bale Kulkul.*"

"Don't tell me, that means *drum tower.* Sort of like a church bell-tower in a Christian country?"

Deor smiled. "Right you are, Your Highness. There are different beats for each occasion, weddings, funerals, ceremonies, assemblies."

Grimly: "That's the call to arms. I can feel . . . see . . . no, not really either. There's a feeling . . . as if the drums were the rumble of feet and the crackle of lightning . . . and a warrior riding an elephant taller than the sky, a warrior king with a blue face and a spear in his hand that *is* the lightning . . . no, that's not it . . . an army of the air with the heads of beasts . . ."

He took a deep breath and shrugged. "Just say that it's also a summoning beyond the world we know. And if they are going to war, they do not go alone."

Then he frowned, and Thora touched the silver Hammer she wore around her neck the way a Christian did a cross.

"And there's the oddest sense of very distant kinship, too," he said.

And there was war in Heaven, John thought with a shiver. *It's the same one here—against Principalities and Powers.*

Folk gathered in clumps, bowing and pointing, chattering and waving their conical straw hats to the colorful cavalcade as it passed by in a glitter of plumes and steel and gold, or stopped their work in the fields to do likewise. The big black water-buffalos they used for draught stopped too and stared, their ears twitching and huge liquid eyes mildly curious. He thought he heard their ruler's name in the shouts, and they had the feel of loyal cries, something he'd heard all his life. It was difficult to fake.

"So, Raja Dalem is popular?" he said quietly.

Toa was trudging along beside Pip's horse with his huge spear over his shoulder, sweat shining on his tattooed skin but no sign of strain on his heavy-featured face. The local horses were well-made, with a strong trace of Arab ancestry, but fairly small. John felt as if he was back on the pony he'd had when he was ten, and for the big man it would be like trying to ride a very large dog. An elephant would have done much better for someone his size.

"Pretty much," he said. "They got good reason to like him, see? Or cling to him like a fucking life preserver. For starters, the Carcosans are sodding maniacs when they aren't worse."

John made a wordless sound of agreement and pushed the memory of being *somewhere else* out of his mind. It tended to fade like a dream anyway, but now and then it came flooding back.

Toa went on: "And everyone else on this island hates the Balinese like poison, so if the Raja loses—"

He drew an eloquent thumb across his neck and made a horribly realistic gargling sound, very much like a man drowning in his own blood. John nodded, and winced inwardly as sounds very much like that came back into his memory with an unpleasant, full-sensory vividness. You were supposed to get used to such things, but so far he hadn't and he wasn't sure he wanted to. He'd met plenty of people for whom killing was just hard disagreeable work, like shearing a struggling sheep or mucking out stables, and there was something at least slightly wrong with them.

Besides the village fanes and little shrines there were some substantial temples by themselves a little distance aside. The latest one by the irrigation canal had a red-plastered wall around it, a tall pillared gate split in the middle and flanked by guardian fanged *raksasa* figures holding their clubs, and a triangular capstone carved with what might be worshipers, gods, demons or some combination. Within rose the tall pagoda-like arrangement of multiple roofs of decreasing size one after another on a tall narrow building. It looked strange to Montivallan eyes, like square mushrooms on a skewer of shish kebab, but it was impressive in its way.

A group of warriors were waiting by the temple gate, squatting on their hams or sitting cross-legged. As the column passed the spearmen and archers trotted out and fell in with the Raja's infantry. By their looks they were peasants most of the time and only a few had so much as a helmet, though there were plenty of straw hats or head-cloths tied at the front; skinny-wiry-muscular men with bare or sandaled feet, bare brown chests, sarongs drawn up between the legs and tucked into broad sashes in a way that made them look like baggy shorts. Their weapons were simple, rattan shields covered in hide, seven-foot bamboo spears with steel heads, bamboo bows and quivers of long steel-tipped arrows slung at the waist, the inevitable keris and parang, but they looked tough and determined as well. Many had healed scars that *didn't* look like the result of agricultural accidents.

"What's that?" he said, nodding towards the temple; as they passed he could see it was new, probably no older than he was, though parts of the foundations were older.

"Sumbak Temple," Pip said; she rode with the same easy lifelong skill as he did, but in a rather different style, with more bend to the knees. "Water temple."

Her shirt and shorts were khaki today, but she still wore the suspenders and the odd hat she called a bowler. Evidently that was how she dressed for active work.

His mind supplied other references to *Pip* and *active*, and he shifted in his saddle and forced himself back to business.

"Every dozen or so of these little villages belong to a Sumbak, and come together to do rites in the temple . . . and also to manage the water distribution system, planting and harvesting times, that sort of thing. The farmers meet with the Sumbak priest presiding and vote on how to keep the system up and fine anyone who doesn't do his share. Then a couple of dozen Sumbaks join around a larger temple and so on to manage canals and dams. They use it to organize a lot of other things as well as watering the fields. It's all a bit . . . fractal?"

John made a gesture with his left hand to indicate he'd understood the reference.

"Like those militiamen," he said. "Well organized!"

"They do organization a treat here," Toa observed. "You might not think it the way they dress fancy and they're always beating gamelans and dancing about and processing back and forth to some temple or another and go into fits if someone uses the wrong inflection talking to them, but give the word and my oath! They swarm out like bloody army ants."

He looked over at the First Mate of the *Tarshish Queen*, who was along to ride herd on the catapults and their crews.

"Is that some sort of Hindu thing, mate?"

Radavindraban shrugged. "It depends on which Hindus, yes indeed, and even now there are very many of us turning up like a penny wherever you go and in many varieties and types and kinds. These are not much like my people. Or those bloody maniacs in Sambalpur who treat everyone else like a dalit, even good Nagarathar like myself."

At their incomprehension he filled in, tapping himself on the chest: "Merchant caste, very respectable."

Deor nodded. "These folk seem more . . . they're harder than those I met on Bali itself. Not braver, but . . . harder."

Thora snorted. "They've had to become so, brother. If they weren't hard, they'd be dead."

More groups of warrior-peasant militia joined them as the day went on until there was a fair little army on the road, with scouts riding or loping along to either side in the middle distance. There was more brush, and the land began to rumple a bit as the mountains grew closer, fingers of forested higher land extending into the plain. The crosshatch of bunds between the rice fields became shallow stepped terraces as the terrain acquired more of a roll.

Thora was right, John thought. *These people's parents or grandparents fought their way ashore, desperate and hungry, and their children look ready to fight just as hard now for their homes and families.*

About an hour after noon they stopped by yet another temple; the troops simply squatted by the roadside, or dismounted and saw to their horses. The mahouts had the elephants kneel, which was a fascinating process in itself, before their burdens were removed. Besides more militia this temple had a field kitchen set up and ready, forewarned by the Raja's messengers and the drumbeats and manned—or rather largely wom-anned and childed—by the local folk. They served bowls of rice, and of a spicy, garlicky soup called *soto bali* thick with pork, vermicelli, peppers, mung beans and sprouts, and bore off a special tray of vegetable dishes for the priest and priestess with much humble bowing as it was handed through the gauze curtains that surrounded them. They were too holy to be exposed to common view, or to eat flesh.

The chance to take off his breast-and-back and arming doublet was inexpressible relief. After a moment to cool he found himself sharp-set for his rice and soup, though he was starting to get nostalgic at the thought of a good wheat loaf . . .

With a crackling-crisp crust, warm from the oven and slathered with sweet fresh butter and eaten with a hunk of sharp cheese, he thought.

More villagers brought fodder and grain to the horses and oxen, and heaps of grass and sugarcane and melons to the elephants, who stuffed it all into their mouths with their trunks and ate with noisy crunching drib-bling enthusiasm before ambling over to the canal to drink hugely and blow water on each other with their trunks and be scrubbed down with coarse-bristled brushes on long sticks by the mahouts. That seemed to be something they enjoyed as much as eating and drinking, though some-times they showed it by playfully shooting a trunkful of water over their attendants.

Tuan Anak Agung, the commander of the lancers and the expedition as a whole, came over to John as he sat finishing his soup; they hadn't had much chance to talk yet. The cheek-flaps of his pointed helmet were pushed up, and he handed his bowl back to an aide as he halted with a slight scowl on his scarred face.

Ishikawa calmly kept moving rice and pieces of meat and vegetable into his mouth with his chopsticks, handling them with a finicky delicacy; the locals used forks and spoons and their fingers. He and the Baru Den-pasaran officer exchanged cool appraising glances and small polite bows. They had common enemies; that didn't necessarily make them friends.

Anak pointed north, to a very faint thread of smoke above the mountains, and addressed John:

"Very dangerous from too soon now," he said in passable but thickly accented English.

"Carcosans?"

"Yes, at fort, maybe also in jungle. Smoke, that is dirty forest savage dog-people. Burn trees for fields. That makes ponds and . . . cuts for water . . ."

"Canals," John said.

"Yes, canals full with soil. Lazy, murdering, ignorant stinking sister-fucking filth-pigs."

Don't be shy, tell me what you really *think of them,* John thought, his face impassive; it wasn't his place to tell the locals how to deal with each other, but he could have an opinion.

Aloud: "Are they"—he paused briefly while he sought a tactful term—"the previous inhabitants?"

"Some," Anak said. "The ones in hills fight for Carcosa, most often. Some *Orang Iban.* Push in from north coast, over mountains. Steep there," he added, making a gesture to indicate land falling vertically into the sea. "Not good land for rice."

"Iban?" John asked.

He'd picked up the word *orang,* which meant *man.* Used collectively the translation was *tribe* or *folk* or *nation* depending on context. Thora and Deor had come up quietly, with Ruan behind them carrying his strung longbow.

"Iban, the Sea Dyaks," the poet-adventurer said.

Thora added: "From Borneo, but they get around these days."

John wasn't surprised. Folk-migrations had happened all over the world where people survived at all, and it seemed the ocean made it easier here in this world of archipelagos. There was a good road to everywhere if you could sail, and the distances were short enough for even outrigger canoes to go anywhere along the island chains.

Deor went on: "We had a . . . bit of a meeting with some of them when we came through the islands a year and a half ago. That was before we sailed from Bali to Hawaii, but I didn't know they'd gotten this far."

"Great sailors and traders, but also pirates often enough, and dangerous," Thora said, and shrugged cheerfully. "Mind you, I've been called dangerous myself, Johnnie."

Anak eyed her carefully, as with some wild and perilous thing he didn't quite believe he was seeing and didn't understand except that it *was* perilous. A fighting-man of his experience would know that, at least; would absorb the knowledge from the other's gestalt in a process as unconscious as it was certain. She'd left off her armor for now, though she was belted with backsword and pukko-knife, and wore simply trousers and what Bearkillers called a *sports bra* for some reason. It showed her tigress build, and a fair collection of scars, mostly on the left flank and right arm; cavalry scars. Of course, she was also missing a bit of the little finger on her left hand.

Marks like that on someone of their quite similar ages meant you'd stayed alive in an environment involving homicidal strangers bearing edged metal, and done it for a decade or more. Which meant a fair number of others hadn't survived *you*. The way she held herself and moved would reinforce the lesson.

"Yes, Iban dangerous, *wanita ningrat* is wise," he said, using a respectful honorific for her.

Which is wise, John thought.

"Users of *sumpitan*, takers of tops."

The Raja's officer mimed lifting off his head and then squeezed as if to shrink it. John frowned in puzzlement, and Deor exchanged a few words with Anak in either Malay or Balinese; they didn't sound different enough for the Montivallan to tell them apart.

"*Sumpitan*, blowguns," Deor said. "Poisoned darts in the blowguns. And they take their enemies' heads and preserve them as trophies."

Toa snorted. "Not that they know how to do it right," he said. "Secret's getting the brain and eyes out and then steaming the head and using shark oil and smoking at a low heat before you sun dry the bloody things, see? That's how you make a real *mokomokai*. Last forever, straight up."

Everyone looked at him for a moment and he grinned and lolled his tongue, a gargoyle figure with his scars and tattoos, leaning on his great spear.

"Iban hunters of heads, yes," Anak said, clearing his throat and visibly deciding to ignore him.

"They are allies of the Carcosans?" John said.

"Allies of selfs. Fight us, fight them, fight before-people, fight each other, fight for pay."

He scowled, his brown face flushing ruddy with anger as his hand clenched on the worn ivory and gold of his parang-hilt.

"Come here when our great hero fathers did, take advantage steal part of this our beautiful island. Thieves!"

I wonder what irony *is in Balinese?* John thought.

Deor's gray eyes flicked to his, and they shared a brief . . . and ironic . . . smile.

"We must careful very scout, now," Anak said. "Fight anytime after next while."

He signaled to his underofficer, who blew on a whistle, and the column went to work. The elephants' burdens had included their own bundled war-gear as well as rice, pickled vegetables and salt fish and spare arrows. Great blanket-like coats of metal rings fastened to leather backing and spiked plates for their foreheads armored the beasts. Their tusks had been cut off at about three-quarters of their length and tipped with brass balls; now those were unscrewed, and vicious-looking curved blades like great scythes edged on both sides substituted, and a man with a sharpening-stick went from beast to beast touching them up while he hummed a cheerful song. Knock-down howdahs were assembled and went on their backs, and four archers and a pikeman with a sixteen-foot spear climbed into each, hanging extra quivers over the sides.

Much of the elephant's gear had been silver-washed, or even studded with semiprecious stones, and the rest trimmed in bright colors and plumes. The mahouts shouted and tapped the beasts with their goads, and the elephants lurched upright, glittering like living tapestries; one curled its trunk up and trumpeted deafeningly, a huge hoarse sound. The others shifted from foot to foot, grumbling low in their massive chests. John had heard legends about the wisdom of elephants . . .

And these are at least smart enough to know what having armor and weapons strapped on means. Of course, so are horses.

"Sigh," John said as Evrouin helped him back into the half-armor.

The valet snorted unsympathetically; his olive face was running with sweat too, and he was encased in similar gear.

"Shield over the back, please, Your Highness," he said, the words absolutely respectful and the tone fairly close to a file-closer's admonition to a recruit. "I'll be standing by with the rest if it's needed."

"Not while I'm mounted. The only people on this island that I don't have two-score pounds on are a few made of blubber."

Toa cocked an eye on him; he had at least eighty pounds more than John, and not an ounce of it was fat.

"Anyone born on this island, that is," John clarified. "Throw in another forty of extra armor and this poor little thing will drop dead underneath me."

"It's no destrier, but better it drop dead than you do with an arrow through the groin, Sire," said Evrouin.

John winced and kept his hands from cupping protectively over his crotch by an effort of will.

He does know how to motivate a fellow. Except that he's also making me want to run away.

"Here, let's sling the helm to the saddlebow where you can get at it quickly. Wouldn't want one in the eye, either."

"And something for the heatstroke I'll be collapsing with, I hope," John grumbled.

"Ah, that reminds me!"

The valet-bodyguard crumbled some salt into one of the bamboo mugs the local women were handing around, and watched while John drank it. The taste was fairly vile, not as bad as seawater but bad, and John breathed carefully for a moment to put down a brief spell of nausea. Evrouin tossed off his with irritating nonchalance.

"Wouldn't lemonade be better?" John said, and grinned.

"When you're in a hammock afterwards, Your Highness," Evrouin said.

"Milady," he added respectfully with a bow to Pip before dropping back behind them and swinging into his saddle with the butt of his glaive socketed in his stirrup-iron.

"Old retainer?" she said, as they walked over to the horse-lines and mounted their own. "I recognize that tone of smug bullying insolence they usually get."

"I heard that!" Toa grinned as he went by. "Comes of having paddled your backside when you got into the Bundaberg and puked all over your dad's heirloom family etchings in the study and your mum was falling about laughing. Never could handle your rum."

"For God's sake, I was six!"

"Still can't," he said over his shoulder.

John coughed; so did Evrouin, though his might be cover for a snigger rather than a pause for thought. He waited until the valet-bodyguard was out of immediate earshot before he went on:

"Evrouin's sort of a retainer. Old retainer of the family, at least. And mine . . . sort of . . . for the last three years. As much of a minder as anything else."

He quirked an eyebrow. "Though . . . well, I told you this voyage was more or less unauthorized? Let's say Evrouin was extremely surprised to end up sailing off from Newport."

"It's creditable that he didn't stay behind."

"No, he's brave and loyal to a fault . . . though if he'd stayed he'd have had to face *my* mother, of course. *God's* holy Mother, was that only a few months ago?"

Pip smiled too. "I feel the same way about my exit from Darwin—

probably Daddy's lawyer arrived panting on the quayside waving a writ just as our topsails disappeared beneath the horizon."

The column reassembled itself without undue formality but commendable speed. John found his head swiveling to either side as the land grew rougher and steeper and the brush thicker, shading up into outright forest; and the roadside trees stopped, evidently a security measure. The villages grew fewer, too, clinging to the lower land along the watercourses, and here the space around the walls of the conjoined compounds was kept strictly clear even at the cost of fruit, convenience and shade. Less was cultivated, so that you could see what had been hidden on the coastal plain; nearly all this had been tilled before the Change, then recolonized by the Baru Denpasarans in ways that ignored the previous field-boundaries and layout save for the roads. At last there were signs of land that had been reclaimed and then abandoned once more when war and raid went through. Small groups of herders armed with bow and spear watched herds of horses and cattle, and pigs whose backs were nearly lost in waist-high vegetation. They were making use of what couldn't be farmed more intensively because field-workers weren't safe without implausible numbers of guards, but they looked thoroughly wary.

Then the column passed through a set of ruins, a town that might have held several thousands, but lacking the tall buildings or steel construction he was used to in works of the ancients. The wreck was old, broken walls and fragments of glass thickly overgrown with brush and tall trees here and there driving roots through shattered concrete and broken stone, but with the roadways in between still showing where sparse vegetation revealed ancient pavement.

In half a dozen places the rusted hulks of ancient vehicles and tumbled wreckage of other sorts had been pushed across the roadway to make barriers, and then a path cleared through them again—from the state of the vegetation, about the same time as the town burned. Mounds of white jasmine vines covered much of it, the cream-colored flowers filling the air with their incongruously sweet scent.

One larger stone building had been treated more savagely still, burned and smashed and then leveled with some effort, and the remains of a round tower lay across it.

Where snags of wall still stood you could see the scorch marks, particularly around the gaping holes that had once been doors and windows. A few skulls peeked out of the underbrush with grinning mockery, or lay in fragments and clumps where bodies had been dragged and heaped, though time and insects had long ago reclaimed bones less obdurate in this climate. They showed the marks of cutting and smashing, which wasn't surprising. In any battle or large-scale killing most died from blows to the head, usually given while they were lying wounded on the ground; he'd heard that often from veterans of the Prophet's War while he was growing up and seen it himself since.

This all happened at about the same time, he thought.

It reminded him of Topanga and the lands near it. Not because of any similarity of climate or terrain, but because there also were places where the bones struck the eye; more of them, in fact, because southern Westria was so dry and had been so very heavily peopled before the Change. In the settled parts of Montival where he'd spent most of his childhood such things had long since been tidied up or reclaimed by nature—Christian clerics and pious lay-folk buried them as an act of devotion, and pagans collected them for burning to give the ashes to Earth and lay unquiet spirits they thought might walk.

Anywhere remote, though, a cave or still-standing structure from before the cataclysm or hollow tree or beside some unused ancient road through the ranch-country you came across the skulls now and then, where those fleeing death in the terrible years had met it unawares. Or at least the teeth—those lasted like stone.

Pip was looking around with her slingshot in her left hand and the arm-brace unfolded. "I've seen places like this in Oz, abandoned since the Change. They always gave me the willies."

"Not long after the Change, yes. But not because of famine or rioting. It's too . . . systematic," Thora said quietly, and turned her eyes to where Tuan Anak Agung rode for a moment.

"Hai," Ishikawa said, giving her a slight bow in the saddle. "Battle here, strong . . . no, fierce battle."

"How can you tell?" Pip said curiously.

The Bearkiller nodded: "This was a sack, done with intent to utterly destroy, destroy the place and its folk both, by someone who knew their work."

Pip and Thora hadn't spoken much to each other beyond essentials. John was glad to see that stop . . . but what the Bearkiller woman said was entirely too plausible. Despite the muggy heat and the flies buzzing about his head he felt an inner chill, as if some echo of that old savagery lingered, desperate valor and bloodlust equally driven by desperate necessity.

Thora pointed to the southern end of the ruins, then traced a line to the north with her forefinger.

"See where the bodies lay?"

"How . . ." Pip began, then nodded as Ishikawa made a sort of affirmative drawn-out grunting *hnnnnn* sound his people used.

"Oh, the skulls," she said. "They last longest."

"You can tell the first attack came in from the south, from the direction we came, and probably at night," Thora said.

"Or just rittle . . . little . . . before dawn, Thora-*gozen*," the Japanese officer said. "For raid, best time. Watchers relax, think they are safe. Sleep is deep for others."

"Or around dawn," she agreed. "The town's fighters met it, to give the rest cover to run for the woods. And fought a delaying action from house to house, and one barricade to the next, they must have been expecting it for a day at least, enough to block the streets a little."

John frowned. "Doesn't look like many got away."

"Right, Johnnie," Thora said. "Because whoever was doing the attacking sent another group in beforehand, swinging wide and through the jungle to come in from the north and then hiding and waiting."

"Like huntsmen waiting for game driven on by the beaters," he said with a shiver.

"Right, they were there to kill, not just take the town. And they came out to catch the fugitives running from the fighting . . . probably the town was burning by then too, because the first attack used fire-arrows and lots of shouting and noise to spread panic."

"Force from jungle come out in—" Ishikawa made an embracing gesture with both arms, indicating a formation like a deep semicircle. "Catch, kill all, then pile the bodies. You say in Engrish . . . clean sweep."

John looked; the signs were obvious once they'd been pointed out. His storyteller's mind filled in the details: darkness, shrieks and war-cries, flame arcing through the night, the able and the brave snatching up weapons and dashing towards the sound of battle where the first screaming onset struck the sleepy guards. Mothers and the sick and old and the plain fear-struck grabbing children out of bed and running in the other direction and then rows of silent blades rising out of the bush . . .

Thora nodded judiciously: "Neat professional job, though, coordinating two concentric attacks like that. Much easier to plan on a nice clear map than actually do through brush and darkness and not just get fucking lost and start going in circles or blundering into each other and fighting your own until the sun comes up and you go *wooopsie-oooopsie!* Careful timing, and a force that could keep very good noise discipline."

"Like Rangers?" John asked; the Dúnedain were very good at moving quietly and undetected.

"You'd need some scouts to lead, but patience and obedience would do for the rest."

She took another long look. "You can see the place has never been reclaimed or mined for salvage and building material since, just the road cleared and the rest left to lie from that day to this," she finished. "Forty-five years or so, I'd say, give or take . . . the first Change Year."

"Yeah, she's right, Pip," Toa said; he pronounced it more like *shay's roy-eiyt.* "Seen a lot places in ol' N-Zed when I was a youngster that had this look. Lot of fighting there after the Change. In North Island where everything went to shit."

He pronounced *shit* more like *shut.*

With a touch of bitterness: "Down in South Island they were eating

spuds and fat mutton and shaking their heads and sighing and doing sod-
all and telling each other how hard they had it."

John looked around at the haunted ruin and crossed himself; Thora
and Deor made the sign of the Hammer, and they passed on. The scop
murmured as he did, lyrics from some tune the prince had never heard:

> *"Flames lick the corners*
> *Of each hungry horseman's smile;*
> *For they have locusts in their scabbards,*
> *And deserts in their eyes."*

The road north beyond the ruins was still well-made, obviously kept
up until recently.

The column slowed, and the war-elephants moved back and out to the
sides beyond the roadside verge, each with one rider standing upright for
a better view as the forest closed in around them. It had been cut well
back sometime in the last year, but the trees beyond that strip grew taller
and taller as the land rose, more bound together with lianas and creepers,
trees that had been growing long before the Change. Orchids and flowers he couldn't name were thick, and bright-plumaged birds flew chattering and fluting. There were gray-furred manlike things flitting through
the branches that he realized with a start were monkeys.

It was all beautiful . . . but John found the hot green heaviness oppressive, more so than the thickest woods in Montival, even the rain-forests
of Olympus where everything had moss inches deep. The Baru Denpasarans had scouts out there, but he still felt nervous. He shifted his balance
to send his horse forward, and drew rein beside Anak.

"*Tuan* Anak, the enemy fortress interdicting . . . stopping . . . your
water supply is about another . . . two hours march?" he said.

The Baru Denpasaran nodded. "Two if go fast-fast, Prince. Three better, need to make sure no ambush."

"Shouldn't we camp, if we want a day's fighting time when we get
there?" John replied. "It's not as if they aren't going to be expecting us."

"Yes, good, Prince sees clear," Anak said, eyeing him with genuine respect. "So do soon, before sundown, time to make strong camp before sun falls."

"Why not here?" John said, pointing back to the ancient wreck. "There's more open ground and the old buildings would give cover."

Anak looked over his shoulder at the ruins, a brief glance and then away. "No. Not there. *Leyak* there."

"Leyak?" John asked.

"Hungry, angry ghost, bad spirit. Very evil, curse there, curse on Bone Place. We go on till out of sight."

John was tempted to argue, until he remembered the fight in the harbor and the figure they called the Pallid Mask. And the crocodile with the sigil-band on its forelimb.

After that, I'll believe anything *might happen. We in Montival have our mysteries, and I suppose that's true everywhere. Let leyak remain a mystery to me! And it's his command and his land; I'm a stranger here.*

When the sun approached the western horizon and shadows fell heavy on the jungle hills around them, Anak called the halt. They were in a stretch where the forest pulled back a little and was lower where it did grow, evidently rock fairly close beneath the soil, and a small swift stream ran across the sloping ground to provide plenty of water. The Baru Denpasarans set to, with a good deal of shouting and arm-waving but not much real fuss or confusion. Nobody bothered with tents except for the High Priest and Priestess. It was more than warm enough to sleep wrapped in a cloak or blanket, and evidently if it rained you just got wet until you dried out again.

The marching camp wasn't the sort of instant temporary fortress Boisean legionnaires would make every night as a matter of course, but the levies cleared brush and dug a ditch and used the soil to pile up a low berm that they packed down by stamping on it en masse while the Raja's professionals stood guard. Then they set the earthworks with a bristle of stakes from the scrub and branches they'd cut, each trimmed to a razor point with a swift blow from a parang and woven around an abatis of felled trees with sharpened branches pointing outward.

Having elephants to help with heavy hauling made it possible to do an astonishing amount of work quickly. When they dragged a weighted chain between them even considerable trees just ripped out of the ground like a clump of weeds; they pushed the biggest over with their foreheads; they lifted the timber in their trunks and dropped it where directed; and they disposed of a good deal of greenery by simply stuffing it into their mouths and eating it. Everyone looked as if they were camping in a set place on a mental north–south grid, by village or band or Sumbak association or *something*. Plenty of sentries were posted, not just pacing up and down the berm but hiding out in the growing darkness.

John still looked about a little as he sat with his back against the wheel of one of the catapults and toes towards a low campfire. They'd lit it for the primal comfort of the thing rather than warmth or cooking; supplies came from a series of field kitchens with big cauldrons. He accepted a bowl of what everyone was eating, brown rice cooked with dried vegetables—tomato and onions and mushrooms and a few others he couldn't place—and some dried salted shrimp.

The sharp savory taste was surprisingly good, and he was hungry. Anyone who thought riding all day wasn't hard work had never done it, particularly if your thighs had had time on shipboard to forget the strains involved. He cautiously took a cup of the tea brought around in tin kettles. It was strong and bitter, and experience had shown that more than one would keep him up even if he was tired, like coffee, but it was refreshing.

Ishikawa made a surprised, pleased sound as he lifted some of the rice mixture to his lips with the chopsticks he kept in a case tucked into the sleeve of his kimono.

"*Umami*," he said, and looked around at the camp. "Not bad. Salty, a little like *dashi*. This green tea is truly very bad, but at least there *is* tea."

"What do you think of the camp?" Thora asked him.

The catapults and prang-prangs were more or less in the middle of the little army, a sign of the value the Baru Denpasarans attached to them. Thora was shoveling her rice in with a spoon and the air of someone who'd eaten much worse. Deor sat a little way away, absently listening to the conversation, absently listening to a raucous round-robin song some of the local folk were passing from group to group, and absently moving his lips in a preoccupied way that John added together and recognized as *composition in progress.*

"Sloppy," Ishikawa said, and then grudgingly: "But the most important things have been done. More or less. I do not like more or less. Even more, I do not like in war. Mistakes kill you."

Thora grunted agreement at his appraisal of the encampment, and there was a spell of rock-scissors-paper as they decided who of the ship's parties would take each watch; she and the Japanese and the huge Maori didn't need a discussion to decide they weren't going to slumber serenely and rely completely on their hosts. John couldn't quite decide whether to be glad his rank spared him such chores, or too anxious to sleep at all.

Deor uncased his harp Golden Singer, tuned it and began to play something low and melancholy. He looked up with a smile as Ruan slipped unobtrusively back into their group. The green-brown-orange tartan of his kilt and plaid and his green-surfaced brigandine were as handy at camouflage here as they were back in Montival, or better.

"I saved dinner for you," the *scop* said.

"And I'm ready for it, my heart, and give you thanks!"

The young Mackenzie unstrung his bow, gave it a quick check before he slid it into its waxed cover, shed his gear and then sat and signed the bowl with a murmured ritual.

"And this, though it's less tasty," Deor said.

He handed his lover a cup of the decoction of sweet wormwood they were all taking; it was good protection against the local fevers, and the *Silver Surfer* had brought plenty of it. Ruan made a bit of a face as he drank, and Toa chuckled.

"Good for what doesn't ail you yet," he said.

"I am a healer," Ruan said dryly. "That doesn't mean I have to like the taste of a bitter potion."

"You'd like those manky little burrowing buggers they get on these islands even less, and it's good for those too."

"*Larva migrans*," Pip said.

John joined in her shudder. Plant life wasn't all that flourished in this climate.

Deor went on:

"What did you see?"

Ruan swallowed a spoonful of the rice mixture and frowned. "A great deal of nothin' much," he said. "These aren't my woods, and nothing's quite the same; not by look or touch or scent or even the feel of the air on your skin or the dirt between your toes. I saw something like deer, and wild pig of a kind, and plenty of birds I couldn't name. Many are the faces of the Mother!"

He made a sign of propitiation. "I did see that our friends here are no woods-runners themselves; I don't doubt they're brave enough and tough fighters when it's a matter of face-to-face, but save for a few they're like so many north-country peasants for wilderness work."

There was a mild scorn in his tone. In the Association lands, the chase was mostly a pursuit for nobles and their paid retainers, beyond the level of throwing rocks at rabbits trying to raid the garden. By contrast most Mackenzies were good hunters and woodsmen as well as farmers and craftsfolk; his folk got a good deal of their meat from the wild, or as they'd put it by the grace of Lady Flidais and the Horned Lord. The Clan's war-training built on it, given how much wilderness there was in the dùthchas.

"I near got speared twice myself because their sentries were so jumpy, password or no," he added. "And that they didn't see me until I was on top of them, when I thought I'd made enough noise to waken the dead in Mag Mell."

"Their sentries aren't any use, then?" John said in alarm.

"To be sure, there's enough of them to warn the camp by screaming as they're killed by anyone sneaking about. Well, that may be drawing the longbow, but they're not the best I've ever seen. Which is why they've got so many out, I'd be thinking."

"Quantity has a quality all its own, as the old saying goes," Pip supplied.

John wondered why Radavindraban gave her a glance and snorted with what was half laughter. He finished the rice and began to scour out the bowl; you had to be careful about that, and even more so here than at home given how fast and thoroughly rot set in with this climate.

"Nothing else?" Thora asked.

"Not now. But there's man-sign in those woods, right enough, if you've eyes to see. Using the game-trails, mostly, but human-kind, and lately. Whoever they were they knew how to move in thick cover, the which the most of our friends here do not; also they were barefoot, and from the tracks of their feet they go that way all their lives."

Toa grunted agreement. "Different shape to the foot," he said.

"How many?" Thora asked, and Ruan shrugged.

"Less than a score, more than two or three. Speaking of the fresh tracks only."

"Scouts," the Bearkiller said decisively. "We're being watched."

John sighed. "Well, we knew there were hostiles nearby," he said. "The people in . . . the large building to the east of the bay . . . saw us leaving, come to that. I'd have us under observation, if I were them. Thank you, Ruan."

The younger man shrugged and laid his blanket-roll next to Deor's, sitting with his hard-muscled arms about his knees.

"You're welcome, Prince. Though it's my neck too!"

Evrouin handed John his lute-case at a gesture, and he tuned Azalaïs; they were all tired, but a little music was never amiss. The instrument was holding up well, but the hot damp made him anxious about it, and he worked a little oil with a cloth into the gleaming intaglio surface. His fingers seemed to find the softly haunting tune by themselves. After a moment he heard a few faint pings from Deor's harp as the other man adjusted the tuning and then the first full chords as he joined in. It was one of his aunt Fiorbhinn's compositions, and the scop had apprenticed to her long ago.

"The Voices Speak" had become popular throughout Montival lately, so much so that there was talk of making it the anthem of the High Kingdom. He and John began:

> *"Speak to me, they speak to me*
> *Of this place they speak to me—*
> *Of sky and wind, of sea and stone*
> *Of moss and fern and cedar tree*
> *Of cliffs where wild arbutus grow . . ."*

One by one all the Montivallans joined in, a wistfulness in their voices.

> *"Speak to me, they speak to me*
> *Of orcas gliding through the deep*
> *Of eagles balancing the wind*
> *Above the waves where salmon leap."*

The song was like a cool breath in the hot alien night; he closed his eyes for a moment and saw the walls of Portland, and the waterfalls like silver threads down the cliffs of the Columbia Gorge, and the hang-gliders dancing with the sky at Hood River. The voices rose:

> *"Speak to me, they speak to me*
> *Of deer that browse the twilight fields*
> *Of stony heron keeping watch*
> *For what the silver sea might yield*
> *Speak to me, they speak to me*
> *Of what has been and what endures*
> *Of summer's bloom and autumn's fade*
> *In the circling of the years!*

The last verse turned soft with longing:

"Speak to me, they speak to me
In voices humming in my bone
In whispers rising on my breath
In languages that tell of . . . home."

Pip looked at him a little strangely. "Well, that was . . . interesting."

Then with a raffish smile: "Do we all have a bit of a nostalgic weep for the old rose-embowered cottage we grew up in now?"

John laughed, and shook his head as he leaned back against the wheel of the catapult. "Just feeling a bit homesick. And come to that, I grew up in castles and manor houses, mostly."

"Ah, well, I'm closer to home. Though that does make me want to see Montival the more. It sounds spectacular—a bit like New Zealand, in fact."

"There's a lot of world to see!" John said, and they shared a smile that meant: *young, and the world before us.*

Then she yawned. "Though right now, I could use a good bit of sleep."

Pip wrapped herself in her blanket at arm's length away from John, using her light pad saddle as a pillow and leaving her bowler hat, cane, kukri-knives, sandals and slingshot within easy reach. John smiled at the way her face relaxed as she went quickly to sleep, making her look much younger. He felt a rush of . . .

Wait a minute, that's affection, not just lust. Well, mostly not. You're in danger here, Johnnie!

He was impressed by her uncomplaining ease with the rough circumstances, too. She was a ruler's daughter and her mother had been a successful adventurer and very wealthy in her own right by the time she bore her only daughter, but while she exuberantly enjoyed the finer things in life she could switch to field living without breaking stride.

Deor had put his harp away and was pacing a circle around their campsite. Every few feet he stopped, faced outward, and drew a sign in the air. The intoned syllable that went with it was felt more than heard. When he had finished, he saw John watching and smiled.

"It's a thing I learned in Norrheim," he said. "I *galdor* the *thurs* rune to make a hedge of thorns. It won't stop a determined attack, but it can delay and confuse them. Humans aren't the only wights in that forest. This place is full of strange Powers. Time to invoke a few of our own. I follow Woden, but tonight I'll be calling on Thunor, who defends us against the etin-kin."

John nodded and crossed himself.

"I'll be invoking the Saints, and for the same reason!" he said.

Then he checked that his belt with sword and poniard were within easy reach and sank back, pulling up a blanket that smelled strongly of horse and listening to the unfamiliar whines and rustles of the alien night.

Even the constellations were different. The stars were bright, though, and a wisp of cloud turned translucent as it drifted across the moon . . .

Same moon at home, he thought. And how I wish I was there! Well, if Pip was there too, that would be even better.

CHAPTER EIGHTEEN

DÚN NA SÍOCHÁNA

(FORMERLY SALEM, OREGON)

CAPITAL, HIGH KINGDOM OF MONTIVAL

(FORMERLY WESTERN NORTH AMERICA)

OCTOBER 31ST

CHANGE YEAR 46/2044 AD

"As the sun bleeds through the murk
'tis the last day we shall work—
For the veil is thin and the spirit wild,
And the Crone is carrying Harvest's child!
Samhain! Turn away
Run ye back to the light of day;
Samhain! Hope and pray
All ye meet are the gentle Fae—"

The *Tennō Heika* of Dai-Nippon looked down from the balcony of the guest quarters at the masked and kilted revelers who sang as they danced through the wet, darkened streets. The newly-lit gaslights along the sidewalks flickered in their opalescent glass globes, casting a glow through the misty air where the torches made whirling red streaks. Later there would be bonfires and a feast where an empty place was left, for the spirits and the ancestors, and tales of ghosts and night-creatures. There were interesting similarities to some festivals in Nihon. This half-inhabited ruin was on the border of the Mackenzie dúthchas, an area that encompassed most of the eastern half of the Willamette Valley south of Mithrilwood and Mt. Angel and stretched nearly to the remains of Eugene and up to the crest-line of the High Cascades, and many of those who worked or dwelt here were clansfolk.

Reiko was comfortable enough in her iro-tomesode with five *kamon* in the Imperial crest, made of dark-blue silk subtly patterned below the waistline, since she had a good under-kimono and *hadajuban* beneath it. If anything it was refreshing out here, since the Montivallans tended to overheat their buildings by her standards and her newly-arrived staff were still working on adjusting the ingenious but shockingly wasteful wood-fired central heating system more to their liking. Back in the home-land you didn't heat a *house* at all; you heated the people, or a small enclosed space.

The air was full of the peculiar heavy chill-wet smell of fog, with wood-smoke, damp earth and conifers beneath . . . nothing completely strange, yet not *quite* like the early part of winters in her own country. Perhaps it was the absence of the sea-scent, never far away on Sado-ga-shima or the other island refuges or costal resettlement beachheads. Homesickness was bitter, and linked to the thought of her father.

Perhaps the home I remember is as lost as Father, existing only in memory. For I am no longer the girl who left it; I am Tennō, and the person within the rank is also new. When I return, I will see it differently.

Then: *Father.*

The thought brought back the shock of seeing the arrow in his breast and his face gone inhumanly still. A shock that overlaid all the other memories. Even the earliest, of his hands guiding hers as she first made a water-offering or popping a sweet *ohagi* into her mouth, of the way his eyes would turn to Mother and light with a secret smile sometimes . . .

Let the breath out slowly. Let the pain flow with it; through you and over you, and then it will be gone.

The mental exercise worked, more or less. It worked better now than it had when the wound was fresher. Time helped, having things to do did as well. She had had a very great deal to do indeed in the long months since, things terrible and strange, the dangers of battle and the threat of death by thirst and other things more grisly. Challenges that could be met only by a total focus of will and mind. That had given the inner bruises time to heal a little before she had the leisure to pay them attention. She did not have the luxury of collapse.

The guesthouse with which the Nihonjin delegation had been gifted was large—

About as large as the Imperial Palace back on Sado-ga-shima, she thought with a quirk of the lips.

That was also a pre-Change structure though quite an old one, built for the Tokugawa governor before Meiji, and a museum just before the Change, extended since and surrounded by a small castle they'd improved as time and resources permitted. *This* building had been part of some institution of learning, abandoned in the disaster, then roughly repaired and boarded up for later use when the Montivallans decided to make this their capital. It had been swiftly but skillfully remade to suit her people's tastes before it was turned over to them as an embassy, property of the Empire and under its law.

Or at least made over to a Montivallan's *ideas* of those tastes taken from old books. The results ranged from the very close to homelike in the case of the tatami mats and the bathhouse to the weirdly disconcerting— nobody she knew used that type of toilet—but you had to give them credit for trying. It would have been impossible for them to know precisely how customs had developed in her country since the Change. It had been easy enough to get buckwheat-stuffed pillows.

High Queen Mathilda is a woman of strong giri, Reiko mused. *She does not like me—I know I am not a charming person.*

One of the reasons she liked Órlaith so well was that Órlaith *did* like her and had from their first meeting, and that from someone who was rather charming themselves.

But Mathilda cannot help but associate me with the death of her lord the High King, the rebellious behavior of her daughter and heir, and the disappearance of her son Prince

John. Yet her behavior towards us is impeccable, because she knows that duty leaves her no choice. I am not drawn to her either as a person—but I admire her sense of duty very much. We are monarchs, bound to it as to a wheel of fire, whatever the consequences for the person behind the mask of rule. This we share absolutely.

This second-floor verandah looked out across very beautiful gardens, in the alien Montivallan style but including promising-looking ornamental cherry trees of the true sakura variety, everything now trimmed and mulched for winter though the grass was still a faded velvety green.

"Winter solitude—" she said, indicating the leafless trees with an incline of her head.

Egawa Noboru, the commander of the Imperial Guard, spoke the next line from behind her, in a voice like gravel moving in a bucket:

"In a world of one color."

It had been Egawa who introduced her to the poetry of Bashō; her father had had no ear for it and never pretended otherwise though he had been a calligrapher of skill, and her mother preferred Chiyo-ni.

"The sound of the wind," she finished.

There were times when the absence of cherry blossoms was as potent as their presence.

Beyond was a broad avenue and then the meeting-hall of the Congress of Realms, which was a rather odd-looking rectangular structure sheathed in marble and topped by a high and broad fluted cylinder like a giant drum, in turn supporting a column topped by a great bronze statue covered in gold leaf, like the building, a work of the ancient world skillfully transformed after the Change.

Whatever the statue had been before the Change, it now showed Rudi Mackenzie—High King Artos—dressed in kilt and plaid and holding the Sword of the Lady. For a moment she closed her eyes, taking a deep breath.

Reiko had seen the High King alive only for moments before he died on that terrible day when her father fell, but she thought the statue did in fact resemble him. Of course, that might be because it had always been a statue of a handsome, athletic *gaijin* man with a short beard. Even now the odd beaky faces here tended to blur into one another, unless she knew the individual well.

Dún na Síochána meant Citadel of Peace when translated into English; Reiko's command of Montival's common tongue was quite good now, and she had no intention of wasting time on Gaelic, since virtually nobody here spoke it as opposed to the way some were always mining it, plucking names like umeboshi from the center of a rice ball. She caught herself before she sneered at that, even in the privacy of her own mind.

After all, do we Nihonjin not also mine our history for things useful in the modern world? Picking and choosing from every era—and from every era's myths of every other era besides its own. Here an institution, there a tool or a way of doing or dressing or speaking, mixing them as they were never mixed before. Until the return of the old becomes something very new, though most of us do not know it. Nor is this time after the Change the first occasion when we have looked to our past, or to dreams of it, in that fashion. Not the first, not the tenth! We have such a great deal of past to use!

On her quest for the Grasscutter Sword she had been granted visions—perhaps dreams, but she thought perhaps much more than that—of her people's long, long history. Of herself, a presence in times when the intertwined destinies of her dynasty and the Sword of the Gathering Clouds of Heaven had touched turning-points of fate for the entire Yamato folk, from the days of the legends to her own great-grandmother's lifetime. It had given her a new appreciation of the depths of the ages involved.

In the street beyond a carriage went by behind six glossy black horses, their hides catching gleams from the streetlamps and the vehicle's own lights. There was a coat of arms on the door, the odd complex busy-looking local equivalent of the spare elegant Nihonjin *mon;* perhaps a northern noble, perhaps the blazon of some merchant prince from one of Montival's city-states. A streetcar rumbled by on its tracks, also drawn by horses, but the huge platter-hoofed beasts seemed almost of a different species.

"Their heavy cavalry is fearsome, but they make such wide use of horses for other purposes here, Majesty," Egawa said.

"They can afford it," she said ruefully, without looking around.

Envy tinged her voice. Nihon was sparsely populated now, very sparsely if you thought in terms of the home islands as a whole, but the long war with the raiders from over the Sea of Japan had kept them tightly packed for survival's sake. There were some horses for military use and oxen for plowing but apart from that little land to spare for pasture, little that could be used for anything but growing food that humans could eat, and sometimes just barely enough of that. Which meant that work which did not come from wind or water mostly had to be done by human muscle. It would be a great thing to lift some of that burden from the shoulders of the common people.

And also the burden of war, this eternal war into which Father was born and I after him. We must turn so much of what we make and grow to supporting warriors and war machines! Shōhei *is the era-name I chose,* Victorious Peace, *and so much more would be possible if we had that!*

She smiled slightly at the vision that suggested. The ancient fields on the main islands cleared and cultivated once more, of course, generation by generation, and the great ancestral shrines restored. Mountain streams channeled for workshops and mills; the huge blight of the pre-Change ruins mined for their metals and to free the land they so wastefully covered; carefully tended mountain forests yielding timber for ships to carry goods around the world and bring back more.

And what that would mean, she thought.

Scenes drifted through her mind, bright with longing; a cheerful crowd at a festival dancing around an image carried down a street; friends laughing as they drank sake and ate yakitori and sang in a little cookshop; poets in a pavilion topping each other in a line-finishing competition as they looked out on an autumn landscape of water and reeds and trees slowly dropping their leaves; men stripped to their *fundoshi* and headbands chanting together as they hauled on the ropes and the beams of a temple rose; a mother in a small neat peasant house proudly serving her family white rice and *tsukemono* and *tonkatsu*; a brush leaving a spare curve on white paper; deft hands making a spray of yellow flowers on blue silk.

We will always be warriors and farmers, and that is good, she thought. *But there should be more in life than toil and discipline, duty and the sword. We should be play-wrights and painters and explorers and scholars too, and dancers and clowns and storytellers and young lovers lost in each other beneath the cherry-trees as petals drift like snowflakes on the wind. It is for this I fight, and that I stand for my people before my kinsfolk the Great Kami.*

She shook herself mentally, back to the present and the alien winter's night.

The half-built capital of the High Kingdom was part construction site, part the ruin of the pre-Change settlement; that was familiar enough from her own life back in Nihon. Right now it was crowded with the influx for the Congress of Realms. She could see that in the wildly varied passers-by; Christian clerics, including a warrior monk with tonsure and dark robe, telling his rosary in his right hand with the left resting on the hilt of his longsword; a saffron-robed bonze in an odd crested hat spinning a prayer wheel; the brass studs and blue denim and broad white Stetsons of those from the Free Cities League of the Yakima; archaic suits and ties marking the self-proclaimed heirs of the ancient Americans from Boise, though to her they looked like the salarymen of legend; and more, and more. Including a minor constellation of what they called the First People here, autonomous tribes ranging from tiny hamlets to the mighty *tunwan* of the Seven Council Fires. A Lakota chief and his followers rode by as if they had grown in the saddle, eagle-feather bonnets sweeping down the backs of fringed war-shirts of bleached elk-hide.

And more important for her purposes and the Empire's, there were troops, too, the growing muster of the High Kingdom gathered over distances she found almost inconceivable, in a range utterly alien to the small, tightly organized and quite uniform population of her own country. Armored knights and men-at-arms, light cavalry in mail shirts with bow and saber, field catapults rumbling by on their way to a camp outside the little city, kilted archers in green brigandines, once the serried swaying points of a pike-phalanx marching by beneath the banner of a golden honeybee on black and singing in a deep male chorus:

"Awake, ye Saints of God, awake!
Tho' Zion's foes have counseled deep,
Although they bind with fetters strong,
The God of Jacob does not sleep;
His vengeance will not slumber long!"

Then a company of Boiseans behind a wreathed standard topped by an upraised golden hand, with hobnail boots slamming down on the pavement in earthquake unison to the rattle of a kettle-drum and brassy scream of a trumpet and a harsh cry of:

"Make way, make way!" from their officer with the transverse red crest on his helm and vine-root swagger stick in his hand.

"We have accomplished much, Majesty," Egawa said. "We have set all this in motion, and turned it to our purposes."

The commander was an inch or so less than her own five foot six in the local system—medium height for a man in Nihon, short here—but broad-built and squat, in plain dark black-and-gray *hakama* and kimono and five-kamon *haori* jacket, fan and the two swords through his sash. He had grown a little gaunt since he had lost his left hand on the beach at Topanga; Montival had fine doctors, as good as any in Nihon, but that was a grave injury and more so for a man in middle age.

Yet despite the fresh lines in his square, rather brutal face and the extra gray in his hair where the topknot stood up above the shaved strip, there was less hidden tension in the set of his stance. He still looked ready to draw and strike instantly, but less as if he wished something would give him the opportunity.

Every now and then his eye would stray to the sword tucked through the moderate-width modern-style sash she wore around her own kimono. Yellow gleams seemed to move in the black depths of what was no longer a simple sheath of lacquer and wood. Just as the blade beneath was no longer simply steel, not even simply a marvel of seven laminations from the hand of the ancient master-smith Masamune.

He looked aside, cleared his throat, and made a slight show of glancing over the railing of the verandah at the samurai who stood motionless as statues at the street gate, water beading on the lacquered lames of their armor and the plates of their broad-tailed helmets, the dim light glittering on the long heads of their tall *su yari* spears. Two flags flew there; one the *Tennō's* personal banner, red with the sixteen-petal stylized chrysanthemum *mon* of her House in gold, the other the Hinomaru, the red sun-disk on a white ground. More guardsmen stood beneath the balcony, almost invisible against the dark red brick with its coat of ivy, save for the wet gleam on the blades of their *naginatas*.

"Yes," Reiko answered. "It is for that that my father sacrificed himself. So that the generations of our people might live. For that, and this."

Her hand rested on the hilt of the transformed sword for a moment before she went on; they both inclined their heads.

"That we of the Dynasty may have the power to guard them through all time to come. There is much yet to be done, but we have made a good beginning . . . to be sure, with the help of our enemies! They will long regret killing the Montivallan High King when they slew our *Saisei Tennō*."

"Hopefully they will *not* regret it so very long, *Heika*," her officer said with grim humor, and she nodded acknowledgment before she said:

"Come, let us examine the circumstances."

The sliding doors behind them were of glass and metal, salvage of the ancient world rather than modern paper and lath, but the principle was the same. Egawa worked them, then preceded her and bowed her into the room. She stepped out of her zōri sandals and across the mats to a low table that held several maps and stacked reports, along with ink-blocks and brushes and a lever-worked mechanical calculator.

The Montivallan ship that had borne her Grand Steward to the homeland had returned recently with a suitable retinue for her—the bare bones of one, at least. As she and Egawa sank back on their knees and heels on the mats in *seiza* and set their katanas by their right sides the inner door slid open and lady-in-waiting Egawa Chiyo appeared—a stern-faced woman of about thirty, the guard-commander's sister and named for the poet. She directed two maids, young cousins of hers in their early teens, and also related to Reiko as grandchildren of her grand-father's sisters; personal service to the Empress was a post of much honor, eagerly sought among women of high birth. Chiyo wore a rather plain iro-tomesode, and the youngsters the more colorful *furisode* suitable for young maidens.

All three had *wakizashi* shortswords thrust through their modest-width modern *obi*, steel *tessen* folding fans tucked away inconspicuously, *tantō*-daggers, and lead weights sewn into the bottom hems of their long hang-ing sleeves, which could be grasped and instantly swung as deadly flails. Their brothers and uncles and male cousins served in the Guard, but like them the attendants were expected to instantly throw themselves between she whom they served and any danger, if necessary with bare hands or the long pointed pins that secured their piled hair.

The pleasantly spare room was large and comfortable, softly lit by biogas lamp fixtures overhead. It had bookshelves, map-stands, a few flowers, armor-stand and racks for *naginatas* near the inner door, and an alcove where she had hung a scroll she had made herself; she had always found calligraphy an aid to a tranquil mind. The other side bore a *kami-dana* where she could make offerings, at the proper above-eye-level height with a circular mirror in front of a stylized miniature shrine and the other necessary objects. The mirror was customary . . . but for one of her birth, it had a special significance.

Reiko sighed inwardly as the maids laid a *kakeban* serving table by each of them, very much like a lacquered tray with four legs and stretch-ers. She knew all the women who served at Court by name and had grown up among them, and she felt the gentle, invisible, unspoken and irresistible pressure of their presence and their gaze shoving her back into her own appointed role as firmly as they performed theirs.

Both tables came from Japan originally, but had been in a museum here before their allies supplied them, and she felt slightly guilty as the heated sake flasks were placed on them and poured with due ceremony into shallow *sakazuki* cups.

They are so very old, and so very beautiful.

Abstractly she knew that she was much less enmeshed in ceremony and ritual than most of her ancestors. It had been two thousand years, perhaps three, since so few people dwelt in the Land of the Gods. The modern court reflected that, that and the ceaseless pressure of the *jinni-kukaburi* raiders and their sorcerer lords. The very knowledge of some of the more arcane rites had been lost, because only Reiko's grandmother and her nurse and one or two others had survived from the Imperial household; others were well-recorded in writing but impossible because their sites were haunted ruins that would not be reclaimed for generations at best.

But even so, in many ways my time here was like . . . what is the ancient word . . . a vacation, despite hardship and peril. Odd to be alone among strangers, even when some became friends. Yet, also so oddly liberating for a time.

"Kanpai, Majesty!" Egawa said, lifting the cup formally, then pausing for an instant as if he'd been caught in some solecism he couldn't name or define.

Poor Egawa, she thought, as she shook back her sleeve and drank delicately, one hand cupped around the other. *I am his superior officer, but also his Tennō, and I am a woman, yet also a student of the arts of war who he knew and trained as a child. And he has seen me be the vessel of my Ancestress, a living God for a moment. He is a most intelligent man, but he is not particularly subtle or at ease with contradictions, with ambiguities. Like a cat, he prefers things to be . . . tidy.*

She sighed again; she missed her cat, but it would have been cruel to have subjected Aiko to the sea voyage that had brought the reinforcements. Cats loved people, but they loved their homes as much. And to be sure, now there was Kiwako—more rewarding than any pet, a whole personality blossoming like a flower. It was well to have something in your life besides the grim necessities of power.

The papers on the table occupied them for some time; occasionally she reached out and adjusted one of the supplemental stands nearby, each holding an alcohol pressure-lamp before a movable curved mirror. Ruling, even ruling less than four hundred thousand people, involved a great deal of dealing with numbers and reports and maps. She had been raised to that even before her brother was lost and she received a prince's education as heir to the throne; women of the upper classes did much of the routine administration at home these days to spare men for battle, and they set policy more often than the men liked to acknowledge.

When war was involved, it generated still more paper. At least these reports indicated fewer raids than usual back home since she and her father left on their mission. Perhaps the enemy was occupied elsewhere, since Japan was far from their only foe. Or drawing back their strength to strike later, or for once preoccupied with defense rather than attack.

Or a dozen other explanations. Do not speculate beyond the evidence. Good advice . . . but it is like saying that you should not scratch a mosquito bite. True, yet so much easier to give than take! But already some of our people live who would have died or worse if we had not made this voyage.

When you put war and ruling together, there was no end to the administrative trivia, and it was a constant struggle to remember that each figure in the columns represented a person, a bundle of loves and hates and longings connected to so many others.

At times you must disregard that, for the greater good; that is giri. *But* ninjo, *feelings and compassion . . . that must have its place too, or you become an empty suit of armor that walks and kills, and then a blight upon the world.*

"At least now we are no longer perpetually trying to make one tatami cover a whole tsubo by shifting it around very quickly," she observed.

"*Hai, Heika!*" Egawa said cheerfully. "Don't the *gaijin* have a saying about robbing one to pay another. . . ."

"*Robbing* Peter *to pay* Paul," she supplied, dropping the English names into the Nihongo smoothly.

"Yes, exactly. We have been robbing Ichirō to pay Jirō all our lives."

"And Jirō to pay Ichirō," she said.

"Now, we may bestow gifts lavishly on both sons!"

She made a single swift nod and indicated the papers: "This all seems quite satisfactory. Not perfect, given the transportation difficulties and how long it takes to build a ship, but satisfactory. Especially if we can hire vessels from Hawaii, and that looks to be possible even if their king

Kalākaua does not enter the war—and eventually, it seems likely he will. From the reports he is an intelligent, farsighted man, and many of his people are partly of our blood. They are Hawaiian now, but they remember."

He made an affirmative sound and bowed again in acknowledgment.

"General Egawa," she said, as she put her cup down after a sip.

Hot sake was comforting on a cold day, as much for reasons of the spirit as the body. There was a reason they called winter the Black Months in this part of Montival; it was as far north as northern Hokkaido, though not as bitterly cold. Short days and little light went with the wet chill.

"There is something that I wish you to most particularly remember and bear in mind."

"*Hai,* Majesty?"

"We have been through a very great deal together. Battle and worse. You have seen me . . . wield great power."

"*Hai,* Majesty!"

This time his tone was fervent rather than merely politely deferential. What had happened on the beach at Topanga was like nothing since the time of legends, as the Divine Wind struck down the enemies of the Empire. And she had killed one of the *kangshinmu* adepts who had tormented them as much or more than the soldiers of their foes. For much of her people's history the *Tennō Heika* had been less a worldly ruler or commander than an intermediary between the living and the world of the Kami and the ancestors, serving the whole people thus as the head of a household did an individual family. In that moment she had been both, and that was her destiny now.

There were three of the Sacred Treasures. The Jewel we retained; the Mirror is still lost; the Sword I have reclaimed. That was no accident. The Mirror confers the wisdom to use power rightly, but first we must have power to survive at all.

"You have seen me be the vessel of the Immortal One Shining in Heaven, for that moment."

She stopped for an instant to emphasize what came next; and closed her own eyes. Memory burned with a fire that sustained, the memory of being suffused by that glory, touching something vast beyond human conception. And that greatness speaking, Her voice warm with pride and love:

Daughter of the Empire. Daughter of the Sun. My beloved child.

She sighed and opened her eyes again. "But please remember that I was Amaterasu-ōmikami's vessel, not the Sun Goddess' very self. I am Her descendant, and by Her own choice Her daughter . . . but not Her. And while the Great Kami are other than we, and while they are vastly more than we in knowledge and in power, even they do not know all things. They are not omnipotent, nor infallible. And neither am I!"

Reiko pointed with her fan to the stump of his left hand; it was healing well with no infection, but not yet strong enough to bear more than bandages:

"What did I say to you on the beach, after you took that wound in my service, and you asked me what good a one-handed swordsman could be?"

He bowed from his sitting position, and spoke with his harsh growling voice made soft:

"That I would serve you with what was here"—he lifted his right hand—"and here"—he touched his breast—"and what was here."

His hand moved to his forehead, and she nodded.

"So, please bear that in mind, my *bushi*. If our people's great virtues are loyalty and discipline, so we have a besetting vice, and it is telling superiors what they want to hear."

"*Hai, Heika*, that is unquestionably true," Egawa said.

Reiko suppressed a laugh she would have had to hide with her fan.

Truly his spirit is lighter since we have recovered the Sacred Treasure. Irony from Egawa Noboru! Playfulness from forged iron!

He nodded a touch too solemnly. "So my father also said, Majesty, numerous times. Everyone agreed with him."

This time she *did* laugh. Egawa Katashi had formed and led the Seventy Loyal Men who had rescued her toddler grandmother from the unimaginable horrors of Change-stricken Tokyo, and he had also ruled what was left of Japan with iron hand and iron will almost from the day he arrived on Sado-ga-shima. Arrived with one injured little girl who was the sole survivor of the dynasty, and a few score remaining followers equipped with swords and armor from museums or his own collections. And a vision of the future based on his lifelong dream of Nihon's past, in a time when all certainties had vanished in that single moment of light and pain and its terrible aftermath. Only his own sense of duty had made him step aside to become an elder statesman and councilor when her father came of age, when he might have continued to rule from behind the Chrysanthemum Throne like many a warlord before him.

And in Kamakura times not only were the Emperors often obedient to the Retired Emperor, and both were puppets of the Minamoto Shoguns, the Shoguns themselves were puppets of the Hōjō clan regents. For a while Lady Masako, she who they called the nun-Shogun, was the real power behind the Hōjō leaders! *It is often the way of our people to come at power indirectly, behind screens and solemn pretense, layer upon layer.*

But not Egawa Katashi, and not his son.

It is not only fitting that I take Egawa Noboru's youngest son as my consort when we return to the homeland, it is wise in several respects. He is healthy, intelligent, of good character—not surprising, he comes of very good stock on both sides, his mother is an excellent person—and it will cement his family's place as a pillar of the Throne in years to come. And if he is rather young . . . well, so were my father and grandmother when they wed. The link of blood between our generations still balances on the sword's edge. Giri, neh? The first duty we owe the Ancestors is to give them descendants.

"Or even worse, we tend to assume that our superiors' thinking is correct simply *because* they are superiors," she said, serious once more. "Do not let your loyal heart betray you so. I need your *wits*, General-san. If you think I am in error, you are *ordered* to tell me. In the appropriate manner, of course. The final decision must be mine, but you taught me much when I was a child; you were *Saisei Tennō's* most valued councilor and commander, a living sword in his hand. A sword forged of will and intellect. So you will be to me, and your sons after you to my heir."

"I beg the Heavenly Sovereign Majesty's pardon for my excessive humility," he said—and she caught the twinkle in his eye and smiled slightly.

"Excellent. To business," she said.

She leaned over the table and traced the path across the Pacific and back with her *tessen* war-fan, a loop to the south westbound and then north again for the return with the prevailing winds, a pattern like the hands of a gigantic clock.

"The Montivallan ship made most excellent time. Forty-four days sailing, very fast indeed; and its very presence and size bore witness to the messages I sent with Grand Steward Koyama."

And this means I need not be the first to bear Mother and my little sisters the news of Father's death . . . and that our brother Yoshihito is truly and finally lost. Is this an evasion of duty? No, I do not think so. For negotiating the details of the alliance here is of the very greatest importance. When I bear Father's ashes home, we may grieve together; but I will come with the Grasscutter Sword reborn to be a terror to our enemies, and a fleet and an army to free our people of the terror that has haunted them since the Change. Father considered those things a good bargain for his life, and so must I. As it would be for mine.

The commander of the Imperial Guard ducked his head. "*Hai, Heika,*" he said. A hesitation, and then: "You have full confidence in the Grand Steward, of course."

That was a question disguised as a statement; evidently Egawa was taking her instructions to heart. The two men—the most important in the Empire's government—had been quiet rivals for some time. They had never let it impede their efficiency, but it was there. One thing that had divided them was their attitudes towards this expedition; Koyama Akira had gone along reluctantly, only half-convinced at most by her father's visions. He was older and more conservative, and though he had been a small child at the Change, at times he still clung to the outmoded mechanistic ways of thought of the ancients.

"I have full confidence in him now," she said dryly, glancing aside and sipping.

Egawa glanced aside as well. "I have rarely seen a man so chastened as he was when the Majesty showed him the Grasscutter Sword," he said, carefully keeping any satisfaction out of his tone, since it would be known just the same.

"I have entrusted him with great authority," she said, just as carefully keeping warning out of hers for the same reasons.

Koyama was also a valued servant, who now *was* chastened—he had been struck dumb with awe and trembled with remorse, in fact—and she had no intention of wasting his talents. Among her people bowing the forehead to the ground was a standard formal courtesy to the Throne, but she had seldom seen it performed as sincerely as the Grand Steward had done when she drew the Grasscutter and the steel had lit with the supernal fire at its heart. Together with her mother he would be ruling Japan in her absence, both at the head of the *Dajō-Kan*, the Council of State.

Which I intend to keep quite separate from the military commands. I trust Egawa, but there is still prudence, and there is still the matter of not setting bad precedents. Father taught me that institutions must be built for average people to use and use safely and well. If they cannot function without extraordinary talent and virtue at their head, then they are failures.

"And he certainly organized matters well and quickly with regard to the party that returned with the Montivallan ship," she said, and Egawa nodded. "And now we will have our own transport once more, without having to deplete the Navy further . . . though I do miss Captain Ishikawa."

"Yes, Majesty. Ishikawa-san is a brilliant ship commander, probably our best, but the Navy officers who the Grand Steward dispatched are very competent men, and have already fully familiarized themselves with the new ship. It is somewhat different from our designs, but of comparable performance; they are particularly enthusiastic about the quality of the single-trunk large masts and spars used on the new vessel."

"The *Arī no Okurimono*," she said; that meant *Gift of the Ally*, a rather unconventional name for a ship in their terminology.

He frowned; the ship was in fact a gift, from Princess Órlaith personally, a near-duplicate of the *Tarshish Queen* they had sailed on to seek the Grasscutter Sword. It was closely similar to the largest class in the Imperial Navy, much like the *Red Dragon* that had borne them here. Egawa was ruthlessly willing to wring every advantage possible from the alliance with Montival, but he also resented the degree of dependence it implied. His father Egawa Katashi had still been in the womb when *his* father had driven his flying machine into the side of an American warship off Okinawa a century ago, in the last doomed effort to hold back the overwhelming might of the invaders by raw willingness to die. That memory was cherished in his family.

"Remember what I said when we first saw Montival's strength, General."

He did, and his face lightened at the thought: she had said that it was good to have powerful friends . . . and even better to *be* a powerful friend, which they would be someday once more. When the *jinnikukaburi* menace was removed, their people could grow. The alliance they made now would provide essential shelter for that growth at first, but in the end it would tower to the sky.

"We will lay the foundations strongly; on them our descendants will build," she said. "One day the Montivallans will be glad indeed to have earned our lasting goodwill. Then our alliance with them will be an alliance of equals, a steel bond of peace throughout the Pacific, and will greatly advance the Empire's interests."

He cleared his throat and continued:

"The logistics will be very tricky. There are ample troops and ample supplies, which is a most pleasant change! But they are here on this side of the ocean; in the Empire we have neither and the one is useless without the other. Shipping will be the bottleneck, and assigning priorities essential."

She made a gesture of agreement. Did you send a hull full of troops first . . . or were shiploads of dried noodles more important, to have a reserve of food available when they landed? Her people remembered the Great Pacific War of a century ago, when utter valor and blood and suffering poured out in oceans had not sufficed for victory; the warrior spirit was crucially important, but spirits needed bodies to inhabit and bodies needed food and weapons to fight. A few cargos of grain would enable them to mobilize more of their own people as well, if they did not need to fear famine after taking too many strong backs and skilled hands from the paddies and workshops. Every shipyard in Montival was working triple shifts now, and she had ordered the same at home regardless of longer-term effects, but it would take time.

He shook his head. "I am disturbed that all resources are not being dedicated to the point of main effort. If you try to be strong everywhere, you are weak everywhere; if you try to do everything that is desirable, you accomplish nothing that is important."

Reiko nodded. "In the abstract, General, your logic is excellent, undeniable. But the additional resources we have secured are our *ally's* troops, and our *ally's* supplies and for the most part our *ally's* ships. Furthermore—"

Her fan made a graceful looping gesture over the Grasscutter Sword lying on the mat beside her, so quiet and still . . . and to the inner eye that could see, like the spirits of Air and Fire, a torrent of the living Sun locked in steel.

"The storm I raised did more than shatter the *jinnikukaburi* squadron. It sent Prince John, the High Queen's son, to only-the-*kami*-know-where, not to mention a major Montivallan warship with hundreds of her loyal troops aboard. Consider that governments are made of human beings, not the passionless thinking machines of the ancients, and try to see it from her point of view. A point of view which we have *no choice* but to take into consideration, since she will be ruler here for another four years. And while the Crown Princess and I are close comrades who share a loss, and we are convinced that our nations must stand united in this war, it is still *her* brother and *her* troops as well. Our interests are well aligned for the most part, but not identical."

He snorted, recognizing the point but obviously wishing he didn't have to. "*Hai, Heika.*"

Then for a single moment he grinned like a shark.

"Whenever my frustrations grip me, I think of the surprise the *jinni-kukaburi* raiders will encounter when the first squadron of Montivallan frigates meets them in our waters. Remember how the *Stormrider* pounded one to burning fragments in the Bay? I would prefer that we had such ships ourselves, but this is an acceptable second-best."

She nodded. "That is indeed a happy thought. But our allies cannot station them there forever; they have their own raiders to guard against here, if not so many and so dangerous, and the seas are large and ships relatively few. We must strike the enemy a heavy blow on their own ground— and this is not simply a contention of nations, so we cannot expect the minions of the *kangshinmu* kings and the evil *akuma* they serve to act rationally when faced with superior force. They care little for the welfare of their kingdom, and nothing at all for the sufferings of its ordinary people."

"*Many* heavy blows, then, Majesty."

The prospect didn't seem to displease him. He inclined his head.

"I am developing a plan in conjunction with the High Marshal d'Ath," he said, mangling the Montivallan commander's name and title. "It is fortunate that they have found more interpreters, even if they speak a very odd archaic dialect and speak it badly at that. My written English is now enough to be useful, but I am too old and my ear too set to learn the spoken tongue well. Writing leaves less possibility of ambiguity in any case, but in the field speed is often essential."

Reiko nodded. "That is why I specified that a number of young persons familiar with written English be sent with the return voyage. Young minds are more flexible in such matters, and in a few months we will have several dozen interpreters of reasonable skill. With hard work."

"*Ganbarimasu*, yes," Egawa observed.

That capacity for intense, sustained grinding effort was one their people had always prized highly. He went on:

"Interpreters of our own. And there are other English-speaking powers in the Pacific we may need to deal with now . . . through our own people."

"Precisely. We must plan for the long term, neh? Human beings die, and their personal friendships and hatreds with them, but nations must go on. Now I will consult with Princess Órlaith and her *hatamoto*; do you think your presence necessary?"

He bowed, taking the hint. "With permission, Majesty, no, if this will be strategic and political matters?"

At her gesture of assent he went on: "I should concentrate on drawing up a preliminary schedule of movement orders for use when we reach home, and a summary for your approval. Mobilization will be under way even now. Our first blow must be not only heavy, but *swift*. Surprise multiplies force."

"Yes, General. We must cripple them beyond recovery, striking quickly many times from more directions than they can guard, like an *oni* with an iron club."

"Hai!" he said with cheerfully ferocious enthusiasm. "Your *bushi* will crack their bones like an army of *oni*, Majesty, and lay their land at your feet."

"Excellent, General." She made a small grimace. "Not that I particularly desire to have Korea at my feet, but better there than at our throats. After that we will have to make it something that is not a threat to its neighbors . . . Thankless work, but preferable to the alternative."

Egawa chuckled harshly and went to one knee, bowing briskly with the fist of his sword-hand pressed to the mat; she had stated that etiquette here was to be that of an army in the field, which simplified matters.

John was . . . is . . . an interesting person, she thought. *How fortunate Orrey-chan does not hold his loss against me! To be sure, she knows he is not dead. Not now. But what peril might he be in? Peril of spirit as well as body.*

CHAPTER NINETEEN

John Arminger Mackenzie dreamed that the shadow of his soul lengthened in the afternoon . . .

He looked up from where the cloud-foam beat on the black sand, endlessly different, an intricate structure that ate meaning and changed it so that even to think was impossible in ways that were attractive and loathsome in even measure.

Something flashed across the sky where black stars moved, something blue. A blue diamond of light, a blue mantle draped over the head of a figure taller than the horizon yet somehow shadowed with his mother's face against a background of infinite light, and then the blue flash of a sword. A sword that was not a sword in the hand of a knight whose beauty was terror and protection, and rearing back snarling from its power a dragon that was no dragon. The substance of his mind seemed on the edge of shattering into fragments as it strained to comprehend things beyond its uttermost abilities. He knew that what he was seeing was true, but that the symbols his consciousness used were less than a child's stick-figure scrawl compared to the unthinkable realities they tried to show.

And there were words, thundering in his mind across gulfs where stars were like motes of dust, syllables of ringing crystal carved from the hearts of ancient suns:

Sancte Michael Archangele—

He woke, gasping out: *"Defende nos in proelio, contre nequitiam et insidias diaboli esto praesidium!"*

There was none of the usual transition between sleep and waking. The memory of the dream vanished, leaving him with only the quickened pulse and breathing that went with danger. Ruan—it was his watch—had an arrow on the string of his bow, standing and peering about uneasily. His brows went up when he saw the Prince awake, and he nodded with visible relief at the sharp gesture with a rising hand: *get them up.*

He went to Deor first, but the scop threw back his blanket as the young Mackenzie reached for him. John tapped his foot against Pip's, which was the safest way to quietly wake someone who slept with a blade close to hand . . . which both his parents had done most of their lives. She stirred, blinked, opened eyes pale in the moonlight and gave him a quick nod as he pulled his feet into his boots. By then the others were all stirring or up, reaching quietly for weapons and harness, helping one another in darkness lit only by embers and a few distant lanterns but keeping low. The moon was down and it was as quiet as an encampment of several thousand humans, seven elephants and many score of lesser beasts could possibly be.

Ishikawa murmured very quietly as he slipped into his light flexible seaman's *kikkō* cuirass and tied the thick silk cords that secured his helm:

"Yumi."

Two of his sailors strung the seven-foot asymmetrical weapon and then handed it and the quiver to him. A crewman from the *Tarshish Queen* began a querulous question, and there was a faint *mmmmff!* as Radavindra-ban clapped a hand over his mouth.

"Arm," he murmured to the *Queen*'s sailors. "Quick, quiet!"

Pip's gang of ruffians from the *Silver Surfer* were faster, if anything, coming awake and ready to fight with the feral intensity of so many coy-dogs. Evrouin helped John into the arming doublet and snapped the clips that held his back-and-breast at hip and shoulder, then pushed the helm down on his head before he started in on the rest of the armor, working from the chest down, buckling the parts together and threading the laces through the eyelets and tying them off. An expert was supposed to be able to do that with his eyes closed, and Evrouin managed it without a fumble in the darkness, his fingers flying as swiftly as a court typist.

You certainly couldn't do it all yourself, not without half an hour, six hands and a contortionist's flexibility.

Even with the visor up the helmet felt stifling as the sponge-and-felt pads within gripped John's skull, and it made the darkness seem blacker. That was no less unpleasant for being mostly imaginary, though it did cut off peripheral vision. The fear wasn't completely imaginary anyway, not when your testicles were making faint whimpering sounds as they crawled up into your belly for shelter, driven by the conviction that someone was creeping up on you from a direction just beyond the corner of your eye.

Sergeant Fayard knelt beside the prince, and John made a circling motion with one hand just after Evrouin slipped the gauntlet onto it. The underofficer nodded, touched two fingers to the brim of his helm and moved crouching to set his dozen crossbowmen out in a ring. There was a multiple *crink-crink-crink-crink-crink-crink-click* sound as they cocked their weapons and slid bolts into the firing grooves; their half-armor was light gear by Montivallan custom, but it made them heavy infantry here.

Think, John, he told himself, forcing his mind into tactical mode.

He'd been educated by warriors, even if it wasn't his first choice of occupation. Then again it hadn't been his mother's either, and she'd been very good at it by all accounts, and his father had always said he'd rather have kept a good inn on an interesting highway, with a horse-paddock and garden and some fishing and hunting in the neighborhood.

If I was an enemy attacking this camp, what would I do? If I wasn't strong enough to overrun it and kill us all, that is, which would take a major force and couldn't be done by stealth.

John carefully refrained from looking at the scattered red-gold dots of firelight, despite the impulse to do just that, remembering the old joke about the drunk who'd lost his house-key looking for it under a streetlamp because that's where the light was. The last thing he needed now was to kill his night-vision. The shield slid onto his arm and he put one hand to his sword-hilt. One deep breath and then another, and another; if you forced your body to behave as if it was calm, the mind followed.

Silence stretched as the Montivallans and their allies finished readying themselves. He shivered a little; it was far from being anything you could call cold, but it was much cooler than the daytime and the heavy moisture in the air produced a lot of dew. Drops of it ran gelid down his spine. On the one hand he was hideously afraid of embarrassment if this turned out to be a false alarm. Not to mention how everyone would resent him for getting them up in the middle of the night. On the other hand . . .

If someone's creeping through the dark, I don't care about being embarrassed! Let's see, why would they do a night attack? I'd go for the artillery and the prang-prangs. This expedition is all about them, when you come right down to it. They're the point failure source. Even if they didn't damage anything else, losing them would mean we couldn't do anything but turn around and go back. You can't attack a fortress with artillery of its own unless you've got catapults, even if you're prepared to bury it under bodies.

He started to relax, pleased with his analysis . . .

"Wait a minute," he murmured to himself, feeling his eyes going wide in the dark. "That means they'd be coming right at *us*."

Then something went *tick* and he felt a sharp rap on his shield. Not nearly as hard as an arrow hitting it, but the same *sort* of feeling, somehow.

Thoughts tumbled through his mind like gearwork in a mill, and he leapt to the side and swept the shield up in front of Pip, putting her between it and his armored body and raising it so that the upper curve covered her face to the brim of her hat.

Tick.

Something struck the side of his helmet. In the same instant Deor shouted a warning:

"*Iban*, blowguns! *Tejem* poison on the darts—deadly! Hold up your blankets to shield each other!"

Tick—tick—tick—tick, as they scrambled for the cloth and someone screamed. There was something about the words *poison* and *deadly* . . .

Blows on his shield and helmet, one heart-stoppingly close to the side of his face, striking the lower edge of the sallet helm. He swept his visor down and another *tick* struck just below the eyeslit. It was hard, a sharp rap like someone knocking a knuckle on a door or hail hitting a roof-tile, but not the punch-hard hammer strike of a crossbow bolt or an arrow from a heavy war-bow. Somehow knowing that the slivers flying invisibly through the night were coated in something that would destroy his nervous system was just as frightening. He expelled a breath, and in the same moment forced terror out of his head, an almost physical sensation.

"Agi Idup! Agi Ngelaban!" someone screamed nearby.

War-cry, John thought, tense and waiting for more darts that didn't come.

And it wasn't any of the local battle shouts, he'd made a point of learning those. There was a clash of steel on the heels of it, and a scream of pain, noise spreading like the ripples from a stone dropped in a pond. However few they were and however stealthy their approach, the attackers had roused the Baru Denpasarans now. They had only moments before they were overwhelmed . . . though the thought of a melee in pitch darkness was enough to make the hair bristle on the back of your head. A small band of infiltrators would have the advantage of being able to strike at anyone around them. Everyone else would be likely to do that too, regardless of who they hit, and might well inflict more casualties on their own folk than the foe did. There had been a battle centuries ago where an entire army had defeated *itself* in exactly that way.

Toa loomed up in the darkness, visible mostly as eyeballs and a glint of steel. The Maori was wrapped in something dark, mottled and shaggy. John had assumed it was the outer cover for his bedroll, and perhaps it was, but it was also a long cloak of flax fabric sewn all over with strips of leather with the hair still attached, constructed so that it fastened at the front and covered his whole body from throat to ankles save where one hand held his great spear and the other a bundle. The garment rustled in the dark as he threw another like it to Pip.

"*Kahu koati,*" he said, which might mean something to her.

It did; she ducked out from behind John's shield and swept the cloak about her shoulders, giving John a brief white smile of thanks in the dimness as she did so. There was a dart standing in the brow of the bowler that she wore, just visible when the tuft of feather on its base waggled. The eyes beneath the brim went wide as she looked out into the darkness and whipped up her slingshot.

"Heads up!" Thora barked, shield up and backsword moving in a wrist-loosening whirl that shimmered in the darkness as the firelight caught the honed edge. "Here they come!"

Things began to happen; there was another clash of weapons, and more shouts. Almost instantly, basketfuls of dry brushwood that had been left ready were tipped into the fires in a dozen places throughout the camp by the simple expedient of kicking out the sticks that supported them. Red-yellow light flared up instants later, dazzlingly bright. It was a mixed blessing as he squinted against it . . .

Those are men coming our way! he thought.

He opened his mouth to shout the order to shoot as the figures were silhouetted against the blaze. The enemy were short, slight brown men like the Baru Denpasarans, or several of the Montivallans for that matter—he'd felt big, pink and conspicuous ever since the *Tarshish Queen* made landfall here—but their fringed loincloths and circles of feathers standing up from headbands made them easy to pick out once they were upright and moving and the fires really caught.

Fayard beat him to it. All twelve crossbows went off together, in a single prolonged *tunnnggg-whap,* and the sailors from the *Tarshish Queen* followed albeit more raggedly and an instant later than the professional soldiers of the Protector's Guard. Ishikawa and Ruan both shot twice in the span of the sound of the crossbows loosing. Figures fell, seeming to vanish from the earth as they dropped out of the fiery background.

Though their screams remained all too audible. Others might be dead . . . or might be crawling towards him on their bellies.

And nearly impossible to see with this God-damned helmet on! And the bolts that missed will go off blind into the night and like as not hit one of our allies.

The weapons the Montivallans carried could smash through armor at close range and were deadly at three hundred long paces. Against naked opponents at point-blank like this they were perfectly capable of punching all the way through a man's body and sinking home in anyone standing behind him. He still wasn't going to try to tell his followers not to shoot at attackers trying to kill them, and if some of their allies suffered because of it . . . well, Holy Church taught that the Fall of Man meant life was a vale of tears full of suffering. He ignored an image of his confessor gibbering in indignation at that piece of sophistry and dismissed the thought of the penances that would follow.

The Iban were moving forward *quickly* now that they'd been discovered, sprinting behind snarls and the red-silver glitter of steel seen by firelight. They had probably expected to finish off men still half-asleep or paralyzed by the darts in a final burst of hand-to-hand slaughter, but they were still doing the right thing—charging home across the missile weapons' killing ground. He thought a few of the sailors from the *Queen* were lying still or writhing on the ground, but there wasn't time to check, and most of their party were on their feet and armed. And shooting. The wet crack of bolts striking flesh sounded beneath the harsh twanging of steel prods and wire string.

A clump of the Iban were heading for his all-too-visible self; polished chrome-steel armor glittered even in the firelight, not to mention the ostrich-plumes on the top of his helmet, marking him out as a leader. They might or might not know what a suit of plate was, but they definitely knew it was conspicuous. The first few seemed to be carrying spears. He had just enough time to realize that they were spearheads on the end of eight-foot blowguns made from some iron-hard dark wood and think *very clever* before they were too close for anything but reflex.

"Haro, Portland! Holy Mary for Portland!" he screamed behind the muffling visor.

In the same instant he leapt into a full-tilt charge, sword up over his head with the hilt forward. At close quarters men-at-arms didn't just *have* weapons, they *were* weapons, and the most deadly ones known to human-kind. Six stamping strides and he tucked the big curved kite shield into his shoulder, leading with it as he lunged in what was almost a headlong fall. The first Iban was skilled and quick as a striking weasel, stabbing for his face and ready to block the sword, but he'd never fought a knight in plate before and wasn't going to have the time to benefit from the experience. John tucked his head a little, and the spearhead banged off the pauldron over his right shoulder with a screech of metal on metal without throwing him off his stride.

He rammed straight forward to contact without pausing or trying to use the sword, something only the confident and well trained—or drunken or reckless—did. There was just enough light to see his enemy was surprised; his concept of normal would have been for John to slow down and use the blade. Then the sheet-steel facing of the shield struck along a quarter of the smaller man's body, including his face and collarbone and part of an arm he'd started to fling up in reflex.

Naked, John would have outweighed the Sea-Dyak warrior by forty pounds of bone and muscle. Armed cap-a-pie and counting the shield it was more like a hundred and twenty, and they met with their full combined velocity. Bare flesh rammed into unyielding steel. The check made John grunt as the shock ran down from shoulder into bent knees and bounced him back fully upright, but this sort of collision was a frequent experience in training to fight as a knight and he knew how to use it. Bone cracked loud enough to hear over the gathering tumult, and that included the Iban's jaw, cheekbone, elbow and eye-socket.

He'd just been struck very hard by a very large club.

The wounded man's limp body tangled up the two following him. John's sword slashed down at the half-glimpsed figure to his right, not aiming, just trying to hit *something* on the bare moving form. If seeing things through a visor's slit in the daytime was a strain, at night it was like fighting in a bad dream . . . or a crowded closet with the door closed. The longsword was a brief shimmer through the night.

The ugly wet crack of impact jarred through the leather inner surface of his gauntlet and into his hand and tight-strapped wrist, with the solid chunking feel of a straight-on hit that you got used to practicing on hog carcasses. A man lurched away grabbing at his right arm with his left, and then ran shrieking for a few steps as it came off in his hand before he collapsed bonelessly limp and face-down. Evrouin stabbed past his liege's sword-arm with the glaive, and someone half-seen grunted in shock as the heavy butcher-knife shape of the blade went home with two strong arms behind it along the mountain-ash shaft.

"Hakkaa päälle!"

That was the Bearkiller war-shout; probably, almost certainly, the first time it had been heard on these shores. It meant *Hack them down!*

Off to his right Thora deliberately took a spearpoint on the breast-plate. That was painful and risky, but left her enemy shocked into an instant's immobility. In the same moment she caught another man behind the knee with a vicious slashing backstroke, punched the steel-shod edge of her dish-shaped shield into a third's face just below the eyes with a crack like an axe blade striking, and then lunged with a beautiful econ-omy of motion that sent six inches of point into the throat of the spear-man drawing his weapon back for another stab. Then she withdrew into guard position with a quick twist of the wrist that opened all the large veins and probably killed the man almost as fast as cutting off his head would have done. It all took about as long as counting one-two-three, graceful as a dance and done with a hard smooth quickness.

"Ha, Woden! Woden!"

Deor Godulfson called on his God as he finished the man Thora had hocked with an economical chop of his Saxon broadsword; the Iban had been trying to stab her in the foot, which showed commendable focus with a leg cut halfway through at the back of the knee. Then he caught another spearpoint on his round raven-blazoned shield, stabbed under-neath it and punched with the boss that covered the grip within.

"Woden!"

Victory-Father's name was probably also a first for this island, and the poet's voice rang like a trumpet. He was on Thora's right, guarding her unshielded side, the oiled steel links of his mail hauberk gleaming like a dragon's skin in the dark. The two of them worked together like the fingers of a single hand. Some fleeting, buried part of John's mind—the part not focused on staying alive in this blindfolded scrimmage—was glad to see it. He was a passing part of their story, but those two were really what mattered to each other, at seventh and last.

He glared around, shield up under his vision-slit and head turning in the automatic side-to-side motion you used to compensate for the loss of your peripheral vision. Then he staggered, and staggered again as something grabbed at his ankle and tried to jerk his foot out from under him, probably failing only because they underestimated his weight.

Evrouin tried to get a clear path for a stab at whoever it was and cursed foully as he couldn't and then had to take on another attacker, glaive to blowgun-spear. John kicked reflexively as he swung the shield to balance himself and felt the rounded toe of his sabaton hit *something*, but not hard enough to break bones.

He was blind downward, and flicked his visor open with the back of a gauntlet as he jerked the shield up to chop down with its lower point, the standard move against someone on the ground—a kite shield was heavy enough to make a very effective bludgeon. That gave him a view as an Iban came erect off the ground like something on springs, rising up between the shield and John's body and dropping the wavy-bladed knife held in his teeth into one hand. The stab at John's face was quick as a lizard's tongue.

Someone had learned the lesson of the last Iban's attempt to fight a knight on his own terms, and learned it very quickly indeed. That someone went around in a fringed loincloth, but it didn't mean they were stupid.

A wasp had darted at John's eyes once when he was a child. The memory flashed as he tossed his head back and to the side with frantic speed and the point flashed by his eyes close enough to part a lash.

Too close!

The motion made his visor click down, blinding him again. He pulled the Iban into a frantic bear hug, which was like embracing a large, very strong writhing anaconda, and smashed his head forward in a butt with the forehead of the low-crowned sallet helm again and again. Even with the padding between him and the steel that hurt his head and neck and lights starred in front of his eyes, but in his current state he ignored it. The Iban didn't have that option as metal pounded into his face, though he stabbed twice and the knife screeched off the breastplate and the faulds over John's thighs. Blood spattered over the front of the Montival-lan's helmet and visor, a hot, salty, metallic smell. The wild man made one last faltering try for the vision slit before he went limp.

One of his teachers—it had been John Hordle of the Dúnedain, still bear-strong at sixty, scarred and jovial and immensely experienced—had told him that in a fight to the death technique was good but raw aggression, a living will to do harm and always going forward made up for a great deal. The hearts of the Sea-Dyak warriors were definitely in the right place by those standards. Against locals—or the Montivallans and Japanese and the *Silver Surfer*'s cosmopolitan gang of toughs, if he hadn't been woken by that nightmare he couldn't remember anymore—they might have broken through to the catapults.

Something isn't right, he thought as he let the one he'd clubbed into a daze with the head-butts drop.

Evrouin finished his man in the same moment with a sweeping two-handed overhead slash that put seven feet of leverage behind his blow. Glaives were about as effective as a battle-axe that way; they were designed to give infantry a chance against mounted men-at-arms, and they could cut a knight's armor if it was one of the thinner parts and they hit it just right. When it came down on the unprotected junction of neck and shoulder . . . well, bad things happened.

John knocked up his visor again, and they stood side-by-side panting as rivulets of sweat poured down their faces and more oozed out of the padding of their helmets. Nobody seemed to be fighting at that instant;

Ruan slung his bow and attended to the wounded, who seemed to be mercifully few.

How were they planning to destroy *the catapults in a few moments in the dark, even if they'd overrun them? Especially when they've probably never seen one before?*

His sister Órlaith had wiped out a battery of Korean field catapults back in south Westria, in the time it took her to walk between them and swing a two-handed cut for each . . . but she'd known exactly what to hit. And she'd used the Sword of the Lady, whose razor-sharp invulnerable blade really could be used over and over again on thumb-thick steel rods and springs. He looked around, with shield and sword in hand. There was a cracking, crunching sound as Evrouin thoughtfully smacked the steel cap on the other end of his glaive's haft into the fallen Iban's head a couple of times, much like someone pounding herbs in a mortar and pestle.

"There!" Pip shouted.

She must have eyes like a cat. The end of her double-headed cane dripped blackly as she pointed, the serrated gold alloy hidden. Toa stood a little ahead of her, crouched with the great spear rotating smoothly in his ham-sized hands and a scatter of bodies—and parts of bodies—lying in front of him. There were feather-tufted darts sticking in the cloak that hung from his shoulder, and he seemed . . .

A bit peeved, John thought as the Maori grimaced like a gargoyle and bellowed:

"Tika tonu mai
Tika tonu mai
Ki ahau e noho nei
Tika tonu mai I a hei ha!"

If that isn't some version of Step right up and lay right down! *I'm a McClintock,* John thought; it was heartening, to have someone like that on your side.

Another band of Iban came running out of the darkness; Pip dropped the cane and whipped out her slingshot from its holster on her thigh, flicking the brace open against her forearm with the same movement. There were at least a score of them and they all seemed to be carrying something besides their personal weapons . . .

Follow-up squad, went through his mind in an instant. *The others were supposed to clear the way. It would have worked, if they'd surprised us, but they don't know it didn't work . . . or they're going to try anyway. But even if it had worked perfectly, there's no way they could have gotten out again, not most of them. It's a forlorn hope, and a very forlorn one at that.*

According to *Tuan* Anak the Iban here fought for Carcosa as mercenaries sometimes and according to him and Deor and Thora all three, they were fierce warriors by nature and custom to boot, but this wasn't the sort of plan you expected of men fighting for pay. Or that anyone with their wits about them would expect hired men to follow with this sort of headlong sacrificial valor. Not just because some master resting someplace safely distant told them to do it. He'd heard his father say more than once that physical courage was simply not that rare a quality, and you could often hire men to *risk* their lives. To pour out their lives like water they had to be fighting *for* something of transcendent value—though that might be an intangible, like honor or reputation or their given oath. Or their employer might have something their families needed for their lives, or held hostages they loved more than life.

All that flashed through his mind in wordless instants. There was only one way this could be worth *anything* to the attackers, and that was—

"Thermite charges!" he yelled; it was the only thing capable of destroying large steel machines quickly. "Stop them!"

Pip stopped one; she drew and loosed with her slingshot. Pure accident smacked the ball-bearing into the nose of the pointed cylinder one of the Iban was carrying under his left arm, with his parang in his right hand. It was a warhead from a firebolt, something substantial made for a twenty-four-pounder catapult or bigger, and the half-inch steel ball hit the detonator pin to smash it back against the friction igniter and the magnesium booster within. Evidently the safety lock had been removed, or this model didn't have one.

The warhead flared into blue-white actinic brightness instantly, spewing stuff hot enough to melt steel in an eyeblink all over the upper half of his body in the most destructive chemical reaction the Changed world allowed. The man carrying it barely had time to begin a scream amid a stink of scorched meat and acrid burning bone. His skull cracked open along its seams as brains and blood boiled within the rigid cage.

A few of the crossbowmen shot, but not enough to blunt the second charge—there hadn't been enough time to reload after they slung their crossbows and drew sword and buckler. Ishikawa loosed a shaft from his *yumi*, and after a moment Ruan rose and drew and loosed as well; both hit at least one man. The first dropped straight down and the point of the warhead clutched in his arms hit the ground hard enough to trigger it. It was trapped between the Iban's midsection the ground when it ignited and the result was . . .

I really wish I hadn't seen that, John thought, feeling queasy even in the rush of battle and turning his head and blinking against the afterimages of intolerable light. *I'm going to remember that and I don't want to.*

"Eyes on!" Evrouin snapped, before adding: "Sire."

Not Eyes on, *you idiot,* at least, he thought.

John forced himself to squint and blink watering eyes. That was enough to show the final despairing rush break on a serried rank—the Guard crossbowmen in their half-armor had come up with their swords and bucklers in hand to stand with the leaders, and the sailors held their flanks with knife and cutlass and *naginata*. It was hard to be sure in the darkness, but he thought the Iban were fewer than his band now, as well as more lightly armed. Each advantage magnified the other.

He stabbed at one attacker, but the man jumped backward with frantic agility and the Montivallan pulled back into guard. Toa's great spear flashed in a circle trailing blood, then struck out underarm in a stab like a frog's tongue. That killed, but the broad head caught in bone and the rearward jerk didn't clear it as the body flopped loosely and came back with the weapon. The moment of immobility was near-fatal; the big Maori went down as another Iban appeared out of nowhere and cracked the firebolt warhead he carried against the side of his head—fortunately not with the point, and he had to reach up to do it, which robbed the stroke of some of its force. Blades poised to finish the fallen man.

"*Tennō Heika* banzai!"

Ishikawa drew and cut horizontally with his katana in a single arc of movement, topping a man's head like a boiled egg; even then John blinked at the sight, shocked that the steel hadn't locked in bone, and the dead man dropped and knotted into a convulsion at the same time.

Pip screamed as Toa went down, a sound composed of fear and sheer raw fury. She moved so quickly that suddenly she was just *there* standing over Toa's body, a kukri in one hand and her cane in the other, and they were blurring even faster, chopping and blocking and smashing into the sides of heads or down onto collarbones or elbows. Blood flew, trails of black in the night, adding to the metallic stink. The last of the raiders went down under multiple attacks.

Then she was standing still and poised, glaring around them as the light grew brighter; more armloads of brush were being thrown on the fires, some of them on the earth berm that surrounded the camp. She used the illumination to administer a series of whacks with her cane to the heads of half a dozen recumbent writhing figures, an unpleasant almost vegetable-sounding crunch-crunch-crunch as she swung it like a flail with her hand tucked right under the knob at the other end.

"Do you have a *flaaag*, you creeping little poison-dart sods?" he heard her mutter between blows, under her panting breath. "No? Didn't bloody *think*"—another full-armed swing and a last crunch—"so!"

Another thing his father had told him once was that you should never just *frighten* a brave enemy if you could help it, because in a courageous mind fear tripped over into killing rage almost immediately.

The fighting was over, as far as he could tell, but the noise all around was building instead of dying, shrieks and what seemed to be chants.

"Deor, I'm going to need you to talk for me if Tuan Anak's down—we have to find out what's going on," he said firmly. "Mr. Radavindraban—"

He was still standing, thought bloodied by a cut on the forehead and holding an arm to it to keep the flow out of his eyes.

Never show the doubt or the hesitation.

"—you're in charge here. Sergeant Fayard, maintain the perimeter around the catapults. It's essential to the mission," he added as the Guardsman looked rebellious.

He was probably going to say: *you are our mission, Your Highness,* but John had a counter to that . . .

"And if the mission fails, none of us are getting off this island alive. Myself included."

Deor nodded agreement, but the scop also looked for Ruan; the young healer was busy—he was threading a needle and telling Radavindraban to sit—and spared him only time enough for a smile and a wave.

Pip bent over Toa, who winced as she felt at the injured spot on his head and groaned as he rose using the shaft of his spear as a lever, with the other hand on Pip's shoulder. He winced again when he shook his head.

"Getting too old for this," he said with a groan. "Time for a rocking chair on the verandah and a bottomless bottle of beer."

"It's not cracked," she said with relief. "You need to remember that big doesn't mean immortal!"

Then she nodded to John. "Bloody right we have to know what's going on," she said.

Her head went up, as if she was a gray-eyed tawny cat sniffing for a scent.

"Something's not right," she said. "That doesn't *sound* like people who just won a fight. It sounds like someone whose puppy got run over by the post-coach."

"Exactly," John said, as the remark crystalized his unease.

The five of them set out—Evrouin wasn't going out of glaive-distance from John, and Thora came along rubbing a swatch of fringed cloth from an Iban's clout along the blade of her bloody sword.

"This has the feel of a decapitation strike," she said, and at their puzzlement: "Term of art in the A-List. Trying to weaken an opponent by cutting off their leadership or their specialists. Like a jab to daze and a kick to finish."

John nodded as he unclipped his helmet and bevor and handed them to Evrouin, cutting off his protest with a gesture.

"I don't want to talk to the locals looking like a man with half a head, or . . . what were those clockwork mechanical men the ancients had called . . ."

"Robots, Your Highness," the older man said. "Or Terminators, in some of the stories."

John nodded; he wasn't sure how many of the stories were true, anyway, but you used metaphor on instinct. A faceless moving thing of metal was intimidating, especially if you weren't used to seeing the like.

Thora tossed him the cloth, and he carefully cleaned the blade of his longsword as they walked; blood was essentially salt water, and that didn't go well with steel. Walking up to excited foreigners in flame-shot darkness with a red-running sword in your hand wasn't the smartest thing to do, either. As he slid it home with a *cling* sound when the guard hit the metal plates of the scabbard's mouth he noticed the stickiness on his right arm and side as the blood ran under the armor and into the cloth beneath. It met the sweat that soaked the doublet and fused into a thick gelid mass that stung in places where his skin was grazed; he hadn't noticed that happening, but if something hit the armor hard at a joint you got rasped as the friction was transmitted through the metal sheets and coarse cloth below.

He grimaced in disgust, and then hid it as he turned to look at Pip. She was casting little glances at Toa, and relaxing a bit as his stride grew more confident.

I'm starting to like her even more, he thought.

The big man was obviously a sort of unofficial uncle and had raised her as much as her parents had. He wiped at the black glinting mass on the side of his head with a folded bandage she handed him from a pouch on her belt, wincing as the alcohol-based disinfectant it was soaked with cut through the clotted blood and met the raw flesh beneath.

"Just stunned a bit," he said to her. "Nothing cracked, not dizzy or seeing lights or feeling like a chunder."

"Technicolor yawn," he added to John's puzzlement. "Puke, like?"

John blinked at the colorful vocabulary, but nodded. Those were the symptoms of a concussion, which was no joke. It didn't matter how big or strong you were, either, if you got hit in the right—wrong—place. A human head and brain were just jelly in a pottery case, regardless of the size of the body attached, and Toa's wouldn't be much more resistant to a whack with a heavy steel weight than his, or Pip's for that matter.

The problem at Tuan Anak's headquarters was obvious when they got there, and visible enough because there were lanterns on poles and fires built up enough to mostly dispel the darkness. The tent the High Priest and Priestess had used—it was the howdah from their elephant set on the ground, basically—was down, and parts of it still smoldering where it had fallen into the nearby fire. There were bodies lying about, Baru Denpasarans and attackers. A few of them were Ibans. The rest of them were Carcosans, wearing vests made of mail and small plates but with the same build and coloring as their enemies, save for two. Those had looked a good deal more like John or Pip—or probably had, since between darkness and the way they'd been hacked about long after they fell it was difficult to be sure.

The two bodies that really mattered had been covered with matting and blood pooled beneath them. John knew immediately from the stunned grief or wails from the others that it was the local clerics. Tuan Anak was standing with his parang almost dropping from his nerveless hand; there was blood on it and on his arm and chest, the more visible because he'd started up in nothing but his loincloth and had apparently fought that way too. A few thin wounds marked his torso, adding to a truly impressive collection of healed scars, but the loss of his holy Pedanda was probably what was causing the stunned look on his face. As John watched he swallowed and gave his parang a considering look and began to turn it in his hand.

Uh-oh, he's thinking that death would spare him having to explain this to the Raja, John thought. *It must be even more serious than I thought.*

"Deor," he said quietly. "Translate for me as I speak—until Anak answers, at least."

He stepped up smartly—ignoring leveled spears in the hands of men wild-eyed with grief and horror and ready to lash out against anyone not of their blood—and thumped his fist to his chest in salute.

"Tuan Anak," he said.

He also made his voice a little louder than was strictly necessary, but not shouting. It was very difficult not to sound angry if you shouted, and even more difficult to not be *perceived* that way. His sword was sheathed, but the blood spattering his armor and face was plainly visible, showing that he'd been fighting the same enemy.

He was rewarded when the Baru Denpasaran commander looked at him.

"We have beaten off the attack on the catapults."

Deor echoed it; John hoped very much that his Balinese was up to this. Then he bowed deeply to the dead priest and priestess and saluted again. It wasn't the sort of gesture the locals used, but it was visible respect, which was what mattered.

"My condolences on your tragic loss. These holy folk must be avenged in enemy blood!"

That got through, he realized as the locals growled agreement. He made himself not let out a breath of relief.

His parents had said that you could pour heart into another like water into a jug; it was part of the mystery of ruling or commanding. Anak straightened, obviously thinking now . . . and thinking that success was the only way he could justify this when he returned to his ruler. The Baru Denpasaran commander looked around at his own folk; he was obviously a very brave man under ordinary circumstances, quick-witted and with the self-confidence that came of high birth and long experience in war. He made a quick calculation and shouted in his own language, waving his blade aloft. Deor stepped up and spoke softly in John's ear:

"Vengeance, he cries," the scop said. "Vengeance, and victory. He calls on Indera—the God of theirs who protects human-kind against the beings of darkness, who rides the elephant and wields the lightning, the smasher of citadels—reminds me a bit of Thunor. He calls on Him for vengeance on the enemies of their faith, the defilers of holiness."

John did let his breath out in a *whoof* of relief then, as he stepped back and motioned the others with him. Tuan Anak gave him a single glance and a hard nod as he turned to snapping orders to his subordinates.

Well, we'll give it a good try, at least, John thought.

As they walked back to their encampment Thora spoke thoughtfully.

"The enemy tried for the one thing we need to take their fort," she said. "And they failed; as long as we have the catapults and prang-prangs we can keep going. And they didn't get Anak, either."

Pip spoke, slow and thoughtful. "No. They tried for the *two* things we need," she said. "I've been here longer. Believe me, against Carcosa, we need those Brahmins too. Needed them, that is. I suggest you all pray *really hard* to Whoever you think is listening."

Toa grunted agreement. Deor nodded slowly. "She's right," he said, and made the sign of the Hammer.

It occurred to John that they might be needing some of Deor's other skills as much as his undoubted worth as a fighter.

Oh, that's a wonderful thought to try to sleep on, John thought, looking up at the stars. It was about four hours to dawn, and tomorrow was going to be . . .

More of an adventure than I wanted, he thought. *I've daydreamed about being out from under Órlaith's shadow. Be careful what you ask for, because God may give it to you!*

CHAPTER TWENTY

Dún na Síochána
(Formerly Salem, Oregon)
Capital, High Kingdom of Montival
(Formerly western North America)
October 31st
Change Year 46/2044 AD

A few moments after the commander of the Imperial Guard left, Chiyo knocked softly at the door—a polite scratch was impractical with thick portals of solid wood. Then she came through, made obeisance to Reiko and turned as she announced in a high soft voice that didn't mangle the foreign names and titles too badly:

"Crown Princess Órlaith, the heir of the High Kingdom."

She bowed deeply, though not to the forty-five-degree angle with head inclination reserved for her own royalty.

"Lady Heuradys d'Ath, her *hatamoto*."

Another bow, not quite so deep, as to a highborn bannerman . . . bannerwoman, rather. That was rarer at home than here, but not so rare as to be totally outlandish in these days of desperate need and straitened means.

"Admit them, thank you," Reiko said.

How to address people was going to be even more of a puzzle as *Tennō* than as heir-apparent, and being among her own people once more brought that back to mind. Speaking English all the time had made her more conscious of how Nihongo had distinctly different registers for men and women—and *onna no kotoba*, women's speech, tended to be rather deferential, at least in its surface forms. In fact her language made it oddly difficult for a woman to be assertive at all without being grossly, obtrusively impolite. Which was inappropriate for her position—much more so now that she was *Tennō*. Extreme formality helped, since both sexes sounded more female when they were being very polite. With men like Egawa she could use the male register suitable to one of higher rank and they just acknowledged it without much thought, but addressing women was a little more difficult if she didn't want to seem . . .

Rather onabe. *Rather butch, as they say in English.*

There was a slight stiffness in the lady-in-waiting's manner. as well. That would be the Sword of the Lady at Órlaith's side. Reiko could feel it herself, the more so now that she bore the Grasscutter. The Lady's gift to the line of House Artos was something that was a sword to the eye . . . but to the inner eye a force like the planes of continents meeting and grinding beneath earth's surface. It would require someone more than human not to be affected when such a thing was near.

The more so if you were not Montivallan. Besides great power, what Reiko sensed was a friendly apartness; as *Kusanagi* was bound to her blood and that of the Yamato people and to the fabric of their homeland, so the Lady's gift was to Montival and its folk and the bloodline of he who had been gifted with it. She suspected that to others the uneasiness would be more profound.

"And bring the meal now, Chiyo-san," she added gently.

Órlaith entered, in kilt and plaid, Montrose jacket and knee-hose, with Heuradys beside her in Associate dress—a belted green kirtle under a sleeveless open-sided surcoat, and a fawn wimple on her head bound with rose-gold chains. Reiko rose, and Órlaith made a bow just slightly deeper than hers, suitable from the heir to a throne to a ruling monarch; Heuradys' was impeccable, deep but not so deep as would have been proper to her own ruler. Lady Chiyo was respectably impassive as she withdrew at the gesture of the *tessen* fan, but Reiko could sense her satisfaction, overriding outrage that foreigners were admitted with swords at their waists at all.

Órlaith grinned as she sat across the table, probably sensing the same thing and feeling she'd scored a point in a mildly amusing game. *Seiza* was excruciating to the point of impossibility for many Montivallans since they generally sat on chairs, but Mackenzies used something very like it for some of their rituals and for unarmed-combat training, which she had found to her surprise had strong similarities to the style she had been trained in and even incorporated mangled *Nihongo* terminology. Heuradys was almost as supple.

"Aren't you glad to have a proper retinue once more, Reiko-chan?" Órlaith asked in her perfect Japanese and with only the very slightest tint of irony, still smiling, as she laid the Sword of the Lady by her right hand.

That was the courtesy position, where your blade was hardest to draw. Courteous if you were going to carry a long blade indoors at all, but her declaration had made this like a war-camp. Which had had several purposes, starting with the fact that they had both been on the receiving end of assassination attempts more than once. Heuradys kept hers by her left, ready for draw-and-strike, which was obligatory given her position as Órlaith's liege woman; she was much more than a bodyguard, but that for starters. From the way her clothes moved, Reiko suspected a vest of light mail beneath.

"I can virtually feel your joy at it radiating like the sun," Órlaith continued dryly.

Reiko used her fan to conceal a chuckle, feeling more at ease than she had all day. She dropped back into English, since Heuradys could follow only the simplest Nihongo and spoke no more than a few words.

"That is not fair, Orrey-chan!" She indicated the Sword of the Lady. "I cannot be polite with *that* at your side!"

Her friend's smile grew wry. "If you think this is stressful, imagine what it's like when I'm talking to my mother with *this* beside us, and both of us entitled to bear it."

Reiko blinked, then half-laughed, half-shuddered in genuine horror.

"You would have to say *everything!*" she blurted. Then, more slowly: "If you were to say anything at all."

"And not speaking is not an option; not with your mother, and not with your sovereign, and when it's both . . . So telling the whole truth of the matter is what I did all afternoon, and she to me. It's not precisely mind-reading, but it's not entirely unlike it, either."

Reiko made a sympathetic noise. Órlaith shrugged, but gave a grateful smile.

"It's helped, in a way. Painfully, but it's speeded our coming together again. It makes an *I love you* a different thing; and now I understand the way things were between my parents better. But to business. It's agreed, I'm to take the expeditionary force. With Lord Maugis de Grimmond as my second-in-command of land forces and Admiral Naysmith for the Navy."

"You are to command? Excellent!" Reiko said. "Maugis-sama is Grand Constable of the Association, is he not?"

"Yes; the baron's a very capable man, and almost as important, well-respected outside the Protectorate . . . outside the Association territories."

A thought struck her. "But was not his son Sir Aleaume, who died with us in the fight at the Bay?"

Órlaith sighed and nodded. "Sir Droyn took him his son's sword and shield, and told him how he met his end; that was fitting, since they were brothers of the sword. His grief won't affect his actions—he's proud that Aleaume fell blade in hand and face to the foe in his liege's service."

Reiko inclined her head slightly. "Duty, heavier than mountains," she said softly; she'd liked the grave young noble.

"Death, lighter than a feather," Heuradys finished.

Órlaith nodded; Reiko had discovered that the saying had long been current here as well as at home. Which was odd, since it originated in an Imperial rescript of Meiji times.

But the sentiment is universal, I suppose. How else could warriors live?

They were silent for a moment before Órlaith went on. Sir Aleaume hadn't been the only young warrior who would never come home save as a token and a memory tinged with grief, nor would he be the last.

"Admiral Naysmith is a Bearkiller of the A-list; that's convenient, and her career a bit remarkable, since they're not a seafaring folk for the most part. And I'm to have Edain Aylward Mackenzie for my chief-of-staff."

"A very capable man," Reiko agreed.

"And *not* an Associate. Mackenzies are well-liked by most; and we've always been close, Uncle Wolf and I."

Reiko nodded; at this level, politics and military command were very much the same thing.

"He knows his business," Heuradys said. "But Orrey . . . just *because* he grew up with your father, he does tend to forget you're not fourteen anymore, sometimes. Or possibly around eight, when he's not watching it."

Reiko sighed; Órlaith wasn't the only person in this room who ran into *that* problem with her father's close retainers.

And in the Montivallan system the Chief of Staff of an army is about as important as the commander; they give a command to one of sufficient birth and rank, with an experienced professional by their side. In this case with another experienced professional in the position immediately below. And yet . . . not only does Orrey-chan have the raw ability, she has the Sword of the Lady.

As she understood it, the Lady's gift to the line of House Artos did much more than show truth; in time of war it amplified the native abilities of the wielder with a preternatural grasp of the things a ruler—or commander—needed to know, amplifying the powers of memory and thought, observation and calculation, making planning swift and sure. The bearer could be their *own* staff.

The door opened again, and Lady Chiyo came in with the maids—three this time—to remove and file away the documents and maps with quick skill, remove the writing-table, to put an additional *kakeban* by Heuradys, and set out the meal she'd ordered. Two of them went to the end of the long room to be ready to shuttle the succession of courses to the three diners, and the third began to play softly on a samisen.

Heuradys ran a quick appraising eye over them. "Not just for giving you consequence and serving the drinks, are they?" she murmured.

Reiko acknowledged it with a slight twitch of the fan and flick of her eyes. She'd repeat the remark in Nihongo later, where it could be overheard; they would be pleased. They were too far away to overhear a quiet-spoken conversation, and of course *spoke* very little English as yet. Now and then she felt sorry for the isolation that must mean, though from subtle signs they all seemed excited and intrigued by their surroundings and were working very hard on improving their command of the spoken tongue. They were only the second group of Nihonjin to travel abroad since the Change, after all. Unless you counted captives bound for extremely unpleasant fates.

Then Reiko looked at the first trays of food and sighed entirely to herself as her friends praised the pretty arrangements; she'd ordered an informal meal suitable for three persons of high rank, and had expected perhaps three dishes and some miso to go with the rice or noodles.

But while she and her party had been housed at Montinore Manor on Barony Ath in the spring, their hosts had found cooks who could produce somewhat Japanese-style dishes . . . except that they had been entirely too rich and elaborate for every day.

Though better than the local styles. Which are very tasty sometimes, but they bolt huge chunks of meat like wolves on a carcass! And the dairy foods range from the repulsive and indigestible to pleasant and indigestible.

She'd been looking forward to a more normal diet when the Palace cook arrived with the ship . . . but he'd been at the banquet laid on to greet the newcomers, and now he was apparently determined not to let the Montivallans show him up. What was before her was a *sakizuke* course, traditionally the first in a *Kaiseki Ryōri*, a formal Court feast. A small aperitif of plum wine, then a few little bite-sized pieces of baby carp simmered in sweetened shoyu with ginger, radish and asparagus and mint leaf, shrimp, flounder rolled in kelp, and black bean with *tsukushi* bud, all set out in artistic combinations in patterned ceramic boxes and bowls.

Very spare compared to the Montivallan equivalents, but a full *Kaiseki Ryōri* had *twelve* courses.

Well, at least I managed two hours of sparring practice today.

In theory she could just set a menu and order it done. But besides being unfitting to her rank, no matter how theoretically absolute you were there were orders that it was wiser not to give. If only because when you devalued another's work, you stepped upon the sleeve of their honor, and doing that without grave need was . . .

Uncouth, she thought. *One must take motives into consideration.*

"*Itadakimasu,*" they murmured with their hands pressed palm to palm, and then their respective prayers at food.

Heuradys picked up a single grain of the rice in her chopsticks and dipped it in the plum wine before burning it delicately in the flame of one of the candles, as her offering to the *kami* she called Hestia of the Hearth.

Out of the corner of her eye, she could see the surprise of the attendants when both the Montivallans used the chopsticks with courteous skill, though they remained outwardly impassive. One knee-walked forward to fill their cups—the situation and various status considerations would make the usual Nihonjin custom of doing that for your neighbor awkward—and then retired.

"And Heuradys is to be my aide-de-camp and head of Household, which means we can keep it down to something reasonable. Mother doesn't care about keeping state, though she doesn't actively dislike it the way I do or Da did—she sort of endures it without really noticing it much. But Lord and Lady, there are plenty of people in Todenangst and the City Palace in Portland who are obsessed with it even now, reason, common sense, offending the rest of Montival, and military necessity be damned. If my father and mother between them couldn't really budge it, I doubt I can. I'll be working around it all my life, I suppose. It's like pushing on a spring, it comes back as soon as you let up."

"For a lot of Associates it's such a big part of what they are . . . who they are," Heuradys said. "And for some it's their work, their calling."

"It would be cruel to just disregard that," Órlaith said.

"Hubristic, and unlucky," Heuradys added.

"But so tempting, sometimes!"

Reiko put her fan before her lips. "I was just thinking very nearly the same about some of my own followers!" she said, and they shared a chuckle.

"*Such* a surprise I got that aide-de-camp job," Heuradys added contentedly, eating a morsel.

"Well, the General Staff—" Órlaith began.

"Meaning Mom Two. It would take a brave general to cross her, my liege!"

"—*offered* to let you lead a menie from Barony Ath instead," Órlaith observed, and Heuradys rolled her eyes.

"As in the Platonic Ideal of *pro forma offer*," she said. "My beloved brother Diomede has that job, and welcome he is. He should, anyway, he's the heir to the barony and he had field experience as a junior officer towards the end of the Prophet's War, when he was Mom Two's squire for a while. It's hard on Ysabeau and the kids, but hey, that's part of being a baron. She's going to settle down with Mom One for another course of intensive how-to-administer-a-barony instruction, together with a social whirl, and trying to prevent my lady Mom One from *totally* spoiling the grandkids."

The grin grew a little wider, and a teasing light came into her eyes; not cruel, but slightly wicked.

"I notice that Alan Thurston *did* get a company command, light cavalry scouts."

"It's fitting, given his birth, and I think he'll do it well," Órlaith said.

"And that company is part of the central reserve, so he'll be close to your Royal headquarters," Heuradys began. "Not to mention close to your Royal hind—"

Órlaith held up a hand. "And please, spare me the next cavalry joke, and the cracks about *riding well*."

"Well, he does," Heuradys said loftily. "If very briefly, in my case. The things I do for my liege."

"Or in this case, don't do. There are some things even vassal and liege shouldn't share. It would be unsanitary."

Reiko hid her laugh, mildly shocked. She'd never had young women friends she could relax and gossip and tease with. At home that wasn't really possible for someone in her position; sisters weren't the same, however dear, and they were all younger than her anyway.

"Could be worse," Heuradys said cheerfully, finishing the last of her sea bream. "You and Reiko here could have fallen in love. Mom One would have loved the tragic romantic thrill of contemplating it, but think of the scandal! Among the Catholics, particularly; they still give *my* parents grief occasionally and we're a lot less conspicuous than monarchs."

"*Itai!*" Reiko said in horror, and did laugh at that. "Even more scandal in *my* home! Not as bad as it would be if Órlaith were a man, but even so . . . a terrible, terrible scandal. Unthinkable."

The thought of the Empress being involved with a foreign lover was mind-boggling; she felt an impulse to keep giggling, as much nervousness as humor.

"Do your parents arrange for your marriage here?" she asked curiously instead.

There hadn't been time to talk of such things before. Negotiations among parents were the usual form at home, though in her case it hadn't arisen and there had been covert speculation that she wouldn't wed at all, leaving the continuance of the line to her sisters. There had been occasional ruling empresses before her, but her own grandmother had been one of the very few such to hand down the Chrysanthemum Throne to the child of her own body. Before the Meiji lawmakers copied the German succession law—before the West—it had been merely usual for the *Tennō Heika's* child to succeed, rather than a nephew or such, not a fixed rule. If your grandparent or great-grandparent had sat the Chrysanthemum Throne you were eligible. That had led to problems too—in particular, it had made it possible for the ambitious to find puppet Emperors to use as a façade.

Perhaps we should adopt the same system as the Montivallans, she thought.

With the eldest child taking the Throne, but regardless of male or female. Hmmm. It might be fortunate if I were to have only daughters. Then I could make a decree, and since there would be no son in any case it would arouse little opposition, and by the time my successor had heirs everyone would be used to it. I will discuss it with Mother. Such things require a delicate touch.

"It differs from realm to realm, like everything else in Montival," Órlaith said. "Among Mackenzies, no—nor McClintocks. Nor in Corvallis or Boise. Not formally, at least, though there are often sort of understandings between kindred. I think the folk of New Deseret have some sort of system where younger people are introduced at Church meetings."

"Among Associates, yes, sometimes, since so much in the way of politics and power and property are involved, but it's more a matter of the parents seeing that the youngsters meet the right people so they think it's their idea," Heuradys said. "Got the idea from old books, my lady Mom One tells me."

"Not the only case where they did that!" Órlaith snorted. "The Protectorate *is* an old book—and a historical novel, at that."

"Yes, but it's Jane Austen in that *particular* case, not Sir Walter Scott or Cecelia Holland or Alfred Duggan or Bujold or Barringer," Heuradys said. "If you're a Count's heir, there just aren't that many *right people* even now. God, some of the intrigues . . ."

"Your father didn't make alliances for your brothers, did he?" Órlaith said.

Reiko remembered that Rigobert de Stafford was a great *daimyo*, Count of Campscapell, though she hadn't met him yet. Heuradys was the adoptive child of her second mother, too.

"Or your mothers," Órlaith added.

Heuradys smiled fondly. "M'lord Dad found the whole thing funny and washed his hands of it when the subject came up; he said that if he'd known reproduction was going to make life so complicated he might have had second thoughts, even via a kitchen appliance. Mom One started making wedding plans—she loves weddings—whenever Lioncel or Diomede wore some maiden's favor to a tournament, until Mom Two threatened to go on a year-long hunting trip to Dawson and take them both along."

Reiko joined the laugh. She wasn't in the least shocked by the domestic arrangements of House d' Ath or de Stafford. Among her people *shudō*, love between men of the warrior class, usually an older mentor and a younger man, had a long and honored history; it didn't affect matters of marriage and children, of course. The custom had returned since the Change, along with much else. The equivalent among women had traditionally been considered so unimportant in the larger scheme of things that before the West came there hadn't even really been a special name for such things; it was just something that one did do or didn't do according to inclination and circumstances.

They fell silent for a moment as the maids replaced the sakizuke with the *hassun* course—named for the measurements of the tray, eight *sun* on each side. This had a selection of small pieces of grilled octopus on octopus eggs and rice, and lily root with salted plums—always one of her favorites, and she hadn't thought you *could* get lily root here. The chef was a man of great energy to locate it, especially considering that he didn't speak the language.

"Now, that's interesting," Heuradys said after the first morsel. "Normally octopus is like trying to chew off someone's ear, but this is exquisite."

Reiko made a small *tsk* sound. "So sorry, but people here really don't know how to handle seafood well. Too much cooking. And putting cream sauces on it . . ." She shuddered.

The *Mukōzuke* course came next, in two parts; three small slices of salmon each and then three of *kampachi*—amberjack—served with fresh grated wasabi and a bright *shiso* emulsion and tamari. All three of the young women concentrated for a moment on the complex medley of flavors and how they complemented one another. That was respect to the cook's skill, and to the *kami* of earth and sea who had provided the ingredients. To despise food, or to take it for granted, was to despise life itself. Their grandparents had seen what happened when Earth withheld Her gifts.

When they had finished it and were cleaning their palates with a little plain rice—how odd it still was to think of rice as an exotic foreign luxury!— Reiko hesitated, then spoke:

"Orrey-chan . . . there is something that has occurred to me since we came north again. Your mother . . . understand, I do not blame her . . . I sense that she cannot help thinking that if we Nihonjin had not come to these shores, pursued by our enemies, your father would still be alive. Yet though your loss is as terrible as my own, I do not think you have ever felt so, or blamed us. Why is that?"

I might have blamed you Montivallans for coming just a moment too late to save Father, if it had not been that your sire fell also, she thought, with a trace of hidden shame.

Órlaith sighed and looked down at the table for a moment; she and Heuradys still made more eye contact when talking than a Nihonjin found comfortable, but Reiko had become accustomed to it as she had to the odd catlike eye colors of blue and amber.

"I think . . . that's because Mother is a Christian. I knew in my bones that he was fated; so did he, for he'd had it from the Powers themselves that he would fall in battle before his hair went gray, the which he'd never kept secret. And . . . not long before he died, he pulled the first gray hair from his beard, and then saw the Washer at the Ford in his dreams."

At her puzzlement Órlaith chuckled sadly, and spoke in Nihongo for a moment: "Ah, and we're close enough something in me forgets at times that you weren't raised here."

Then in English again: "Among Mackenzies . . . and McClintocks too, it goes back to the old Gael . . . There's a belief that if you dream you're crossing a river and see an old woman washing a shirt at a ford with blood running downstream from it . . . well, the clothes are yours. A sign, and that sign is of death not long delayed."

Reiko shivered slightly, as at the touch of something cold on the back of her neck. *You didn't need a miko, a shrine-maiden, to interpret a dream like that for you!*

"You were expecting . . . What happened, then?" she said.

"No. That is . . . sometime, yes, sometime soon; but not just then, for he didn't tell me. Or Mother. The one because he didn't want to spoil our last time together, the trip to Westria, by making my grief start early."

Reiko nodded somberly. "Hai! I *feared* for my father constantly on our voyage, but that was a matter of war anyway. If I had *known* . . ."

"And he didn't tell Mother for the same reason and because she was pregnant and because . . . well, she *is* a Christian. He knew that the time had come when the King must die that the folk might live, and the land be renewed by the willing sacrifice of his blood. So it was he walked to the Dark Mother consenting, with a smile, savoring every moment the more because it might be the very last."

"Clotho spins, Lachesis measures, Atropos cuts," Heuradys said with a sigh. "We don't choose our fate, only how we meet it."

Softly she went on: "And you did that well indeed, my King. In your dying you united your people for this war. Your spirit will lead us, as well as the heir of your blood."

Órlaith was silent for a moment, then nodded. "Yes. But the White Christ's followers don't think that way, despite the fact that He did the very same thing. And had foretelling of it from His Father."

"Strange people, Christians," Heuradys agreed. "Even my own relatives."

"It is easier for us, since everyone follows the Way of the Gods in Japan," Reiko said. "Well, and we honor the Way of the Buddha too, of course."

A mixture of the two had been her people's manner of dealing with the divine and the world of spirit for a very long time. Since the Change the balance had swung heavily to the older, native Shinto side of the mixture, but the Eightfold Way was far too closely woven into the fabric of Nihon to ever be removed.

Órlaith went on: "She'd have driven herself frantic trying to avoid it. He told Edain, and Uncle Wolf told me afterwards. He was Father's right-hand man and battle comrade, and his heart-brother since they were children."

"Like you and Heuradys-*gozen*," Reiko said, and Órlaith nodded.

"Father knew that if you run from your fate, you run towards it, for it's always before you, waiting, whichever way you turn," she said.

"*Hai*, very true," Reiko agreed.

Grief never went away; hers for her father was still a dull ache. But it did . . . get out of the way of things as time went on, so that it no longer required a mental effort like battle to deal with normal life.

The *takiawase* course was traditionally items cooked in broth separately and combined just before serving; this was fried tofu balls with prawns, something very like home's black fungus, and ginkgo nuts and water chestnuts simmered in broth.

"Yoshihito always loved ginkgo nuts," she said with a sigh.

The conversation had reminded her of how she'd lost him twice, when his ship disappeared, and again more terribly when trying to hold the unsheathed Grasscutter Sword had burned him to talc-fine ash in an instant. That had proved him corrupted by his captivity; *Kusanagi* itself had chosen which of her generation was worthy of the Chrysanthemum Throne. But with the pain she would also remember there had been gratitude in the last look on his face. She would remember that until her own death. Only that made it bearable at all.

"When we were both very young . . . I remember he would ask for them and pout a little when he couldn't have them all the time."

"Why not?" Órlaith asked.

"They cause convulsions," Reiko said, then smiled with a flash of amusement as Heuradys stopped with one halfway to her lips. "Only if you eat them all the time and while you are young," she added.

She finished the motion and ate it, but Reiko thought her enthusiasm had diminished, and suppressed an impulse to giggle.

The *futamoto* course in its elegantly simple lidded stoneware bowls was soup made from *suppon*, what the Montivallans called snapping turtle, which turned out to be very common here. The broth was gelatinous and silky, and viscous enough for the little bits of sweet corn, winter melon, snap peas, scallops and tiger prawns to appear suspended in time and place.

"Now that's a winter soup," Órlaith said appreciatively.

They chatted through the other courses; the real meat of the meeting had been Órlaith's appointment, conveyed to Reiko first by her own words as a mark of regard. It came to Reiko with a shock that she was going to miss Órlaith very badly when the war was over. And Heuradys and the others as well.

Or perhaps really the freedom of action I had here.

"It was a feast," the two Montivallans said as the last trays were removed, which was both polite and in this case literally true, and prepared to make their good-byes.

Then there was a brief scuffle at the door.

"Kiwako!" a young woman called in Nihongo. "Kiwako, you wicked little *gaki*, come back—oh, *masaka*! No, not there!"

A child just past the toddler stage ran through, with a maid in close pursuit. The little girl in her colorful double kimono over a shift plumped herself down in *seiza* and made a fair approximation of an obeisance, then gave a brilliant gap-toothed grin. She was shooting up, already taller and a little plumper than the skinny feral thing Reiko had found chained by an ankle amid the cyst-like horrors of the castle in the Valley of Death.

"Majesty! So sorry!" the maid said. "She scampers about like . . . like . . ."

"Like a scampering child," Reiko said indulgently. "I seem to remember one named . . . oh, I think her given name was Misako . . . who was prone to that. Even to climbing through windows from trees. Scandalous!"

The maid of honor, who was twelve and who of course had been that girl a few years ago, sighed almost inaudibly and waited with patience. Most Nihonjin were mild with young children, however stern life became later, and the Heavenly Sovereign Majesty favored the *Gaijin* infant.

Kiwako—Reiko had given her the name, for she had had none in that place of abominations—was still slender, but longer-faced and bigger-nosed than a Japanese infant, pale and ginger-haired and green-eyed. To modern Nihonjin eyes she looked like a fox, or the fox spirits who went by the same name, which was why Reiko had carefully avoided calling her *Kitsune*, except sometimes as a joke between them in private. The name she had bestowed meant *One Born on a Border*, among other things, and was entirely fitting. She had been born in a shadowy place between worlds.

Kiwako had just called herself *th'kid*, and had not even imagined other children.

"*Heika!*" she said; that was the polite informal form of address, but Reiko rather thought Kiwako used the title as she would have a given name. "I had dinner! There was noodles and miso and piece fish and pickles!"

Precisely what I was hoping for, Reiko thought fondly, as she absently corrected the child's grammar.

Food was still a wonder to Kiwako; as the youngest and last descendant of the little clan who'd been trapped in the lost castle—descendants and slayers of the man who'd stolen the Grasscutter Sword from Nihon after the Pacific War—she'd grown up eating insects and vermin and possibly other things. She was already forgetting and the nightmares growing less, but nourishment fit for a human being still delighted her. So did clothes, bathing, and language—she'd had a little slurred English to begin with, but in the months since she had absorbed Nihongo like a sponge soaking up water.

The child shuffled sideways on her knees and leaned into Reiko, a small solid weight, her hair bound back and smelling of herbal wash. The contrast with the filthy feral creature she'd met was utter . . . but it had been that creature who warned her in time to turn a descending blade. She put an arm around the girl's shoulders. Versions of that crucial aid had also passed to the newcomers from home, and everyone had seen how the *Tennō* helped the girl make offerings to Inari Okami. Who was patroness of rice and swordsmiths . . . and served by white foxes who were Her messengers and agents.

Little Fox, your life will not always be easy in Dai-Nippon, however much I protect you. We of the Land of the Gods have never been a folk easy with outsiders, and now less so than ever. But with Inari as your guardian, it will be easier than it might. And many fear my namesake the Ghost Fox.

Heuradys and Órlaith grinned at the girl, who hid herself for a moment behind a fold of Reiko's kimono sleeve before she peeked out again. The two Montivallans each extended a hand to cover the other's eyes, and they played at peeking at Kiwako, repeating the little game until all four of them dissolved in laughter.

"*Kagome kagome!*" Kiwako pleaded.

"No, little one," Reiko said firmly.

That was a children's game that required multiple partners; Reiko had played it with her sisters when she was small. She and several of the entourage had played it with Kiwako, and she'd become entranced with it. Unfortunately there weren't any other children here for her to do it with as often as she wished.

"Here, play with this."

She pulled a *kendama* out of her sleeve; Egawa had whittled it for her in his spare time, as he had for his own children back in the homeland when they were of an age for such things. There was a flared handle ending in a wooden spike, and a ball on a string with a hole in the center. You tossed the ball up, and then caught it either on the spike, or on one of the two cups that flanked it.

Reiko demonstrated, carefully keeping it slow and using the cups on the sides first, which was easier, and then the spike. Besides being amusing for small children it was good for training their hands and eyes to work together smoothly and swiftly. Kiwako took it eagerly, and tried the toss with her tongue protruding slightly between teeth clenched in concentration. The ball ticked off the edge of the cup, and Reiko showed her how to damp the swing before she tried again.

In a few moments the child was lost in the toy, eventually giving a squeal of delight when the ball caught in the cup, which showed commendable persistence.

"*Ganbaru!*" Reiko said, her voice warm with praise, and was rewarded with another brilliant smile. "See, little one, if you keep trying and do not give up you will learn! This is true of many things. Always try hard!"

"I'll get one of those for Vuissance," Órlaith said, naming her youngest sibling, or at least the youngest until the upcoming birth.

"I'll get a couple made for my nieces and nephews. I've got four about the right age," Heuradys said, her usually cool catlike amber eyes warm and fond.

"My sisters and I would sit about playing with them, seeing if we could catch the ball at the same time," Reiko sighed.

The adults made their farewells. "*Ittekimasu*, Reiko-chan," Órlaith said, which would have been very casual from anyone but a monarch or their heir; it meant *I'm off*, more or less.

Heuradys bowed. "*Shitsurei shimasu*," she said, more formally, and with slow care for the sounds.

CHAPTER TWENTY-ONE

Kerajaan of Baru Denpasar
Ceram Sea
November 6th
Change Year 46/2044 AD

J ohn woke with a convulsive reach for his sword. Six inches of steel hissed free of the scabbard in the beginning of a draw-and-strike.

"Sorry, Sire," Evrouin said.

He'd tapped his booted toe against his liege's foot. That had brought John up convinced for a second or two someone was about to kill him, with his heart pounding and mouth dry. The gathering noise of the camp would have awakened him eventually anyway. But he *had* said to get him up just before the sun edged up over the horizon, and it meant Evrouin had to get up earlier himself, and that foot-tap was the safest way to wake someone so to be fair . . .

"No problem," John said tightly, and the guard rang against the mouth of the scabbard as he pushed the blade back.

The man didn't *look* sorry; he looked as if he'd be grinning if he could. He also had a large steaming mug in his hand, which made up for a great deal. John threw off the dew-sodden horse-blanket and pulled on his boots after a quick check for scorpions and centipedes, and took the tea. The medley of buzzing, tweeting and clicking sounds from the forest was picking up as the pre-dawn hush ended, and the murmur and clatter of human waking joined it.

"Thank you," he said, and blew on the surface, sipping as fast as the hot liquid allowed, and running his free hand over his chin, which rasped. "Another, please, and I'll shave today."

"Sire."

He knelt as he handed the man his empty cup to take to the nearest kettle, kissed his crucifix and held it between his clasped hands as he bowed his head. Remembering last night, after his usual morning Paternoster he added softly:

"St. Michael the Archangel, defend us Christians and our allies in battle. Be our strong shield against the wickedness and snares of the Adversary; and do thou, O Prince of the Heavenly Host, by the power of God, cast down into hell Satan and the other evil spirits who prowl about the world for the ruin of our souls. Amen."

"Amen, Sire," Evrouin said as he came up with the cup and handed it to him, crossing himself with his free hand as well. "Amen with all my heart."

He fetched water for a splash and brushing teeth as well; John was glad of that, because his mouth felt as if a small rodent with bowel-control problems had crawled in there and died of scabies some time ago, and there was dried blood on his hands and face, still faintly sticky in this damp climate. He'd been too tired to do anything much about it last night.

More tea helped as well. The acrid liquid was heavy-sweet with sugar this morning, and had some sort of spice in it too. Though the locals didn't use milk, which had Radavindraban complaining worse than the sting of the stitches in his forehead even as he gulped his and asked for more. Captain Ishikawa was quietly appalled at the thought of putting milk in tea—or anywhere but the mouths of calves, for that matter—and regarded other additives as foul desecration as well, but he drank nonetheless. John found the sugar and the caffeine helped him get his eyes open and the sand out of the edges of his mind; he felt a moment's smugness at how much faster that was for him than for some of the older members of the party.

Toa gave him a jaundiced look as he emptied powdered willowbark extract from Ruan's healer's chest into *his* tea and drank it. He grimaced as well, always spectacular with his rough features and tattoos; the swelling bruise on the left side of his head added to the gargoyle effect.

"Enjoy bouncing back like a fucking rubber ball while it lasts, mate," he said in John's general direction. "Because it doesn't last and I'm here to tell you. You and the bloody blooming frangipani-flower of Tanumgera Station here."

Pip looked at him fondly. "You can still do anything you could when I turned ten, you old fraud," she said. "Whether you're just up or not."

"Too right I can!" he said. Then, quickly: "But it hurts more every year."

"And speaking of hitting the Bundy, I remember you got chockers at my tenth birthday party and punched a camel unconscious when it spat on me. Shocked and scarred my tender young mind, rather."

"It would have bitten you if I hadn't. Likely I'd have to use an axe now-adays."

John did come fully alert quickly; unfortunately that made him more aware of how he felt, and even at a few months short of twenty you didn't wake refreshed after blowguns and blades in the dark hours of early morning. It wasn't just the loss of sleep, or even the way hard effort wrung you out. There was a peculiar set of sensations that came in the aftermath of fear and rage and tearing effort, like some sort of toxin in the blood and muscles.

The tense feel of louring, sullen anger that drifted through the camp along with the woodsmoke and cooking odors didn't help. He found that when he thought about last night he felt a little that way himself, and even more as if he were looking at the world through a sheet of glass and not quite through his own eyes.

Better to put that aside for now.

"Ah, darling, was your beauty-sleep interrupted by those rude naughty men?" Pip said as he stretched and something cracked in his neck.

A wink took the sting out of it, and they both yawned hugely, though he thought she was looking offensively chipper even for someone their age. He'd never been one of those people who leapt out of bed unless there was something specific he was looking forward to eagerly that day, and besieging a fortress didn't count the way a dance or concert did.

And lying on the ground with a horseblanket and a saddle doesn't really count as bed, either. Should I start including more of this in the epics I keep meaning to get around to composing, or not? Hmmmm. I could write Father's . . . but the frightening thing about that is, am I worthy of doing that?

Sleeping on the ground here also exposed you to a lot of mosquitoes, which this island seemed to have in abundance once you weren't on the beach with the sea-breeze in your face. They were not nearly as pretty as the equally ubiquitous butterflies, and in his admittedly jaundiced opinion nearly as large. One of the *Silver Surfer* crew who came from Papua—where the bugs were evidently even worse—handed around an herbal-smelling ointment that helped with the itches, a little. Evrouin appeared with a basin of hot water, and John lathered up and snapped open his straight razor; it wasn't the first time he'd shaved sitting on a saddle with the water between his feet, and it had become a lot less painful since he stopped getting pimples.

The thought brought a little reminiscent amusement tinged with sadness. The first time had been on a hunting trip when he was fifteen, in the high forest country on Mount Hood around the Royal preserve of Timberline Lodge. And now John could see with the eye of hindsight that his father had carefully hid his smile at John's insistence on scraping off the light dusting of peach-fuzz, though that was less time ago than he liked to remember.

I miss you, Father. If you'd lived . . . we'd just be getting to the stage when we could be men together, and friends, as well as father and son. You would have been my captain and my King, as well as Dad.

These days he really did need to shave at least four or five times a week if he didn't want to have patches of bristles over his cheeks and chin, the more conspicuous because it was two shades lighter than the dark-brown hair on his head and with a disconcerting orange undertone. There was something oddly soothing about the warm wet feel of the suds, the smell—he was still using the last of the lavender shaving soap from the *Tarshish Queen's* stores—the familiar feel of the horsehair brush and the slide of the keen-honed steel over his face. Many of the other males in the Montivallan party were doing likewise, possibly on the theory that you should meet death looking your best, or because it raised morale, or just because the sticky heat here made facial hair unpleasant. It was a sign of Divine planning that the locals had so little of it.

"Have you ever tried a beard?" Pip said. "You'd look good with a nice thick short-cropped one. Spade-shaped."

John finished shaving the delicate bit under his nose before he answered, then spoke as he wiped his face on the towel and carefully cleaned and stowed his razor.

"Maybe when I'm thirty. Right now it would be sort of . . . tufty," he said.

A grin. "Prince Tufty? Well, I see the problem."

"My father said he tried twice and gave up in despair before he got one worth having, at about that age. You women don't appreciate the drawbacks of growing whiskers on the face."

"If you've forgotten that *I* shave, you shall be pummeled mercilessly," she said with mock ferocity.

Several women nearby stuck fists into the air with thumbs upraised. One muttered something on the order of *tell him, sister,* and John winced at the snickers.

Pip went on thoughtfully: "Your father . . . do you take after him? I rather resemble Daddy, with different plumbing, of course, and I'm tall like him; mentally I'm more like Mummy."

Mummy must have been half shark, John thought. *That was admiration . . . mostly. I think Grandmother Sandra would have liked her, which is an ambivalent compliment.*

He remembered Queen Mother Sandra as a kindly old lady devoted to her grandchildren and a font of shrewd cool advice, usually with a cat in her lap and a scent of lavender and peppermints. She'd been a notable and highly intelligent patron of all the arts, too, and it had been a high compliment to his very embryonic talents when she had given him his lute Azalaïs just before she died and he was barely eleven.

On the other hand, he was now uneasily aware she'd been at least half the partnership with his grandfather Norman Arminger, who'd been a model for bloodthirsty tyrants. There was a joke older folk in the Association told, of

Sandra being bitten by a rattlesnake once: the punch-line was that then the *snake* died. They'd called her the Spider, then: the Spider of the Silver Tower. In whispers.

I think she'd have liked Pip, too. That would have been an interesting meeting to see!

He shook his head; there was no need to show off all the family linen right away.

"No, Father was taller than I am; about six-two. And fair—blond hair with a touch of red, and light eyes like yours—well, blue and green as well as gray, it depended on the light. I look more like my mother's side of the family, her father Norman Arminger and her mother Sandra—née Whittle. The Armingers and the Whittles both tended to be brown-haired and have hazel eyes, with the odd towhead, judging from the old family scrapbooks I've seen. I think in terms of character I'm more like Grandmother Juniper— we're both musicians, at least, and one of her daughters is too."

"Arminger? Whittle? Those sound like English names," she said.

"They are, far back. Quite far back, for the Armingers; the first one arrived in North America about four hundred years ago. It's Anglo-Norman, originally; the word means armor-bearer, squire . . . or someone with a coat of arms."

Pip laughed. "I know, darling. Balwyn comes from the same stable— one of the leaders of the First Crusade carried it. It means *Noble Leader,* and not *Baldy With A Wart,* as you might think. We converted it to a surname around eight hundred years ago."

He laughed as well. It was pleasant to have this sort of link with a girl he was . . .

All right, admit it. You're falling in love with Pip.

He was falling in love with a girl his mother couldn't object to, as well: daughter of a ruler and of impeccable background—it would give the Arminger line more prestige in Associate eyes. They'd been rather envious of the way the Lorings had married into the ruling lines of the Mackenzies and Dúnedain.

There! Falling in love, thinking of taking her to meet Mother. You said it, at least to yourself.

It was also pleasant to have this sort of distracting chitchat when someone, several someones he'd never met and who had nothing personal against him, had tried to kill him last night. And when he'd be riding all morning to give someone else a crack at it. Popular legend said young men his age were supposed to think that they were immortal. If he ever had, it was wearing very thin indeed—and had been since he saw that monster wave coming at the *Tarshish Queen* back in South Westria.

Knights were supposed to know that they'd die by the sword, and to despise death despite that.

And I do despise it, how I do. Just not in quite that way. Life's too much fun and there's too much I haven't done yet. And nobody in their right mind is eager to face Judgment. That's why smart people ask God for mercy, not justice.

John went on aloud: "And the Whittles were descended from an English sailor who settled in Portland in the eighteen-sixties; he married a local girl who was the daughter of a Québécois trapper for the Hudson Bay Company who'd settled down to farm in the Willamette with a Niimíipu woman . . . Nez Perce, the tribe's called by outsiders. On my father's side . . . his mother Lady Juniper was Gael from Ireland and Scotland, mostly, some English, a little Cherokee. My father's father was Mike Havel, the first lord of the Bearkillers . . . he was half Suomi and the rest Svenska and Anishinaabe in about equal measure."

"I thought you said your grandmother married an Englishman, Sir Nigel Loring? Daddy's people, the Abercrombies, were Scots before they left for Oz about two hundred years ago, of course. But the Balwyns are related to the Lorings, if I remember Mummy's tales. It would be difficult for two families who'd come over in the Conqueror's train *not* to be related, after all this time."

"Yes, but my father was . . . err . . . conceived . . . in the first Change Year. Sir Nigel arrived about eight years later . . . when the British had their little problem. My aunts Maude and Fiorbhinn are his daughters."

"Little problem? When Charles the Mad went absolutely barking, and before Queen Hallgerda put a pillow over his face and then William did his little coup?" she said. "People heard about *that* in Oz, believe me, news still did travel even then. Mummy wasn't surprised at all, and she'd known Charles before the Blackout . . . the Change."

Then she winked. "Apparently he tried to get into her knickers at least once . . . Well, princes are randy bastards, you know."

"Right," Prince John said dryly.

She's a bit disconcerting. I like it.

Breakfast was bowls of the same rice mixture that they'd had for dinner, just cooked until the rice was softer, with a banana from a bunch that had been on the carts. John's stomach was clenched in the fading darkness of the swift tropic dawn. The bodies of the dead had been carted away immediately but they'd mostly been slashed open during the fight, and the climate meant the smell of rotting blood and fluids soaked into the earth was already plain. That certainly didn't help, nor did thinking about what the buzzing flies had on their feet, but he made himself eat, and smile as she handed him another of the yellow fruits.

"It's still odd to think of having these every day," he said. "I'd eaten them maybe twice in my life before we arrived in these seas."

Pip laughed. "Common as dirt where I come from. The Mexicans call us bananalanders, in fact," she said.

"Mexicans?" John asked.

Mexico . . . that was what the realm south of the old Americans was called, wasn't it? But the Change hit them even harder.

There were a few shadowy groups of dusty villages and ranches in remote parts there that claimed to be the heirs of the Mexican realm, the way Boise had with the United States, but he couldn't see what that had to do with Australia.

"Mexicans are what we bananalanders call people in Oz from points south, the Tasmanians and so forth, and all the dozens of little whatevers that've sprung up in the last couple of generations. Mostly we call them that because they hate it, even if they don't remember *why* they hate it."

After a moment John groaned at the geographical pun, then winced as he began the standard loosening-up exercises. You did *not* want to pop a tendon. Not at any time, and especially not in a foreign country where killers could be waiting under every brush.

"Neck stiff?" Pip asked, cocking an eye at the way he hitched for a second halfway through a stretch.

He nodded cautiously; it hurt, in fact. She knelt behind him and kneaded the muscles skillfully with strong slender fingers. That hurt even more at first, then he whimpered as the iron cords started to relax, and the incipient headache faded to a throb. That made the effort in the offing less ghastly.

"Knock on the noggin last night?" Pip asked sympathetically.

"Deliberate one," John replied. "An Iban got far too close with a very sharp knife, so I embraced my outer savage and head-butted him unconscious. It hurt me, but a *lot* less than it hurt him."

"Ah, the fabled Glasgow Kiss of legend," Pip chuckled, drumming the edges of her palms into his deltoids. "Even more charming with a helmet on."

"Are *you* all right, *chérie?*" he asked, feeling a little guilty. He would have noticed if anything was really wrong, but . . .

"Oh, fine. Just a few scratches. Though I loathe those poisoned darts. Not cricket at all."

She grinned and patted the prang-prang behind them waiting to be harnessed to its team. "Of course, neither are these, and I absolutely adore *them.*"

John looked over at the wounded. Nobody had actually died from the darts; evidently that was only likely if they struck you somewhere like the neck, and the paste on them was very fresh. But all four of the men who'd been hit were unconscious—or possibly suffering from paralysis—and very sick indeed, with a tendency to long pauses in their breathing. The locals had been giving them concoctions that included belladonna and other dangerous stimulants, and they were going back under guard in wagons when the main force went forward. That was very light losses, but the fact that they'd been awake, alert, armed and in their gear when the enemy struck accounted for it. The Baru Denpasarans hadn't been, and they'd suffered several score dead or crippled besides losing their High Priest and Priestess. He'd been carefully vague about why he'd woken up.

Not least because I'm not really certain myself.

"There, all better?" Pip said.

"Much better, and thank you, sweetie," John said. Then he looked up: "Ah . . . good morning, Thora."

The Bearkiller nodded to him, a slight smile on her face. Then she looked at Pip, who was returning her stare with a raised brow and an implacable politeness.

"Talk a bit?" the Bearkiller said.

"Of course," Pip said; he knew her well enough now to see that there was caution in her courtesy.

They walked a little aside. There was little privacy in a war-camp, and that had been awkward. If only a few spoke your language you could have a conversation, though. John watched warily, caught a stare from both women, and turned away to ostentatiously go over his longsword. It didn't need it—Evrouin saw to it—but it gave him something to look at, and anyway you should check your own gear. He remembered to be conscientious about that . . . most of the time. When he'd been a squire, the others had played a game of substituting a hilt with a stub blade on those they thought were slacking, which could be *extremely* embarrassing if a knight barked *draw* in an unannounced inspection.

Toa was sitting crosslegged nearby, going over the blade of his great spear. There was a nick in it; bone could be surprisingly resistant, and the file made a steady *wheep-wheep* sound as he worked on it.

"I wonder what they're talking about?" John said after a moment, then cursed silently.

Toa laughed, a sound like a lion grunting in the bushes, and rolled his eyes in the direction of the two women. He had a better angle to observe them.

"What the fuckin' hell do you think they're talking about? You, mate.

And not just the length of your donger. Though I figure if they were going to have a knockabout over you, it'd have happened by now."

. . . and John suddenly noticed that he was sitting in a way that meant he could rise very fast. Neither Pip nor Thora were the type of shy retiring maiden you heard about in some of the romaunts, looking wistfully out of a castle tower and waiting for other people to make events happen. It would take an ogre on Toa's scale to separate them if things went wrong.

Suddenly he laughed—softly, and facing away from them. Toa looked at him with an expression of gargoyle curiosity.

"I've heard a lot of songs where knights fight for a fair lady's favor," he said. "Not all that many about two fair ladies fighting for a knight's."

Toa's bellow was loud enough to make a nearby yellow-and-blue bird that was pecking at something on the trampled dirt fly up cheeping in an aggrieved tone. Then he cocked an eye at Thora and Pip again.

"Well, bugger me blind," Toa said. "They're shaking hands." Dryly: "No hug or kiss on the cheek, though."

Pip returned, looking more relaxed; in fact, the contrast made John suddenly realize how tense she had been. He almost blubbered in relief for a moment. It also showed that Pip was taking Thora seriously, which was a very good idea. Toa went back to honing the nick out of the blade of his spear.

"That was odd," Pip said, frowning a little. "I think we were talking about you, darling."

"You think?" John said, feeling a little indignant.

"Well, first she said I handled myself fairly well last night," she said, and frowned a little more. "Fairly!"

Toa grunted. "You're a natural and quick like a taipan," he said.

John made a puzzled sound.

"Taipan . . . snake that likes to hide in sugarcane fields," the Maori explained. "First thing you know it's bit you six times and you're not breathing anymore. Seen it happen."

Pip preened a little. "Well, then."

Toa went on: "She's a natural and she's got a lot more experience. That *fairly* bit's a compliment from someone like her, straight up. Don't get too full of yourself. She's fucking dangerous and no mistake."

Pip blinked thoughtfully. "Well, if you say so. I did the pleasant thing, of course. Then she said . . . ummm, some things were worth fighting for and some weren't, and you should know when you've got what you're going to get out of something."

Toa laughed again. "That's the voice of experience, too," he said. "Different type but it still helps."

The younger pair glared at him. "What's that supposed to bloody well mean?" Pip said. "That we'll understand when we grow up?"

Toa shrugged. "Pretty much," he replied, grinning at her throttled fury. "Because you're just a nipper yet," he said. "And you're bloody right to be relieved. It could have gotten bad."

John met her gray eyes. "I don't entirely understand that either," he said, and shrugged.

"Oh," Pip said. "*And* she said that she'd wanted more than one thing and gotten all she wanted of that and now she'd go off and set up house, after this fight was done, and to thank you very much for the gift."

This time Toa's laugh was more like a snigger, an alarming sound from someone his size. He shook his head as they glared at him again.

"Oh, not for the sodding world," he said. "Mum's the word! Right, mum's the word!"

That set him off again as he slung his modest bundle into one of the ammunition limbers and the locals brought up the six-horse teams that would pull the artillery.

"Let's hope we get the chance to get older and be initiates of all these mysteries," Pip said soberly.

Then she laughed, young and beautiful and arrogant. "And I expect we will."

"Yes, seeing . . . I see?" Tuan Anak said later that day.

I hope you do, and I hope I remember those lessons well enough, John thought.

The Carcosans had pulled back into their fortress when the Baru

Denpasaran force arrived, or at least all the ones they'd seen had done so—those jungle hills on either side of the rolling open land of the valley weren't far away, and quite a bit could be hiding there. The fortress itself had a deep water-filled ditch around its perimeter and a thick sloping wall of compacted earthwork about twenty feet high pounded down around a lattice of bamboo rods. The outer surface of the pentagonal construction was covered in turf that was patched with yellow but mostly the green that showed it had taken root to guard the soil against the washing of the rains.

Higher sections marked the corners, with breastworks of earth-filled bamboo baskets and firing ports for the catapults there; John thought there were probably four in all, and from the descriptions they were nine- or ten-pounders. There was a tall wooden tower on a mound in the center, made of logs notched together and acting as a sort of keep; the fort as a whole was big enough for about a thousand men, and it strongly resembled the motte-and-bailey castles the Association had built just after his grandfather seized power there in the early days after the Change.

Though there was no way of telling if that many garrisoned it. Or of how many had just faded into the surrounding hills.

There *was* a sparkle of steel on the ramparts, the brightness of spearheads. The black-and-yellow flag of Carcosa fluttered at the highest peak of the tower, and elsewhere on the walls. John blinked at it and then away. There was something *wrong* about it . . .

Looking at the steep ground that ran in ridges from southwest to northeast and a tangle of cross-grained hills wasn't much more reassuring. All was covered in three-layer jungle a hundred and fifty feet high, bound together with liana and vine. Tags and tatters of mist filled the folds as far as vision reached, until it faded away into blue distance. Occasionally a flight of birds went by calling raucously and then settled down into the rustling green silence again. It was a loud quietness somehow, lingering there in the background despite the chatter and hum and rattle and thump of several thousand men.

Ruan said the ground was fairly open once you were into the deep

woods—the upper layers shaded the ground densely—but the outer surface was dense as a hedgerow for several hundred yards. The young
Mackenzie found the interior oppressive too; a fine mist drizzled down
much of the time, or there was a long olive-green gloom occasionally
speared by beams of brightness. Where a giant had fallen life roared in,
twisting in slow vegetable war for light.

John realized now that most of his local allies hated and feared the
jungle and were no more able to operate in it than he was. Less so, if anything, because he was at least well used to hunting in hilly woodlands.
Temperate forests with completely different trees and plants, but the basic
principles were the same, and the Baru Denpasarans were peasants who
tilled cleared land, most of it rather flat. And then stayed within the gates
of their villages after dark, believing—rightly—that the forest-dwellers
hated them as invaders and would kill them on sight.

Tuan Anak said he had specialists who understood the wildwoods and
that they were out there checking. John believed him, but it still made
him nervous.

The hills hung brooding over the valley, the arched concrete of the
pre-Change dam, the lake that snaked northward from it, and the new-built
fort at its foot. A fair stream of water ran foaming over the spillraces and
down into a river that hugged the eastern edge of the valley; the enemy
were drawing the lake down to deny it to the takeoff for the canal upstream
whence water flowed to the western coastal lowlands of the island.

From Baru Denpasar's point of view that *had* to be stopped, and soon.
He sympathized and understood their fear and rage. Rice needed a great
deal of water, and anything that interfered with the round of the farming
year was a mortal threat, one that hit you on a visceral level every time
you looked at your family eating or felt hunger in your own belly. More
to the point, he couldn't really expect the Raja and his folk to make a
major effort to get the Montivallans and Townsvillians free of Carcosa's
threat unless they helped him end this menace. A ruler's duty was to his
own folk before strangers.

Anak used his parang to point. "Scouts say forest empty. We outnumber garrison. Fuf . . ."

He looked down at his hand and moved his fingers to recall the English numeral. *"Five to one."*

Then he made a side-to-side motion with the blade. "No rice here, comes long-long way on bad road for enemy, much up, much down."

Hilly, John thought; the local noble's English was very basic, but it got meaning across. And he understood logistics.

"No big rice, no big army men," Tuan Anak said as if to confirm the thought.

The Baru Denpasaran commander scowled, a thoughtful expression exaggerated by the scars and lopped nose.

"But we no stay long, same for us, too must cut rice soon. Must take quick but lose too many men, if we try to take walls while engines shoot us from this side, that side."

"They're there, and we're here," John said, pointing to the fort. "It will cost, taking those works, but not ruinously if we can suppress their catapults and then rake the ramparts with our prang-prangs when the assault goes in."

And every one of the non-ruinous losses lying gaping at the sky with sightless eyes is someone's beloved child. Holy Mary, Mother of God, Lady pierced with sorrows, pray for us sinners, now and at the hour of our deaths!

"You have such fort, many," Anak said; it was a statement rather than a question, but a request for reassurance too.

"Yes, many," John said, and didn't continue aloud:

And most of them make that look like a pimple, unless you count Mackenzie duns.

For one thing, it was very fortunate indeed that the enemy fort was rather small and improvised. He couldn't tell Tuan Anak how to take a major Protectorate castle or a walled city anywhere in the High Kingdom, because to the best of his knowledge nobody in Montival ever had, save by treachery or starving it out. Smaller works, yes, though at terrible cost . . .

He put calm confidence into his voice, copying his instructors:

"Now we have to work forward, establishing sheltered positions, until we can dominate their fort and suppress its fire."

He sketched a standard siege operation, with trenches zigzagging forward, parallels dug, redoubts established, and then the whole procedure repeated. His instructors had called it a *Vauban Approach*, after some great French warrior of the ancient world. The problem was that even the best modern catapults weren't as powerful as the black-powder cannon Vauban had used, and the ones they had were light warship machines turned field pieces, not a battering-train meant for siege work. Even the *Tarshish Queen*'s eighteen-pounder bow and stern chasers were only just in that class, and the prang-prangs were for use against troops only.

"Then it can be stormed," the Montivallan prince finished confidently. "Getting up the walls of an earthwork like that isn't the problem; it's getting the troops to the foot of it."

Not that I've ever done anything of the sort.

He'd never really enjoyed learning fighting much, but it was good to be fit and he *did* like doing well in tournaments—it was a quick route to popularity with girls well-born and otherwise—and he'd realized long ago that it might well keep him alive at some point. That had happened about the time that he grew old enough to imagine what the scars so common in his parents' generation actually meant.

But while jousting and sparring could be at least not terminally tedious, lessons in siegecraft had bored him like a hydraulic drill. It made his breath catch to think all these people depended on his remembering it right.

Then he glanced across to Thora. She gave him a single slight nod to signify *fine so far* and he managed not to slump in relief—if you slouched in armor it clattered, and looked ridiculous. She'd talked of sieges she'd seen here and there, without much detail on her own role; but he was absolutely confident that she knew how to do it far better than he did. Fortunately he had her with him and so didn't have to do it alone. And Captain Ishikawa was standing tactfully behind her, looking preternaturally calm, which was also reassuring. From what he'd said, he'd both defended and attacked forts as well.

The Baru Denpasaran lord wouldn't take *orders* from any outsider what-soever, which was reasonable enough. And he wouldn't listen well to advice on warcraft from a Japanese stranger or a woman of any variety, even if he grudgingly respected both as individual fighters. He would take suggestions from a Prince, provided the Prince was from very far away in the land of the fabled American ancients, and provided the Prince had brought equipment he couldn't do without and most of all provided his ruler had ordered him to do so, point-blank and in public. Especially now that he was desperate for victory to make up for a stinging loss.

He's no fool, but custom is king over all lands, John thought, trying to be charitable and tolerant though he thought the basic attitude idiotic. *Still, I'd like to see even the stiffest Associate noble treat Grandmother Sandra like that, or Baroness d'Ath!*

He almost smiled at that, then sobered. From what he'd heard—heard whispered, it wasn't spoken aloud—a number of them had *tried* to do just that after his grandfather died and Nonna Sandra became Lady Regent of the Protectorate. Somehow they'd all come to bad ends in ways that left their heirs no way to strike back, or sometimes left them with no heirs at all. The survivors had learned wisdom, or at least how to act as if they had wisdom, motivated by a miasma of fear, until the pretense had become reality. His grandmother had said to him once, smiling slightly, that if you compelled people to behave as if they believed something eventually all but the strongest-willed really *did* start to believe it, because it was easier on their pride than admitting every moment in the privacy of their soul that they were pretending.

Tuan Anak sighed. "Men born, men fight, men die, men reborn."

Well, that's a little surprising. But what was it Father liked to say? Wasn't it: A man's mind is like a forest at night, always full of the unexpected.

The Baru Denpasaran forces had put folding umbrellas up over the command post; that seemed to be a matter of status, but John was very glad of it. It had been midmorning by the time the little army had debouched into the flat sloping glacis before the enemy fort, and the sun was fierce. This was the only practicable approach; its flanks were within shot-range of the woods on both sides, and the eastern side was close to the river too, which was too swift-moving and deep to ford.

It's a murderously simple approach, John thought. *But at least it's so simple I can't make any major mistakes if I have to decide something on my own when there's no time to consult. Hopefully. God, I never asked to have the fate of men in my hands!*

A voice seemed to whisper: *Take up your cross, and follow Me.* He shivered and put the thought out of his mind.

"We do," Tuan Anak said decisively. "Camp first. Make safe base."

That was much like the marching encampment they'd run up yesterday, except that the trench was deeper and the wall higher and topped with a substantial stockade and fighting platform, and the field of sharpened stakes and bamboo knives in covered pits stretched out farther. The Montivallans and Townsvillers watched from beneath the commander's umbrellas, the common sailors squatting or sitting nearby. When Tuan Anak moved his command post to a completed section of wall northward, facing the Carcosan fortress, they followed. John looked down over the vast construction site that was the camp and whistled softly.

"Very impressive," he said.

Pip and Toa and First Mate Radavindraban were watching with interest, but when John spoke Ishikawa and Thora and Sergeant Fayard all grunted in agreement in their different ways. The Nihonjin officer's concurrence was reluctant, but genuine.

It wasn't so much that the Baru Denpasarans were disciplined the way Boiseans or Reiko's samurai were. They were disciplined *enough*, in a rough-and-ready way, but their regulars had little of that polished snap and the peasant militia none. He thought for a moment, and decided that the remarkable thing was that they were so self-organizing. Their leaders had told them what to do, and which group was to do what, and then the men simply went at it without needing to be watched or driven by anyone except themselves. They were like Mackenzies that way, but even less formal.

He thought they were competing with each other too, in a comradely fashion, village against village and one Sumbak association against the next. The result wasn't particularly neat, but it was massive and it went up *fast*. So did the essentials—a hospital section roofed with woven bamboo, watering points for men and livestock and kitchens, and latrines safely deep and distant from the rest. Then they started in on thatched temporary huts, or at least shelters to keep the rain off; there was even an improvised temple.

Anak nodded. "Now, make fort little small to see," he said, turning to look at the Carcosan position again. "And diggings, small."

That led to some confusion, and consultation with Deor. It turned out the Baru Denpasaran commander meant making a model of the whole operation in miniature on a sand table, so that John could mark out the way the siege works should go for Anak's monoglot officers. That was deeply reassuring, since it was the standard way *he'd* been taught and gave them a common language beyond words, but . . .

That will be about as much fun as watching mud dry, John thought, and carefully didn't sigh.

I wish I was back to doing this with models, John thought four days later at the bright height of noon.

"Down!" someone shouted.

John ducked his head below the rampart of earth-filled bamboo baskets on the edge of the pit, knocked his visor down and raised his shield up from his side in the same motion until it was like a roof overhead. As he did so he realized that he didn't even know which *language* the call had been in—and didn't care.

At least it's not a catapult bolt, he thought; *that would have been here already*.

A flight of arrows lifted shrilling from the ramparts of the Carcosan fort, and this forward bastion was only about two hundred paces from it, well within range. They were close enough now that the enemy bowmen could fire from behind the parapet, down in the relative safety of the fortress courtyard.

He looked up sharply, though only for an instant, and there was a perverse beauty to the flickering threadwork against the blue sky as the shafts rose to their apogee and the steel heads glinted like starlight on water as they tipped over and began to fall. Another flight followed them, and another.

Starlight on water. That's a good image! I think there's something about that in the Bible . . . no, it's Byron.

Once he had the reference the words came into his mind complete:

The Assyrian came down like a wolf on the fold
And his cohorts were gleaming in purple and gold;
And the sheen of their spears was like stars on the sea
When the blue wave rolls nightly on deep Galilee.

His Aunt Fiorbhinn had told him once that mediocre poets had influences; great poets *stole*. And if you were going to steal, steal from the best. And Byron had been an adventurer too, leaving comfort and wealth to fight for the Greeks in their uprising against Turkish oppression. It was something to be a man of deeds as well as words.

As he thought he ducked his head down again, back to a view of pounded mud and mats making trails through it and the smell of wet earth and wastes and fear-sweat and, faintly, death. Getting an arrow in the eye while looking up put you into a special category of human being: *too stupid to live* summed it up.

"For what we are about to receive—" he began, reflecting that he'd be sweating like a pig even if it wasn't like a sauna and even if he weren't in his suit of plate complete.

Which it is, and which I am.

"—may the Lord make us truly thankful, Sire," Evrouin finished.

Fayard and his men from the Guard were grimly silent; John thought the underofficer would be really happy only if his charge spent his time in a deep bunker. There was a rising whistle, and he winced. There might be something more wearing on the nerves than being shot at and not being able to do anything except passively wait it out, but if there was he hadn't run into it yet. Evrouin and the rest of those in the bastion stepped back under the overhead protection that covered the rear half, layers of three-inch saplings crisscrossed on a framework of bamboo lashed together with strips of the same material and covered in a foot of earth.

Crack.

An arrow punched into the sheet-steel covering of his shield, dimpling the metal but not piercing it, and bounced off. Then hundreds fell, in a hissing, thudding, snapping rain. He suppressed the impulse to squeeze his eyes shut, and instead simply endured. Ten arrows struck his shield, and several penetrated to the plywood core and stood vibrating. Another glanced off the curve of his sallet helm, a hard blow like a quick punch from a fist on the top of his head. More sprouted suddenly from the packed earth around him, or plunged into the roofing above the crew of the catapult and the guard detail or cracked and rattled off the big killing-machine itself.

The last shaft had scarcely fallen before Ruan leapt out and sprang onto a stack of ammunition boxes. He had an arrow on the string of his longbow and two more between the grip and the forefinger of his left hand. He drew and shot all three in a quick ripple of effort, the great yellow limbs of Montivallan mountain yew flexing smoothly and the flat snap of the bowstring sounding hard and fast.

John risked a peek himself. The central wooden keep of the Carcosan fort was still burning fiercely; it had been made of green wood and covered in hides, but a flurry of napalm shells and firebolt had set it alight during the last night-time bombardment. A huge plume of black smoke drifted northwestward away from them, carrying all but a bitter hint of the reek with it. The pounded dirt of the walls merely looked scorched and chewed, being immune to fire and nearly so to impacts, though the palisade on top of it had been knocked to flinders.

More to the point, that pillar of smoke meant that the Carcosans had no tall lookout post to direct the fire of their missile weapons. A man standing on the rampart doing duty for that dodged as the first of Ruan's

shafts hissed by his head, then toppled with a distance-thinned shriek as
two more thumped into his upper chest.

"*We are the darts that Hecate cast!*" Ruan shouted, and then something in
Gaelic that John thought involved the words *your mother.*

Mackenzies didn't really speak the language of Grandmother Juniper's ancestors, but they swore in it full often. . . .

"Good work!" Deor said, cautiously looking over the parapet himself
and thumping his lover's back as Ruan jumped down.

Fayard and his men cheered a fellow-shooter and the scop went on:
"Wuldor couldn't do better."

While he spoke the crew of the catapult sprang to readiness; it was
already cocked and the hydraulic lines ran back to the covered section.
Locals manned the pumps, and waited ready to move the trails behind
the machine if it needed to slew around more than the traversing mechanisms could handle. Despite Ishikawa's worries the frames had held
up . . . so far, and with a little hammer-and-wrench work. A few others
gathered in the arrow-shafts; the whole ones could be shot back by the
Baru Denpasaran archers, and the broken ones would provide heads for
their fletchers to use.

"I think we haven't dismounted all the enemy machines in that bastion
on the left," John said. "Give them another brace of roundshot."

They had plenty of those; the foundry in Baru Denpasar had run up
hundreds, since it needed only the ability to cast a metal sphere and they
were willing to sacrifice as much as needed even if it meant melting down
tools. The surprisingly small nine-pounder ball was slapped into the
groove—it was about four inches in diameter—and the gunner's foot
stamped down on the firing-pedal.

Tung-WHACK!

The locals finished picking up the arrows and threw themselves onto
the arms of the pump as the throwing arms slapped forward into the stops
and the mechanism recoiled. John flicked up his visor again, put his binoculars to his eyes and watched. The range was short and the ball didn't
have time to slow down much as it covered the distance in a blurred

streak of speed. Then it plowed into the tumbled, smoldering ruins of the squared-timber bastion that had been built into the wall of the fort. Splinters and clods of dirt flew skyward.

"Again!" John snapped. "Keep it up, sustained fire."

I hadn't realized how you can be keyed up, exhausted and terminally bored at the same time, he thought as the next ball thumped home. *This is like overseeing a construction project while being shot at.*

A hail from the guards at the point where the zigzag communication trench entered the pit was answered in Thora's unmistakable flat Bearkiller tones.

"Good to see you," John said sincerely.

Thora pushed up the three-bar visor of her helm and grinned at him; her face was red and running with sweat like his, but unlike him she seemed totally indifferent to it.

"Tuan Anak is taking all your *advice* seriously, Johnnie," she said with a grin and a wink. "Even when I carry the *message.*"

In fact she'd been solemnly passing on . . . her *own* opinions, with Deor helping out when the Baru Denpasaran commander's uncertain English ran into a wall. He was quite certain the whole business would have had her sword out and blood shed if it had happened back home, but since they weren't going to be here for long she regarded it all as a joke.

"Your delicate little flower has the prang-prangs ready, too," she went on.

There seemed to be genuine respect in that, even liking, as well as a tinge of sarcasm; John decided he wasn't presumptuous enough to think that he understood how Thora's mind worked. Instead he nodded to the bosun's mate in charge of the catapult.

"Cease fire for now," he said. "Be ready with the assault fire plan at the signal."

The man nodded, blue eyes bright in the ruddy tan of his face. "Will do, Your Highness."

John and Evrouin, Thora and Deor and Ruan turned into the zigzag communication trench, walking slightly bent over. The big ditches had been dug by the local folk to suit themselves, and by that standard even Evrouin's five-foot-six was tall, and he was the shortest of the five of them. None of the Montivallans wanted to show their heads over the parapet. The Carcosan catapults were supposedly suppressed . . . but they might just be biding their time. He carried his sallet under one arm, as well. The white ostrich plumes would be just too tempting if they bobbed along over the edge.

And damned if I'm going to take them off! In fact, he'd bought a new set in town before they left.

"They've got the trebuchets set up," Thora went on. "And Tuan Anak is very taken with *your suggestion* about those."

That one had been Captain Ishikawa's. John felt as if he ought to blush. Still, there was no way on God's green earth the Balinese noble was going to take *suggestions* from a foreign woman, or from an *Orang Japon*. From a Prince of a great realm in the fabled land of the Americans . . . then, if they were politely phrased, yes.

Thora grinned. "What's being a great monarch but a lifetime of getting the credit for what others do tacked on to your own deeds?" she asked.

Ouch, he thought.

Tuan Anak was waiting in the foremost parallel, the trench facing the enemy ramparts, just beyond bowshot from the Carcosan fort.

To get there John and his party passed the row of six trebuchets. The lever-principle machines were mostly made of wood—they had plenty of good timber within reach, albeit it was green—and the metal parts had come along from the city on the carts, along with artificers. Each was sitting in a circular pit dug more than ten feet deep with a berm piled around it. As far as he could tell—more to the point, as far as Captain Ishikawa could tell—they were well designed. The principle of a heavy weight hinged to one end and a much longer throwing arm with a sling on the other was simple enough. The devil of efficient energy transfer was in the details of proportion and angle, though, and while he remembered the basic formulas he was profoundly glad someone with practical experience was along.

The Baru Denpasarans used similar machines to command their western half of the harbor back at their capital. Without the *Tarshish Queen's* longer-ranged weapons to suppress their Carcosan equivalents they couldn't have built these massive things close enough to the fort's wall, and even so it had cost lives. Now they were ready. Each sling was loaded with a ton-weight ball of rocks the size of a baby's head, bound together with tight nets of coir rope made from coconut husk. Geared winches would pull the arms down surprisingly fast after each shot, and more bundles were ready to be rolled into the sling-cups.

There was a strong fruity odor as they passed; the nets that held the rocks had been soaked in vats of triple-distilled toddy before they were filled. No open flame was near them, but lidded clay pots of coals were standing ready. The connecting trenches leading up to the commander's position were thick with troops, crouching on their hams with their bows or spears standing up between their knees and their shields propped against the mats that revetted the earth walls. Many of them nodded and grinned at the Montivallans as they passed; it was nice to be popular, although a little alarming when some of the smiles were dyed blood-red with *paan*, the combination of lime paste and betel nut and leaf many hereabouts chewed.

They spat when they chewed, too, though in town they used wooden buckets. Nobody was taking that much care here.

Thora chuckled grimly. "Hides the blood a bit, eh, Johnnie?"

"Just what I was thinking," he said tightly.

Tuan Anak was talking to his officers when they debouched into the forward trench. John waited quietly; it wasn't his country and he wasn't in command here. As he did, he heard Fayard talking to his men, a few last instructions and then:

"We're a long way from home. But our oaths are here, and our honor, Guardsmen, and so is the one we swore before God to protect with our lives."

"God's enemies are here too," one of them said quietly; his name was Ernoul, John remembered.

Fayard nodded agreement, and finished: "And we all saw what the Prince did for a shipmate. Can we do less?"

The Prince blushed, then turned and settled the plumed helmet on his head.

"And I know you're here, comrades, brothers of the sword," he said, meeting the eyes of each. "We've come a long way together, and shed our sweat and blood side by side. I'm glad of it, and I won't forget who was here with me either."

The squad came to attention and smacked right fist to heart in the Association's salute. John kept his face grave as he returned it, but he swallowed nonetheless. The men of the Guard would have fought for him regardless; that was their oath. But he thought he saw genuine respect for him, the individual and not just his rank and blood. The golden spurs on his heels seemed to settle in a little more comfortably.

Evrouin stepped near and murmured, "And remember, Sire: if you die, we all have to face your mother. So don't, eh?"

John chuckled. "I see your point, goodman. You've certainly done everything you could to keep me alive."

Deor and Thora and Ruan were talking softly, their heads together.

"There'll be room for you at Hraefnbeorg, Ruan, when we make our steading," the scop said. "If you choose."

The young Mackenzie grinned at him and laid a hand alongside his cheek for a moment. "Sure, and there's Dun Barstow now only a few days' journey away from your brother's holding, my heart," he said. "I could visit my own folk full often. If your oath-sister agrees, of course."

"What, turn down another pair of hands around the place? Not likely!" she said. They all chuckled at that, having grown up as folk of the land. "If wyrd will have it so, then."

Then she turned to Deor. They each laid a hand on the other's shoulder, covered that hand with their own free one and spoke in unison:

"Lo, there do I see our Fathers . . .
Lo, there do I see our Mothers . . .
Lo, there do I see the line
Of all our people from their beginning . . .

They do bid us to take our place among them . . .
In the Halls of Valhalla,
Where the Brave may live forever!"

Pip came up with Toa, and a few of her followers. She'd changed into her white costume with the suspenders and what she'd said was called a bowler hat, her cane jauntily over one shoulder. The big Maori was scowling; first at her, and then at John. Two of the *Silver Surfer* sailors carried local shields, fairly large ones, and they were casting the odd apprehensive glance at the blade of the great spear in the older man's hands.

Ah, John thought. *He's told them that if she stops an arrow, they might as well kill themselves and save him the trouble. And they believe him. So would I.*

"Shouldn't you be looking after the prang-prangs, Pip?" he asked.

She snorted, and used the serrated head of the cane to adjust the jaunty angle of her hat. John was glad of the secret—as a hidden steel cap was called—within, but he wished with all his heart that she was carrying more protection than a set of metal-capped boiled-leather knee and elbow pads. And he was glad Toa had had the idea for the men with shields.

"The prang-prangs? That's technician's work, darling," she said airily.

Then, her face completely serious for once, without the usual edge of ironic mockery: "Leading . . . that's what I was *born* for, John."

He sighed, nodded, and made himself smile. *There's absolutely nothing I can say to that,* he thought. *Not without more hypocrisy than I could get away with.*

"Well, you can certainly handle yourself in a fight, I've seen that," he said. "But I'm better equipped for a slugging match, so I hope you don't mind if I stick close? And perhaps make the point of the spear?"

"Wouldn't *dream* of objecting, my dear," she said. "Isn't this where we came in, rather?"

"Ah . . . yes," he said. "I won't say *we have to stop meeting like this,* but . . ."

Tuan Anak finished his briefing and his officers saluted in local fashion and trotted off to their bands. He looked at the two parties of foreigners— three if you counted Ishikawa and his sailors—and nodded approvingly.

His lancers were the only substantial group in the Baru Denpasaran force with much body armor, and they'd be following him straight in.

"Good," he said, inclining his head to John. "We fight together, so friends do."

Then he barked a command in Balinese. Half a dozen archers dipped the heads of arrows wrapped in cloth into clay pots full of embers and then shot skyward. Red smoke trailed behind them. John turned his head southward. The throwing arms of the trebuchets showed over the heaped earth surrounding them, since they were twenty feet in the air; those were the shorter ends, the ones with huge boxes of rock hinged to them. They trembled as the retaining hooks were knocked out of the eyelets and then began to fall—slowly at first, then with ever-gathering speed.

The parts on the other side of the axle that pivoted the arm were sixty feet long, and they had slings half that length attached to them to throw the loads. The netting around the great balls of rock was already wrapped in pale-blue flames as the slings dropped away at the top of the arc. The rushing passage of their high curving path through the air fanned the fire into a blaze, and they were trailing black smoke as they began to fall. Four of them burst apart before they struck behind the wall, spraying the courtyard of the fortress with scores of fast-moving chunks that weighed twenty pounds or so each. The others would disintegrate instantly on the ground, sending their loads out in circles almost as lethal.

Tuan Anak barked another order. This time the fire-arrows trailed green smoke, and a set of trumpeters raised their instruments as well—long straight things with flared mouths called *Pérérét*, and they sounded a high, complex, modulated wail that his musician's ear recognized as a repetitive tune.

With a roaring scream two thousand bowmen burst out of the Baru Denpasaran trenches and ran forward. Calling war-cries he didn't know, or the name of their ruler, which he did recognize, but behind them would be . . .

Deor was close enough for John to hear him speak in quiet natural tones; those could carry better through loud noise than a shout, something any good musician knew.

"For the food our children eat," the Hraefnbeorg man said. "There are few cries to make a man fight more fiercely."

"Or a woman," Thora said, working the fingers of her sword-hand.

The tumbled, smoking remains of the bastions on the wall stirred, as men pushed aside the charred remnants with poles and metal glinted behind. John felt a moment's vindication; just as he'd thought they hadn't managed to silence all the enemy machines. Then three roundshot snapped out into the gathered mass of archers as they raised their bows, skillfully aimed grazing shots that bounced and tumbled through the dense ranks shattering bone and flesh as they passed. He lowered his glasses and swallowed as he cased them.

Dozens died or fell screaming in instants. The rest drew their weapons and let fly. John whistled softly, impressed: he'd heard of men standing under catapult fire, but he'd never seen it before. Fayard had, since he'd fought in the tail-end of the Prophet's War.

"Brave men," he said.

The catapults from the *Tarshish Queen* cut loose in the same instant from their advanced positions, pushed forward from the main parallel along the Baru Denpasaran line; all of them aiming at the enemy machines. Then:

Prang-prang-prang-prang—

The ratcheting mechanical clamor of the *Silver Surfer's* rapid-fire weapons sounded, as the grass-covered woven matting was thrown off. They were aiming at the Carcosan catapults too, but any of the glinting stream of projectiles that missed would rake the interior of the fortress as well. The Baru Denpasaran archers grouped in three rough battalions and shot, and they had extra quivers slung. Arrows flickered skyward in shoals, probably six hundred or better every second, and the target zone inside the fort's walls was only about six hundred feet on a side. John rinsed out his mouth with water from his canteen, spat, and took a long drink before capping it and settling his helm on his head and his shield on his arm.

The forward edge of the trench had sturdy wood-and-bamboo staircases built into it at intervals, opposite the access paths stretching backward. Tuan Anak shouted again. The trumpets sounded their high wailing squeal, and banners swung upright—narrow flags of colorful silk secured to the poles along the long edge. As they waved a tearing scream sounded from thousands of throats, and the massed troops waiting in cover began to move forward. The first parties that thundered by carried long stout ladders, built with steps rather than merely rungs and each borne overhead by twenty or thirty men. They had headbands tied tightly about their foreheads and crimson marks on their cheeks, and the glazed look of . . .

Men sworn to win or die, John thought, as they went up the steep access steps without breaking stride or faltering.

The Baru Denpasaran leader made a further gesture—words would have been impossible in the clamor—and led the way up the nearest flight of stairs himself, one reserved for the commander and his immediate followers. The raja's armored lancers came after him carrying their horsemen's weapons like pikes, and the Montivallans and their friends followed. John hadn't drawn his sword yet, and was glad of it as he clutched at the railing to steady himself as he followed. The stair hadn't been designed for a man his size in eighty pounds of gear, and the prospect of breaking it or just slipping and falling flat on his face didn't bear thinking about.

The banners went forward in three groups towards the gaps between the blocks of bowmen, and the assault-parties with the scaling ladders. Behind them the roaring spearmen followed. John swept out his sword and shouted as he ran:

"Órlaith and Montival! *Follow me!*"

CHAPTER TWENTY-TWO

Free and Loyal Chartered City of Astoria

Portland Protective Association

(Formerly western Oregon)

High Kingdom of Montival

(Formerly western North America)

November 10th

Change Year 46/2044 AD

"Why do we have to have *so many* investitures?" Heuradys d'Ath muttered as the Crown Princess' party halted outside the city's eastern gate for the ceremonial entry.

She was in full armor with the visor raised. Her sword was in its scabbard, but her shield with the d'Ath arms—sable, a delta or on a V argent, quartered with Órlaith's Crowned Mountain and Sword crossed with the baton of cadency—was on her arm, and if you knew her well she was bristling like an aggrieved cat.

Órlaith could tell she was also trying to look in all directions at once without being conspicuous about it, which was difficult even with your helmet still at the saddlebow and a faint mist of rain drifting down out of a lowering sky. There was a strong smell of the damp horses whose breath puffed out in gray snorts, woodsmoke from the town, and the brackish water of the Columbia's tidal estuary northward.

Their escort waited patiently behind them, kilted archers standing by their bicycles, the lances of the men-at-arms shifting a little like a swaying leafless forest tipped with wet steel as the horses moved their weight from hoof to hoof as they stood. The light cavalry company were a little more casual, easterners on quarter horses who were ranch-hands in civil life, armed with curved sword and horn-backed saddlebow; only the mail shirts and helms and round shields were different from their ordinary working gear, and those were hidden under grease-wool cloaks and hoods right now.

Alan Thurston was their commander. Órlaith carefully did *not* look in their direction. Things with her mother were better now, and she didn't want to risk another row just as the expeditionary force was leaving. She might have heard—Órlaith had been discreet, but not secretive—but at least they didn't have to have a public fight about it.

Avert the omen, she thought, and made a protective sign with her left hand. *But I really like Alan.*

"Couldn't we just have the proclamation you're in charge read out, and get you and Reiko on the bloody ships and *go?*" Heuradys went on.

"Only *three* investitures," Órlaith replied patiently; it was her liege knight's job to fret, and there was plenty of stress floating around in this last whirlwind of effort. "If you count the informal one where Mother just told me. Then the formal announcement in Dún na Síochána in front of the Congress of Realms, and this time."

"This one's in a *city.* Not Dún na Síochána, a real city with a wall and thousands of people we don't know."

"Tsk, being prejudiced, are we the now?"

"I like cities. Well, I like visiting them occasionally. But it's not a controlled environment like a castle . . ."

Then she chuckled ruefully. "I just realized I'm . . . what did Captain Feldman call it . . . *kvetching* . . . at taking you through a place full of your loyal subjects so I can hustle you off across thousands of miles of stormy ocean to battlefields full of demon-worshipping madmen . . . where you'd be *safe,* presumably. Athana witness, the human mind is a wonderful thing."

Órlaith nodded; she was in plate too, and likewise helmless. The armor was fulfilling the other half of its miracle, being as miserably cold in chilly weather as it was unbearably hot in summer, and letting cold drops trickle down her neck into the arming doublet.

"And we're doing it because Astoria is stuffed with troops and panjandrums from all over the kingdom. They need a chance to see it done," she said.

"And there may be real enemies here," Reiko said tactfully, her lacquered harness bright even in the chill gloom.

Her face was expressionless, but there was a slight smile in her tone, and Órlaith gave an equally slight wink to her as they reined in side-by-side. They both spent their days surrounded by loyal-to-the-death paranoid vassals convinced that assassins lurked behind every tree and barn.

Heuradys sighed, and Sir Droyn cleared his throat with a slight exasperated sound as he fell in behind the senior knight of the Household. Egawa Noboru was riding behind his Empress, and with him two samurai carrying the flagstaffs for the Hinomaru and the *Tennō Heika's* personal banner. *His* face might have been carved from amber-colored stone as he looked up at the great gates.

Astoria had been a city before the Change, albeit a small one by the standards of the ancient world, and remote. Fish and grain from freighters drifting down the Columbia had brought it through the first few months, and Órlaith's grandfather Norman had taken it early in the Foundation Wars. Either he or more likely Nonni Sandra had seen the long-term need for a window on the Mother Ocean.

The site of the city was shaped almost exactly like a clenched fist seen palm-down with the town on the thumb jutting out to the west. The city wall across the base of the thumb was typical of major works from the early Protectorate period, made of steel shipping containers filled with rubble and concrete and then cemented into a homogenous mass and stuccoed. It loomed sixty feet above a dry moat studded with sharpened angle-iron. The parapets were machicolated out over the edge and the whole wall studded with round towers half again as high at hundred-yard intervals, with steel shutters masking the catapult-ports. The gatehouse before them where the road and railroad ran through the wall was a castle in its own right, with a tower at each corner.

The whole was grossly in excess of any rational military need; even today something half the size would be impossible to storm. It was meant to crush an opponent's heart before a blow was struck.

The flame-wreathed Lidless Eye of the Armingers flew from the staffs atop the towers' conical witch's-hat roofs, alternating with the City's banner. That bore Saint Nicholas, patron of merchants, sailors and fishermen, shown as a bearded brown-skinned man with a Roman bishop's crosier and mitered hat, standing in a boat with three children at his feet and three gold coins in his hand.

And from the center . . . the Crowned Mountain and Sword of the High Kingdom, green and black and silver.

Órlaith made a small gesture with her right hand, a flick of the fingers. Sir Droyn rode forward clattering across the bridge that spanned the moat, followed by two mounted trumpeters; his plumed helmet would have looked a little more impressive if it was less damp, but he was still a fine and martial sight in his polished plate. The knight ceremoniously thumped his gauntleted fist against the gates. Since the portal was closed by a solid slab of welded steel girders twenty feet high and six inches thick, the *clunk* was rather undramatic.

The trumpeters behind him in their colorful tabards raised their polished brass instruments and sounded a long descant. Then Droyn's deep voice rang out in formal challenge:

"Her Highness Órlaith Arminger Mackenzie, Crown Princess and heir to the High Queenship of Montival, calls upon her loyal city of Astoria to open its gates and render homage!"

There was a moment of silence, just long enough for her to think how hideously embarrassing it would be if something had gone wrong with the machinery—normally the gates were closed only for drills—and then a dozen more trumpeters raised long oliphants and blew from the rampart above. A whirring rumble of gears and winches sounded, and the great steel slab of the gate slid sideways into the bulk of the gatehouse wall with a grind of steel on steel—several dozen railway wheels were set into the lower part of the mass on the inside, running on a solid smooth steel plate set into the roadway.

City militia double-timed out of the great arched tunnel of the gateway and formed up to either side, looking quite martial in their helms and breast-plates and rapping their glaives down to stand at attention on either side. The Lord Mayor, the Aldermen and guildmasters—or guildmistresses—and the bishop came pacing out in robes and chains of office, faltering only a little as they realized it was going to rain on their finery and they couldn't use umbrellas because that would make the ceremony impossible.

Well-to-do townsmen were among the few people in the modern world who *weren't* used to getting wet to the skin fairly often.

Órlaith sighed as she set her face into a mask of stern courtesy. These folk had a right to it, and to know their contribution was valued, and that their city was paid due honor through their own leaders . . .

Twenty minutes later as they rode through the gate and the local notables fell in behind as part of the procession she whimpered almost inaudibly:

"The rest of my life! And I think the Syndics were a bit peeved that I cut their speeches as short as I did by jumping in at a pause!"

"It's not *all* going to be like that," Heuradys said. "Some of it will be worse!"

Órlaith could feel Reiko struggling between laughter and sympathy without giving any exterior sign of either. Something like: *You should see what it's like for me before you complain,* perhaps. At least a High Queen of Montival wasn't expected to be what amounted to the hierophant of a state church, which a *Tennō Heika* was with regard to the Way of the Gods in Nippon.

When a crowd was making this much noise—and the cheering was very loud indeed—you couldn't shout *over* the blanketing white roar, but you could talk through it without being overheard, or anyone noticing, if you were careful about it and had the knack. Folk lined the road all the way from the gates, over the broad strip of the open *pomery* inside the

wall and into the stretch of forest carefully managed by the Burgh Council to protect the watershed and furnish fuel-wood. The mass grew even
thicker as they approached the built-up districts, both townsfolk and
soldiers from as far east as the High Plains.

The road ran quite close to the river and the thicket of mast and spar and
bowsprits that lined the docks there, and the scores more of ships anchored
offshore for lack of room, with lighters and barges shuttling back and forth
to the shore. Sailors were cheering too, from perches on the spars and in the
ratlines, and flags flew from every masthead and bunting from the rigging.
From here you could look northwest and see the ramparts and tall towers of
the massive castle of plastered concrete that anchored the southern approach
to the bridge across the Columbia—that was Crown demesne, and also gay
with banners today, though pointedly *not* including the image of Saint
Nicholas.

"Sooo, Wardancer," she said, running a hand down the arched neck
of her mount, who was rolling his eyes a little. "Sorry to be doing this to
you, boy, but sure and we all have our sacrifices to make."

This was one of the destriers she was taking with her, a sturdy, muscular, long-legged roan of sixteen hands with a mane almost blond, six
years old and beautifully trained. None of the beasts were going to enjoy
the weeks they faced in the dark tossing holds of ships; that and the prevailing winds were one reason they planned to break the journey in
friendly Hawaii. They'd be three months at sea even with very good
weather.

"Suspecting that we *are* going to get good weather, my liege?" Heuradys said quietly as she saw that Órlaith was glancing at the Grasscutter
by Reiko's side.

"Yes, Herry, somehow I do," Órlaith said as they fell in behind the
carriage.

Reiko overheard. "I cannot guarantee it," she said. "But . . ."

The slightest hint of a smile. "Yes, Orrey-*chan*, I also suspect we will
have favorable winds."

Reiko was cheerful, if you knew her well enough to read the signs.

Well, this is the fulfillment of a dream for her, Órlaith thought ungrudgingly. *I'm leaving home. She's going home with the force that will free her people of fear and secure their futures; and to her mother and her sisters. Will she find it hard, to be in those familiar places and her father always absent? I think so. It's hard enough for me here. I am looking forward to being places where everything doesn't remind me of the first time he put me up before him on his horse, or taught me how to draw a bow or make paper birds to fly out the window, or where we ate a summer peach together with juice running down our chins and hands like laughter. Or wishing I could introduce him to Alan—I think he'd have liked him, Da was never one to hold your parentage against you. Or he wouldn't have handfasted to Mother!*

Her mother had told her stories of that, how her father had been her only friend when they were both ten and Mathilda Arminger a hostage among Mackenzies, taken by accident in a raid during the old wars against the Association. Young Rudi Mackenzie had stood the lonely girl's champion and sworn the oath of *anamchara* with her.

The others who'd followed her and Reiko to the Valley of Death and the lost castle were there too just behind the monarchs, including Diarmuid Tennart McClintock and his caterans and Karl Aylward and his Mackenzies, with Macmac padding along with the other greathounds and taking the cheers as his due with raised ears and looks cast to either side—he wasn't a dog of excessive humbleness. Suzie was in her best between the Dúnedain cousins, including ceremonial feathers in her hair—deeply meaningful to a Lakota—which her kinfolk found rather shocking for a woman to wear, something which bothered her not at all.

The mounted heralds in tabards sounding their horns at intervals rode before them. The crowds thickened as the procession moved on into the more densely peopled sections, cheering wildly and calling blessings. Here the militia faced outward, with their polearms held horizontally to keep the crowds off the pavement.

Órlaith never felt entirely at home in cities, but this was also Montival—and a part of it that her blood had nurtured. Astoria had nearly twoscore thousand people now, and like its great rival Newport to the south the number was greater than it had been on the day of the

Change, and still growing. There was little farmland immediately around it except for some pasture and hay meadow, but railcars and barges and riverboats brought the Columbia's wealth downstream. Fishing-boats from dories to deep-sea schooners waged their grim immemorial struggle to harvest the ocean's riches, nearby wrecks provided abundant metal, water-power sawed and hammered and turned lathe and drill and helped skilled hands. Daring skippers carried the yield of its hinterlands to many lands, and also the products of its own craft guilds, and returned with wealth and a breath of strangeness. There were foreign ships as well, more every year. Folk from three continents walked these streets, bringing not only wealth but songs and tales, their legends and their Gods. Astoria had prospered under the Lord Protector and Lady Regent Sandra after him, and under the High King's long peace it had flourished.

That showed in streets lit by gas lamps in cast-iron stands, buildings as likely to be new as repurposed work of the ancients; tall houses of four or five stories, half-timbered frames and whitewashed brick noggin beneath steep shingle roofs, blazoned with the crests of magnates or guilds. City-folk crowded the sidewalks and clustered thickly in window and balcony, cheering and waving or holding up children who fluttered tiny flags on sticks.

Laborers in canvas smocks and baggy trousers and wooden clogs or long gowns and wimples, sailors in striped sweaters and shapeless caps, rowdy apprentices in blue jackets, leather-aproned journeymen, master-craftsmen in their Sunday best, merchants brightly clad in bag-sleeved houppelandes and hose and curl-toed shoes, Catholic religious in cassock and biretta or the robes and habits of their Orders, all bore themselves proudly.

City air makes you free, as the saying went.

The shops and worksteads which occupied many ground-floors were shuttered for this day of her departure, but street-sellers circulated amid the dense crowds, with trays of sausages in buns and candied apples or cups of hot spiced cider or chips and batter-fried fish wrapped in sheets from old issues of the *Astoria Intelligencer and Herald*. Others sold scarves printed with the faces of the Royal household. Mostly the cheering was a shapeless white roar of noise, but Órlaith could pick out her mother's name now and then, or her own, or her father's. Bells rang from the numerous churches and choirs sang; someone had gotten them all doing the same hymns, at least.

The docks were on the ball of the thumb. Slipways stretching eastward along the riverfront held the frames of a dozen ships, bare ribs or partly-planked hulls, and four more were in a fitting-out basin getting their masts and standing rigging. This part of town was equally crowded, though more of the spectators were troops waiting to board, and it was more purely workaday. Any home in the city might be a workplace too, but the blocks nearer the waterfront held the trades that needed more space or more elaborate facilities, vast warehouses and equally vast timber yards, machine-shops and foundries, fish-packing sheds and soap-boiling plants; there were tramway tracks set into the pavements, more for shifting heavy cargo than people. The usual city smells of horse and woodsmoke were supplemented by a strong waft of fish, and scorched metal and hot oil and burning charcoal. Here the work of the day went on without cease and the labor had gone on all through the night, for right now that task was stowing the last of the expeditionary force.

It was important to get the whole fleet over the tricky, dangerous mouth of the Columbia as fast as possible. As they went by netloads of bales and boxes—and once a blindfolded destrier with a sling-band under its belly—swung through the air as cranes pivoted to a whirring ratchet of hydraulic engines, and officers and dockmasters waved clipboards and shouted. Troops filed up gangplanks bent under their bundled gear; a band of Mackenzies did a sword-dance on one wharf as they waited their turn, whirling kilts and flashing steel and faces painted for war, the drone of bagpipes and a snatch of song:

"As the world turned dark, I lighted the log,
With Yule burning bright and piercing the fog.

I lay with my lady in the dark of the year,
And I'll be reborn when Spring draws near!"

A chanting rose as an oar-tug pulled a transport away from the dock, the towing cable rising and spritzing water as its fibers tightened.

Órlaith would be crossing in the Royal Montivallan Navy frigate *Sea-Leopard*, and the big warship was just completing its stores as they passed; caterpillars of sailors were trotting up its gangplanks with massive sausages of rolled canvas and bundles of tarred cable. Reiko's smaller *Ari no Okuri-mono* was tied up on the other side of the pier, with the crew on their knees and bowing their heads as she approached. From here the estuary mouth northwards was a mass of hulls and sails and swarming small craft tending to them.

"To hold such power in your hands!" she heard Egawa Noboru say beneath his breath.

Admiral Naysmith was not far away, conferring with some of her captains and the Columbia pilots in their gold-worked blue jackets, a short thickset woman of about forty. She'd punctiliously offered Órlaith the captain's cabin at the stern for herself, and smiled when the Crown Princess snorted and told her to be serious. Eight of them would be bunking in it, and Macmac curled up in a corner. The rest of the ship would be packed as tight as Astoria sardines in oil, despite the fact that *Sea-Leopard* was just finished her shakedown cruise and big, seventeen hundred and fifty tons and two hundred eighty-five feet from stem to the tip of her bowsprit.

Órlaith nodded to Naysmith as they passed and received a salute and a doffing of the fore-and-aft hat; the Bearkiller admiral had pleaded press of business to avoid the ceremony up on Astoria Column Hill. That made her unusual, but people expected an almost-rude bluntness from her folk.

Everyone else is going to get as close as they can! Órlaith thought as they turned up the curving road and the city unfolded like a map beneath her, streets and roofs and church-spires.

Her mother awaited her under the awning of a great open-sided pavilion in the robes of State and bearing the silver lacework of the crown on her gray-shot brown hair, her care-worn face still the center of all eyes among the pomp of delegates and great lords, steel and silk and jewels. Órlaith swung down and took a knee briefly, bringing her fist to her chest and bowing her head, then striding forward as Mathilda made the slight palm-up, crooked-finger gesture that meant *rise and approach*. They kept their faces grave, but there was greeting in their gaze as their eyes met. Reiko halted beside her with the slight mutual inclination of the head that signaled a meeting of equals; then they pivoted to flank Órlaith's mother.

"Folk of Montival!" the High Queen Mathilda called. "Our lord the High King Artos was slain by foreign men from across the western sea, men who landed unheralded on our own soil with weapons in their hands to shed his sacred blood. For this and for their many other crimes I and the Council of Realms have called with one voice for war against the evil sorcerers who rule and oppress the realm of *Chosŏn*, who our ancestors fought even before the Change. It is Our intent that they be cast down and utterly destroyed, and their slaves freed from misrule and set at liberty to choose their own fates. What is your will?"

"War!" half a dozen voices shouted among the crowd on the rain-drenched hilltop.

Blades were drawn and brandished beyond the silent files of the green-clad High King's Archers, the grounded glaives of the black-armored Protector's Guard and the long spears and *naginatas* of the Nihonjin samurai. The short speech had been repeated down the road to the city, and all the way to the docks, by nomenclators with printed copies. More and more took up the cry, down the twisting road and into the streets packed with knight and burgher, lord and dame, with townsfolk and with soldiers from every member-realm of the High Kingdom. Even the newest; there were a few Topangans and Chatsworth men and riders of the *bnei Yaakov* already on the ships.

The cry spread farther. "War . . . War . . . *War!*"

Órlaith felt a shiver as the thing turned from human voices into an elemental roar like storm-surf beating on cliffs, as if Earth and Sea and Sky themselves cried out for vengeance against her father's killers. It vibrated through the titanium-alloy plates of her armor into her very bones.

"WAR . . . WAR . . ."

Mathilda raised her hands, the ermine cloak falling back from her shoulders as she did. The sound died down gradually, falling away to a grumbling murmur in an outward wave of quieting.

"We will fight this war with all our strength; and our allies will add their strength to ours. The Empire of Dai-Nippon has suffered many wrongs from the same enemy. As their enemy is ours, so our cause will be theirs!"

Reiko stepped forward. She was in the black-and-scarlet lacquered armor her people wore, with the chrysanthemum *mon* on her helmet and a bearer to either side with the Hinomaru flag and the *Tennō's* personal banner. She and Órlaith faced each other and bowed gravely. Then they turned westward and put their hands to the weapons at their sides. Slowly they drew them, and raised them skyward.

Shock.

There was always a feeling of flexure when she drew the Sword of the Lady, even for practice. As if the substance of the world could not quite contain it and bent beneath the strain. Today it struck through her like a wash of cool fire, a taste like the granite bones of the earth beneath her, a strength like the rumble of avalanche in the mountains and sun baking black rock in a desert and the roaring wrath of the great bears on the ice-flows of the north. She wasn't sure if there was physical light, but everything seemed to sing for a moment. And with it another light, more golden, from the Grasscutter; a hot wrath that could send worlds down in slow flame. The light drizzle stopped. Then above them the clouds parted, and the rising sun behind them painted the world in shades of green and gray.

The High Queen flung her arms upward. "However you may call on Him and by whatever names, *God wills it!* Through all toil, all terror, all grief, *to victory!*"

Total silence reigned for a long moment until they sheathed the swords; then the sound washed over them, stunning even in that vast landscape of mountain and river, sea and sky. When it had died down a little Órlaith knelt before her mother and extended her hands with the palms pressed together. The High Queen took them between her own; the winter sun glinted coolly on the gold and jewels of the crown and the embroidery of her cotte-hardie.

"As High Queen of Montival and all its peoples, I put the fate of our warriors in your hands, Crown Princess Órlaith of House Artos," she said, in a clear carrying tone. "Treasure their blood and their lives, for each is precious to Us and to their kin. Yet they have sworn those lives to the service of the High Kingdom and to our just cause in this war our enemies have forced upon us. When you must strike, do not hesitate! Strike like a hammer and hold nothing back."

The pavilion was open to the sides and they were holding the ceremony atop the Astoria Column Hill so that they could plead necessity to keep the numbers and problems of precedent from ballooning completely out of control. The hundred-and-sixty-foot height of the column stretched upward behind them, with scenes from the ancient history of the region spiraling upward around its surface and a cast-iron staircase within; the lookouts on the platform at the top would have been within the clouds until a few moments ago. Their view would be even more breathtaking than hers, the Coast Range eastward rising green-gray and streaked with fog and cloud above its forests, the great bridge swooping northward over the Columbia, and the infinite white-streaked gray of the waters, the tumbled roofs of shingle or tile sloping down to the docks, the white sails dancing with wind and sea beyond.

"I will take up this charge, my Queen," Órlaith replied. "For it is the duty laid on my blood by the Powers. And that blood I stand ready to spill when the need of my people calls. It binds me to this soil and this folk through all their time past and to come, wherever I go. So I swear to fight with all my strength of body, soul and mind; never relenting until the day is won, be the cost what it may. Unless the sea rise and drown us, or the sky fall and crush us, or the world end."

There was a short cheer as she stood and embraced her mother, careful of her still-healing body beneath the robes of State. The infinitely familiar voice whispered in her ear, the mother now and not the ruler:

"And come back to me, my golden girl. You remind me of him so. Come back to me."

The various dignitaries were present in their carefully calculated proportions and places from all over the High Kingdom, down to the city's Lord Mayor and the Bishop of Astoria and the heads of the various confraternities and guilds, and they all moved to fall into line in their places behind the Royal coach as the stewards directed. The air was cold; not freezing, but full of a penetrating damp chill. You could go months without seeing the sun here in this time of short days, and it made the light that was blossoming with the offshore breeze more welcome. It smelled of wet earth and horses and wet wool and a hint of the incense in the censers of the Catholic clerics and, strongly, of tree and rock behind them.

Blue eyes met brown, and shared love and concern as they spoke the words of fealty and command. Ceremonial words, yet speaking to a deeper truth.

Mother still looks drawn, Órlaith thought with concern. *And she gets tired so easily. She needs more rest than she allows herself.*

Her fifth and last labor was only a month past and it had been hard; there had been heart-stopping moments of fear, though in the end mother and babe had come through. The child—a girl named Juniper Sandra Arminger Mackenzie—was thriving; in fact, she was kicking and gurgling in her small woven-wool suit, in the arms of a Mackenzie nurse not far away. With her grandmother-namesake occasionally sneaking glances at her out of the corners of her eyes, beneath formal dignity of arsaid and carved staff and Triple Moon headband.

And Mother knows I'm going to war, Órlaith thought. *I've got the responsibilities, and the Morrígu knows they're heavy, but I can be excited and look forward to doing something. All Mother has to look forward to is waiting for word from half a world away—and worrying about me and John.*

She turned and held out her arm, and her mother leaned on that armored strength. This close together the Sword linked them somehow, and she could feel the older woman's response to the complex of emotions that ran through her, the feelings that turned to:

You bore me, and nursed me and held me close to your heart all my growing years. You fought for my life against men serving evil when I was as baby Juniper is now. Lean on my strength today, because that strength is the gift you gave me.

And in return: *I will.*

She handed her mother up into the State carriage, with the six black horses waiting in as near to stillness as their kind could, their coats gleaming and the dark plumes tossing on their headstalls. A score of lancers on barded destriers sat their horses before and behind. The rest of the Royal family followed.

"Look after Mother, and the Mother-of-all and the Lord bless you, brother," she said softly as the next figure stepped in. "She's going to need you. It won't be a short war."

Her brother Faolán was fifteen now, a handsome if gangly lad despite the few spots and many freckles that marked his milk-white skin, shooting up towards their father's height. He wore his fox-red hair down his back in a clansman's queue and a kilt and jacket and plaid and Scots bonnet with raven plumes in the clasp—he'd been very Mackenzie for the last few years, the more so since the news of Father's death came north. Right now she judged he was half consumed with envy that she was going, and half still floored by her little lecture last night on how if she and John didn't come back he would be next High King.

"That I will, sister and Lady, by the Lady and Her Lord," he replied gravely, his voice wobbling a bit.

"And remember me in your prayers every night, eh?" Órlaith said to the last figure before the nursemaid. "When I come back you'll be bigger, but no fairer."

Vuissance was ten, black-haired, clad in a child's wimple and surcote and simply sad that yet another fixture of her life was departing for God-knew-how-long, but controlling her tears with a desperate earnestness that showed in the white-knuckle grip on her rosary.

"I will. I'll ask St. Joan of the Bow to protect you!" the girl said.

"A strong shield, my darling," Órlaith said, hugging her and kissing the top of her head.

She held the baby for a moment and kissed it too before handing it up and stepping back.

Vuissance leaned down. "And find Johnnie. Please!"

"I will. I promise. And he'll have a song to sing for us all."

Then she stopped, stumbled, gasped as she turned to her own mount.

Heuradys was at her side instantly, a hand under her elbow.

"What's wrong?" she said sharply.

Órlaith turned her head to look at her knight, and saw by the shock on her face how pale she must have gone.

I have to pull myself together! she thought. *Too many are watching.*

"John," she whispered, her hand going to the hilt of the Sword. "Something's happened to John. Something terrible."

"Órlaith and Montival!" John shouted again.

The space between the Carcosan fort and the Baru Denpasaran lines had been in tall grass and brush. Now it was burnt and pockmarked with rocks and a bristle of arrows nobody had been suicidal enough to try to retrieve. More bundles of rock bound in flaming rope went by overhead, and John was acutely aware that if one burst prematurely the stones within would pulp his head, helm or no. The streams of catapult shot and prang-prang bolts would kill him just as surely. You were supposed to forget such things in the heat of the moment, but so far that wasn't happening.

And I'm glad it isn't. I'd hate to be in danger and *crazy too,* he thought as he knocked his visor down; it was time to start worrying about stray arrows coming his way.

The storming parties with the ladders were within a hundred yards of the fort's battered wall now. Suddenly men showed there, archers. Bolt and ball and prang-prang and arrows tore into them, but enough shot that the ladders staggered. Men ran forward from behind to take the place of those who fell, and suddenly they were at the edge of the moat. They let the base of the ladders fall—the legs there were sheathed in metal, like big spades—and the tall contraptions toppled forward. More men appeared on the ramparts as they fell forward, trying to fend them off with long poles with Y-forks at the end. One scaling ladder went sideways into the ditch, but most of the two dozen thumped home—and they had long slightly curved iron spikes beneath to bite into the target, raven-beaks they were called back home. The Baru Denpasaran archers had lowered their trajectories to sweep the ramparts too, and the slender bamboo shafts were going overhead uncomfortably close; he hoped they had the fire discipline to stop when the assault troops, who included *him*, were up there.

Then they were at the foot of one of the ladders, just in time to see a man with two arrows through his body topple shrieking off to land and drown in thin stinking mud of the moat. The wailing sound of agony and despair was lost in the roaring crush. Thora and he hit the first step side-by-side, their shields up. Despite the unpleasant springiness of the construction beneath his feet, this he *did* know about, having run up more scaling ladders than he cared to recall during his squire training. The storm of shot going by overhead lifted, which was one worry out of the way, but immediately men who'd been lying flat behind the crest of the earthwork sprung up and started shooting frantically.

One lead bullet from a sling made the edge of his helmet go *ting* with a wrenching force that nearly punched him off the ladder. Arrows cracked into his shield and Thora's, hard enough to stagger a man at this point-blank range. All he could see through the vision-slit was a narrow strip of men trying to kill him.

Admiring their courage didn't mean he didn't feel an overwhelming flash of hatred at their *existence* at this precise moment.

There were feet pounding the ladder behind them; he couldn't tell who, and would have bet on Sergeant Fayard, until he and the Bearkiller leapt the final few feet, tucked behind their shields and desperate to punch the waiting crowd back from the head of the ladder to make space so more attackers could join them. He landed on broken wood and earth and staggered and a man with a spear poised to thrust at his eyes . . . then snapped backward as if he'd been kicked in the face by a horse. It was a crossbow bolt that had done it, and Fayard was one of the best shots in the Protector's Guard and he was less than a hundred feet away. Eight more men attacked him and Thora, all there were room for, and three of them died with crossbow bolts in their heads and chests in the next few seconds—the rest of the squad must be handing their weapons to Fayard as they reloaded. Two more went down with Mackenzie ashwood shafts driven through their bodies—that would be Ruan shooting. Those two he trusted to support him so, and few others.

He slashed a bare-chested man with a parang and threads of spittle hanging from his lips, and then hacked him again with frantic haste when he ignored the wound. Nobody ignored a half-severed neck, or at least he hoped they didn't, and this one fell. Thora cut into a thigh, punched the boss of her round shield into a face and then stabbed over it with economical precision. Blades punched at him, banging into his shield and squealing off the steel plates that covered him, making him stagger and bruising him even though they didn't penetrate. The two Montivallans' armor and size and the fire support was giving them . . . moments of extra life facing so many opponents.

"Thor with me!" Thora grunted.

They took advantage of the gaps and stepped a long pace forward, relying on *someone* to slide in beside them before they were flanked. People did; Deor was there beside his oath-sister, Evrouin's glaive snaked out and caught an ankle with the sharpened hook on the reserve of the blade. Toa's huge spear flashed to his shield-side, and Pip was behind him coolly firing her slingshot from point-blank range behind the first line with eye-punching accuracy.

The fight swayed for an instant, and then John was standing and sobbing in breath and coughing and knocking up the visor to bite for air again. Baru Denpasaran fighters streamed past him, down into the open court of the fortress where the garrison had gotten up out of its dugouts just as the storm of trebuchet fire broke over their heads. Fayard and his crossbowmen were around him now, glaring as they leveled their weapons.

"We've done enough," he wheezed, leaning on his shield and fumbling at his sword until someone took it away and wiped it for him—he thought it was one of the Guard crossbowmen. "Let them finish their own fight."

Someone thrust a canteen into his mouth and he pulled in water and choked and coughed and shot it out his nose and then drank again anyway.

"You've got it," Thora said to him.

"What?" he sputtered.

"The *Baraka*, the thing that pulls others after you. Your father had all there was to have, and your sister has plenty, but you've definitely got some. It's a magic, the Gods and the *alfar* give it or they don't."

They moved along the wall top, ignoring the bodies tumbled in the graceless ungainly sprawls of death and found places to sit. The air was thick with stinks and smoke; the haze from the burning keep lay like water in the enclosure of the fort's walls, a patchy cloud of dirty brownish-white. Pip moved off a little to see to one of her men who needed first aid, but stretcher-bearers would be coming forward soon. He was very tired, and let his head sag back against a snag of broken timber as he sank to his heels and then let his legs splay out in front of him.

"*Watch out!*" a voice screamed.

That started him awake. What he saw froze him for long seconds. The burning tower had . . .

Broken apart, he thought, as the crackling, banging rumble grew with rushing speed. *Broken apart and most of it's falling at* me. *God, you're not playing fair!*

He made it halfway to his feet and then was knocked over backward as several men threw themselves over him.

Blackness.

For a moment John heard two voices overlapping: one was Pip's:

"He's not bloody dead! Dig! They were on top of him, he's got to be there some sodding where!"

Another was speaking, and he didn't understand it. Then realized it was in another language . . . French, and an archaic dialect at that. Few living men could have followed it, but he'd studied that tongue for his art, and not only the book-version but scholarly writings on how it had sounded. The clangorous syllables assumed meaning, a version still harsh and nasal, closer to Italian than the langue d'oil, and closer still to the Latin bones of the speech.

Who the hell is speaking the way someone from Toulouse would have seven hundred years ago?

"My lady is most kind, of a certainty," it said.

He blinked his eyes open and wished he hadn't, because with consciousness came pain. It took moments to realize that the pain was in his shoulders, and that he was being carried on a pole—one run behind his shoulders, then in front of his elbows, which were tightly bound to it. The pole flexed again, and his toes touched the ground lightly and agony lanced through his joints. The path he was on had ended before what looked like the side of a hill in the gloaming just before sunset. Then he saw that it was a temple, though of no faith he knew, a tall gate heavily carved and even more heavily overgrown, with fallen statues on the steps leading to it. The air was mildly cool, full of a smell of moist rock and things growing and rotting, perfume and decay.

I'm dreaming, he thought. *That's it, I got hit and I'm dreaming.*

"What is the world but a dream?" the same voice said; to him, this time.

He could see the tall, robed, hooded figure turning to address him over his . . . its . . . shoulder. His eyes went wide in fright, meeting those lambent yellow slits and he frantically looked aside. It was the same . . . not a man, but something that walked upright . . . that he'd fought on the harbor. The mask was inhumanly beautiful, in a way like a sketch of humanity, and it made him want to pound his head against a rock so that he wouldn't have to *see* it. Listening was worse, but he couldn't do anything about that.

A shorter, lumpier figure was beside it, carrying the longsword he remembered. The fingers that held the weapon's scabbard were unpleasantly puffy and soft-looking.

The mask spoke; somehow he couldn't tell if the carved lips moved, or not:

"We walk in dreams, and wake, and find ourselves still in dreams within dreams, as the black stars shift and the moon sets before the towers of the sacred city. And who is the dreamer, and who, messieurs, the dream itself?"

A deep rumble came from within the hill-high ruin before them. A line of brightness ran down the middle of it from the tall peak to the base, and the rumble grew. The great mass parted, like a door swinging open, ponderous and sure. Through it poured . . . things.

At first he thought they were men, but then he saw that they would reach no higher than his standing waist. Naked and stick-thin, childish faces and huge dark eyes below shocks of hair and a thin bristle of whiskers around withered lips, loincloths and spears and hatchets tipped with chipped volcanic glass. They piled on one another until there was a seething heap of them, and then they looked at him.

And blinked, in unison, hundreds of eyes vanishing in the purple gloom and opening in a single glinting motion. Then the mouths gaped, showing pointed teeth and fluttering tongues, and they *squealed*. John felt himself grunt and his head went back in an arc of pain as the sound trilled and drilled into his ears.

"*EEEEeeeeeeEEEEEeeeeeeEEEEE—*"

He sagged as it stopped, feeling blood running warm and salt from his ears and nose, eyes and bitten lips. A figure danced down from that opening, and at first he thought it was the dancer of the *tari Cendrawasih*. But the hair that tossed about her head was white-blond . . . or rather the white of polished bone. When she stopped in the final figure of the dance he saw that her fingernails were long and had the glint of razors, and the necklace about her neck was of gut and skulls. Then she lifted her head and the hair parted, and he made a hoarse sound of denial at muzzle and tusks and narrow red eyes, the flesh with the moist living pliancy of real life.

"Most beautiful Madam Rangda," the Pallid Mask said, with a flourishing bow and movement of his hands that was as much Old Europe as the language in which he spoke.

"Dearest ally of my monarch. I kiss your hands and feet at this most generous aid. It shall be repaid in overflowing measure."

There were men following behind those who carried John, men bloodied and weary and still bearing weapons. The Pallid Mask gestured towards them, and the little lemur-eyed creatures chittered and *flowed* towards them. The shrieks were brief, and a long red tongue lapped at the dancer-thing's fanged chops.

"A good appetite, my lady," the robed man said. He turned to John. "Now to Carcosa . . . the earthly Carcosa which strives always to be worthy of its namesake . . . for our better acquaintance, most well and high-born guest."

John forced himself to look into the lambent eyes. "I doubt you'll get much satisfaction from it," he said. "If you don't dare face me without a mask."

The man signaled, and the bearers began to drag John towards the cleft in the rock.

He chuckled as the young man was borne past him. "Oh, my Prince . . . I wear no mask."

"No mask?" John said numbly. The scream bubbled in his throat, choking him. *"No mask?"*